AND
THE
STARS
KEPT
WATCH

AND THE STARS KEPT WATCH

PETER FRIEDRICHS

atmosphere press

For Irene

Faith, Hope, and Love, your time abide!

Let Hades marshal all his hosts.

The heavenly forces with you side,

The stars are watching at their posts.

--Rev. Frederic Henry Hedge,
from "The Northern Lights and the Stars" (1859)

PROLOGUE

Returning to consciousness was, for Catherine, like ascending from a deep-water dive. It happened slowly and in stages. At first, surrounded by darkness, all she noticed was her own breathing. Then, she became aware of other sounds, muted and distant. Next came the awareness of touch and, with it, pain. Her head throbbed, and every breath delivered a stabbing sensation to her ribcage. Then there was light, as waves and particles danced behind her eyelids in a kaleidoscopic display. Even after she broke the surface and opened her eyes, she laid no claim to full awareness, lacking as she was both comprehension of her surroundings and any memory of recent events.

"Nate, can you turn the lights off?" She recognized her husband by his scent before her eyes adjusted to the harsh light and he came into focus. "They're giving me a headache."

"Hey there." Nathan reached for the switch on the wall of the hospital room. "You gave us all quite a scare." He gripped Catherine's hand as if he alone were holding her on the surface, the sole force keeping her from going under again.

"I'm so tired."

"You took quite a beating." He stroked the back of his wife's hand. "The best thing you can do is rest. I'm just glad to have you back." Nathan bent down and kissed her on the forehead, just below the bandages that wrapped her fractured skull. "Carey is on her way up from New York. She should be here tonight." Catherine would be glad to see her sister.

"I don't even remember what happened." Catherine's voice was a feathery whisper, all she could manage. "But I had some amazing dreams. Remind me to tell you about them."

"It'll all come back to you. The doctors said it would just take some time."

Catherine tried to gain her bearings. She could tell she was in a hospital bed. She had a splitting headache and sharp pains every time she took a breath. She had a vague memory of a noisy, bumpy helicopter ride. But beyond that, her memory ended abruptly, as impenetrable as an August fogbank hanging off the Maine coast that lay just a few miles to the east.

"Nate, what happened to me?"

"You don't remember?"

"Right now, I couldn't tell you if I fell out of an airplane or wrecked the car. Are the boys okay?"

Nathan squirmed in his seat and avoided answering his wife's question.

"The most important thing is you're all right. Why don't you close your eyes and get some rest?"

Catherine didn't need to be coaxed. Without conscious thought or intention, she succumbed to the inexorable pull of sleep. She was a stone dropped into a lake, the force of gravity dragging her down. Her senses departed in stages, just as they had returned only a short time earlier.

4

CHAPTER ONE
NATHAN

Lost? How could I be lost? Nathan peered through the dense understory of the woods he thought he knew so well. He'd grown up traipsing around the spiderweb of trails that crisscrossed the hills and valleys of this part of southwestern Maine with his father, hunting rabbits and game birds. If you blindfolded him and dropped him down anywhere in York County, he'd know his way home. Or so he thought. But now, as he sat in the driver's seat of his all-terrain vehicle, his two boys in the back, he had to admit that he wasn't sure where they were.

"Dad, let's go." Six-year-old Jacob had reached the limit of his interest and his energy. They'd been out for a couple of hours already, and he was ready to get back home. Jacob's little brother Joe piled on to express his dissatisfaction. "Why are we stopped?" Then, in his best four-year-old whine he added, "I'm bored."

"This is a special adventure, guys." Nathan looked around, hoping to see a familiar landmark. "I want to be sure we're on the trail that leads us to the treasure." The boys in the back seats, each strapped into the four-place ATV with elaborate harnesses for their safety, perked up at the mention of treasure.

"Is it gold from a pirate ship?"

"Will it be guarded by a monster?"

"If it's buried, how will we find it?"

"Keep your eyes peeled. You'll know it when you see it." The diversion worked its magic. Nathan switched on the RZR's headlights in the darkening woods and kept searching for the trail that would lead them home.

"Dad, don't the bears like to come out at night?" Jacob was always the worrier.

"Not at this time of year, buddy." Nathan hated to lie to the kids, but he didn't want to give them yet another reason to be concerned. "They're still hibernating."

*

It had been six months since Catherine had surprised Nathan with his birthday gift.

"I hope you like it." Catherine guided her husband out the front door, blindfolded. She had sworn their two sons to secrecy, and the boys actually managed not to give away the surprise. But as the four of them walked into the yard, the children couldn't contain themselves any longer.

"Look, Daddy! Look!" The two young boys grabbed their father's hands and pulled him forward. Catherine peeled off the bandana so that Nathan could see his birthday gift.

"You didn't." A wide grin spread across Nathan's face. His eyes grew wide with glee. "It's amazing!"

Nathan rushed to the showroom-new ATV, the exact model he'd been talking about for months. The boys were already climbing into the back seats.

"It's the one, right?" Catherine nodded toward the Polaris RZR. It was a beefy, side-by-side 4-seater with knobby tires, headlights, a front winch, and a full roll cage, with room for the whole family. Nathan suspected that his wife had checked with his best friend, Jim, before making the purchase.

"Oh, yeah." Nathan beamed, walking around the vehicle.

"What are you waiting for?" Catherine tossed him the keys. "Aren't you going to take it for a spin?"

Their home in southwestern Maine, just a few miles from the New Hampshire border, sat perched on a western-facing hillside on twenty acres of land. It was surrounded by fields and forests, ponds, lakes, and swamps. The perfect environment for four-wheeling.

Nathan noticed that Jacob and Joe had already donned their helmets, which Catherine had strategically placed on their seats in the back. He and his wife fastened their chin straps and buckled them into the car seats she'd had installed. The seats had special four-point harnesses that added a degree of safety beyond the standard lap belts. Nathan donned the blue helmet that sat in the driver's seat, which matched those of the two boys and the ATV's paint job. Catherine did the same with hers, which was neon pink. Nathan plugged everyone into the on-board intercom before taking his place behind the steering wheel.

"Everybody ready?" Nathan put the key in the ignition and turned it. The engine roared to life.

"Yay!" The boys squirmed in their seats, their arms and legs cartwheeling with glee.

"No hot-dogging." Catherine grabbed her husband's arm with one hand as she braced herself against the ATV's door with the other. She knew him well enough to issue the warning. "At least, not on the first day out."

Nathan gave a small nod to his wife. He knew that she worried about his risk-taking tendencies. She admonished him regularly about driving too fast up the Maine Turnpike when they went out to dinner in Kennebunk or Portland. He'd given up some of his more dare-devilish activities when he'd become a father. He'd sold his hang glider, and his rock-climbing gear hung untouched and gathering dust on the wall of their garage. When they were dating and then in the early years of their marriage, Nathan had kept up such pursuits. But he respected Catherine's more conservative, safety-conscious perspective and the responsibilities that came with being a father. His wild side still revealed itself occasionally. Just not usually in his wife's presence.

Nathan revved the engine a few times, threw the ATV into gear, and the family gleefully rattled down the path that led into the woods. The boys were giggling in the back, and Catherine could see the joy in her husband's eyes, even behind the visor of his helmet.

The land around Catherine and Nathan's house in Newfield was remarkably untouched, even though most of the property along the larger lakes and ponds in southern Maine were ringed by summer homes owned by doctors and lawyers from Boston. It was true that some large parcels had been clear-cut to provide wood for the paper industry when mills still dotted the landscape, but that was a century ago. Most of the region now held at least second-growth forest, meadows, lowland bogs, and large swaths of deciduous trees. The area was home to a wide variety of indigenous wildlife, including white-tail deer, coyotes, porcupine, beaver, and fox. Black bears were occasionally seen robbing a birdfeeder in somebody's yard, and northeastern songbirds, owls, hawks, and other birds of prey abounded. It was a perfect environment for hiking, camping, fishing, and four-wheeling, a place where a family could be close to nature just a few steps out their back door.

After an hour of bouncing around the wilds of York County, Nathan announced over the intercom "Let's take her back to the barn" and he turned the rig toward home. They'd run the machine through its paces, throwing mud and dodging trees.

"Come on, Dad." Jacob's voice crackled over the intercom. "Just a little more!"

"Yeah, Dad." Joe used his squeaky voice, the one that made Nathan laugh as it seemed to jump two octaves when he begged him for something. "Please?"

"Your mom's got to get back and make us a birthday dinner." Nathan aimed the ATV up the trail that led back home. "Remember, it's Nacho Night!" This news seemed to mollify the kids as they both let out a whoop of glee.

With the RZR safely parked back in the driveway, Catherine pulled her cell phone from the pocket of her jeans as Nathan unbuckled the children from their seats. "We need to take a selfie!" She motioned them all into place in front of the RZR. The four of them, splattered in mud, but beaming, crowded together for the picture.

*

With the kids splashing around in the bathtub, Nathan walked up behind his wife as she prepared dinner. He put his arms around her waist and nuzzled her neck.

"You like your birthday present?" Catherine leaned into her husband's arms.

"Mmmm," Nathan tightened his embrace and nibbled affectionately on his wife's ear. "I can't wait for my other present, too."

"Well, if you're talking about the nachos, they'll be ready in half an hour."

"You know that's not what I'm talking about." Nathan pressed his body against his wife's.

"Settle down, Birthday Boy," Catherine broke away from her husband and began setting the table. "Why don't you go check on your sons."

*

After an initial flurry of intense use, the RZR saw less and less action as its novelty wore off. Throughout that fall, Nathan occasionally invited the family out on an adventure with the four-wheeler. Most of the time, Catherine would decline and send her boys out on their own. Nathan knew that she preferred to spend a lazy afternoon on the deck watching the hawks soar over the house or reading a novel uninterrupted to bouncing around the woods in a noisy, gas-guzzling machine. And so, on an unseasonably warm Saturday afternoon in March of the following year, when spring was teasing all of New England into believing it just might arrive early, Catherine declined Nathan's invitation to take the RZR out for a spin.

"You guys go. It looks like it could be really muddy, and I know you'll have fun. I'll have dinner ready when you get back." Catherine gave Nathan a peck on the cheek before easing herself into a chair in the living room. Nathan knew it was her favorite spot to catch a nap, and he was glad to give his wife a break from the kids.

"Hey, guys!" Nathan called the boys, who were upstairs playing in their rooms. "Wanna go sling some mud?" Jacob and Joe bounded down the stairs and threw on their jackets. It had been a long, bitterly cold winter, and this was the perfect antidote to their cabin fever.

"Put on your boots and gloves, too. It feels warm now, but it'll be colder once we get going." The boys did as their father instructed and stood by the RZR as Nathan pulled off the tarp that had covered it all winter. Nathan helped the boys into their seats as the ATV warmed up, checking to make sure their harnesses were snug, and plugging their helmets into the intercom.

As Nathan expected, it was a muddy, glorious day in the woods. The patch of warm weather released the frost's hold on the ground, and the RZR slogged through the muck like a black lab chasing a tennis ball. With every bounce and turn, Jacob and Joe let out squeals of delight, encouraging their father to repeat the maneuver.

"Faster, dad!" Joe yelled from the back. Jacob, who was older but the less adventurous of the two, held on for dear life, but the look in his eyes showed Nathan that he was enjoying the ride.

After an hour or so of careening along the network of trails, Nathan decided it was time to turn back toward home. It was only then that he realized that, at some point, he'd veered off the marked trail. He stopped the RZR in a grove of maples that soon would be tapped for syrup and assessed the angle of the sun in the sky. He trusted his gut and turned the RZR in what he thought was the general direction of home.

"Time to head back, boys!" Nathan swung the ATV around a large oak tree and dodged a granite outcropping.

"Aww, do we have to?" Joe craned his neck forward as he

pleaded with his father to extend their adventure.

"Yep. Mom's got dinner going, and we'll have quite the clean-up to do from all this mud."

Picking his way among the trees, Nathan steered a northeast course in hopes of finding a familiar trail. He felt a slight tightening in his belly as he realized he was going to be playing it pretty close to the edge with the still-early sunset. Although the RZR was equipped with headlights, he didn't want to be too far from home when it got dark, knowing that Jacob, especially, would be scared in the woods at night. Nathan picked up his speed slightly as the path widened, and he saw the darkening sky of approaching night through the trees.

After following a deer path for nearly 20 minutes, Nathan was surprised not to have come across a marked trail. He thought he knew these woods like the back of his hand, and he was growing concerned that his instincts hadn't yet paid off. He stopped the RZR, flipped up the visor of his helmet, and looked around, unsure which way to turn. He decided to set a northerly course using the compass he'd installed on the dashboard, hopeful that he'd intersect with a road or trail that would lead them home. He told the boys a story about some treasure they were looking for as he threw the RZR into gear.

Nathan stuck to his intended course as best he could, dodging rocks and trees and bushwhacking through the thick underbrush. Because the trees had yet to leaf out, the late afternoon light penetrated down to the forest floor despite the low angle of the sun. After another half-hour of picking his way through the woods, with the kids becoming increasingly agitated, Nathan was relieved to reach a point at the bottom of a gentle slope where the dense forest thinned out, revealing a familiar sight. He knew exactly where they were: by the south shore of Franklin Pond, a small and undeveloped body of water that he and Catherine had kayaked on before they'd had kids. Home, Nathan knew, was about two miles north of the far shore. He also knew from fishing this pond as a boy that there was a perimeter trail around it. He recalled that the trail wasn't much more than a footpath and knew that navigating the RZR along it would be tedious and time-consuming. He glanced at his watch and at the darkening sky. He knew he was going to be getting home much later than he'd planned, and that Catherine would be worried about them.

CHAPTER TWO
CATHERINE

Catherine was glad she'd decided to stay home and send her boys off on their own. She'd only read a few pages of her book before falling soundly asleep in her favorite easy chair, snuggled under an afghan blanket her grandmother had crocheted for her when she was in high school. She often joked with Nathan or her sister Carey that it was her "grown-up blankie." At least she'd broken her thumb-sucking habit. Catherine stretched her arms wide as she shook off the sleep and then lowered them to touch her belly with both hands, amazed at how much energy it took to grow a baby, even when it was only about the size of a lima bean. She was looking forward to the moment later that night after the boys were tucked away in bed when she would share the good news with her husband that their third child was on the way.

Catherine brewed a cup of green tea for herself and returned to her La-Z-Boy, gazing out the window at the late winter sky. She listened to the slow drip of snow melting off the roof and hitting the deck that surrounded three sides of the home that she and Nathan had built. *We've built more than a house. We've made a home. A life.* She allowed her thoughts to drift back to their earliest days together.

They'd met when she was practicing law in Boston, and he was getting his business off the ground in Portland. She was on the fast-track to partnership at Goulston & Storrs, a shining star in the bankruptcy practice group, and Nathan had recently returned home to Maine after a brief but successful stint on Wall Street. His Babson MBA had given him the tools he needed to make a small killing in the market, enough money to start his own financial planning firm in Portland.

Catherine let out a contented sigh as she realized that nearly ten years had passed since their wedding. She looked out the sliding glass doors at the now-familiar view and remembered their chance meeting at a gas station on the way home from Sugarloaf. They'd both, separately, had a glorious day of spring skiing. Catherine had stopped for a snack and was walking across the parking lot of the Irving in South Paris when a pickup truck lurched out of a parking space. She had to jump out of its path as it backed out, the driver clearly not paying attention. She felt a surge of adrenalin tinged with anger at the careless driver. But in this case, the driver noticed his error, pulled the truck back into its space and jumped out with hands held high and a look of shock on his face.

"I'm so sorry. You were in my blind spot and I didn't see you. Are you okay?" Catherine was taken aback by this unexpected apology, and when the driver offered, as compensation for the near-miss, to buy her a coffee, she agreed. She was immediately attracted to Nathan's ruddy good looks, accentuated by the sunburn he'd gotten that day on the slopes. He told her later that it was her shock of red hair and her quick wit that had won him over. That and, he always joked, the athletic ability she'd displayed as she dodged his oncoming vehicle.

They grabbed an empty table in the dining area of the mini-mart, sipping their coffees and making small talk.

"Your cat-like reflexes are impressive." Nathan smiled broadly as he joked, revealing some adorable dimples. His face was boyish but manly.

"Clearly, you like to keep people on their toes." Catherine blushed as she nervously pulled her hair into a ponytail. She was aware that this very attractive man with dark, wavy hair and piercing blue eyes was seeing her at less than her best. Their conversation covered the usual topics, like where they lived and what they did for work.

"So, did you always want to be a lawyer?" Nathan took a sip of his coffee.

"Pretty much. If they were alive today, my parents would tell you that every meal, every bath-time, every bedtime was a negotiation with me. I guess I was born to it."

"I can't say I always wanted to sell stocks as a kid."

"If that wasn't your dream, what did you want to be when you grew up?"

Nathan looked around to make sure no one was within earshot, then leaned across the table. "Promise not to laugh?"

"No." Catherine flashed a quick smile and blushed again. There was something about Nathan that put her at ease. It felt natural to be herself with this total stranger.

"I'll tell you anyway." Nathan paused and shifted in his seat before he continued, looking around again at the nearby customers as he spoke in a near-whisper. "I wanted to sing in a boy band."

Catherine nearly sprayed her coffee in his face, but she managed to choke back her drink.

"I knew you'd laugh." Catherine noticed that it was his turn to blush. "Remember 'Making the Band' on MTV?"

Catherine nodded and blurted out the name of the band that the reality show had produced. "O-Town!"

"Right. That's what I wanted to do. To front a band like NSYNC or Backstreet Boys."

Catherine noted that he had the looks to be a frontman, and she wondered if he had the moves. She also appreciated that he was sharing something serious with her. "Do you sing at all these days?"

"Just karaoke. And I don't even have to be drunk."

"That's a long way from being a stockbroker on Wall Street."

"And if you ever say a word to anyone, I'll deny it to my dying breath." Nathan smiled broadly.

Their courtship was brief and intense. As a New England spring turned to summer, they split their time between Boston and Portland, alternating weekends at each other's place. They bonded over their shared love of the outdoors and of the Boston Red Sox. They spent weekends hiking in southern Maine and New Hampshire or paddling kayaks along the coastal Maine Island Trail. They went to Fenway or out to the Cape. By fall, they were engaged, and in June of the following year they strode out of the chapel at Mt. Holyoke College – her alma mater – as newlyweds.

*

Catherine took the last sip of her now-cold tea and walked to the far end of the house, where the third laundry load of the day awaited her attention. *It's amazing how much laundry two little monsters can generate.* Hefting the laundry basket onto her hip, she glanced at the clock on the wall and was taken aback to see how late it was. She was surprised that Nathan and the boys hadn't returned yet and wondered whether the RZR had gotten stuck somewhere. She pictured her husband slogging through the muck to pay out the winch cable and hook it around a nearby tree, as they'd had to do once last fall. She imagined Jacob and Joe standing by, watching. Jacob would be anxious and concerned, while Joe would be right there beside Nathan, up to his knees in the swamp water.

The two boys were so different, Catherine mused. They always had been, right from the start, even in how they came into the world. Jacob's delivery was a marathon, with a labor that lasted more than 30 hours. It was as if the boy was happy to stay safely tucked into his little cocoon and refused to come out. Joe, on the other hand, burst forth less than 20 minutes after Catherine and Nathan had arrived at the hospital. He'd been a bold and brash kid ever since. The two boys even looked completely different from each other. Jacob sported the dark, wavy hair and blue eyes of his father, while Joe favored Catherine with his fair skin, mop of red hair, and sea-green eyes.

Jacob, older than Joe by 30 months, was a sensitive, empathic child. He was plugged into the world in a way that Catherine hadn't seen in other children. When the boys went hunting for newts in the yard, he was happy to find them. But he worried for their happiness and was always anxious to return them to their home. Jacob loved books, especially the "Magic Tree House" series, where he could imagine traveling through time and space with Jack and Annie, the main characters. And like most boys his age, Jacob was obsessed with dinosaurs. He had dozens of the plastic prehistoric animals strewn around his room, and he pored over the books that identified each by name and trait. Catherine could leave Jacob for hours in his room as he spun out stories of dinosaur families and their adventures.

In contrast to his older brother, Joe was a wild child. He was Catherine's ultimate patience-tester, but even when he did something outrageous, it was impossible to stay mad at him. Whenever Jacob and Joe conspired to misbehave, Catherine could count on Joe to be the instigator. It was Joe who convinced Jacob to fill the two raised garden beds with water from the hose, shortly after Catherine had planted the peas last spring. When she found them lounging, naked, in identical pools of mud, Joe told his mother that he had wanted to make "matching hot tubs." While Joe was a source of endless frustration for Catherine, he always made her laugh with his antics and his devil-may-care nature.

Catherine put the laundry away and turned her attention toward dinner. She pulled together the cheese, chips, meat, and pico for the kids' favorite nachos, so they'd be ready to put in the oven the minute they got home. Nachos were a staple in the Osgood family, and Catherine had raised the simple food to an art form. She still remembered when she and Nathan had discovered the small Mexican restaurant in Portland that would become their "go-to" spot when they were dating. They had spent an afternoon poking around the shops of the Old Port when they'd come across Tortilla Flats, a hole-in-the-wall place that advertised three-dollar margarita specials. They decided to duck in for a drink and a bite, and it was there that they discovered their shared love of both nachos and chicken fingers.

After placing their order at the counter, Nathan and Catherine sat down at a table by the window. Catherine took a sip of her icy drink and gazed over the rim at this man to whom she felt such a strong attraction. "When I was younger, I dreamt of opening a restaurant that served nothing but chicken fingers and nachos. And maybe a side of mac and cheese."

"We should definitely do that someday." Nathan grabbed a chip and dipped it in guacamole. "We could call it "Nacho Mama's Chicken Fingers."

That simple witticism convinced Catherine of what she'd been feeling already: she and Nathan had a future together.

"We could have chicken fingers with different coatings and dipping sauces." Nathan was munching loudly, a dab of sour cream staining the corner of his mouth. "And wine pairings, too, with different nachos."

"Oh, I'm way ahead of you." Catherine swiped her napkin across Nathan's lip. "I've been tearing recipes out of cooking magazines since I was twelve."

*

Tonight, Catherine had prepared one of their favorites: BBQ pulled-pork nachos with pepper-jack cheese. As she finished spreading the shredded cheese over the chips, Catherine glanced out the kitchen window at the setting sun, then down at the clock on the front of the oven. Noting both, she felt the first pangs of real concern. *Why is Nathan keeping the boys out so late?* Catherine grabbed her phone to make sure she hadn't missed a message from Nate and then tried to distract herself by looking at dog rescue sites. She and Nathan had recently agreed that it would be good for the boys to have a canine companion and that they were old enough now to take some responsibility for its care. From there she switched to her Pinterest boards and her Facebook page, the rabbit holes of social media serving their intended purpose of distracting her from her growing concern.

When she resurfaced from her deep dive into home makeover sites and spa getaways, Catherine looked out the windows facing the New Hampshire hills just across the state line to the west and noticed that the sun was grazing the treetops. Her stomach clenched at the sight and her pulse began to race as her anxiety sought to blossom into full-blown panic. *Where could they be? Why hasn't Nathan called to let me know what's going on? Has something happened?* She tried to calm herself, remembering all the times she had worried needlessly about her husband's whereabouts. In the past, every time she'd felt her fear response kick in, Nathan had come bounding through the door, clueless to her concerns. Catherine tried to take some solace in these memories, but they only succeeded in making her mad. She had been singularly unsuccessful in getting Nathan to appreciate her anxieties and to check in with her to ease them.

Catherine grabbed her phone and texted her sister, Carey, as much to take her mind off her worry as anything else.

Nathan and the kids aren't back from their RZR ride yet.

Hmm. Seems late. Sorry.

He pisses me off when he doesn't check in.

I know. You can let him have it when he gets home.

There was no love lost between Carey and Nathan, and Catherine realized expressing her frustrations about her husband to her sister would only fuel the fire.

Oh, I will. After kids are in bed.

Catherine was worried. She was angry. And, she realized, these weren't the sentiments she had planned to greet her husband with this evening. Not with the news she was holding. Now she started to think that she'd have to wait a few days to let him know that they were going to have a third child.

Let me know when he gets home.

Will do. Bye.

Love you.

You too.

Catherine checked that her ringer was on and set the phone down. Standing at the kitchen counter, she recalled the first time she'd felt this way.

*

They'd only been together a couple of months, but both of them knew their relationship was serious. Nathan had decided to go rock climbing with a friend. He'd been to a rock gym a few times and liked the physical as well as the mental challenge of the sport. But, as he told Catherine, he felt limited by the confines of the artificial wall and wanted to take it to the next level. A friend of his was an experienced climber, and one Saturday had invited Nathan to go climbing with him on Cathedral Ledge outside of North Conway. Catherine saw him off with her customary "Be careful!" and "Call me!" as he got into his friend's truck to head north.

Catherine didn't hear from Nathan all day, nor did she really expect to. But by about 4 o'clock she'd begun to worry. She was, she knew, a "catastrophizer." She'd even consulted a therapist about it when she was back in college. Catherine was comforted to learn that there were lots of people like her who, when faced with an uncertain situation, immediately spin out a story of the worst possible thing that could have happened. But that information and the therapy had done little to break her of the habit.

As the minutes, then hours passed, Catherine convinced herself that her boyfriend – the love of her life – had plunged to his death from the top of a cliff and that his mangled, lifeless body was at that moment being carted off to the local morgue. She wondered who she should call to see if anyone had died hiking that day. By 6 o'clock, she was bouncing off the walls of her apartment, unable to think of anything but the fact that Nathan was dead. She put in a call to her sister to share her concerns. Carey was usually pretty good at talking her off the ledge.

"Cat, you know how this goes, right?" Carey tried not to let the frustration show in her voice. "He's fine, and he's going to be back any time now."

"That's easy for you to say." Catherine paced the apartment as she spoke. "And even though my head knows it's true, try telling that to my body."

"Take a few deep breaths. Have a drink. Pop a movie into the Blu-Ray to take your mind off it."

Catherine breathed a sigh into the phone. "I know you're right. Thanks for being there."

"That's what big sisters are for, kiddo." Carey clicked off the line.

About fifteen minutes later, Catherine was startled by a knock on the door. By now, she was convinced that it must be the state police, there to inform her of her boyfriend's violent, tragic, and untimely death. When she mustered the courage to turn the knob and open the door, Nathan was standing before her wearing a goofy grin on his face, the picture of contentment. His dayglo chartreuse climbing helmet sat at a jaunty angle on top of his head. He seemed completely taken aback when Catherine fell into his arms, sobbing with relief. Catherine later learned that Nathan's cell phone had fallen out of his pocket shortly after they'd gotten to the climbing spot. It, not he, had been the one to take a fatal plunge off the cliff. It simply hadn't occurred to him to use his friend's phone when they'd gotten off the rocks at the end of the day.

*

No matter how many times Catherine impressed upon Nathan her need to know where he was, what he was doing, and that he was all right, he almost always failed to stay in contact enough to keep her from going crazy with fear and anxiety. As Catherine paced the rooms of their Newfield home, getting more and more wound up about what might have happened, she tried to remind herself that this was "typical Nathan" behavior. She tried to comfort herself by thinking that, at any minute, he and the kids would come bounding through the door with tales of an amazing adventure.

CHAPTER THREE
NATHAN

Nathan eyed the sun settling near the horizon, the dark, narrow trails that led in both directions around the pond, and the snowpack that blanketed the ice in front of him. He estimated that it would take more than an hour to pick his way along the shore path. But by making a beeline across the frozen expanse, which he guessed to be about half a mile wide, they could make it home before nightfall. He pulled his cell phone from his jacket pocket to check the time and to call Catherine to let her know where they were. Noting that it was 4:25, he also saw that he had no service. He tucked the phone back into his pocket without bothering to dial.

Jacob was tired and cranky. "C'mon, Dad. Let's go. I'm hungry."

"Yeah." Joe took his cue from his older brother. "What are we waiting for?"

With that, Nathan eased the RZR onto the hard-pack snow of the pond. When he got all four wheels onto the ice, he paused to see if anything untoward would happen. He figured that if the ice wasn't going to support their weight, it would be here, near the safety of the shore. He idled there for about thirty seconds, long enough for the boys to whine again through the intercom. Not hearing or feeling any instability, Nathan gave the RZR some gas. He gained confidence and picked up speed with each passing yard, and soon they were past the halfway point and closing the distance to the far shore.

The trees along the pond's edge cast fingers of shadow across the ice as the sun reached for the horizon. Nathan scanned the far shoreline to pick out a place where he could guide the RZR back onto solid ground. Out of nowhere, the front left tire bounced into the air and landed with a hard thud. The left rear wheel quickly followed. Recalling this moment later, all Nathan could figure was that they'd hit a hidden log or rock, or maybe an ice heave that he'd failed to notice.

The ice, weakened by the blow of the front wheel, received the impact of the rear tire with a sickening "crack." Before it could gain purchase on something more solid, it broke through to open water, and, within seconds, the ice beneath the back half of the RZR disintegrated. Both children screamed in terror.

"Daddy, what's happening?" Jacob's panicked voice crackled over the intercom before the battery and electrical system shorted out. The rear of the machine, which housed the engine and most of the vehicle's weight, was sinking fast. With a surge of adrenalin, Nathan popped the lock on his harness and dove out through the space between the RZR's door and the roll cage above it. Grabbing onto the top bar of the cage, he swung himself toward the rear of the machine, which was now immersed up to the doors. He took a quick glance toward the shore, trying to gauge the distance to safety and to get an idea of how deep the water might be. It was farther and deeper than he hoped.

Turning back to the boys, he saw that they were now both waist-deep in water and sinking fast. Both children flailed against their harnesses. Nathan could see the panic in their eyes, and he didn't need the intercom to hear their desperate cries. The water was climbing rapidly to the level of Jacob's chest and Joe's chin. Nathan grabbed for Joe's now-submerged harness and fumbled with the latch. Releasing his son should have been as easy as pressing a button, but something was wrong. Either the mechanism was jammed, or Nathan's fingers were losing their ability to function in the icy water. Whatever the reason, as the RZR continued to sink and the water began to fill Joe's helmet, Nathan was unable to free his son.

Nathan's own helmet was filling with water now, and he realized that the sinking machine was pulling him down with it. Instinctively, he broke for the surface while simultaneously wrenching the helmet from his head. He took a huge gasp of air and plunged back down into the dark water, blindly feeling for the bars of the roll cage. Nathan was ungainly in the water, clad in his winter gear, and he was unable to reach the RZR on his first attempt. As he felt his brain begging for oxygen, he again broke for the surface. He treaded water momentarily and tried to catch his breath. Summoning all his strength he took in a giant lung-full of air and dove again.

Nathan forced himself deeper than the last dive. Groping head-down in the dark water with his hands outstretched in front of him, this time, he was able to locate the top-most bar of the roll cage. He pulled himself down into the rear passenger compartment of the vehicle between the two rear seats, facing them. With his left hand, he again tried to unlatch

Joe's harness while he blindly groped to locate Jacob's. It registered somewhere in Nathan's subconscious that neither boy was struggling any longer, as they had been just a few moments earlier.

Before he could manipulate the harness locks and release the boys, searing pain shot through his lungs, driving him to the surface. He tread water, gasping for air until he could fill his lungs for another dive. On his third attempt, Nathan felt awkward and uncoordinated. He couldn't get his legs and arms to drive him down to the bottom of the pond. The frigid water had begun to take its toll on Nathan's body. He resurfaced without reaching the boys and again gasped for air. He made a fourth, flailing attempt, but barely got a few feet below the surface before he had to turn around again.

The primal part of Nathan's brain - the part that puts survival above all else - was kicking in as hypothermia threatened to rob him of his strength and his senses. Torn between his duty as a father to protect his children and the instinctual demand for self-preservation, Nathan decided to make one more try. This time, though, he accomplished little more than splashing just below the surface. In a moment of pure anguish, he resigned himself to his impotence. He was unable to save his boys.

Nathan awkwardly paddled himself toward the edge of the ice. There, finding handholds in the frozen snow, he drew upon his dwindling physical reserves and heaved himself to safety. He lay there, face down on the snow, his wet clothes sticking to his skin, as he tried to catch his breath.

Less than a minute passed before Nathan willed himself to get up off the ice. Maybe, he desperately thought, if I can get someone here in time, they'll have a chance. He remembered reading an article about something called the "mammalian dive reflex." The article had explained how cold water would slow down a whale's or a dolphin's metabolism to the point where they could survive for hours without taking a breath. That same article told stories of children falling through the ice and being submerged for long periods of time and who, when rescued, due to this same phenomenon, were successfully revived. It was only this memory, and the hope it offered, that propelled Nathan to move on from the hole in the ice beneath which Jacob and Joe lay.

Nathan knew that his friend, Jim, lived just a few hundred yards beyond the far shore. If he could get to Jim's house, he could call 911. He could still rescue the boys. With fierce determination, Nathan trudged and then ran across the remaining expanse of ice and climbed onto the shore, following the path away from the pond. Blood returned to his extremities as he ran, and he found renewed energy to quicken his pace. With his blood circulating again, he shed the encumbering outer layers of his frozen clothing and sped forward toward his children's hoped-for resurrection.

Nathan crested the hill that he knew led to Jim's house and was relieved to see light streaming from the windows. His labored breath blew out in plumes ahead of him, his icy beard and his panic aging him beyond his years. He mounted the stairs to the front porch and burst through the unlocked door.

The anguished father's desperation was etched on his face. "Jim! Where's your phone?"

"Nate, what's happened? You look like crap." Jim jumped up from his chair beside the woodstove.

Nathan spotted the phone sitting on the coffee table and grabbed it. He punched in the three-digit emergency number. The dispatcher picked up on the third ring.

"911. What's your emergency?"

"My ATV fell through the ice on Franklin Pond."

"Franklin Pond? In Newfield?"

"Yes, hurry. My sons are still strapped in."

"Slow down. Tell me exactly what happened."

Jim was already donning his snowmobile suit as Nathan explained, with all the urgency he could, that his boys were trapped in the ATV at the bottom of the pond. The dispatcher asked where Nathan was calling from and then instructed him to stay where he was. "We'll send someone out right away."

Jim was strapping on his helmet as he tossed a dry snowmobile suit to Nathan.

"Get out of those wet clothes and put these on. I'll get my sled fired up."

Nathan began to undress. There was no way he was going to sit around the house waiting for the rescue squad to arrive, with his sons out there in the cold, dark water. But his fingers fumbled with the buttons of his shirt as he tried to strip down, and soon his whole body was wracked with tremors from the shock and the cold. Jim poked his head in the front door.

"C'mon, Nate. Let's go!" But when Jim saw the condition his friend was in, he knew there was no way he'd be able to retrace his steps and return to the lake. Tossing his helmet aside, Jim grabbed a blanket off the back of the couch. As he reached out to wrap it around him, Nathan collapsed into his arms.

Jim took his shivering friend by the shoulder and eased him down onto the couch. "Wait here. I'm going to get the shower started. We need to get you warmed up." He returned a moment later and guided Nathan up the stairs to the bathroom. In an act of tenderness, intimacy, and mercy that neither man could have imagined possible, Jim disrobed his incapacitated friend and guided him into the shower. Nathan

30

was unable to stand on his own. He collapsed to the floor and let the hot water course over his body. Slowly, the spasms subsided and then disappeared altogether.

*

On paper, Jim Richardson and Nathan Osgood were unlikely friends. Nathan's status as a successful financial planner stood in stark contrast to Jim's grease-stained shirts and parochial perspectives. But on the Saturday morning more than three years ago when their paths first crossed, something clicked between them. Jim had been nursing a cup of coffee and reading the newspaper at the Hungry Hollow Café in Limerick when Nathan came in to buy some cider donuts for the kids. Nathan decided to order an egg sandwich for himself and took a seat at the table next to Jim's while he waited.

"Hey." Nathan nodded to Jim, trying to be friendly but not intrusive. "How's it going?"

"Not bad, I guess." Jim looked over the top of his paper.

Nathan pointed to the headline in the local weekly Jim was scanning. "So, I see they still haven't caught that bear yet." The authorities had been trying for months to trap and relocate a large black bear that had been raiding bird feeders and generally scaring folks around town.

"Nope. And I hope they never do." Jim laid the paper down on the small café table and took a sip from his cup.

"I know. Right? What do people expect when they live out here? Isn't that why we don't live in a city?"

"If you don't like it, move back to Boston. That's what I say."

The men introduced themselves and discovered that they

31

were neighbors, living about three miles from each other as the crow flies. After that first Saturday, they began an unspoken ritual of meeting at The Hollow for coffee on Saturday mornings. Over time, their friendship deepened to the point where Jim, a single father, was coming by Catherine and Nathan's for dinner once or twice a month. When Jim's daughter turned twelve, Catherine had her begin doing some light babysitting for Jacob and Joe.

*

"Help should be here pretty soon." Jim waited on the other side of the shower curtain. "They'll do everything they can for the boys, and I hear they're really good at what they do."

Nathan didn't have the energy to respond. But when he recalled the terrified look in Joe's eyes from behind the visor of his helmet as it filled with water, and Jacob's flailing to get free, he was wracked with gut-wrenching sobs. Jim padded out of the bathroom and let his friend work through his pain in private.

When Nathan had cried himself out, he pulled himself up and turned off the water. As he stepped out of the shower, he saw that his friend had left a pile of clothes on the vanity. They were several sizes too big for him, but at least they were warm and dry. He dressed and went downstairs to the living room and saw flashing blue lights pulsing in the dooryard. Jim was outside on the porch talking to a Sheriff's deputy and gesturing toward the trail down to the pond.

Another shot of adrenalin surged through Nathan's body. He jumped into a pair of boots by the door and sprinted outside. "You've got to get people down there! My boys are trapped under the ice!"

"Sir, we're doing everything we can right now." A female Sheriff's deputy answered, then peeked at her watch. "The Warden Service is on their way and we're mustering search and rescue as quickly as possible."

"But we've got to go *now*!" The desperate father found no reassurance in the deputy's words or passive demeanor. He paced around the porch, oozing anxiety. "They can't last much longer."

"Sir, I know this is hard for you --"

"Hard for me? You know this is hard for me?" Tears burst forth as Nathan lost all composure. Jim had to restrain his friend from physically confronting the deputy. He tried to wrap a comforting arm around Nathan's shoulder, but the desperate father shrugged it off. "We've got to get to them while there's still a chance! Jim, do something!"

"Nate, c'mere." Jim took his friend by the elbow and led him to a corner of the porch, away from the deputy and lowered his voice to a conspiratorial whisper. "Listen, I already decided we can't wait until the wardens get here. I've made a few calls to friends who've got snowmachines and ropes and stuff. They should be here any minute."

No sooner had Jim offered these words than the two men spotted a pair of headlights coming up the driveway. Nathan charged down the porch steps, Jim close on his heels. A Ford F-350 crew cab pulling a trailer with two snowmobiles parked beside the sheriff's cruiser. Three burly men climbed out of it, all cradling helmets under their arms.

"Hal, Sam, Greg, I'm glad you're here." Jim shook each of the men's hands in turn. "This is Nate. It's his boys I told you about." The men nodded at Nathan, their eyes downcast. "Let's get your sleds unloaded and get down to the pond. You've got the ropes?"

One of the men nodded in response as they all grabbed gear from the truck bed and lowered the trailer's tailgate. Jim moved off to fire up his own machine.

"Now wait a minute, boys." By force of habit, the deputy had a hand resting on her service weapon as she came down the steps from the front porch. "Where do you think you're going?"

"We're going to go try and get those boys." Jim swung a leg over his snowmobile's seat and indicated to Nathan that he should get on behind him.

"We've got experts on the way." The deputy approached the men sitting astride their idling machines. "I don't want to make a bad situation worse by having a bunch of you fall through the ice. Let's all calm down and wait here."

"You can wait if you want, but we're going to go give it a shot, and there's nothing you can do to stop us." The deputy watched, powerless to restrain the men, as they revved their engines and careened down the trail into the night. She knew he was right. There was nothing she could do.

Jim led the small caravan of three snow machines down the forest trail toward Franklin Pond with Nathan seated behind him. They came to a stop when they reached the edge of the pond and dismounted. Standing in a tight circle, they consulted Nathan.

"Nate, how far out is it to where you fell in?" Jim scanned the ice that glowed in front of him in the glare of the headlights from the snowmobiles.

"I'd say about 200 yards or so." Nathan pointed toward the dark center of the pond. "Come on! What are we waiting for? We've got to get out there."

Jim glanced at the faces of his four friends. "Okay, here's the plan: Hal, you've got a climbing rope with you, right?"

"Yeah, three lengths of 75 feet each." Hal held up a coil of red, braided rope.

"Good. I'll tie that around my waist and head out onto the ice while the rest of you wait here on the shore. Pay out the line as I go. That way, if I break through, you can help pull me out. Once I know it's safe, I'll tug on the rope and you can follow. We'll leap-frog like that and get as close to the hole as we can. Nate, you stay here with these guys."

"No way, Jim." Nathan moved toward Jim's sled. "I've got to get to my boys."

Jim put his hand on his friend's shoulder and looked him in the eye. "Nate, you've got to trust me on this. You're going to be better off following with this crew than you are with me in the lead. It's a lot less likely I'll break through the ice with just one of us on a sled, so you've got to let me go alone. Got it?"

Nathan couldn't argue with Jim, and he didn't want to delay the rescue any longer. He nodded his agreement.

Hal tied the red rope around Jim's waist and Jim eased his snowmobile out onto the ice. Just as Nathan had with the RZR, Jim stopped close to shore to see if the ice would hold. When he felt secure, he guided his sled forward as Hal paid out the rope. The other men spliced the remaining lines together.

Out on the ice, beyond their view from the shore, Jim crept along, listening as best he could over the noise of his machine for any sign he might lose his purchase. After traveling what he estimated was about 50 yards, he stopped and gave a strong tug on the rope.

Hal felt the line in his hands go taut. "That's our signal." The men climbed onto their snowmobiles and slid out onto the ice. They rode single file, spread out for safety, following Jim's track. When they were within ten feet of Jim, Hal stopped and dismounted, and Jim resumed his forward progress. The crew repeated this maneuver with what seemed to Nathan excruciating precision until he could see Jim had stopped about 30 yards from the edge of a small expanse of open water.

Jim walked back to where the others were standing. "I don't dare get any closer with these machines. We'll have to go the rest of the way on foot. Let's all get roped up." Hal, whom Nathan later learned was an experienced alpine climber, produced a set of carabiners from a tote bag and quickly linked all the men to the rope, which he anchored to two of the snow machines. They trudged forward toward the hole as a unit, Jim taking the lead with a bright flashlight. When he came to within 10 feet of the hole, Jim heard a loud "crack" from underfoot and froze in place. He put his hand up to stop the others from advancing. "I'd say that's as far as we go."

"Now what?" Nathan's tone reflected the urgency all the men felt.

"I've got the hook back in my bag." Hal freed himself from the rope and headed back to the snowmobiles.

It was clear that Jim had a plan. "Nate, your rig's got a full roll cage, right? Did it land upright on the bottom of the pond?"

"Right, yeah. It does. And I'm pretty sure it was upright when it sank."

"And you think it's in about fifteen feet of water?"

"I think so."

"Good. Here's what we're going to do. We're going to use the grappling hook to snag the roll cage. If we can do that, we'll tie the other end of the ropes to our sleds and see if we can pull the ATV up to the surface. It's a long shot, but it's the only shot we've got."

For the first time in the 90 minutes since the sinking, Nathan felt a glimmer of hope.

Hal returned to the group with the grappling hook. He quickly removed the men from their safety ropes and attached it to the line. "Who's gonna try and fish for the machine?"

Before Nathan had a chance to offer, Jim grabbed the hook and started to walk toward the hole in the ice. When he'd gotten to where he'd felt the ice shift beneath his feet he sank to his knees and crawled on all fours. As he approached the hole, he got down on his belly and wriggled forward until his hands could reach out and touch the edge of the ice. He fed the hook forward and gingerly lowered it into the water. When he thought he'd let it sink deep enough, he began to pull it back up, hoping it would snag on something.

Three times Jim let the hook sink, each time a little deeper. Three times, he came up empty. On the fourth try, he decided to let the hook sink until it hit bottom. He paid out the rope until it went slack. Jim wasn't a religious man, but he prayed to God that this time he'd catch some part of the machine with the hook. Slowly, he pulled the rope up off the bottom, meeting no resistance. Just as he was about to give up, he felt the hook catch on something. He pulled back as hard as he dared while lying at the edge of the ice. Whatever it had caught on was heavier than he could pull up.

"I think I've got it!" The excitement in Jim's voice was palpable, but everyone knew it was premature to celebrate.

Jim eased himself away from the hole. "Take up the slack and hold tension on the rope." By the time he had returned to the clutch of men, they had already secured the ropes to the snow machines. "We'll have to pull in unison. Our three rigs will need to be side-by-side for this to have any hope of working."

To a man, they knew they were risking their own lives in this rescue attempt. They had no safety net themselves. If their machines broke through the ice, they'd all be on their own. But they also knew the stakes were as high as they could get, and if they were worried about themselves, they didn't show it.

With the ropes secured, the four men climbed onto the snow machines and started their engines. Nathan sat behind Jim, but this time faced backward toward the hole in the ice and the point where he hoped his two sons would soon emerge.

Jim signaled to the others, giving them the sign to move forward. "Take up the slack!" He shouted over the din of the machines. The men eased their snowmobiles forward until they held tension on the ropes.

"On my count now. Three, two, one, go!" The men gunned their sleds, and they lurched forward in unison as the ropes stretched to their limits. The roar of the snowmobiles was deafening. Slowly, though, the machines inched ahead. It felt like there was movement on the other end of the ropes. The men's hopes rose as they edged forward.

"Keep it going, boys!" Jim's voice was drowned out by the snarl of the straining engines. But their treads, which had dug down through the snow to the ice below, started slipping in place, and their progress stalled. Jim gave the signal to stop.

Nathan jumped up from the back of his friend's sled. "What are you doing? We were getting there!"

"It feels like we're stuck." Jim addressed the crew. "Here's what I'm thinking: What if we put some slack in the ropes, gunned our engines, and kind of shocked the rig out of the mud?"

Hal looked hopeful. "Might work."

"Might snap the ropes." Greg was unable to bite back his skepticism.

Jim rallied them around the idea. "I don't see that we have any other choice. Let's back up about ten feet and get a running start at it."

The others followed Jim's lead and again positioned their machines side-by-side. Once more, on his count, they gunned their engines, and their sleds raced forward. As the ropes snapped taught, the unexpected happened. Instead of the RZR rising from the bottom, it dragged forward, causing the ropes to chew into the ice at the edge of the hole. Acting like saw blades, the ropes tore a deep gash in the ice in a direct line between the hole and the snowmobiles. Suddenly, on both sides of the ropes, the ice began to disintegrate. The jagged laceration was widening fast as it approached the three snow machines.

"Get out! Get out!" Jim clambered off his machine, and the others followed suit.

Over his shoulder, Jim watched the ice split apart behind him like a zipper, open water approaching with alarming speed. The men scurried to safety moments before the opening reached their sleds. Once safely away, they looked back to see that two of the machines had disappeared completely. The third was half-submerged, with its track below water and its skis dug into the ice, pointed toward the night sky. The men stood there panting and speechless. None of them dared to look at Nathan, who was sitting in the snow with his head between his knees. They could tell by the way he was shaking that he was sobbing with the realization that his children were dead.

After a time of respectful silence, Hal was the one to speak.

"Best be getting back."

Jim nodded and broke from the group, moving toward Nathan. He crouched down next to his grief-stricken friend.

"Nate, there's nothing more we can do now. We need to wait for the Warden Service to get here. Let's get you back to my place."

"I can't leave them, Jim."

"I know, I know. But sitting here's not going to help them. Let's go get some coffee, see what the rescue team has planned. Maybe we can do something when they get here."

Nathan hung his head once more between his knees, shaking it slowly. "I just wanted to get us home before dark. It was just a shortcut."

"I know. I know." Jim put his arm around his friend and eased him to his feet. As one, the five men turned away from the hole in the ice and made their way back to shore. Jim trailed behind his three buddies who had given their all to help, guiding Nathan by the arm like a lost child.

*

"Mr. Osgood?" the female sheriff's deputy approached Nathan as he returned to Jim's house with the rest of the unsuccessful rescue team. "I'm afraid I'm going to need to get a formal statement from you."

"Now? Can't it wait?" Nathan spoke into the ground, not making eye contact with the deputy.

"I'm wondering whether you've been in touch with your wife. Does she know where you are or what's happened?"

"Oh my God." Nathan was seized by a new level of panic. "She has no idea. I tried to call her from the trail before I crossed the pond, but I didn't have any service. What am I going to tell her?"

"Here's what I suggest." The deputy placed a comforting hand on Nathan's arm. "Why don't we let the pros handle things here. I'll drive you home so you can tell your wife you're okay. She's probably worried sick."

"I'd like to go along with you." Jim draped a heavy wool blanket over Nathan's shoulders. "I know both Nate and Catherine pretty well. Maybe my being there will help."

"Fine with me as long as it's okay with you, Mr. Osgood." The deputy rose to her feet. Nathan nodded, thankful for Jim's steadfast friendship, and followed the two of them to the cruiser.

CHAPTER FOUR
CATHERINE

Catherine was climbing out of her skin. It was well past sunset and still no word from Nathan. She was a cyclone of emotions. Fear, anger, and anxiety swirled through her as she repeatedly dialed Nathan's number only to get the same straight-to-voicemail result. The unbaked nachos sat on the kitchen counter, the soggy chips wilting beneath a dried crust of meat and cheese. *Where could he be? Where could he possibly be?*

Catherine didn't want to alarm anyone else, so she picked up the phone to call Carey, who knew from her earlier text that she was worried. "I'm going out of my mind here. I hate to cry wolf again, but I'm really scared that something's happened this time."

"I know that you're afraid right now, Cat. It's hard not to know what's going on. Can you take a few deep breaths? Let's try and breathe together."

Ever since they were little girls sharing a bedroom in their family home in Saratoga Springs, New York, Carey had used this technique to help calm her anxious little sister. She encouraged Catherine to find a comfortable spot to sit and then led her in some breathing exercises. While it distracted her briefly, the frantic mother couldn't sit still for more than a minute, and she let Carey know.

"Thanks for trying, Carey. I don't think anything's going to calm me down except holding those boys in my arms." Catherine was pacing around the house again, wearing a circular path from the living room to the kitchen to the dining room and back to the living room again. "And wringing Nathan's neck for being so irresponsible."

"Keep me posted, Cat. Let me know when they're all home, safe and sound." Catherine hung up the phone and resumed her fearful vigil, feeling like a trapped mama bear who's been separated from her cubs. Desperation disoriented her. She lost all track of time as wave upon wave of adrenalin surged and then subsided, the emptiness of not knowing stretching out before her. Catherine's ears buzzed with anxiety, her body vibrating like a high-tension electric wire.

It could have been ten minutes or two hours after she'd hung up with Carey that she spotted a pair of headlights coming up Mountain Road. Her heart soared when they turned into her driveway. *A neighbor gave Nathan, Jacob, and Joe a ride home after they'd gotten stranded somewhere. Maybe they'd just run out of gas.* But her breath caught in her throat when she saw the rack of blue lights on top of the car. She tore out the door and ran to the driveway as the cruiser came to a stop, and a sheriff's deputy stepped out and turned to pull the handle on the back door.

Catherine's heart leaped again, this time with joy, as she saw her husband step out of the car. She barely noticed that he was wearing someone else's clothes and that he was wrapped in a blanket. Catherine flung herself into his arms, all the anger of the past few hours melting away with the relief she felt, knowing that Nathan and the boys were safe. She closed her eyes to blink away tears of joy as the deputy went to open the rear door on the other side of the cruiser. Catherine expected to see her two beautiful boys leap out, both eager to tell her the story of their adventure. What she saw instead didn't register. *What is Jim doing in the car? Where are Jacob and Joe? Maybe they're still in the back seat.*

Catherine tore herself away from Nathan and noticed for the first time that he was crying. She pushed him out of the way and dove into the back of the now-empty vehicle.

"Where are the boys?" Her panicked voice echoed from inside the car. "Where are my boys?" She desperately searched for the precious, but absent cargo. "Where are they? Where are they?" She ran to Nathan, frantic in her quest.

"They're gone!" Nathan blurted between sobs.

"Gone? What do you mean, gone?" Panic was cutting off Catherine's air supply.

The sheriff's deputy moved closer toward the couple. "Ma'am, I'm afraid there's been an accident." With those words, Catherine felt the world tilt on its axis before it all went dark.

*

It was all a dream. A really, really awful dream. Catherine slowly awoke from what felt like a deep sleep, her eyelids heavy. *I must have fallen asleep, waiting for the boys to get home. What a nightmare.* Feeling a cold washcloth dabbed on her forehead, she opened her eyes and saw her husband's face. Then she noticed, standing behind him, their friend Jim, and a woman she didn't recognize, wearing a uniform and an equipment-laden utility belt. A surge of adrenalin shot through her as the scene in the driveway came rushing back, and she knew it was real. An all-too-real nightmare. The young mother sat bolt upright on the couch.

"Tell me right this minute where my babies are."

Nathan tried to respond. His lips moved, but nothing came out except a sob. He looked to Jim and the deputy with pleading eyes, unable to bring himself to utter the words that needed speaking.

"Ma'am, I'm afraid it's bad news." the deputy stepped forward. "The worst news a mother can imagine."

Jim approached the couch and took a seat on the opposite side from Nathan and took Catherine's hand in his.

Nathan stared at the floor in front of him and finally managed to utter a whisper. "Cat, Jacob and Joe are gone."

"Stop saying that! What do you mean 'gone?'"

Jim took the leap that Nathan couldn't. "They're dead, Catherine. Drowned."

The news simply didn't compute, and her confusion was the only thing that Catherine could hang onto. "Drowned? It's the middle of winter. How could they drown?"

Her mind clouded over as she tried to come to terms with the devastating news. She felt herself growing faint again. But the faces of her boys came floating into her vision, and the mama bear in her erupted.

"I need to see them." She turned to the sheriff's deputy. "Where are they? Where are they right now?"

"They're on their way to the hospital." The deputy edged toward the front door. "I can take you there if you'd like."

"I need to be with them. I need to see them. I need to hold them." Catherine jumped up from the couch.

Jim rose with her, but Nathan seemed glued to his seat, his head in his hands. Catherine had her jacket on and her hand on the doorknob. Jim looked down at his friend and, from his time in Operation Desert Storm, recognized the signs of shock. He reached down and roused the grieving father with a gentle shake of his shoulder.

"Nate, you need to go with Catherine. C'mon. Get up." Nathan slowly rose and walked toward the front door. He clearly wasn't all there. "You can drop me by my house on the way." The deputy gave the large man a nod and strode out to her cruiser.

The drive to the hospital seemed interminable. Catherine kept probing Nathan for more details, but he just stared out the window, lost in a catatonic state.

"Nathan, you need to talk to me!"

He turned his gaze to face his wife, but his eyes seemed to look right through her, into the dark woods passing by the window.

"I killed them." With that simple, devastating declaration he returned his vacant gaze out the window.

The sheriff's deputy swung the cruiser into the emergency entrance of the hospital and parked by the front door. She let Catherine and Nathan out of the back and walked them through the sliding doors. Catherine felt like she was walking through Jell-O. Each step was an effort, her breathing labored, like she was hiking at 15,000 feet.

"Down the hall this way." The deputy pointed. She had alerted the medical examiner that they were on their way, and he had held off on starting his autopsies of the boys' bodies.

Catherine's legs turned to rubber when she saw the sign on the wall, pointing them toward the morgue. *Can this be happening? This can't be real.*

Nathan trudged along beside her, looking like a zombie. It occurred to her that he might need medical attention.

The Medical Examiner met them at the door to the morgue. He turned to the couple and tried to prepare them.

"They weren't in the water that long, so you won't see any outward signs of deterioration. We've cut them out of all their clothes, and their bodies are very pale. Other than that, they'll look like they're asleep." Catherine heard the words but couldn't process them.

The Medical Examiner began to turn toward the hall, then paused and made eye contact with Catherine. "They're lying on tables, side-by-side. Would you like to see them one at a time, or together?"

Catherine knew what she wanted without hesitation. "Together."

"I'll let my assistant know. Please, wait here one moment." He disappeared through a pair of swinging doors that let out a small whooshing sound, like a whisper, as they opened and then closed behind him.

Catherine felt wobbly on her feet, and she reached for Nathan to steady her. He was unblinking and absent, still as a stone.

The swinging doors opened again and the doctor gestured them through. "Are you ready?"

Catherine gave the slightest nod, thinking to herself that it was a stupid question. The doctor led them into the sterile, brightly lit room, the sheriff's deputy following close behind. Two metal tables stood side by side, each holding a sheet with a small form underneath. The doctor and an assistant drew back the sheets as Catherine moved closer, until she was standing between the tables. Looking down, she saw the pale, lifeless faces of her two children.

"No!" Catherine tried to process the horror before her. "No. No. No." Her body knew better than her mind that she needed to be protected from the sight that lay before her. For the second time in an hour, she fainted, collapsing between the two tables.

*

Catherine awoke early the following morning feeling groggy and disoriented. She had a terrible headache and, reaching up to her forehead, felt the large egg that had blossomed there.

"Shhh, don't touch that," a gentle voice urged from the bedside. "Just take it easy. You took quite a spill."

"Where am I?" Catherine's head felt like it was full of cotton.

"You're in a room at York Hospital," came the answer. "We've got you sedated, so you probably feel pretty woozy." That was an understatement. Catherine couldn't lift her head off the pillow, and she felt like she was floating four inches above the mattress.

"My children. Where are my children?"

"How much do you remember from yesterday?"

Catherine wracked her brain, trying to remember through the drug-induced fog. Like a television mystery that reveals its clues piecemeal over time, fragments of the day floated by. She finally remembered someone – could it have been Jim Richardson? – telling her that Jacob and Joe had drowned.

"Is that right? Are my boys really dead?" She felt a small wave of anxiety wash over her, but it was flushed away by the meds they'd given her. She fell back to sleep before hearing the answer.

*

Catherine's hand slips easily between Nathan's fingers, and he strokes her forearm, both tickling her and sending a tingling sensation that reaches from her arm into the deepest parts of her body. They're walking in splintered sunlight, through a grove of tall trees. She rests her head on his shoulder as she listens to him pour out his dreams for their future together. It feels like home. That's the only way she can explain it. She hears a mix of sentimentality and level-headedness come from this man, whom she feels like she's known forever. She knows they will be together always.

As they come to the edge of the woods, they find themselves standing at the base of a hill with an open field sloping up and away from them. Catherine spots three children, two boys and a girl, standing at the top. The three wave handfuls of wildflowers when they see their parents below. Then, one by one, they begin to log-roll down the hill toward the waiting couple. First Jacob, then Joe, then the smallest, Hope. They laugh as they watch the children rolling, picking up speed as they descend. The children are giggling, enjoying the thrill of feeling a little out of control.

But suddenly, the sky darkens and a storm cloud billows in the distance. Catherine looks up to see a bolt of lightning ignite the sky, followed by a shattering crash of thunder. When she looks back at the children, they're all rolling down the hill too fast now, completely out of control. The shouts of glee coming from the children have turned to cries. They're screaming for help. Catherine turns to Nathan to see what he's going to do, but he's disappeared. She's all alone. Catherine turns back to face the hill and the falling children, but when *she tries to run toward them, she's separated from them by a wide body of water. She's forced to watch helplessly as each child rolls and bounces, then splashes into the water and sinks out of sight. She paces the shoreline waiting for them to surface, but they never do.*

*

Catherine awoke from her dream with a gasp, dazed and shaken. She looked around, disoriented, as the whole horrible ordeal slipped back into her consciousness. She turned her head toward the door and was surprised to see her best friend Heather sitting beside the bed. Heather grabbed Catherine's hand when she realized her friend had regained consciousness.

"Hey, sweetie." Heather offered her usual greeting, the red rims of her eyes giving away the fact that she'd been crying at her friend's bedside. "I came as soon as I heard."

Catherine lay her head back, realizing that it was all much more than a bad dream. The tears started to flow for both of them.

"I'll leave you two alone for a bit." The nurse who had been keeping watch over Catherine walked quietly from the room, leaving the two friends to share their moment of grief. There were no words to ease the pain, and Heather was wise enough not to try offering any.

As her crying subsided, Catherine looked around the room. "Where's Nathan?"

"He's fine. He can't be here right now." This seemed to satisfy Catherine for the moment. The accommodating nurse returned to the room with a syringe and injected something into Catherine's IV tube.

"This will help take the edge off, dear." Between the nurse's gentle voice and the medications, Catherine was soon floating again. She was aware of being in a hospital bed. She was aware that her closest, dearest friend in all the world was there. And she was aware that Joe and Jacob were dead. But she didn't feel it as the stab to the heart that it was.

*

When Catherine returned to consciousness some two hours later, Heather was still holding her hand. "I'm right here with you." Catherine gave her hand a tight squeeze. Slowly, she opened her eyes and turned to her friend, who could see the sadness in them. They both sighed, tears flowing quietly but freely.

"I talked to your sister. She's on her way and should be getting into Logan around 3 this afternoon."

"Mmmm. Good."

"Nathan's parents were here for a while. Then they went to see him."

"Where is he?"

Heather didn't know any easy way to tell Catherine how Nathan had ended up in the hospital himself, so she just came out with it.

"Catherine, when you passed out in the morgue last night, Nathan tried to hurt himself." She thought "hurt" might land easier than "kill." "They were able to stop him, but they put him in the psych unit for observation."

Still feeling the effects of the medication, Catherine couldn't take in the implication of this news. "Mmmm. Okay." Catherine slowly gazed around the room at the unfamiliar surroundings, and then into her friend's eyes. "Thanks for being here."

"Sweetie, there's no place else I would be, given what's happened."

Catherine noticed, for the first time, the pads between her legs, their meaning slowly dawning on her. "I lost the baby?"

Heather nodded. "I'm sorry. How far along were you?"

"About eight weeks. I was going to surprise Nathan and tell him last night." Catherine paused and looked her friend in the eye. "Heather, what am I going to do? Jacob and Joe...I can't imagine my life without them. And the baby, too."

Once more, tears began to cascade down Catherine's cheeks. Heather climbed into the narrow hospital bed, wrapped her arms around her grieving friend, and let her sob into her shoulder until her blouse was soaked with tears. She stayed there until Catherine returned to an uneasy sleep.

CHAPTER FIVE
NATHAN

Down the hall from Catherine's room, in the community hospital's small inpatient psychiatric unit, Nathan lay heavily sedated on a suicide watch. Leather straps held his wrists and ankles close to the metal frame of his hospital bed.

The psych unit at York Hospital was a suite consisting of three patient rooms and a nurse's station located behind a locked door at the end of the second-floor hallway. Nathan was the only patient in the unit. His room, like the others, was equipped with its own camera that the care team could monitor from the nurse's station. Every 15 minutes the staff looked in on him and checked his restraints. The room itself was austere, and no personal belongings were permitted, not even a "Get Well" card, if he ever received one.

Between the restraints, the medication, and the monitoring, Nathan was no danger to himself. He floated on a raft of sedation that occasionally bumped against the shore of consciousness. But for most of the morning, he was unaware of his surroundings or the circumstances that had delivered him there.

By noon, the medication had begun to wear off and Nathan realized where he was and what had happened. The scene in the morgue replayed in his head like a balky streaming video, jumpy and skipping. The boys' inert forms on the cold metal tables. Catherine collapsing to the floor. Nathan grabbing the deputy's pistol from its holster and raising it to his head. Being grabbed from behind. A scuffle. Someone wrestling the weapon from his hand. Being pinned to the floor. The sharp pain in his arm from an injection. Darkness.

As the fog of the sedative lifted, the terror of the previous day's events came into sharper focus. *What have I done? Jacob and Joe are dead. How could I have been so stupid? I just needed to go around the lake. That's all. How will I go on? How will we go on? Catherine. Where's Catherine?* Nathan struggled against the bands, flexing and straining every muscle in his body as waves of guilt, grief and regret washed over him.

"I'm not going to hurt myself," he shouted into the void. Although he couldn't see anyone nearby, he was certain that someone, somewhere could hear him. He thrashed against the restraints. "Would someone just take these things off of me!" Again and again he called out. "Hello! Is anyone there?"

After what seemed like hours but was only a few minutes, a slender woman with shoulder-length brown hair wearing a long white lab coat appeared in the door to Nathan's room. "Mr. Osgood, I'm Dr. Rachel Susskind, the hospital psychiatrist." The physician, who appeared to be in her mid-40's, pulled a chair up beside Nathan's bed.

"Finally. Would you please remove these things?" Nathan strained against the ties that held him fast. "I can't even scratch my nose."

"That's the idea. They're for your own protection."

"I don't need protecting. I need to get out of here."

"I'm afraid that won't be possible, given what happened last night. At least, not yet."

"Listen, Doc. I was out of my mind last night. Don't you think anyone would be, given what happened? My sons are dead because of me. How do you expect me to live with that?"

"That's what we need to talk about." Dr. Susskind closed the chart she'd been reviewing. "Before we can let you out of here, we need to be sure that you intend to live, no matter how hard that might be."

"It's just a figure of speech." Nathan writhed under the restraints.

"I understand, Mr. Osgood. So, here's what we're going to do." Nathan sensed that the physician was all-business with little concern for bedside manner. "I'm going to spend a little time talking to you about what's going to happen, and you're going to listen. After I talk, we'll have a short conversation. How does that sound to you?"

"Like I have a choice?"

The doctor ignored Nathan's sarcasm and continued. "You attempted suicide last night. It may have been a spontaneous reaction to a stressful situation, a one-time occurrence. But with the trauma you experienced and your guilt over the death of your boys, it may not. It's my job to try and assess that. You're on an involuntary admission here. That means that we can hold you, without your consent, for up to seventy-two hours. If we deem it necessary that you stay longer, for your own safety or that of others, we would need to apply to the court for an extension. My goal is to be able to release you within the three-day period, secure in the knowledge that you won't try to do yourself harm once you're released. That determination will be based, in part, on what you and I talk about over the next couple of days. It will also be based on the support systems you have in place to help you cope with what's happened. Is this making sense so far?"

"Yes." Nathan realized that he needed to at least pretend to be compliant to speed his release.

"Good. And, of course, depending on how this conversation goes, I will determine when we can remove the restraints. Okay?"

"Got it."

"So, let's get started, shall we?" Dr. Susskind pulled a small notepad from the pocket of her white coat. "Walk me through exactly what happened yesterday."

Nathan's eyes widened. "Hold on. You want me to relive the trauma less than 24 hours after it happened? What kind of doctor are you?"

"I'm a psychiatrist, Mr. Osgood. Board-certified. I need to hear how you describe yesterday's events to evaluate your current state of mind. I need to hear from you—what you remember and what you don't. Whether there are blank spots or things out of order. If so, we'll need to explore what you're blocking out. Plus, describing what happened out loud can help to reduce the event's power over you. And that will be critical to your successful recovery from the trauma."

Nathan felt the tension in his body begin to ease as he took in the logic of the doctor's words. As much as he hated to relive the terror of the last day, he sensed that he had no choice.

"Now, let's start with your decision to go for a ride in your ATV with your sons, then proceed from there."

Nathan spent the next 40 minutes describing, as best he could, the sequence of events that had landed him in the hospital and his sons in the morgue. By the time he was finished he was completely spent, ready in his exhaustion to do whatever the psychiatrist required.

Dr. Susskind closed her notepad and slid it back into the pocket of her lab coat. "I'm going to recommend removing the restraints, Nathan. But that doesn't mean you're in the clear, by any means."

"So, when can I get out of here?"

"I think we can do some intensive work together over the next day or two. I know I'm stating the obvious, but there's no quick fix here. While it may recede in time, nothing is going to completely remove the pain of losing these kids, or the guilt you feel for their deaths."

Hearing these words, Nathan seemed to withdraw from the conversation. It was almost as if he had received another dose of the sedative.

"Nathan, I need you to look at me." Nathan turned his head toward the psychiatrist, a vacant look on his face. "I want to be very clear with you about one thing: You can survive this. Right now, it may feel like you don't want to. But you *can*. Whether you *do* will be entirely up to you."

A few minutes after Dr. Susskind left Nathan's room, a hospital orderly entered and removed his restraints. He was free to get up and sit in his chair or walk out to the nurse's station as he pleased. Instead, he just rolled over on his side and stared at the wall.

*

Nathan dozed, the after-effects of the sedatives dulling his senses as he avoided the pain of his ordeal through the escape of sleep. He was roused by a gentle knock on the door and, turning toward the sound, he was greeted by the tearful faces of his parents. Jean Osgood rushed to her son's bed while his father Frank hovered just inside the door. Nathan burst into tears at his mother's embrace. His body was wracked by sobs that Jean received as only a mother could. Frank came and took a seat at the foot of the bed, and soon all three were crying together.

"I couldn't save them, Mom. I tried. Really, I did. But I just couldn't do it."

"I'm sure you did everything you could, honey." His mother stroked Nathan's hair, soothing him like she used to when he was a toddler. "Everything you could."

They sat like that, in their tableau of grief, for several minutes until they cried themselves out.

Nathan broke away from his mother. "Where's Catherine? How's she doing?"

Jean took her son's hand. "She's recovering in a room down the hall. She had a nasty fall and got a bad bump on her head, but nothing serious. But she did lose the baby."

"The baby?"

Nathan's parents saw by their son's reaction that Catherine hadn't yet told him that she was pregnant.

"Oh, honey." His mother sighed. "You didn't know?"

As the reality dawned on Nathan that he and Catherine had lost more than their two sons, a new wave of grief washed over him. This one threatened to drag him under for good.

"I killed our baby, too." Nathan turned his back on his parents and stared at the wall, withdrawing into himself at the realization.

Nathan's father dried his eyes and stared down at the floor. "We'll get through this, son." The elder Osgood feigned confidence, sounding as if he was trying to convince not just his boy but himself too. "I don't know how just yet. But together, we'll get through this."

Nathan was a million miles away now, completely unresponsive. Jean rubbed her son's back. "We'll be back to visit again as soon as we can. We love you." The two bereaved grandparents backed out of the room, leaving Nathan alone in his despair. He left his dinner tray untouched, his own sustenance the farthest thing from his mind. Over and over again, Nathan replayed the prior day's scenes in his head, an endless loop of tragedy and heartbreak.

*

Nathan lost all track of time. All he knew was that the sun had set and he faced a long, dark night alone. He'd never felt so isolated in all his life. Like an astronaut on a spacewalk whose safety tether was severed, he was drifting away from all that he knew and loved and counted on. His heart, the place where love and light had so recently resided, was an echo-chamber filled with nothing but self-loathing.

How could I have been so stupid? I thought it was safe. But that doesn't matter now, does it? What was I thinking? What have I done? The awful thud the wheels made on the ice, the crack that followed, the screams of terror from Jacob and Joe. And then the silence, the unalterable silence that followed. Never, never, never would he hear again the sounds of his sons' voices. Never would they come bounding boisterously into his and Catherine's bedroom at sunrise to jump on their bed and start the day off with a tickle fight. Never would he hold Jacob close during a thunderstorm as the boy shook with fear or toss Joe high in the air to come splashing down in the lake with squeals of delight. Nathan felt the weight of "never" battering and crushing him like an avalanche, threatening to bury him alive. And he deserved it, didn't he? He had no one to blame but himself. But for his own stupidity, his momentary lapse in judgment, he and Catherine and the boys would be sitting around the dining room table together, just like any other night, joking and laughing and loving.

There was so much lost, so much he destroyed in that one fateful moment. Memories came flooding back in a relentless stream. Meeting Catherine for the first time, literally nearly running into her in the convenience store parking lot. Late-night conversations over bottomless bottles of wine about their plans for the future. Would she leave her high-powered legal job in Boston, or would he move there and jump back into the world of corporate finance? Could she be happy living in a small town, raising kids? Finding the land on Mountain Road and designing their house together. The countless drives to the site as their dream took shape and form in reality. Carrying Catherine across the threshold when it had been finished. Making love for the first time in their new master bedroom, with its view out to the hills across the state line in southeastern New Hampshire.

Nathan remembered exactly where they were when she'd told him she was pregnant with their first child. It had been a glorious fall day, the air crisp and clear, and they'd taken the ferry from Portland out to Peak's Island for brunch and a bike ride. They were sitting on some rocks, the gentle waves of Casco Bay lapping the shore. Catherine's red hair, tousled by the wind, blew in and out of her face despite her constant attempts to tuck it behind her ears. Her nose was red from the sun and the wind and the cold. "Do you want to put the baby seat on my bike or yours?" she'd ask casually. Nathan didn't get it at first, and Catherine had just sat there, grinning at him deviously until the light dawned on him.

Other memories came rushing by in a torrent. The births of both the boys, the first one long and drawn out, the second nearly too quick. Nights walking the floors with Joe or Jacob and the bleary-eyed mornings that followed. The scare they'd had with Jacob, when he'd mysteriously spiked a high fever, the source of which the doctors couldn't identify and how, gratefully, it had vanished just as mysteriously as it had erupted. Gleeful Christmases around fresh-cut trees from their own forest. Their decision to go ahead and try for a third child – and realizing that he'd cut short that unborn child's life.

Nathan tossed and turned with the flood of recollections, all held under the pall of the previous day's tragedy until he couldn't stand it anymore. He pounded the nurse's call button with his fist. A voice came over the intercom.

"May I help you?"

"I need something, anything to help me sleep. Please, please," Nathan begged.

"Just a moment" came the disembodied voice. Nathan bolted upright and burst out of bed, pacing the room as he waited. His agitation was like a metal band around his chest, tightening with every breath. After what seemed like an interminable wait, a nurse wearing scrubs arrived with a syringe.

"Please take a seat, Mr. Osgood." The nurse gestured toward the bed, and Nathan sat down heavily on the edge. The nurse administered the shot.

"That should help pretty quickly. I'll wait with you to be sure." Within thirty seconds the injection began to work its magic. Nathan could feel the band around his chest easing and soon he felt like he was floating on a tranquil sea.

"Let's get you back to bed." The nurse encouraged Nathan

to lie back down and pulled the light hospital blanket up to his shoulders as he complied. He didn't remember falling asleep.

CHAPTER SIX
CATHERINE

Heather stayed glued to Catherine's bedside while her friend drifted in and out of consciousness on the day after the accident. The sun was fading behind steely clouds that hung low on the horizon when Carey appeared, breathless, in the doorway to Catherine's room. Catherine gasped out a sob at the sight of her sister and reached for her. Carey grabbed Catherine in a long and desperate embrace, and they wept together as Heather discreetly left the room.

The two sisters had always been close. With only eighteen months separating them, they shared nearly everything growing up on a small farm in Saratoga Springs. Both girls loved the outdoors, and both were athletic. In high school, Carey focused on swimming and softball, while Catherine excelled at field hockey. Catherine loved horseback riding so much that her parents had bought her a horse for her twelfth birthday. Both girls loved to ski, and they spent countless winter weekends at Killington with their parents, careening down the slopes, shoulder to shoulder, pressing each other to push the limits of their control. The biggest differences between them were their looks and their academic interests. Catherine's wavy red hair and freckles set her apart from her sister, who sported straight, strawberry blond hair and an unblemished complexion. Where Carey was a math whiz and loathed subjects that were reading-intensive, Catherine was all about the written word. It was no surprise that, after attending Mount Holyoke College together, Carey had headed to business school and Catherine to law school.

Although it didn't seem possible, their parents' accidental death drew the young women even closer together. They were both in college when it happened, and from the time of the accident until Carey's graduation, the two were inseparable. It had been one of those freak accidents where no one was to blame, there was no one to be angry at. Their parents had been on their way home from Killington on a Sunday night, driving a road they knew like the back of their hands, when they hit a patch of black ice. Their car swerved across the center line, barely missing the oncoming traffic, then catapulted down an embankment. After rolling, it struck a tree that nearly split the car in two.

The sudden loss of their parents forced Carey and Catherine to lean into each other in ways they'd never known possible. They drew strength from each other and together they grieved openly and bravely. The summer after the accident was spent with lawyers and accountants settling their parents' estate, and the girls' complementary skills had come in handy. After a semester away, they returned to school, deciding that they would both benefit from the structure and challenge that college offered. After their leave, they'd received permission from the administration to share a dorm room for Carey's senior year.

Since graduation, Carey had been single-minded in the pursuit of her career in international finance, and she remained unmarried and childless. She had virtually adopted Jacob and Joe as her own and spent hours FaceTiming with them from the far-flung locations her career took her. Whenever she could, she'd hop a flight from LaGuardia to Logan to spend a few precious days with her sister and the boys. Catherine reveled in these visits, not just for herself but for how her boys thrived in the presence of "Auntie Carey."

Catherine eased her grip on her sister and sat back against her pillows. "The doctor said I can go home tomorrow." She wanted to let her sister know that, at least physically, she was going to be fine.

"Carey, I lost the baby, too." Carey grasped her sister's hand. She was the only one who'd known Catherine was expecting, and how excited she was about it.

"Oh, Catherine." Carey pulled her into another prolonged embrace and as she did, Heather reappeared in the doorway to Catherine's room. "I'm going to leave you two alone, but I'm here if you need me. Any time, day or night." She looked directly into Catherine's eyes. "I mean it."

Catherine nodded with tears in her eyes as Heather turned and left the room. A wave of grief washed over Catherine as her sister sat holding her hand.

"I can't imagine my life without them. People say things like 'this is like a bad dream,' and I never really got that until now. It really is. I just want to wake up from this and drive back home. I want to walk in the door and hear them fighting over stupid stuff. I want to make them macaroni and cheese and see them sitting at the kitchen counter. I mean, even the hard, scary times like when Jacob was sick. I'd take those right now. The idea that all that's gone just isn't real."

"I know, I know." Carey let her sister ramble as she processed her new reality.

"Remember when we heard about Mom and Dad's accident? The shock and the pain of that? And, I mean, we were devastated, right? I don't know. Maybe because this is my kids. It's a whole other level of pain. I can't even wrap my head around it. Seriously, Carey, I get why Nathan tried to kill himself. I don't know that I can live with this. I don't know how he'll be able to."

"Let's focus on you right now. Nathan's getting good care." Catherine took in a deep breath and nodded in response.

*

Catherine was cleared to be discharged early the following morning, the attending physician having briefed Carey on post-concussion protocols.

"Let's get you back home." Carey pulled some clothes out of a small bag that she'd brought to the hospital.

"What about Nathan?"

"I spoke to Nathan's father earlier this morning. He told me that Nathan's got to stay a little longer." Catherine didn't ask for details, seemingly satisfied with this vague statement.

By eleven o'clock, Carey was pushing her sister in a wheelchair down the hall toward the elevator, Heather walking alongside. Heather accompanied them to the parking lot, where she gave her friend a fierce hug and waved her phone in front of her. "I'm only a text away." Catherine climbed into the passenger seat of Carey's rental car and managed to give Heather a wan smile out the window as they drove off.

Catherine stared out the window as they left the hospital

parking lot. "What am I supposed to do when I get home?"

"We'll figure that out as we go along." The two sisters drove on in silence, making the ten-mile trek back to the house on Mountain Road.

"I know it's the last thing you want to think about right now." Carey looked over at her sister, concerned about how she'd react. "But we'll need to find a funeral home for the boys and decide about a service."

Catherine's stomach lurched at the idea. She suddenly felt like she had when she was five years old, riding in the back seat of the family minivan on the curvy roads from her house to her grandparents'. She pushed the button to roll down the window and faced the late-winter air, hoping her nausea would pass. They made their way through town, past the familiar landmarks of Catherine's life, and her mind ticked off events which, until that moment, had seemed meaningless and mundane. There was the Starbucks where she took Joe "for coffee" after they dropped Jacob at preschool. There was the library where Jacob played with trains in the children's reading room. There was the park where she and the boys would walk by the river and listen to the peepers on the first warm days of spring. There wasn't a mile between the hospital and home that wasn't suffused with some memory of her children. It was like a perfume that lingered in the wake of a woman who had left a party long before. But now it smelled like old, dead flowers, sickening in their sweetness. Catherine wondered if she would have to move away and never return to this part of the world.

"We'll make a quick stop to pick up your prescription." Carey broke into Catherine's thoughts as she swung the car into the CVS parking lot.

And what about Nathan? What did she feel about Nathan?

How could their relationship bear the weight of this loss? Did she want it to? She felt sorry for the guilt he would always carry, how it had broken him. But that felt like the same feeling you'd have for a stray puppy cowering on the shoulder of a highway, an instinct to care for broken things. Was that love? Would she ever be able to wake up beside him and smile because she was happy that they were together? That thought felt like a betrayal of her two dead sons and their unborn child. He was right, she decided, in his declaration made in the back of the police cruiser on the way to the hospital: He had killed them. He alone was responsible for the fact that her entire world had imploded. It was his fault that the sun, the moon, and the stars had all been snuffed out in one careless and irredeemable act. Catherine could already sense the seeds of anger blossoming into full-blown resentment and rage.

Carey climbed back in the car and handed her sister a pill and a bottle of water. "They said at the hospital to take one of these as soon as you got them." Catherine prayed that the medication would take effect before they walked into the house and she was forced to confront its emptiness and the enormity of her loss.

The drive up Mountain Road sparked an uninvited memory of the day Nathan carried her over the threshold of their new home.

*

It was a warm day in late May, coming up on seven years ago. They had gotten word that the building inspector had issued their certificate of occupancy. They made the drive from their apartment in South Portland to Newfield as they had so many times while the house was going up, but this time the trip had an altogether different feel to it. Nathan's parents had offered to meet them at the house to help them celebrate, but they had politely and firmly declined. They wanted to mark this milestone in their own way.

Catherine rolled down the window and took in the warm air wafting up from the valley below as they climbed the last hill on the aptly named "Mountain Road," leading up to their house. "Our road," Catherine thought to herself for the first time. She noticed a hawk circling lazily above the treetops and took it as a good omen. Nathan eased the Subaru off the road and onto their driveway, which had yet to be paved, and parked in front of the garage. Catherine had been here a hundred times before. She'd seen the house going up, bit by bit. She shouldn't have been surprised, but this time the sight took her breath away. It was done. It was theirs. (Well, it was the bank's and theirs.) Her life flashed before her eyes, but it was a flash-forward in which she actually saw her dreams coming true. She saw the yard and driveway filled with toys and bikes and a trampoline, and she heard music playing through the open windows and the raucous laughter of children, lots of children, wafting on the summer breeze.

"Are you coming?" Nathan poked his head in through the driver's side window, breaking Catherine's reverie.

"Hell, yeah!" Catherine grabbed the handle to open her door. She noticed that Nathan was holding a bottle of champagne, and he had a devious grin on his face. She strode toward the garage doors, through which they'd entered the house so many times on their frequent inspections of its progress.

"Uh-uh." Nathan shook his head and took his wife's hand. "Not this time. This time we go through the front door."

Hand-in-hand, the couple made their way up the slate

walkway to the front door of the classic Colonial structure. Nathan reached into his pocket and pulled out two sterling silver key rings, one marked with a letter "N" and the other with a "C." The single keys hanging from each were identical.

"Here you go." He held out the keys to Catherine. "You do the honors."

"Which one is mine?" She was intentionally being playful, trying to extend this moment of joyful anticipation. She took her key, slipped it in the lock, and eased the door open. She was about to step into the house when Nathan grabbed her by the arm.

"Geez, Cat. Slow down. We're gonna do this right."

Nathan shifted the champagne bottle from his right hand to his left and slid his free arm around his wife's shoulders. Bending down, he slipped his other arm under her knees and she made a little hop to help him take her in his arms. They gazed into each other's eyes, both grinning like little children on Christmas morning. Their lips locked in a very adult embrace as Nathan stepped into the house that would become their home. He eased her back down to the floor in the two-story front hallway, and Catherine did a slow spin, taking it all in as if seeing it for the first time.

"Oh Nathan! Can you believe it? It's actually finished!" Pure joy radiated from her face.

Hand-in-hand they walked through the first-floor rooms, taking extra time in the kitchen – her dream kitchen – opening the refrigerator, the oven, the cherry cabinets, and the drawers of the baking island that Catherine had designed herself. They paused in front of the large sliding glass doors that opened onto the wraparound deck and the view of the surrounding hills that they'd seen so many times before. Nathan wrapped his arms around his wife's waist from behind and rested his chin on her shoulder. They sighed together as they reveled in the moment.

"Okay." He broke off the embrace and turned toward the stairs. "Second floor."

They proceeded up the central staircase, and Nathan directed Catherine down the long hallway that housed the bedrooms, bathrooms, and home office. They poked their heads into each room, enjoying the echo of their voices in the unfurnished spaces. Catherine mentally placed beds, bureaus, and desks in each room as they went along. Nathan then directed her to the master bedroom suite. Unlike the rest of the rooms in the house whose doors had been wide open, Catherine noticed that this bedroom door was closed. She reached for the doorknob and was about to turn it when Nathan stopped her again.

He tugged on his wife's shoulder, holding her back. "You're in such a hurry. Slow down."

Still carrying the bottle of champagne, he repeated the move he'd made outside the front door and scooped Catherine up in his arms. Again, they kissed as he swung open the door. Catherine laughed out loud when she opened her eyes to see curtains hung in the windows, a throw-rug on the floor, and a fully made bed in the middle of the room. Two champagne flutes stood on a nightstand. She looked back into her husband's face and understood the mischief she'd seen earlier in his eyes.

"Well, don't you think it's time we christened the place?" Nathan lowered Catherine onto the bed, popped the champagne cork, and filled the two glasses. Before he had time to hand one over to her, Catherine grabbed them both.

"These can wait." She set the glasses back on the nightstand and pulled her husband down onto the bed. Then they made love for the very first time in their new home.

*

Carey pulled the car into the driveway and stopped in front of the closed garage doors. Earlier that morning, she had policed the yard to be sure it was free of toys to minimize, or at least defer, Catherine's shock in returning home. The two of them sat silently in the car, listening to the sounds of the cooling engine. A minute that felt like an eternity passed, until Catherine let out an audible sigh.

"I guess I can't sit out here for the rest of my life." She reached for the door handle and let herself out. She could feel her anxiety, but with each passing minute, its edges seemed to dull as the pill she'd taken worked its magic. Catherine pressed the code into the keypad by the garage door and it lifted smoothly on its tracks. Carey took her hand as they entered the garage. The first thing Catherine saw when they opened the door to the mudroom was a jumble of shoes, boots, slippers, and sneakers on the mat by the bench. She took in a sharp breath when she realized that Jacob and Joe had sat on this very bench to put on their snow boots before going out and climbing into the ATV. *Could it be just yesterday afternoon? It feels like an eternity.* Never again, she thought. She felt her knees weaken and she leaned into her sister, who slipped her arm around her waist and guided her past this inadvertent makeshift memorial.

As they moved further into the house and the full effects of the pill began to kick in, Catherine felt like she was having an out-of-body experience. She observed herself reacting to everything she was seeing, but she couldn't feel the emotional impact. Everything looked familiar, but at the same time, it was all new. Objects seemed to have an aura about them, especially the pictures on the mantle and tabletops.

"Would you like something to eat?"

"I just want to sit down." Carey walked her sister over to an easy chair in the living room, and she fell into its soft embrace. "Maybe some water." Catherine looked up at her sister with glassy eyes. She leaned back, kicked up the footrest and took a few deep breaths. When Carey returned with a glass, her sister was fast asleep.

CHAPTER SEVEN
NATHAN

Dr. Susskind entered Nathan's room. Both last night's dinner and the morning's breakfast remained untouched beside his bed.

"Nathan, it's Dr. Susskind." She gently shook Nathan's shoulder.

"Go away."

"I could do that, but it just means you'll be stuck here that much longer."

"I don't care."

"What don't you care about?"

"I don't care about anything anymore."

"Is that right? You don't care about your wife? You don't care about your parents? You don't care about all the people who love you?"

"No one loves me after what I did." He turned to her, his face flushed with anger and self-loathing. Dr. Susskind took a seat in the chair beside Nathan's bed.

"Why would they stop loving you because of an accident?"

"This wasn't just any accident. It's not like I dropped a dish on the floor."

"You're right, Nathan. The result is certainly far more serious. But it was an accident nonetheless."

"You can say that, but you weren't sitting in the driver's seat. You didn't make the decision to cross the pond. You didn't see my kids' faces, the panic in their eyes. It's all I see when I shut mine."

"Tell me about that decision."

"It was getting late. I knew Catherine would be worried. The boys were tired and cranky. I tested the ice. I thought it was safe."

"So, you were concerned about your wife. You were cautious. You were trying to do the right thing under the circumstances."

"None of that matters now."

"I disagree. It may be too soon for you to see it, but I think eventually it could make all the difference. Think about that, Nathan, and think about all the people who love you. I'll be back later so that we can talk some more." Dr. Susskind rose from her seat and quietly walked out the door.

After the psychiatrist departed, leaving Nathan alone again to brood, he rose from his bed and stood at the window. He picked absently at the cold slices of bacon on the breakfast tray as he gazed out on the gray March day. Gun-metal clouds scudded across the sky, pushed by a wind that carried with it the possibility of a late winter storm. Nathan knew these kinds of skies, having grown up in the town right next door to where he now stood. He knew how uncertain, how changeable the weather was this time of year. One moment it could feel like you were on the cusp of spring, ready to fling open the windows even while melting snow dripped from the eaves.

The next, you could be caught in a snow squall that dumped a foot of ice and snow on the roads, fields, and forests. Under ordinary circumstances, Nathan enjoyed this kind of unpredictability. He couldn't imagine living in Florida or California, where every day was a cookie-cutter of the one before.

He'd missed not just the weather but the entire environment when he'd spent four years living and working in the concrete canyons of Manhattan. But that had all been part of the plan when he graduated from Babson. He'd read Tom Wolfe's *Bonfire of the Vanities* when he was a senior in high school, and it had given him a vision of an arc, a trajectory for his life. Unlike the protagonists of that book, he would work only a brief stint on Wall Street. Just enough to bank a boatload of cash that would spell freedom for him. He wasn't in it for the rush of the deal, the juice that had hedge fund managers feeding at trough after trough, never sating their appetites. He was only looking for his cut, enough to enable him to get back to his beloved Maine to start up his own company. Portland was a town full of professionals in need of investment advice, and Nathan saw the opportunity both to make a good living and to have some quality of life. He wasn't prepared to sacrifice his happiness in pursuit of the almighty dollar. His goal was to be comfortable. To provide for a wife and children. To spend weekends wandering through the woods, or fishing in the ponds and streams of southern Maine. To instill in his children a love of the natural world as his father had in him.

Nathan's father was his hero and his role model. Although he'd inherited the family business, his dad had innovated and expanded it into one of the largest manufacturers in the State. He employed nearly 200 people, and yet he never let the business consume him. Frank Osgood had found time, when Nathan was growing up, to teach him how to throw and hit a baseball, how to bait a hook, how to start a campfire in the rain. Nathan couldn't remember a single high school soccer game – home or away – when his father wasn't on the sidelines, cheering him on. He knew that his father had harbored hopes that he would take over the business one day, but when he was just a junior in college Nathan had sat his father down and, as gently as he could, burst that bubble. They'd gone out to dinner at their favorite steak house, the one they ritually visited after a day of hunting, fishing, or hiking in the woods. After they'd placed their orders, Nathan took a deep breath and opened up the conversation.

"Dad, you know the last thing in the world that I ever want to do is disappoint you."

"You could never disappoint me, son."

"Well, I know you've been hoping that I'll come join you at the plant after I graduate. At least that's the feeling I've gotten for a long time."

"I think every father hopes his son will follow in his footsteps, Nate." His father gazed down into his scotch. "But every dad wants his kid to be happy, too."

"I know it'd be fun to work together." It was Nathan's turn to stare into his drink, a Coke.

"I hear a 'but' coming."

"Yeah, Dad. There is." Nathan told his father about his plan. He became more and more animated as he mapped it out.

"I'm really glad to hear you're ultimately planning to come back to Maine."

"I can't imagine settling anywhere else. Or raising a family. You and Mom gave me so much."

Nathan's father looked him in the eye. "It sounds like a good plan, Nate. Whatever you need from me, I'll be there. I just want what's best for you." Nathan was relieved that there wasn't a hint of disappointment in his father's voice.

"Whatever you need from me." His father's words took on new meaning for Nathan now, as he noticed the dirty gray piles of snow in the corners of the hospital parking lot where they'd been plowed all winter. He hoped he could count on his father to help him get through this, even though Nathan was responsible for killing his grandchildren.

*

When Dr. Susskind visited Nathan again later that day, he was sitting in the chair in his room. He was still in the hospital-issued gown, robe, and slippers since he hadn't any clothes other than the out-sized ones he had worn in the night before.

"Hey, Doc." Nathan tried to sound as casual as he could.

"You seem to be feeling better than when I last saw you."

"Working on it."

"What's changed?"

"I'm not sure I can put my finger on it. I just know I need to get out of here and want to do what I have to do to make that happen."

The psychiatrist sat down at the end of the bed. "And why are you anxious to get out of here?"

"Look. I know I've got a lot of work to do to make up for what happened. I can't do it lying around here." Nathan nodded toward the hospital bed. "My wife needs me. Or at least I hope she does. Maybe she doesn't. I don't know..." His voice trailed off, and a look of uncertainty and fatigue returned to his face.

"Nathan, I'm glad you're feeling better, but I'm concerned about rushing this process. Let's take it one step at a time."

"Okay. Just tell me what I need to do."

"We need to pull together a strategy that you can commit to and follow through on after your hospitalization. But first, you need to understand that this isn't a problem you can solve, like tackling a new sales territory or training a new staff person. It's going to take a whole different set of skills on your part. You also need to know that progress isn't going to be linear. There are going to be ups and downs, advances and setbacks."

"Yeah, I think you mentioned that before. But I want to get out of here."

"Let's talk about that. What do you think it will be like when you get out of here?"

"I don't know." Nathan leaned forward, his elbows on his knees, and stared down at the floor.

"'I don't know' isn't good enough to get me to punch your ticket." The doctor consulted her notepad and thought for a moment. "Okay, let's make this really concrete. What are you going to say to your wife when you see her?"

The words tumbled out of Nathan's mouth as they occurred to him, his thoughts far from fully formed, much less organized. "I don't know what to say. What is there to say? I mean, I know I'm going to say I'm sorry, right? But that seems so useless in light of what I've done. I know I can't undo it. I'll beg her to forgive me, but it seems way too soon to ask for that. Can she ever forgive me? I don't know how anyone could forgive me. What should I say?" A tone of desperation entered Nathan's voice. "What's the right thing to do? Can you tell me?"

"This is good, Nathan." The psychiatrist deftly evaded responding to his question. "This is the stuff you've got to wrestle with. And it's not only about your relationship with

Catherine. It's about your relationship with yourself. What do you need to say to yourself right now?"

Nathan stared back at Dr. Susskind with a blank look on his face. "That's what I'd like you to think about, Nathan. I'll see you later." The doctor rose and walked out of the room, leaving Nathan lost in thought, feeling off-balance and uncertain.

*

Nathan spent the afternoon sitting in the chair of his hospital room, staring out the window. The scene matched his mood. The parking lot was about half-full, and the bare pavement was grey. The decaying snow was grey. The sky was grey. Nathan's entire world, it seemed, had shifted from full color to black and white. It was just the opposite of what happens in *Pleasantville*, one of Catherine's favorite films. There, love had changed everyone and everything for the better, bringing color and beauty into the world. It had been like that for him when he first met her, and the colors only intensified as their family grew. But now, because of one stupid decision – his decision and his alone – all the color, beauty, and joy had been drained from their world. They'd all been thrust back into a life where nothing would ever be bright and vibrant again.

Nathan squeezed his eyes shut, tears dripping from their corners. But whenever he closed his eyes, scenes from the accident flashed in his mind like a movie. The "bump" that sent the back of the RZR through the ice. The speed with which it sank. Jacob flailing in his seat as the water rose to engulf him. Joe's pleading eyes. The paralyzing cold of the water. His desperation. His helplessness. His devastation when he had to abandon his attempts to save them. It all came to one inescapable, irrefutable conclusion: he should have drowned along with his children. He didn't deserve to live. He didn't want to live. His children were dead, and he had killed them. His life was over. He climbed back into bed and cried himself to sleep.

*

Nathan turned toward the door of his hospital room when he heard the knock and saw the psychiatrist there, accompanied by someone he didn't know.

"Nathan, this is Robert Heasley. He's a therapist whom I thought you should meet."

"Hello, Nathan." Robert extended his right hand. He appeared to be just a few years older than Nathan, and he wore a plaid flannel shirt, corduroys, and loafers. "I'm so sorry for your loss." Nathan sat up and swung his legs over the side of the bed. He shook the man's hand perfunctorily. Robert took a seat in the lone chair in the room, while Dr. Susskind remained standing in the doorway.

"Nathan, you might remember that I told you that it's critical that you have a support system in place to help you get through this. I think Robert could be an important resource for you, a key member of your team. Are you willing to have a conversation with him to see whether that might be the case?"

"Anything that gets me out of here."

"Thanks, Rachel." Robert nodded to the psychiatrist.

"I'll leave you two to it." The doctor took the cue from her colleague and turned to leave.

"Nathan, I know that phrase 'I'm sorry for your loss' sounds hollow, like it's a canned response, but I want you to know that I mean it. I'm a parent, too, and since I heard about your accident, I've been thinking about how devastated you must feel."

"Mmmm." Nathan barely uttered a response.

"So, let me first tell you a little about me, okay?" Robert offered a quick sketch of his history, both professional and personal. Then he described some of his passions and projects.

"So, enough about me. Dr. Susskind, of course, shared with me what you and she have been talking about, but that's really all I know about you. Tell me about yourself."

"Where do you want me to start?"

"Anywhere you'd like."

"Like how my life is over?"

"How about starting a little earlier than that?"

Nathan complied and offered the therapist an oral recitation of his personal and professional resume. After a short time, Robert interrupted him. "What about being a father?"

"What about it?" Nathan shot back with an undertone of hostility.

"I mean, you've told me about your parents and growing up around here. And about how you and Catherine met. And about your time on Wall Street and then starting up your own business. But you haven't said anything about being a dad. Tell me what that's been like for you."

"I'm not sure what you want me to say." Nathan stared down at his hands and idly picked at a hangnail. "It was the best part of my life, and now that's over."

"Hmm. I understand that. But tell me what it was like before yesterday."

"I adored those kids. I'd do anything to turn back the clock."

"Of course you would. But what did it mean to you to be a father?" Robert apparently wasn't shy about pressing his clients – even brand-new ones – to get to the heart of a matter.

"It meant a lot of hard work."

"And?"

"And it put a lot of stress on Catherine and me."

"And?"

"And they were everything to me. I would do anything for them."

"I'm sure."

"And I let them down. The one thing a father does, the only thing, the most important thing, is to protect your kids. To keep them safe. That was my one and only job. And look what I did. I failed. And now they're gone."

"Yes, they are. And you're still here. Those are two truths that are staring you in the face. You can't change the first truth that Jacob and Joe are gone. Do you think changing that second truth is an answer?"

"It would be the easy way out."

"I guess, in some ways, it would. But from what you've told me about yourself, you aren't a 'take the easy way out' kind of person. That doesn't sound like you. You've told me you're a 'face down every challenge' kind of guy."

"I guess."

"So, let's start from there. I'd like to see if I can help you through this if that's all right. Are you willing to let me help you try?"

"I guess so. I really need to get out of here, though. Can you help make that happen?"

"Yeah, I think so." Robert stood up and offered Nathan his hand. Nathan instinctively rose up to meet it. "I'll talk with Dr. Susskind and we'll get the paperwork started."

"Thanks." Nathan accepted the therapist's outstretched hand. Robert surprised him by drawing him into a hug before turning and walking out the door.

*

Nathan felt a glimmer of hope after the therapist's visit. He'd be getting out of there soon. But the more he thought about what was next, the prospect of facing Catherine and the emptiness of their lives, the more agitated he became. As afternoon stretched into evening, he paced around his small hospital room, unable to settle himself down, feeling like he wanted to crawl out of his skin. He was a caged animal. Without a cell phone, he had no way to communicate with the outside world and no way to distract himself from the thoughts churning in his head. The more he thought, the more anxious he got. His mind bounced from despair over the loss of his children, to gut-wrenching guilt over his role in their deaths, to intense anxiety over the prospect of returning home and facing Catherine the next day. Nathan prided himself on always being in control – of himself, of any situation – and he had no control over any of this. He was the sole survivor of a shipwreck, lost far out at sea, alone in the night, bobbing in a vast and hostile expanse of despair.

What will my life be like now? Can I bear this guilt? It feels like it's crushing me. How can things ever return to normal, whatever that means at this point? Will Catherine even talk to me again after what I've done, much less rescue me? How could I even ask that of her? No, I never could, not after taking the boys from her. I can never ask anything of her, ever again. It's up to me to rescue her. But how can I do that when I'm drowning myself? Is this the end of everything? Our marriage?

The perfect life we've mapped out and built for ourselves? How could I have been so stupid? Oh, what I'd give to turn back the clock and take the longer way home. I failed my sons. Those terrified looks on their faces. I did everything I could. Or did I? Did I really? Was there something more I could have done? Maybe one more dive down to the bottom would have saved them.

The howl of pain and grief that rose from somewhere deep inside Nathan brought the duty nurse and orderly running to his room. The nurse offered Nathan a sedative, and he eagerly grabbed it as the life raft he had been waiting for to save him.

*

Early the next morning Dr. Susskind walked into Nathan's room, trusty notepad in hand. Nathan was dressed and staring out the window.

"I heard last night was rough. How are you doing now?"

"It was, Doc. But it feels like I had some kind of a breakthrough, too. I feel much better today. I think if I can just get out of this prison, I'll feel even better. I want to start moving forward and this place is making me feel stuck."

"That's good to hear, Nathan. I talked to Dr. Heasley this morning, and he wants to set up an appointment with you within the next 48 hours."

"Okay. I can do that. What else?" Nathan saw light at the end of this particular tunnel and was relieved to feel some sense of control being handed back to him.

"I'm going to give you a prescription for a sedative. It's like the one the nurses gave you last night, just a lighter dose. It's strong but won't necessarily knock you out. You can take it when you feel you need to, but you should know that it's harder to deal with the pain if you deaden it with drugs. You'll have to use your own judgment, but to help you in that I'm not going to give you more than five pills at a time."

"Okay. Got it." Nathan nodded.

"Nathan, I also want to warn you that there isn't a road map where you're going. You hear about the so-called 'stages of grief,' but everybody's different, and I've yet to meet anyone who follows the formula. You and your wife are going to be wandering in the wilderness for a while. You've got Robert to help guide you, and I hope your wife has someone, too. In some ways, you're both going to be on two journeys at the same time, and that isn't easy. You've got to navigate your way through your own grief, just as she will. And then you'll be feeling your way through your relationship with each other, facing together the reality of the accident and the loss of your children. I don't think I need to say this, but I will: there are no guarantees here. None of us knows how it's all going to turn out. I'm going to release you from here with all my hope and prayers for the future."

At the end of the physician's monologue, Nathan took a deep breath and let it out slowly. "I'm scared."

"I understand, Nathan. But that statement alone means you're in touch with your feelings, and that's what you need to be throughout this process. I'll call your parents and let them know they can come pick you up in about an hour. It takes some time to process the paperwork, but you should be home in a couple hours or so."

"Okay, Doc. I guess I'm as ready as I'm going to be. Thanks for everything." Dr. Susskind shook Nathan's hand and turned for the door, leaving Nathan to pace nervously around the room.

CHAPTER EIGHT
CATHERINE

Catherine awoke from her drug-induced nap to the familiar smell of macaroni and cheese baking in the oven. From the time she was old enough to chew, her mother had offered up this dish as the ultimate comfort food. Whether it was to console her after the time she fell from her horse and broke her arm, when her high school field hockey team lost the state championship game, or simply on a frigid Saturday in the dead of winter in upstate New York when the whole family was suffering from cabin fever, Catherine could count on the communion that happened around the dinner table as the savory dish was served. Her mother had taught both girls the recipe when they were old enough to learn it, and Catherine often served it up to the boys on cold winter nights.

That memory brought Catherine up short. Her heart clenched in her chest when she realized that she would forever be denied that pleasure, and countless others, now. A wave of grief washed over her, and she sat in the chair with her eyes closed, tears streaming down her face. At just that moment,

Carey walked into the room to check on her. Seeing her sister's distress, she squeezed herself into the chair beside her and took Catherine into her arms.

"Oh, Carey." She sobbed. "What am I going to do?"

"I don't know, Cat. I don't know."

"Thanks for the mac and cheese." Catherine sniffled, the wave beginning to recede back out to sea, leaving her washed out in its wake. "But I can't eat anything."

"That's okay. You can have some later. Or just pick at it when the mood strikes you." Catherine held onto her sister like her life depended on it. The two had walked the landscape of grief together more than a decade earlier when their parents had died, so they weren't in completely uncharted territory. And yet, for both of them, this was different and unfamiliar terrain.

"You know, if I had a magic wand..."

"I know. I know." Catherine eased her grip on her sister and wiped her eyes with the back of her hand.

"I'm sure you don't want to talk about this right now, but while you were sleeping, I called Nathan's parents. I hope you don't mind, but we decided on a funeral home for the boys. The hospital released them this morning. You and Nathan can decide where to go from there, but at least they're not sitting in that morgue anymore. They're being well-taken care of."

This news drifted past Catherine like she was watching a movie. She tried to envision Jacob and Joe lying in the basement of a funeral home, and all she could picture were scenes from *Six Feet Under*.

"Thanks." It was all she could muster in response.

"Do you want to take another pill? They say you can take one every four hours."

"I don't think so. Not yet, at least. It really knocked me out, which I guess is the point. But I can't just sleep through this."

"Okay. Well, they're there if you need them." Carey gave Catherine a squeeze and climbed out of the chair. "I'm going to putter around in the kitchen."

"Those are words I never thought I'd hear from my international financier sister," Catherine managed to joke.

"Well, desperate times..." Carey moved toward the door. "This mac and cheese is the limit of my repertoire, so you'd better get used to it."

"I think I'm just going to sit here for a while. Thanks for being here." Catherine tucked her legs under her and gazed out the window at the familiar scene. Tall trees marked the edge of a wide expanse of grass they'd cleared as a play area when the house was built. Catherine knew that, once you entered the forest, you could walk for miles without seeing a soul. She had always been drawn to these intimate experiences with nature, especially as a teenager, riding her horse Annie through the woods for hours on end. As she thought about the forest that extended from the house she and Nathan had built, trees spreading seemingly forever in all directions, these same woods that had brought such comfort to her all these years suddenly felt different. Ominous and dangerous. She knew now that you could go into these woods and never come out again. She knew because it had happened just yesterday. *Could it be only yesterday that I waved goodbye to Joe and Jacob as they drove off into these woods, happy and smiling?* This forest was no longer the inviting escape it had always been. Now it was a foreboding, evil place. It gobbled up small children and consumed happiness the way a black hole devours planets and light and anything else good within its gravitational field.

If anyone had asked Catherine how she was feeling that

afternoon, a day after the incident, the best she could have told them was that she felt empty. Like there was a huge, gaping void inside her, a blackness as deep and as dark as the sea on a moonless night. "Shattered" might be another adjective that floated up out of that void. Her life felt like a porcelain vase that had been shaken from the mantle by an earthquake and, hitting the unforgiving stone of the hearth below, exploded into a constellation of shards that could never be restored to anything resembling its former beauty.

Late in the day, Catherine rose from her chair and slowly walked from room to room. As she went, she grabbed photographs off the walls and shelves where they'd been arranged. Then, she returned to her chair and pulled each one from its frame. She haphazardly spread them in her lap, on the side table, and on the floor around her in makeshift collages. They scattered like autumn leaves that had floated down from a forest made of memories. There were the traditional "coming home from the hospital" pictures of both boys. Catherine and Jacob sitting atop a chestnut horse together, his first time riding. Joe in the bathtub, sporting a Mohawk made of shampoo. Catherine, Jacob, and Joe walking up a wooded trail together, hand-in-hand. They were ordinary moments in the life of a family, unremarkable in every way except that they were hers. To the untrained eye, it appeared to be a random assemblage of photographs. If you had asked Catherine why she had selected these particular images, she likely would have been unable to express rhyme or reason. And while not even the most experienced psychologist could explain whether Catherine had made the choices consciously or unconsciously, there was one thing that all these pictures had in common, one clear thread that united them all: none of them included Nathan.

*

Catherine heard her sister answer the landline in the kitchen. After she got off the call, Carey sat down on the couch across from her, noticing the photographs strewn around the room but saying nothing

"Who was that?"

"Nathan's father. It sounds like Nathan is going to be released from the hospital tomorrow."

"Mmm-hmm."

Carey gave her a few beats before she pressed her sister for more reaction to the news. "How do you feel about that?"

"I honestly have no idea, Carey. I don't know what I'm feeling right now. So, I have no idea how I'll feel tomorrow."

"Well, do you want to go and meet him at the hospital? I could drive you. Or we could let his parents give him a ride home."

Catherine exploded. "I don't know! I told you I don't know!" Catherine jumped up from her chair, spilling the photographs from her lap onto the floor. "I can hardly breathe right now, and you're asking me all these questions! Don't you get it? My children are dead. I'll never see them again. I'm going to have to put them in the ground and they might as well bury me with them." Catherine broke down, sobbing uncontrollably as she fled the living room, leaving her sister in the wake of her devastation.

*

Catherine didn't emerge from the sanctuary of her bedroom until the following morning. Carey was just hanging up the phone when she walked into the kitchen.

"Coffee?" Carey poured a mug for her sister as Catherine reached into the refrigerator for the milk.

"Who was that?" Catherine took a seat at the counter.

"Frank. He wanted to let us know that he and Jean can give Nathan a ride home. Is that okay with you?"

"Sure. I guess."

"Do you want to talk about anything?"

"I don't know, Carey." Catherine held her head between her hands, her face hovering over the mug of warm liquid, her elbows propped on the bar. "I just feel so lost."

"I know, Cat. We all do. Hey, would it be helpful if I called Heather, and we had her here when Nathan comes home? Maybe just for some extra support?"

"Yeah, that would be good, I think. Thanks." Catherine grabbed her coffee and wandered back out to her favorite chair in the living room as Carey picked up the phone to call Heather.

"She'll be over in a while," Carey called out from the kitchen. But the message barely registered with Catherine, who just gazed out the window, her mind a blank.

*

Heather was sitting in the living room with Catherine when Carey poked her head in and let them know that Nathan was on his way home. Catherine visibly tensed at the news.

"What?" Heather noticed her friend's restlessness.

"I don't know if I can even look at him," Tears welled up in Catherine's eyes. "I don't know who I am anymore. Two days ago, I had this perfect life, and now it's all been ripped apart. And he's the one who took it from me."

"I know, sweetie." Heather opened her arms in invitation, and Catherine moved from her chair into her friend's embrace on the couch. "I think you've just got to let yourself feel what you're gonna feel, do what you're gonna do. That's all anyone can expect of you right now."

"The thought of sleeping next to him ---"

"Mmm. Well, maybe that comes later." Heather tenderly stroked Catherine's hair. "Maybe he sleeps in another room for a while." The image of Nathan sleeping in either Jacob or Joe's bed brought new tears to Catherine, and she wept silently in the comfort of her friend's arms.

The house phone rang, and Carey took the call in the kitchen, then delivered the update from Nathan's parents: "Cat, Nathan's almost here. Heather and I will be in the playroom if you need us."

Heather gave Catherine one more hug, then released her grip. "We'll get you through this." Catherine gave a slight nod and wiped her eyes with a tissue. She could feel her chest tightening, and she tried to take a few deep breaths to calm herself as she returned to her favorite chair, which in the past 24 hours had become her nest, her sanctuary.

Catherine startled when she heard a knock on the front door. She hadn't expected that. She thought Nathan would walk right into his own house. Was the knock a simple courtesy, a warning, that would be followed by her husband walking in the door? Or was she supposed to answer the door and invite him in like a guest? Already walking an emotional tightrope, the knock threw her off balance. She decided to stay where she was, in the safe cocoon of her chair, and let Nathan figure it out. She didn't have to guess for long, as she heard Nathan's key in the lock and the click of the deadbolt. Then, the moment she'd been dreading: Nathan poked his head into the living room.

"Cat?" Catherine fixed her gaze at the floor in front of her.

"Cat?" Nathan repeated, frozen at the threshold between the entry hall and the living room. Catherine stirred from her silence and slowly turned her attention to her husband, her eyes brimming with tears. Nathan's filled to match hers as he rushed to his wife and knelt at her feet, the dam breaking for both of them. Wordlessly, desperately, Nathan clutched Catherine's legs, resting his head in her lap. Catherine instinctively reached down and stroked Nathan's hair, her tears flowing freely. Nathan's body was wracked with sobs, reminding her of the countless times her two young sons had come to her in tears after a nightmare or a fall, how they had held her legs, and how she had comforted them in just this same way. The memory brought her up short, and Nathan felt her body go rigid as she stopped stroking his hair.

"I'm so, so sorry." Nathan gasped through his tears. Cat offered nothing in response. She simply gazed out the window, waiting. For what, she didn't know. Her eyes, at least for the moment, had dried, and her face was a blank, tear-stained slate.

After an excruciating minute, Catherine finally summoned her courage and spoke a simple sentence. "We lost the baby."

Nathan lifted his head from his wife's lap and nodded, unable to turn his face up to look into her eyes.

"I know. My parents told me." His voice was barely a whisper now.

"I was going to surprise you when you got back. But then you didn't come home, and you didn't come home, and I waited, and I waited..."

"I got lost in the woods, and the sun was going down." The explanation snowballed out of him. "It was getting late, and I knew you'd be anxious about where we were, so I tried to call, honest I did. But I didn't have a signal. And I wanted to get home so you wouldn't be worried, so I took a shortcut."

"Don't you dare try to blame *me* for this." Catherine snapped at her husband with explosive sharpness, nearly jumping up from the chair, pushing him away.

"No, no. I wasn't blaming---"

"This is all *your* fault." Catherine cut him off. "You and your recklessness." Her rage struck like lightning, igniting a wildfire she couldn't contain.

"What the hell were you thinking? How many times did we talk about staying safe when you had Jacob and Joe with you? I don't give a shit if you want to jump off a cliff to get your kicks. Just don't do it with my boys."

Nathan hung his head. "You're right. I know you're right, Cat--"

"*You* did this. Not me." She cut him off. "Don't try to make it sound like you took a chance because of me. You bastard. How could you even say something like that?" Catherine bolted from the living room. She ran up the stairs to the bedroom, slammed the door, and flung herself on the bed, shaking with anger. It was the first time she'd felt anything but emptiness since she saw the bodies of her children on the metal tables in the morgue.

*

Carey knocked lightly on the bedroom door and slid silently into the room. Catherine was standing at a window, staring out at the valley.

"How dare he!" Catherine wheeled around, her face still flush with rage. "How dare he try and blame me for this! He's the one who wanted that stupid ATV. He's the one who wanted to take joy rides through the woods. He's the one who got lost. He's the one who was stupid enough to drive out on the ice." Tears streamed down Catherine's face. "He's the one who killed our boys and our baby."

Carey tried to take Catherine in her arms, but she would have none of it. "You can't make this better, Carey. Nothing is going to make this better. Nothing is going to bring my babies back."

"I know. I know." Carey held her place by the window, close to her sister.

"I can't even look at him right now. I don't want to see him. I don't want him in this house."

"I get it, Cat. But don't you think---"

"Don't I think what? Don't I think my life is over? Don't I think the man I loved, the man I trusted, the man whose one job was to keep my children safe, betrayed all that? You bet your ass that's what I think."

"He's hurting, too." Carey walked a fine line.

"Good! He should be. He'd better hurt like the Nine Circles of Hell."

"I know you're angry right now, but—"

"I want him out of this house." Catherine cut her sister off and wheeled away from the window to face her. "I want him gone. You hear me? I want him out of here. Now, Carey. You tell him that. You tell his parents that. He can go live with them for all I care."

"Are you sure, Cat? Is that going to help you? You know that's all I care about."

"It's what I need right now." Catherine was suddenly clear. It was as if a veil had been lifted and everything had come into sharp focus. Her determination was palpable, a living thing that had suddenly taken root and blossomed deep down inside her. "I know it's what I need. I need to be here. Alone. Just me and my memories. He ripped my heart out, and I can't try to find it with him hanging around. Go tell him. Go tell them. Would you please go tell them?"

"If that's what you want, of course, I will." This time, Catherine accepted Carey's hug before she left to deliver the message.

*

After Nathan had left with his parents, Carey rejoined her sister up in her room, knocking gently before letting herself in.

"Nathan's left like you asked."

"So, now what?" Catherine lay on the bed, staring into space.

"What do you mean?"

"I mean, now what do I do? I should be picking Jacob up from school. I should be baking cookies with Joe. I should be doing their laundry. I should be dreaming about what color to paint the nursery. There's nothing left to do."

Catherine's eyes filled again. Apparently, the well of her tears was bottomless. Carey sighed and laid down on the bed next to her grieving sister. They both stared up at the ceiling, breathing together. After a few minutes, Carey tip-toed around what she knew would be a delicate subject.

"I wonder how you say goodbye to them?" She spoke the words into the empty space above them, afraid to look her sister in the eye.

Catherine lay inert on the bed, thinking. "First, I have to get past that this isn't all just a dream. That I'm not going to wake up, and Jacob and Joe will be downstairs fighting over who gets to use the iPad or that I won't have to referee arguments between them a zillion times this week. Or that I'll never give them a bath again or snuggle as we read a book before bed." She turned her head to face her sister, a pleading look on her face. "It's a dream, isn't it, Carey? Please tell me this is all a really horrible dream."

"I wish I could." Carey took Catherine's hand and gave it a tight squeeze. "I wish I had a magic wand and could make it all be different."

"I really don't know who I am without them." Catherine sniffled, trying to hold back another wave of tears. "You hear someone say that their kids are their whole life and you roll your eyes and say to yourself, 'Well, I feel sorry for you, lady,' but then you realize that you're that person. Then your kids vanish, and when they go, they take your life with them. That's what he did to me. He didn't just take their lives. He took mine, too."

The two sisters lay quietly on the bed then, knowing there were no words of comfort, no words of grace, no words to repair a heart that had been ripped apart by a moment's poor decision.

CHAPTER NINE
NATHAN

Nathan trudged through the front door of his childhood home and up the stairs to his old bedroom. Out of force of habit, he pulled the replacement cell phone his father had given him from his pocket and saw that he had a voicemail from his friend Jim.

"Hey, Nate. Just calling to see how you're doing, man. Shitty, I'm guessing. Just wanted you to know I'm here if you need anything."

The message felt like a lifeline, tossed to Nathan when he needed it most. He shut the door, hit the "call back" button, and Jim picked up on the second ring.

"Hey, Nate. How you doing?"

"Like you said, Jim, about as shitty as can be." Nathan filled his friend in on what had happened since the accident. Catherine passing out in the morgue. Him grabbing the deputy's gun. His forced stay in the psych unit. His aborted visit back home and how Catherine had thrown him out.

"So, you're at your folks' place for a while?"

"I have no idea for how long, Jim. It's Catherine's call."

"She's a good woman, Nate. Strong, too. You gotta trust that."

"Yeah, but I fucked up so badly, Jim. I don't know if anyone's that good or that strong, that they could forgive what I did."

"Look, Nate, it's been what, three days? You can't expect miracles. You're looking at a long haul. Speaking of which, I know your folks'll take good care of you, but if it gets a little hairy there, you know that I've got a spare bedroom and a fridge full of beer. You can stay here as long as you'd like."

"Thanks, Jim. I may take you up on it."

"Any time, buddy. I'm here for you."

"Thanks." Nathan ended the call and reached into his pocket to retrieve the business card Robert Heasley had given him. His call went to voicemail, and Nathan left word for the therapist to call him back to set up an appointment. He laid down on the narrow twin bed of his youth, the maple headboard still scarred from when he took his jackknife to it when he was twelve years old. He closed his eyes and dozed fitfully until the vibration from his phone roused him. It was Robert returning his call. Nathan told him about his encounter with Catherine.

"When could I see you?" Nathan sat up on the edge of his bed.

"I've had a cancellation this afternoon. Do you want to come in at 3?"

"I'll be there." Nathan stretched, got up off the bed and headed downstairs. He joined his parents, who were sitting in the den, and told them about the call from Jim and the appointment that he'd set up with his therapist.

Frank was prepared to broach a touchy subject with their

son. "We've been busy, too, Nate. I hope you don't mind, but I called Rev. Susan at the Unitarian church in Sanford to talk about funeral arrangements. We talked this over with Catherine's sister, and we all thought it might make it easier for the two of you if we could sort that out for you. Susan said we could hold the funeral at her church on Saturday."

Nathan collapsed into a leather chair in the corner as if he'd taken a punch to the gut. His parents waited for a response, but when his mother saw none was forthcoming, she filled in the silence. "We let Carey know so that she could tell Catherine. We think it's for the best to hold a service soon, but not too soon."

Nathan just stared at the floor. It felt like his parents were tag-teaming him. Now it was his father's turn to speak: "We also looked into buying plots up at Westview Cemetery. You know, that spot up on the hill outside of town? We thought that would be best. I called and put a deposit down."

Now his mother: "If you want, your father and I and Carey can take care of all the arrangements. We want to do what we can to make it easier on both of you."

"Easier?" Nathan felt something snap inside at the word. "Easier? Nothing about this is easy! Don't you get that? I mean, I know you mean well, but really? Easier?"

"Okay, son, maybe that was a poor choice of words." Nathan's father intervened. "We need to try and be gentle with each other here. We're all still reeling from what happened. Please understand that we're trying to help where we can. Just think about it. A funeral at Rev. Susan's church. This Saturday. A burial afterward up at Westview. How's that sound?"

"It sounds horrible. It sounds impossible! I can't even talk to my wife and you're planning the funeral for our children?"

Jean tried to soothe her son. "Just think about it, okay,

Nate?" Nathan gave a brief nod and plodded back upstairs to his room, waiting for the time he could talk to Robert.

*

Nathan eased his parents' car off Winter Street and onto Riverside Avenue. He parked at the curb in front of a blue Victorian house with a simple wooden sign in the front yard that read "Mousam River Counseling." He mounted the steps onto the porch and walked through the front door, entering a sparsely furnished waiting room. Taped to the door opposite the one Nathan entered was a yellowed index card signed by Robert that read: "I will be with you shortly." Nathan took off his jacket and sat in one of the chairs, folding his coat in his lap. He picked up an old issue of "Woodworking" magazine and leafed through it absent-mindedly. Less than five minutes passed before the inner door opened, and Robert appeared behind it.

"Come on in, Nathan."

Nathan entered Robert's office and noticed immediately that there was no couch. He'd never been to a therapist, and he believed the stereotype that they all had couches.

"Have a seat." Robert pointed to one of two Windsor chairs that matched those in the waiting room. Nathan obeyed, taking in the rest of the office. It was furnished in a style that Nathan would call "eclectic yard sale." On one side of the room sat an old oak roll-top desk, papers neatly stacked in piles, with a brass banker's light sitting on top of it. The opposite wall held an alcove with a large window with cut glass that looked out on a small backyard that sloped down to the Mousam River. Next to it was a door that Nathan realized must be the way a client exited the office, unseen by the next person sitting in the waiting room. The walls of the office were painted in a muted earth tone, reminding Nathan of a trip he and Catherine had taken to the Sonoran Desert shortly after they'd been married, and the rock canyons they'd hiked together. The memory registered but felt more like it was someone else's.

Robert took the seat opposite Nathan. He was wearing glasses that Nathan hadn't noticed during their meeting in the hospital. They made him look older and more serious than the open, friendly face Robert had presented in the psych unit. Nathan also noticed that he wore the standard-issue checked button-down shirt and khakis that were the uniform of Ivy League graduates. He looked around for a tweed jacket with suede elbow patches to complete the preppy ensemble, but he didn't spot one.

"How's it feel to be out of the hospital?"

"Strange." Nathan looked everywhere except at the therapist, desperate to find something he could rest his gaze upon. "I mean, I'm glad to be out. But it's weird. Everything is familiar and foreign at the same time. It's the same, and it's completely different."

Robert nodded and remained silent, giving space for Nathan to continue.

"It's like I'm a visitor in my own hometown. Like I've been away for a long time, and everything's changed, but at the same time, nothing has changed."

"But everything *has* changed, hasn't it?" Robert leaned in toward Nathan, his body language indicating his intention to listen closely.

"Right. Basically, life as I knew it is over. And now I'm supposed to start this whole new life. But I'm wearing the same old clothes, driving the same old streets. I don't even know where to start." Nathan ran his fingers through his dark hair in a gesture of exasperation. "Catherine threw me out."

"You mentioned that on the phone. Tell me what happened." Robert sat back to listen as Nathan walked him through his brief encounter with Catherine at their Mountain Road home.

"Were you trying to shift the blame like she said?"

"Of course not! This was totally my fault. I mean, I'm the one who got lost in the woods, and I'm the one who decided to try the shortcut across the pond. I was feeling the press of time, with the sun setting, and I knew she'd be worried about us. But I don't blame her. I only blame myself."

"So, Catherine is another innocent victim, just like the boys, and the baby. But she survived the crash, and they didn't. In a sense, you and Catherine are both survivors."

"Well, she's both a survivor and a victim, I guess. I don't see that I can claim to be a victim, too."

"Why not?"

"Because I did this. I was at the wheel. I had complete control."

"And you drove across the ice."

"And I drove across the ice. It was all my fault."

"I'm not sure I'd agree with that, but let's go there, Nathan. Let's say that you had complete control and that it's all your fault. You're totally to blame. What does that mean?"

"What do you mean, 'What does that mean?'" Nathan was baffled by the therapist's question.

"What's the fallout? What are the implications of being totally responsible? What does it matter, whether or not you're to blame?"

"Well, the immediate fallout is that I'm buried in guilt. I'm feeling so guilty that I feel like I don't deserve to live. It's overwhelming. I can't get out from under it."

"What about the sorrow, Nathan?"

"The sorrow?"

"Yes, the sorrow over the death of your children. Knowing that you'll never see them grow up, or the baby Catherine was carrying. You'll never even hold that child."

"Of course, I feel sorry!" Nathan nearly shouted at Robert. "I'm not a monster!"

"No, Nathan. You're not." Robert leaned in toward Nathan now. "Can you say that again?"

"What? I'm not a monster?"

"Right. Say it again."

"I'm not a monster."

"You're not a monster. You didn't take Jacob and Joe down to the pond and drown them with your bare hands. You didn't commit some heinous, premeditated act. You made a decision and acted on it, and that decision had unforeseen consequences. Yes, they were dire consequences, but you're not a monster."

Nathan sat silently, tears welling up in his eyes and spilling down his cheeks.

"You feel guilty. I get that. But I wonder how much bandwidth the sorrow gets, given how overwhelmed you are by guilt. And I wonder whether the sorrow, the sense of loss that both you and Catherine feel, is where the two of you can meet. Maybe that's the common ground that you can both stand on and from which you can try to start to rebuild a life together. But if all you're really feeling is guilt, that separates you from your wife. She can't go there with you because she doesn't share that blame."

Nathan nodded slightly, trying to absorb the therapist's words.

"So, maybe where we start our work is around those feelings of guilt. I'm not saying we can get rid of them completely. But maybe once we at least tamp those down a bit, and you can make more room for your feelings of grief and loss, then we can work on how you and Catherine can move forward as a couple."

Robert pulled a small calendar out of the breast pocket of his shirt and consulted its contents. "Let's meet again on Friday. Does 11 o'clock work for you?"

Nathan sniffled and wiped his eyes with the back of his hand. "Sure. I guess. I mean, I don't have anywhere else to be."

Robert pulled a couple of tissues out of a box on the windowsill and handed them to Nathan as both of them rose from their chairs. Robert gave Nathan a comforting pat on the back as he guided him toward the door.

*

Nathan spent the entire next day shut up in his room. He emerged for meals when his mother called up the stairs, but he barely picked at his food. After pushing his peas around on his dinner plate, much as he did as a child, Nathan said, "I'm going out for a while." He left the house without further explanation.

At first, Nathan drove slowly around the familiar streets of the town where he'd grown up. Past the town library where his mother had taken him for story hour when he was a toddler. Around the town common that had been the site of family picnics and Fourth of July concerts as a kid, later where he learned to play Ultimate. He drove past his old elementary school and recalled the time he had fallen from the top of the slide onto the hard dirt below, knocking out a tooth, and how it had bled and bled. To his embarrassment, he had cried in front of the older kids, who had mercilessly made fun of him.

Heading out of town, he passed the road where Olivia, his first high school crush, had lived, and he wondered what might have happened had he ever had the nerve to ask her out. Soon, he found himself on Route 109, the main road linking Newfield with the rest of the outside world. As the main route between his home and his office in Portland, he could drive this road with his eyes closed. He knew its every twist and turn, every rise and dip. He'd driven it on bright, sunny mornings and at midnight in blizzard conditions. He knew all the spots where you were most likely to encounter deer and the occasional moose.

As he passed the intersection with Mountain Road, the car seemed to want to steer itself up the winding road, to transport him to his home at the top of the hill. The place where, at this very moment, Catherine, his wife, his life was sitting. He pictured her in the La-Z-Boy, a throw covering her legs that were tucked up underneath her. And he pictured his two boys, sound asleep in their beds upstairs. How many nights had he come home late from work and found his family just so? How many times had he walked into the house, kissed Catherine gently on the lips, and padded quietly upstairs to peek into the boys' rooms, just to see their angelic faces in silent repose, finding their deep, even breathing a comfort to his anxious heart? How many times had he come back downstairs and sat down on the couch and listened to Catherine tell him of the day's events, both comic and tragic, and how much she loved her "little men," as endearing and as frustrating as they always were?

With tears wetting his cheeks, Nathan slowed as he approached the turn that led him home. But he didn't take it.

Instead, he continued down the main road, his mind shutting down the memories it had just evoked. Five minutes later, he found himself sitting in the idling car in front of Jim Richardson's house. He had no idea how long he'd been there when his friend came down the steps from his front porch and knocked on the window, startling him.

"Nate, you want to come in, man?"

"Uh. Yeah." Nathan turned off the engine and followed his friend into the house. There was a warm, amber glow emanating from the woodstove in the corner of the living room, and Nathan detected the faint aroma of stew in the air. His stomach responded with an involuntary growl and, for the first time since the accident, he found that he was hungry.

"Did you eat?" Jim leaned over a pot on the stove, the steam fogging his glasses. "I've got some venison stew still hot on the stove. Remember that ten-pointer I bagged last fall? This is the last of it."

Nathan gratefully accepted the steaming bowl that his friend placed in his outstretched hands as they both took seats at the small, square table in the kitchen.

"What're you doing out here, Nate?" Nate blew the hot steam from the soup spoon and took a bite of the tender, gamey meat. "Don't get me wrong, you're always welcome, but I wasn't expecting you tonight."

"I don't know. The car just kinda drove itself here." Jim waited for him to continue, while Nathan chewed and swallowed the bite. "I'm already going crazy cooped up in my parents' house. The funeral is on Saturday."

"Yeah, I heard. That's gonna be a tough scene. What can I do to help?"

"I want to walk down to the pond, Jim."

"You mean, now?"

"Yeah. Now. Will you come with me?"

"Umm. Yeah, sure," Jim pushed his chair back from the table and took his bowl to the sink. "Have you got some boots and a warmer jacket? It's pretty cold out there tonight."

"I'll be okay."

"All right. Let me just put some more wood in the stove, so it's nice and warm when we get back." Jim went out to the porch where the wood was stacked and returned a moment later with an armful. He stoked the fire and donned his down vest.

"Here, put this on." He held out a parka to Nathan. "I don't want you to freeze."

"Thanks." Nathan took one last spoonful of his stew and shrugged into the jacket that was three sizes too big for him. Jim grabbed a large flashlight from the corner of the kitchen counter, and the two men went out into the night.

The path down to the pond was rutted from all the traffic after the accident. State and local police had used the trail to gain access for their investigation, both on foot and by snow machine. What snow remained was ground down into the soil, making the trail a slippery, muddy mess, and the men had to carefully pick their way down to the pond.

Jim paused by the side of the trail and turned to face his friend. "Are you sure you want to do this?" Nathan nodded and pressed on. Jim decided it was best to walk in silence and to follow his friend's lead. Soon, they could see the white, open expanse of the pond through the pine trees. A crescent moon hung low in the western sky.

Emerging from the woods, the men were met by the three wrecked snow machines, now sitting on the shore of the pond where the police investigators had hauled them out of the water. One machine sat on its side, its wide track exposed to the faint moonlight. Jim leaned against it and watched his friend closely. Nathan stood stone-like on the shore, looking out across the pond. Because the weather had turned cold again, the water that had been opened up by the RZR's plunge and the attempted rescue had re-frozen. In the absence of any snowfall since the accident, the men could easily make out the scar on the face of the pond that their activity had left. Jim sat by silently, ready to tackle his friend to the ground if he made a move to venture out onto the fragile veneer of ice.

Nathan gazed out onto the glassy surface of the pond. Then, without warning, he fell to his knees and let out a primordial howl. It sounded like all the grief in the world being liberated from a well drilled deep into the ground. His anguish shot up and out into the night sky like a geyser whose fragile stone cap had just been breached. The release of energy dwarfed every living thing around it. The sound made the hair on the back of Jim's neck stand up and reminded him of the eerie, almost-human cry that a rabbit makes when, clasped in the jaws of a predator, it is about to die. Jim winced at the heartache he was witnessing.

When he had emptied his lungs, Nathan knelt at the water's edge, panting heavily. Jim rose from his perch on the snowmobile and knelt down beside his friend. Wrapping his arm across Nathan's shoulder, he whispered "Feel better?" Nathan nodded, but barely. Jim stayed there with him until he sensed that the man who had lost everything to this nondescript, icy body of water might be ready to rejoin him in the land of the living. He coaxed Nathan to his feet and the two men turned their backs on the lake. Without saying a word, they made their way up the slippery path back toward Jim's house.

Between being emotionally drained, physically exhausted,

and embraced by the warmth of the woodstove, Nathan passed out on the couch within minutes of their return.

CHAPTER TEN
CATHERINE

"Cat, I think you need to try and eat something." Carey called from the kitchen the next morning when she heard Catherine come downstairs and plop herself into her easy chair. Carey poked her head into the living room where Catherine was sitting, staring blankly.

"I'm not hungry."

"Okay. I hear you. And I'm going to make one of my patented, kick-ass smoothies anyway. Even if you only take a few sips, it'll be something."

Catherine rose from the chair and went to the bathroom. She was shocked by the image that stared back at her in the mirror. The egg on her forehead had receded, but the bruising on her face was turning pale shades of yellow and green.

"You look like shit," she muttered to herself. She picked up a brush and ran it through her hair. Looking down at the vanity, her gaze fell upon two small superhero toothbrushes and a half-squeezed tube of children's toothpaste. Her breath caught in her throat. The most recent bedtime routine for the boys was for her to snuggle with them in the living room as she (or Nathan, when he was home from work in time) read to them. Then they'd brush their teeth in the downstairs bathroom, and she or Nathan would give them piggyback rides up to their rooms.

Catherine opened a drawer of the vanity and swept the toothbrushes and paste into it, slamming it shut with a sense of finality. Would she ever, she wondered, be able to come across some evidence of Jacob's and Joe's existence and not feel like a brittle twig that snaps in half at the sight? Leaning against the counter, her arms spread wide and her head hanging over the sink, Catherine took a few deep breaths to recover. When she regained a semblance of stability, she splashed some water on her face, dabbed it dry, and walked into the kitchen.

Carey was standing at the baking island, two glasses in front of her. She had just switched off the blender and begun to pour the creamy liquid into one of them.

"No kale?"

"No kale." This call-and-response was a ritual dating back to their college days. Both were perpetually trying to stay healthy and eat well, but neither could abide the tough, leafy vegetable.

Carey slid a glass across the counter toward her sister, and then went to the door that led outside to the deck. Catherine took her cue and followed her sister outside, taking a seat beside her. The metal frame of the patio chair held the winter's lingering cold, and Catherine shivered as she sat down. Together they sat in silence, gazing at the view of the hills of southwestern Maine. Winter was releasing its grip. There were hints of the soft green tones of early spring in some of the trees, and the bird songs were shifting away from the plaintive winter cry of the chickadees to include a wider variety of melodies. Catherine thought she even heard a robin. The fact that it was warm enough for them to sit out on the deck without parkas was another sign that spring was on its way. Catherine turned her gaze upward and let the sun warm her face until she realized that it was just this fact – the sun's higher trajectory in the sky and the lengthening days – that had led the pond ice to be unstable and allowed the ATV to break through. She turned her head toward the shadows of the nearby woods at the edge of their yard. Their darkness better suited her mood.

Catherine felt like she was grasping at so much, trying to hold onto everything, fearing that if she let her guard down at all, she'd lose any remaining control, any connection to reality that she still had. But sitting there on the deck with her sister, she realized that she had to relinquish her grip on something or she'd go crazy. "So, I'm fine with whatever funeral arrangements you make. Could you take care of the details and just point me in the right direction when it happens? I can't even begin to think about it."

"Of course. I'll talk to Frank and Jean and work it all out. We'll plan on Saturday."

Without thinking about it, Catherine took a sip of her smoothie. The cold, creamy goodness sluiced down her throat, and she could feel it all the way down to her stomach. She realized that her body was craving nutrition and, with Carey looking on but being careful not to stare, Catherine drained her glass in one long gulp.

*

As darkness descended around the house on Mountain

Road, Catherine became increasingly anxious. It wasn't that she was afraid of what might come out of the woods at night. In their years living there, she and Nathan had seen just about every form of wildlife there was traipse through the yard. Instead, she feared what she would see when she closed her eyes. Carey had padded off to the guest bedroom after getting reassurances from her sister that she'd come ask for help getting through the night if she needed it. The light coming from under Carey's door had gone out not long after she'd turned in.

The house was all Catherine's. And it was filled with spirits. No room was safe because the ghosts were inside Catherine's head. She herself floated like an apparition from room to room, touching a toy here or a stuffed animal there. She lingered in the laundry room, where stacks of neatly folded clothes were piled on top of the dryer. It seemed a lifetime ago when she had sat folding the clothes, wondering why Nathan and the kids hadn't gotten home yet. She placed the neat piles into a laundry basket and carried it upstairs. With the care of a first-time mother cradling her baby, she sorted and gently placed the small underwear, t-shirts, and jeans into their proper drawers in each of the boys' bureaus, every movement a prayer.

When she was done, Catherine curled up on Jacob's bed. Clutching his blankie to her chest, she lay on her side, holding it up to her nose. She inhaled his scent, and her tears flowed freely until the worn cloth, every edge frayed from years of love, was soaked through. How would she go on living? What purpose was there to her life now? Since she'd married Nathan, all she'd wanted was to be a mother. To get up in the morning and surprise her kids with blueberry pancakes. To pack their lunches for school. To plan elaborate birthday parties with ponies and magicians and moon-bounce houses. To be a home-room mom and take cupcakes and juice to their classes. To sit at the dining room table and puzzle over their math homework. To read them the children's stories that she'd grown up with and to snuggle with them before bedtime. To peek into their rooms at night on the way to bed, and see their angelic faces wrapped in mantles of sleep. Now, all that was gone. So suddenly, so terribly lost. These were the thoughts that accompanied her as her body, spent from all the grief and sadness it had endured over the past days, finally succumbed to the succor of sleep.

*

Heather was puttering around the kitchen, putting away dishes, when Catherine came downstairs from Jacob's bedroom. She had lines on her face where the creases in the pillowcase had left their mark.

"Good morning, sleepy-head." Heather used the same line she used on her children after a long nights' sleep.

"Mmmm." Catherine stretched. "I really conked out."

"Carey told me you were up pretty late, wandering around the house."

"Mmm-hmm." Catherine reached for the fresh pot of coffee her friend had made. "I fell asleep without even realizing it. I didn't think I ever would last night. Everywhere I turned, a memory popped up and smacked me in the face."

"I'll bet. I made you some breakfast in case you were hungry." Heather slid a plate with scrambled eggs and toast across the counter at Catherine. "Carey's over at the church with Nathan's folks."

Catherine sat at the counter and picked absently at the

eggs. "Tell me it's all going to be okay, Heather. Please?"

"Look, Cat. I know you. I know you're strong. Probably the strongest person I've ever met. And I know you've just been sucker-punched. You've been knocked down, but you're not out. You're a fighter. You'll come back from this. I don't know what that means, exactly, but you will. I have no doubt."

"Good pep talk, girlfriend. I just wish I could believe it."

"Well, here's how I see it. You're what, four days in so far? Right now isn't the time to be thinking about the future, or what your life is going to be like. Right now is about right now. It's about being in this really shitty place and not knowing if or when or how you're going to get out of it. You don't need the added pressure of trying to figure out what the rest of your life is going to look like. Your job right now is to remember each and every moment you had with those two great kids, and to be devastatingly sad that they're gone."

"I think I'm doing a pretty good job of that."

"I mean it, Cat. You're in a really dark tunnel right now, and it's not your job to try and find the light. It's to sit in the dark until someone or something brings you the light. And my job, and Carey's, is to sit in the dark with you and make sure you know you're not alone."

Catherine let Heather's words wash over her as she stared absently out the sliders that led from the kitchen to the deck, framing her view of the woods and hills that lay beyond. She felt drained, and the day had only just begun. She couldn't bear the thought of all the emptiness, the nothingness that faced her in the next hour, the next day, the next year. The void stretched out endlessly in front of her like the gaping, yawning mouth of a monster, waiting to swallow her up. Heather pulled up a barstool next to her, sitting in silent vigil beside her. Together they watched out the window as clouds gathered in the distance, signaling a change in the weather and the return to a blast of winter. The sky reminded them both that spring was still a long way off.

*

Catherine spent the day before the funeral feeling like she wanted to crawl out of her skin. Nothing could calm or distract her. Her sister's presence suddenly felt like a burden, and even a visit from Heather failed to ease her sense of dread. The overcast grey skies both reflected and exaggerated her mood, the heavy, snow-laden clouds seeming to close in on her from all sides. By noontime, Carey couldn't take it anymore.

"Catherine, do you want to take one of the pills the doctor prescribed?"

Catherine snapped at her sister with a withering glare. "Why? You want to just knock me out so that you don't have to deal with me anymore?"

"I just thought it might help to calm you down a bit."

"I'm sorry." Catherine's mood shifted, and she was suddenly contrite. "I think I've just got to get through this. I can't deaden myself to the pain. I think I just need to be alone for a while."

Catherine turned from the room and retreated up the stairs to her bedroom, where she closed the door. She sat down heavily in the armchair in the corner and dragged a cardboard box to her feet. She reached down and grabbed a random handful of photographs and set them on her lap. Looking outside, she noticed that it had begun to snow. It was coming down hard, and she could barely make out the tree line at the edge of the yard. Perfect, she thought. Now we've got a blizzard, so no one can make it to the service tomorrow.

She sat back heavily and began to look through the pictures.

Why do we only take pictures of the happy times? She pondered the question as she held a snapshot of Jacob at his second birthday party, his shining face smeared with icing. *Is it because we don't want to remember the arguments, the sleepless nights, the slamming doors? Photographs only ever show us half our lives. They don't give us the full picture.*

While the smiling faces of her children that floated up from the images offered a small degree of consolation, she longed for the fuller perspective that was lacking. She wanted to hold onto all of it. The good and the bad. The fun and the fights. She longed for everything she had had with her sons. She felt a sense of desperation emerging, fearing that it was all sand sifting through her fingers, that all that they'd been and done together as a family, everything she'd been for the past decade, would soon be lost to her.

How can I bury my boys? How can I let their bodies be put in the cold, hard ground? They should be pulling on their snowsuits and building forts and having snowball fights. She longed to stand at the door to the deck, watching them fling themselves from higher and higher steps into the snowbank at the bottom. She could feel their cold, rosy cheeks against hers as she kissed them when they came in from outside, tracking snow through the house as they shed their wet clothes. She saw them sitting at the island in the kitchen, waiting for their hot chocolate to cool, chattering about how much snow it would take to cover the house up to the roof. She could hear Jacob's concern for his father's safety, driving home from work in the storm, and Joe's silly laugh as he talked about making tunnels through the snow down to the road into town.

Catherine had no idea how long she sat with her thoughts.

A soft knock on the door startled her, and Carey poked her head in. "Mind if I come in?"

"Sure. But I'm afraid I'm not very good company right now." Catherine wiped the tears from her cheeks with the back of her hand. Her sister sat down on the bed, eyeing the box of photographs.

"May I?" She extended an open hand, and Catherine gave her a random bunch.

"I remember this." Carey held up a picture from one Christmas morning when Nathan had given Jacob a coonskin cap like he'd had himself when he was a boy. Jacob was smiling broadly in his flannel pajamas, wading through a sea of wrapping paper. "Whatever happened to that hat?"

"Joe threw it up in a tree that spring." Catherine chuckled lightly. "He told me he was using it as bait to try and catch an owl."

"That kid sure could make up stories, couldn't he?" Carey had a tone of admiration in her voice. "You never knew what to believe with him."

Catherine nodded. "He was my clown. And Jacob was the sensitive one. He had a sixth sense. Like he always knew when you were hurting, and he always wanted to make you feel better." They sat in silence as they gazed at the photographs. Carey let out a sigh and Catherine looked up at her sister.

"Well, this just sucks." Tears streamed down Carey's face. "I know you're in pain, And we're all in pain. But I have to tell you that, as your big sister, it's the worst feeling in the world not to be able to fix this for you. I feel so helpless."

"I know. I know. But there's no fixing this. Nobody can fix this. Somehow we just have to find a way to live with it."

"I'm sorry." Carey pulled a tissue from a nearby box. "I came up here to try and make you feel better, not to dump my stuff on you."

"It's okay. It actually kind of helps, you know, to get me out of my own head a little bit." Catherine sniffled and wiped her nose with her own tissue.

"Carey, why did this happen? I mean, what kind of world do we live in where one minute you can have the perfect life, and the next it's all blown to bits? It makes no sense."

"I don't know, Cat. Maybe it's a test of some kind. To see what we're made of. It's why I don't believe in God. I can't imagine a God who would do this to someone. It makes me feel like it's all just random chance, and that we can't take anything for granted. But I would rather have learned that lesson an easier way." Carey blew her nose.

"It's like my old life just ended the way a movie ends." Catherine moved to the window to watch the large flakes cascade to the ground. "And you get up from your seat and walk away like it never happened. It feels like I'm being told: 'Forget the past dozen years. It's time to start over from scratch.' But I don't want to start over. Those years and their lives have to mean something, don't they?"

"Of course, they do, Cat. You may be starting from ground zero, but that doesn't mean they never existed. Those boys are with you now, and they'll always be with you. With us. You're starting over, but it's from a different place. Where you go from here, though, who's to say?"

"I don't know how I'm going to make it through tomorrow." Catherine sat down heavily on the bed beside her sister.

"I don't know how any of us will. But I know we'll figure it out together." The two of them sat like that as the snow accumulated outside, laying a soft, downy blanket that covered the fields and forests in reverential silence.

CHAPTER ELEVEN
NATHAN

The steady, dense snow fell all day Friday. Any New Englander would tell you that this storm was what they called a "widow-maker," because the snow is so heavy to shovel that it causes weak hearts to give out. By noon it was falling so fast that Nathan wondered whether he'd be able to get to his appointment with Robert later that afternoon. Thirty minutes later he received a text from his therapist canceling their appointment. Nathan responded immediately, asking if they might at least have a phone conversation, given that the funeral was to be held the next day. In reply, Nathan's phone rang and Robert was on the other end of the line.

"Thanks for talking to me, Robert." Nathan sat on the edge of his bed, upstairs at his parents' house.

"No problem, Nathan. How are you feeling?"

"A little better, actually. I feel like I had some kind of breakthrough last night."

"Really? I'm glad to hear it. Tell me about it."

Nathan told the therapist about driving around town and

ending up at Jim's, and about walking down to the pond.

"Looking out at the ice, I just kind of collapsed."

"Mmm-hmm."

"You know how they talk about alcoholics and drug addicts hitting rock bottom? Well, that's what it felt like to be there. It was like all the pain and the guilt and the shame and the grief just knocked me to my knees. It was just pressing me down into the mud, trying to crush me." Robert remained silent, and Nathan continued.

"At first, I couldn't even breathe, and I just wanted to crawl out onto that ice and break through and sink into the water and drown. But then, something inside of me shifted. I can't explain it, but it was like this ball of fire started burning down in my belly. It got hotter and hotter. And at first, it was really painful. Like the fire and the pain were in some kind of battle inside me. It hurt so badly that I had to scream. And when I let it out, that fed the flames and they started to melt the guilt."

"That sounds like a powerful experience, Nathan."

"I'm not saying that I'm healed, or that I don't still feel like shit about what happened. But it's like I know I don't want to die anymore. Like I can go on. That I've got something inside me that's going to get me through this."

"I'm really glad to hear that, Nathan. That image of the fire inside you is powerful. I hope you can hold onto it. You know tomorrow is going to be rough."

"Oh, I know. I can't even really let my mind go there right now. But I wanted to tell you what happened to me last night. I had to say it out loud, maybe to help make it real."

"It was real, Nathan. Hold onto it and remember that moment. You can draw strength from it."

"I will. Especially tomorrow."

"Especially tomorrow, but after that, too."

"Thanks for calling me, Robert. You'd better get on the road. It looks like it's getting nasty out there."

"Call me on Monday to set up another appointment, Nathan. I'll be thinking about you tomorrow."

"Thanks." Nathan ended the call and laid down. He rolled onto his side and looked across the room at the Star Wars poster on the wall, another remnant from his childhood. "What would Han Solo do?" he asked himself before drifting off into a restless sleep.

*

Saturday morning dawned with a brilliant blue sky. The sun reflected off the new-fallen snow, a carpet of sparkling crystalline prisms. More than a foot had fallen overnight, but this being Maine, all the primary roads and most of the side roads were already clear. Nathan sat at the breakfast table with his parents, who were reviewing with him the plans for the day and reassuring him that they'd be with him every step of the way. Nathan was anxious about how Catherine would react when they got together for the first time since his miscue on the day he'd been released from the hospital.

"I want to be with her. I need to be with her, and I know she needs me."

Jean was concerned about where this was heading. "Nate, this isn't something you can script in advance. You won't know until you see each other what's going to happen. It's not the time or the place for you two to try and reconcile."

"But Mom, I need her to know that we can go on together. That we can get through this and come out the other side."

"Your mother's right, Nathan." His father joined in the conversation. "It's great that you're feeling so certain about that, but you can't force that on Catherine. Especially not at the funeral. I know it's a cliché to say this, but you've got to give her space."

"But what if I give her too much space? What if she thinks I don't want to be with her?"

"I don't know, Nate." Jean took her son's hand and looked him in the eye, trying to offer him the best advice she could summon. "But I do know that it's not going to be helpful to force yourself on her on the day she has to bury her children."

*

A long line of mourners already snaked out the front door of the small church and down the sidewalk when Nathan and his parents pulled into the church parking lot. The grief-stricken family entered the building through a side door to avoid the crowds and, with little notice and no fanfare, they climbed a flight of stairs and opened a door that placed them at the front of the sanctuary. Nathan's father caught him by the elbow as his knees buckled at the sight of the two small caskets that sat along the altar rail. The caskets themselves were identical, and simple in their design, with brushed nickel hinges and handles set off against a polished white lacquer finish.

Frank and Jean quickly ushered Nathan to a seat at the far end of the front pew from where the children lay. Nathan sat nearly doubled over, trying not to hyperventilate. He was completely unprepared for the image set before him, not that anything could have come close to readying him. His tears flowed freely as his mother gently rubbed his back in a vain attempt to comfort him. The bereaved father and husband gasped for breath between sobs, vaguely grateful that

Catherine wasn't there to see him in such a state.

The caskets bearing the bodies of the two boys lay head-to-head across the front of the small sanctuary. Nathan glanced over at the two matching boxes and wondered which one held Jacob and which one Joe. His breath caught at the question, and he let out a quiet sob. His father handed him a packet of tissues and placed a comforting hand on his knee, giving it a squeeze. Beyond the caskets, in the chancel area, stood a low table on which sat a large bowl holding an unlit candle. A simple wooden lectern, which served as the pulpit, was placed off to the side. Against the front wall of the sanctuary, a spray of flowers adorned a low, cloth-draped table that sat beneath a large stained-glass window depicting a sunrise over the coast of Maine. Soft light filtered through the window, bathing the area behind the caskets in a warm glow. A young woman was playing poignant music on a harp as the mourners gathered. Amidst hushed conversations, an occasional sniffle floated on the heavy air.

Nathan noticed when a hush fell over the crowd of mourners and, along with them, he turned to face the back of the sanctuary. Catherine, flanked by Carey and Heather, was silhouetted in the doorway. Even at a distance, Nathan could tell that Catherine's legs were refusing to move her forward and that her sister and best friend were physically propelling her toward the two gleaming white boxes that held the bodies of their young sons. As Carey and Heather guided Catherine into her seat at the opposite end of the pew where Nathan and his parents were seated, Catherine reached out her hand and tenderly stroked the smooth, polished wood of the nearer casket. Then she turned her head away from the caskets and made eye contact with her husband. Nathan could tell by her blank expression that his wife was heavily sedated, and he wished that he were too. The distance between the two –both physical and emotional – was palpable. The harpist concluded her prelude and the church pastor, Rev. Susan Shiland, approached the lectern.

"The Bible tells us that for everything, there is a season and a time to every purpose under heaven. A time to sow, a time to reap, a time to build up, a time to break down, a time to laugh and a time to weep." The pastor paused and took a deep breath before continuing.

"These words ring hollow today, as we mourn the tragic death of these precious and beautiful children, Jacob and Joseph Osgood. This should be the season of laughter and joy, of hope and promise. And yet, here we are, our arms empty and our hearts broken. The earth is upended, seasons out of sorts. The hope and promise of spring is upon us, the season of new life. But the hope and promise of Jacob's and Joe's lives have been stolen from us, and we cannot imagine what purpose under heaven can be served by that." Rev. Susan turned her attention to the front row of the mourners and continued.

"Catherine and Nathan, we share with you the agony of your grief. The anguish in your hearts finds echo in our own. We know we cannot enter all you feel, nor bear with you the burden of your pain. We can but offer what our love does give: the strength of caring and the warmth of those who seek to understand the silent, storm-swept barrenness of so great a loss, that on your lonely path you may not walk alone." The sobbing and sniffling in the sanctuary wafted into the rafters, and despite the pastor's words of compassion, Nathan had never in his life felt as alone as he did in this moment, surrounded by so many people.

The words flowed over Nathan like one who sits behind,

but not under a waterfall: They cascaded past him without touching him. He sat through the service holding his head in his hands, staring down at the floor in front of him. Once, he lifted his head briefly and looked at Catherine, but she looked away without acknowledging anything. The minister continued to speak in what seemed to Nathan an endless torrent of words having no meaning or purpose.

Before he knew it, his father was prompting Nathan to stand. The service had been blessedly brief. The preacher invited them to join hands for the benediction. Nathan was stunned when Catherine took two steps toward him, reached past his father, and extended her hand to him. He grabbed it as a man hanging by his fingernails above a gaping chasm would grasp the hand of a rescuer. It was the first contact Catherine had offered since she'd run from their living room on the day he'd been released from the hospital.

"We are gathered in the presence of a deep and abiding mystery," the pastor intoned. "With humble hearts, we bow before the veil, which has fallen between Jacob and Joe Osgood and us. May the peace which passes understanding, the peace which comes with acceptance, the peace of the Spirit which rises above all the strains of the earth, be and abide with us all, both this day and forevermore. In the spirit of love, we have gathered. In the spirit of love, we depart. Blessed Be and Amen."

The pastor gave a nod from the podium, and once again, the harp struck up a plaintive melody. Pallbearers from the funeral home appeared from the wings and wheeled the two caskets down the center aisle as the floodgate of tears ruptured. The sound of the harp was drowned out by the sobbing of the mourners. As they waited to recess out of the church, Catherine stood staring into the space the caskets had just occupied. Nathan stared at the stained-glass window.

The families followed the caskets out to the waiting cars, the procession to the cemetery having been arranged with military precision by the funeral home director. The long, black sedans transporting the two families were led by two identical hearses, the purple flags attached to their front fenders fluttering in the breeze. Catherine, Carey, and Heather traveled in one limousine, while Nathan and his parents followed in the other.

The procession wound its way out of Sanford, heading north and west toward Newfield. The cars climbed a steep hill on a winding road that was slick and slushy from the prior nights' snowfall. As they crested the hill, a wide expanse opened before them, and the cars turned into a driveway with stone pillars supporting a wrought-iron arch above it, declaring that they had arrived at Westview Cemetery. They came to a stop in front of a piece of open ground that had been prepared for the interment. The new-fallen snow had been cleared and large swaths of artificial turf laid out, covering the ground on which sat two rows of folding chairs. The chairs faced two open gashes in the ground. The pallbearers reverently removed the boys' caskets from the hearses and gently lowered them onto the frames that perched above the openings of the matching graves. The two families took their places in the chairs, some of Nathan's relatives choosing to stand behind them. The funeral home director walked down the row of chairs, handing each family member two white roses. Nathan clutched his so tightly that all the blood ran from his knuckles, and his hands quickly grew cold. Rev. Susan appeared and began the short graveside service. Nathan shifted uncomfortably in his seat, barely able to contain himself. All he could think about was his chance to talk to his wife once this horrific ceremony was over.

Rev. Susan took her place in front of the gathered family. "Robert Ingersoll, a great public speaker of the late 1800s, was asked to speak at the graveside of a friend's young daughter. He spoke briefly, and with the greatest words of comfort he could find. These are his words:

'Before the sublime mystery of life and spirit, the mystery of infinite space and endless time, we stand in reverent awe. This much we know: we are at least one phase of the immortality of life. The mighty stream of life flows on, and, in this mighty stream, we too flow on, not lost but each eternally significant. For this, I feel: The spirit never betrays the person who trusts it. Physical life may be defeated but life goes on; character survives, goodness lives and love is immortal.'"

Rev. Susan raised her arms toward the sky, signaling that she was nearly finished.

"May all gathered here know peace in this time. May we feel the warmth of spirit, and the comfort and consolation of each other's care. And may the courage of the early morning's dawning, the strength of the eternal hills, the peace of the evening's ending, and the love of life be in our hearts this day and all days. Amen."

With that, Rev. Susan took her two roses, turned toward the graves, and placed one on each casket. She then motioned for the gathered family to do the same. Nathan's father was closest and began the painful procession, followed by Jean, and then Nathan. Carey stood and turned toward her sister, helping her from her chair and guiding her toward the open graves. Standing before them, Catherine let out a pitiful cry. Carey helped Catherine extend her arm toward the graves, supporting her with her other arm around her waist. The two flowers fell silently from Catherine's hand as she glided past the caskets and toward the waiting cars.

Nathan waited by the limousine that had carried Catherine to the cemetery, and he noticed that she paused in her progress toward the car when she saw him standing there. Carey shot him a glance that had "Back off" written all over it, but he refused to take her cue. The two women approached him, and Carey stood protectively near her sister as they reached the spot where Nathan was standing.

"Catherine." He didn't know what else to say. Catherine looked down and studied her mud-stained pumps, waiting for him to continue.

Nathan felt a mixture of desperation and fear creep up the back of his neck. His palms were suddenly sweaty.

"All I can say is that I'm sorry. And I'm hurting like you are, and I love you." The words were cascading now out of Nathan's mouth; he didn't know when he would next get a chance to tell his wife how he felt. "I'm begging you to stay together. I'll do anything. Anything. I know I can never make this up to you. I know. And I'm so, so sorry. Please. Please, don't let this ruin us. I need you. I love you."

Catherine turned toward her husband and took a deep breath. She let her eyes drift over Nathan's shoulder to the site of her children's' graves and then beyond, to the surrounding, snow-covered hills. Nathan waited patiently, tears and mucus dripping from his eyes and nose, afraid to move, afraid that if he did, the earth might crack open and swallow him up.

Looking Nathan squarely in the eye, Catherine uttered one word. One devastating word:

"No."

Then she turned, climbed into the back seat of the limousine, and slammed the door behind her.

CHAPTER TWELVE
CATHERINE

Catherine didn't recognize the number flashing on her phone, so she declined the call. After it showed up as a voicemail, she touched the keypad to listen.

"Hi, Catherine. This is Rev. Susan. From the UU church. I wanted to let you know I was thinking about you. I also wanted to let you know that I'm here and happy to sit down with you if you'd ever like to talk. I don't want to be a bother, but I wanted to say that you don't have to go through this alone."

Catherine set the phone down on the table beside her easy chair in the living room and looked out the window. She was surprised to hear from the pastor. It had been more than six weeks since the funeral, and the two really didn't know each other. But the timing of the call was uncanny. Carey had gone back to New York just a week earlier, and those seven days in an empty house had been among the hardest since the accident. Despite Heather's regular check-ins, Catherine had never felt more alone in all her life.

Through the miracle of modern medicine, Catherine was unable to recall many specifics from the funeral for Joe and Jacob, even later that same day, much less weeks afterward. The entire event was like a stop-motion movie, with large gaps in between the shots. Walking into the church and seeing the caskets. Taking her seat in the front and looking over at Nathan, his face red and puffy from crying. Did she take his hand at the end of the service? She's not sure what prompted her to do that, if her memory wasn't playing tricks on her and it didn't actually happen. The void left behind when the caskets were rolled away and feeling not just nothing, but less than nothing. Empty, gone, invisible, a ghost evaporating like early-morning mist over a mountain lake. The gruesome scene at the cemetery, those two bottomless pits they were going to put her children in. Thinking, as she looked out across the surrounding hills that, for the rest of her life, she would come to know this view intimately, in every kind of weather and in every season. Carey's steadfast calm as the sedative began to wear off during the graveside service, reminding her to breathe as she held onto her sister's hand for dear life.

And then there was the encounter at the car. Nathan accosting her. It felt like an assault, really. How could he choose that moment – the moment her babies were being lowered into the ground – to beg for forgiveness, to plead for them to reconcile? What could he possibly have been thinking? Carey was furious and had not been able to contain herself on the ride home from the funeral.

"What the hell was he doing?" Carey shouted into the cavernous back seat of the limo as Catherine sat beside her, visibly shaken. "Selfish doesn't begin to describe it. I can't believe the way he confronted you. I would have jumped in to save you if I hadn't been completely blind-sided."

Catherine patted her sister's hand, the irony of her comforting Carey in this moment not lost on either of them. Carey quickly apologized.

"Are you okay?" Carey turned toward her sister in the seat.

"As okay as I guess I can be under the circumstances." The two women were silent for the remainder of the car ride home.

The loss of Jacob, Joe, and the baby had settled into Catherine's body like a parasite. It made itself at home in her gut, its presence felt by the way it drained her of energy and interest. Each sunrise hailed a new day that promised nothing. Catherine had no way to fill her time, except to reflect on the emptiness of her life. Until now, she hadn't realized how all-consuming motherhood had been. She was like a fish who had suddenly discovered the water in which it had always been swimming, and the awareness itself made her feel like she was drowning. The absence of motherhood's physical demands left her adrift. No "mom taxi" to drive, shepherding the kids from school and daycare to gymnastics and swim lessons. No piles of laundry to process. No meals to plan, shop for, or prepare. No more pre-bedtime dance parties or wrestling on the living room floor.

But more than all that, there was the emotional vacuum. All the love had been sucked out of her when the vessels into which she poured that love were lost. Catherine longed to feel something. Anything. But she felt nothing. She hadn't lost just the feelings of joy, anticipation, satisfaction, and deep gladness that motherhood gave her. Gone, too, was the anxiety over Joe's emerging aggressiveness and the worry about how Jacob was doing in school. The constant brooding over how to raise children with good values and kind, open hearts. The weighing of whether to have any more children and then, albeit briefly, the fears over the new baby's development. She had become a human sieve: Everything – every experience, every thought, every feeling – passed through her like so many grains of sand. She had no capacity to capture or hold onto any emotion.

With nothing to do with her body and nothing to occupy her mind, each day stretched out interminably ahead of her. *Is this what my life will be forever?* She sat for hours in the recliner in the living room or the chair in the corner of her bedroom. She was a moon whose host planet had suddenly been obliterated. Without its gravitational pull, she was released from her orbit and all she'd known before. It was a form of freedom, yes. But it came unbidden and at the cost of her very self. She was free, but only to wander aimlessly forever through the cold, dark void of space and time.

Catherine considered the minister's message, then pressed the "call back" button. After all, she had nothing better to do.

*

Catherine entered the church and followed signs for the minister's office, trying not to hyperventilate with the memory of the last occasion that had brought her to this building. She knocked tentatively on the door, taking a deep breath and wondering why she was bothering with this visit. Catherine had virtually no hope that it would be of value to her. Truth be told, she wasn't even sure she was ready to take a step onto the road of recovery, much less begin to walk down it. For weeks now, grief had been her constant companion. It greeted her when she rose each morning and curled up beside her when she laid down to sleep at night, a silent, steadfast partner. The pall lay like a wrap across her shoulders as she sat, day after day, looking out the window of her home.

Although weighty, its presence had become familiar, something she had come to count on. What if this conversation upset the delicate relationship she and grief had managed to establish?

"Hi, Catherine." Rev. Susan extended her hand to shake Catherine's as she swung open the door. "Come on in."

"Thank you, Reverend." Catherine felt awkward about using the honorific as she entered the office. "Is that what I should call you?"

"Some people call me Reverend Sue. Others just Susan, or Sue. Whatever feels right to you is fine with me."

Catherine noticed that three walls of the office held shelves that were crammed with books. In the corner sat an old, beat-up Steelcase desk. with a matching swivel chair. It appeared out of place to Catherine. Its massive grey bulk dominated the room and made Catherine think of a World War II battleship.

Susan noticed Catherine's gaze. "My grandfather's." Susan nodded toward the desk. "He was a cop for nearly 40 years and that was his desk. I inherited it when he died. I admit, it's pretty dreadful, except for its sentimental value."

Susan motioned Catherine toward two chairs sitting in front of a large double-hung window that looked out onto a flagstone courtyard. A large pile of grey, dirty snow hulked in a shadowed corner where it had accumulated through the winter.

"We call that our 'glacier.'" Susan nodded toward the window. "The sun never hits there, so it usually doesn't melt until sometime in June." The pastor took a seat in one of the chairs, so Catherine obliged by sitting in the other. "I'm glad you came in."

"I'm not sure why. I mean, I'm not a member of the church or anything." Catherine shifted uncomfortably in her seat.

"I can't imagine what you're going through." The pastor deflected Catherine's concern.

"Mmmm," came Catherine's non-committal response.

The two sat in silence, Catherine gazing out the window. The minister's patience was annoying. Catherine fidgeted with her rings and her watch, and crossed and uncrossed her legs, while Susan sat, nonplussed. Finally, Catherine had to say something just to break the tension.

"I thought there were these stages of grief. I always read about that, anyway."

"Yeah." The pastor shook her head. "Dr. Kubler-Ross did more to hurt people who are grieving than you can imagine. After her book came out, everyone thought there was a formula, that there were defined steps to go through, like a progression. The reality is very different. No one I know has ever followed the stages she wrote about."

"Tell me about it. I feel like I'm all over the place. It's more like I'm going in circles than following steps leading somewhere. I'm just spinning my wheels and not getting anywhere."

"It's been, what, two months since the accident?"

"It'll be nine weeks on Saturday."

"That's not much time, is it?"

"No. And it's also an eternity. Every day's the same. Empty. Pointless. The highlight of my day is going to the cemetery and crying for, like, an hour."

"That's awful, Catherine. I'm sorry you've got to go through this."

"At least I'm not alone. My sister calls every day, and my best friend and I text a lot." Catherine glanced at the pastor and then returned her gaze to the courtyard, adding with a sigh, "The casserole caravan has finally slowed to a crawl. I've never eaten so much lasagna in my life."

"It sounds like you've got some good support."

"I'm not alone, but the loneliness is like this weight that's crushing me. And sometimes everyone calling makes me feel like I'm on a suicide watch or something."

Susan's antennae were up, and she suddenly turned serious. "Should they be worried about that?"

"No, no. I'm not going to kill myself over this. I might kill Nathan, but ---"

"So, you're angry with him, huh?"

Catherine could feel tears fill her eyes before the words came out of her mouth. "Angry? I don't think there's a word for it. He's always been reckless. He's like a little boy sometimes, never thinking about consequences. And that reckless, childish behavior killed my babies. You bet your ass I'm angry." Catherine accepted the box of tissues the pastor held out to her and blew her nose. "Sorry for the language."

"No need to apologize. Far worse has been spoken in this office. It sounds like you don't know where to go with your anger, either."

"Well, I've shut Nathan out of my life, at least for now. He's tried calling, but I don't answer. I can't even stand the idea of being in the same state as him, much less actually seeing him." The two of them sat silently, letting the words hang in the air. Then Rev. Susan spoke into the void.

"The image I have, Catherine, is that you're lost in this swamp, and it's all dark and foggy. You don't know which way to turn. And even if you did know which way to go, you couldn't really get moving because your feet are stuck. And not only that, you were put in this awful place by someone you loved and trusted."

"That sounds about right." Catherine nodded as she wiped

her nose, the tears subsiding.

"If you let me, Catherine, I might be able to help you start to get un-stuck. I might even be able to get you moving along a path that could lead you out of the swamp."

"Just don't tell me I have to accept Jesus as my Lord and savior." Catherine was only half-joking.

"No, no. None of that. I'm a licensed pastoral counselor. It's a kind of therapist. It's therapy with a spiritual twist, but I don't force religion down anyone's throat."

Catherine realized that it felt good to talk with someone who was outside of her circle of family and friends. Susan was laid-back but perceptive. She listened carefully, and the image of the swamp that she offered was spot on. Catherine said the words before she had even consciously thought them:

"I think I'd like that." Rev. Susan reached across the small study to pull a calendar off the imposing desk, and the two women agreed on the date of their next meeting.

*

After the third or fourth visit, Catherine found herself actually looking forward to her sessions with Rev. Susan. Her initial impressions of the pastor had been confirmed: she was easy to talk to, an attentive listener, and an insightful therapist. Their conversations even sometimes ventured into the realm of the spiritual, which, surprisingly, didn't make Catherine uncomfortable. During one meeting, Susan asked Catherine a question that led her into some deep introspection.

"Where do you think Jacob and Joe are now?"

Catherine wasn't a religious person, and there were times she wished she were. It would be comforting to believe that her boys were angels up in heaven or that they were walking somewhere with Jesus, safe and surrounded by love. But it all seemed just a sham to her. Some kind of plot to brainwash people into trying to be good so that they could claim a later reward. She knew she didn't believe in heaven, in the traditional sense of a place where people inhabit human-like bodies and are happy all the time. But after her mother and father died, she occasionally got a powerful sense that one or the other was nearby. At her college graduation, she was sure that her father was in the audience, cheering. She also felt her mother's comforting presence while she was in labor with both her boys. She'd never questioned these feelings because no one had ever asked her about them. In fact, she hadn't even told Carey about them.

Catherine experienced Jacob's and Joe's death differently. While she grieved the loss of her mother and father, and she missed them terribly at every milestone moment of her life, losing the boys felt more like someone had taken a machete and chopped off one of her limbs. A big part of her was missing. Gone. Vanished. And yet the phantom pain that amputees talk about was there, too. Somehow, the boys were both gone from her and still present with her.

She looked at the pastor with a mixed sense of curiosity and clarity. "You know, I have no idea. But it feels like they're both close by."

As was her style, Rev. Susan sat patiently while Catherine reflected on the question. Just as she was unable to buy into the idea of heaven, so, too, did she reject the notion that Jacob and Joe simply no longer "were," that they had ceased to exist when their last breaths were taken. *So, if they're not angels in heaven and they're more than just their biological bodies, what and where are they?* In the days that followed, Catherine turned the question over and over in her mind, kneading it like a ball of dough. As she sat beside her children's graves, she began to wonder why she was there. *They're not here. I know that.* And she began to question whether this near-daily ritual was serving any useful purpose.

Catherine knew that she felt closest to her children in her home, especially in their bedrooms. She had left the rooms virtually untouched since the day they'd left for their fateful ride that bright Saturday in March. Their blankies still smelled like them. Their toys still waited for their return. She hadn't even washed the sheets on their beds. But more than the objects that surrounded her in these rooms, she could feel the boys' presence, their essence there. Walking through the house, Catherine felt like the boys were right around the corner, in the next room, close enough that she could almost reach out and touch them. It was as if they were playing a game of hide-and-seek with her, and she couldn't quite discover their secret hiding place. But she knew they were there.

Catherine recently had fallen into the habit of starting her morning by sipping her coffee, standing first in the doorway of Jacob's room and then in the doorway of Joe's. And, lately, she noticed that something was shifting inside her. The ritual was no longer morbid or painful. It had been weeks since she had thrown herself onto one or the other of the boys' beds and sobbed into their pillows. Instead, pausing at their thresholds had become her way of greeting both the day and the spirits of her boys, whose presence she felt and wanted to continue to feel. Just a few moments in that liminal space, gazing at their stuff, brought her a sense of connection and, with it, peace. For a few minutes each day, she would stand there and absently gaze at the remnants of her happy family. Jacob's collection of dinosaurs neatly arranged on his bookshelf. Joe's Lego blocks, some connected and sitting in the corner, others tucked away in clear plastic bins. Jacob's rocking horse, sitting motionless in the corner waiting for a rider, gazing back at her with a glassy stare, and "Bun-Bun," the stuffed rabbit that was Joe's equivalent of the American Express card: He never left home without it. As she stood in the doorways of their bedrooms, Catherine opened herself up to the comforting feeling of Joe and Jacob's presence, and she wondered why she was still making the awful trek up to Westview.

Catherine found herself embracing the notion that the boys were with her. Not as spirits or as ghosts, but as a form of energy. Sometimes she pictured them as orbs of pulsing light floating just above and behind her head. At other times, she experienced them as soft, warm breaths of air that took the chill out of the nighttime air, wrapping Catherine like a blanket as she sat on the deck watching the sunset over the western hills. She tried to put these feelings into words when she next saw Rev. Susan.

"I feel their energy with me all the time. It's like they're outside me and in here all at the same time." She pointed to her heart. "There's something about them that is real and palpable, and it survived their death."

"I know you hate it when I get all religious on you." The minister smiled, leaned forward, and tapped Catherine on the knee. "But that's what I call 'the soul.' It doesn't begin with our birth and doesn't end with our death. Scientists frame it as the 'conservation of energy,' and that's fine if they want to put it in those terms. But the principle is basically the same as far as I'm concerned: Nothing is created, and nothing is ever lost from the system that we're a part of."

Catherine nodded at the thought as the pastor suggested

it. "To tell you the truth, I really don't care what we call it or what others think. I know they're with me in a way that means something. In a way that lets me know that I haven't lost them completely. That's at least some comfort."

The two women sat with Catherine's statement. In that moment, the young mother who'd lost her boys, her unborn child, and her sense of joy and hope realized, for the first time since the accident, that the shattered pieces of her life were beginning to be reassembled. They'd never form the same picture as before, but maybe they'd come together in some new configuration that might just allow her to go on living.

CHAPTER THIRTEEN
NATHAN

"What's new?" Robert opened with his usual wide-open question as Nate took the now-familiar seat in the therapist's now-familiar office. Nathan had been seeing Robert regularly since his release from the hospital, often more than once a week. Robert had helped pull him back from the brink on several occasions. In the time since the funeral, they'd slid, slowly and almost imperceptibly, from the crisis counseling that followed the accident, when Nathan had experienced frequent anxiety attacks and incapacitating feelings of self-blame and guilt, to a new phase of treatment. This one was focused on helping Nathan begin to accept and navigate the "new normal" of his life without his children and, thus far, without Catherine. Corresponding with this evolution in his recovery, Nathan had moved out of his parents' home and in with his friend Jim.

"Nothing. Nothing at all. I tried to call Catherine again, but she didn't pick up, and I didn't leave a message. Just like last week and the week before that and the week before that."

"I'm sorry to hear that. At least you're trying."

"I guess, but it's not getting me anywhere. I feel like she's got me in a holding pattern. Like she's got complete control of my future."

"Why do you think she's still not taking your calls?"

Nathan reflected on Robert's question. He wanted to blurt out "Because I killed her children, you idiot!" but he refrained. Robert waited patiently for his client to frame a response.

"Because she hates me for what I did."

"She hates you?"

"Wouldn't you?"

"Tell me what she's said or done to lead you to believe that she hates you."

Nathan sat with the question, turning it over in his mind, looking at it from every angle. After a few minutes, he realized that all that Catherine had done so far was to put up a wall, a protective barrier, between them. He saw that he actually had no idea how Catherine was feeling except that she wasn't ready to share anything about it with him.

"I dunno." Nathan fidgeted with his hands, unable to find a good answer to the question.

"So who, would you say, hates you? Catherine? Your parents? Your friend Jim?"

Nathan sat in silence for nearly a full minute, hoping against hope that he could outlast his therapist. But out of the silence came a revelation. "I hate myself."

"You do?"

"Of course, I do. I hate myself for what I did. I made a horrible mistake, and I can't undo it."

"No, you can't. So, what are you going to do, Nathan?"

"What do you mean, what am I going to do?"

"Well, you just said you made a horrible mistake, and that

you can't undo it. So, if you can't undo what you did, what are you going to do?"

"I don't know. I need to make it up to her somehow?"

"Really? How are you going to do that?"

"I have no idea. That's what I need to figure out. I need to find a way to get her back. To get her to take me back."

"That's what you need to figure out? Do you think this is about making up for your mistake? About somehow compensating your wife for the death of your children? That sounds an awful lot like buying her forgiveness. Is that what you want?"

Nathan's head was spinning. "You're twisting my words, Robert. That's not what I meant."

"If that's not what you meant, then tell me what you meant when you said, 'I need to make it up to her somehow' and 'I need to find a way to get her back.'"

"I guess I need to find a way for her to see that I'm still the same person. The same person that she married. I don't think she sees that."

"Are you, Nathan? Are you the same person now that you were when you left the house with the boys that Saturday afternoon? I'm not so sure. No, check that. I *am* sure. I'm sure that you're *not* the same person. You can't tell me that you could go through what you've been through and still come out the other side unchanged."

"Mmm. I see what you're saying."

"If nothing else, you started out that day feeling pretty damn good about yourself. And now you tell me that you actually hate yourself for what you did. That sounds like a pretty big shift, at least in perspective, if not personality."

Robert's reasoning made sense to Nathan. He couldn't argue with the logic. "What do I do? Do I walk up to the front door and ring the bell, and introduce myself to her and we start all over again?"

"Maybe. Maybe not. But that's pretty far down the road. I think the first thing we need to figure out is: Who is Nathan now? If he's not the Nathan from before, then who is he? And, for starters, how can we get him to stop hating himself?"

Nathan sank back in his chair, exhausted by the thought. All he wanted from Robert was to help him figure out a way to get back together with Catherine. He was overwhelmed by the sheer magnitude of the work ahead that Robert had just laid out.

*

Living at Jim's, Nathan fell into a morning routine that included a daily hike down the path to Franklin Pond. There, he would sit on a boulder by the shore and gaze out onto the lake, observing the ice as it turned to slush and eventually to water. The first several times he sat by the pond his grief twisted his insides into a knot as he recalled the events of that fateful afternoon. The pain was intense, but each day he forced himself to walk toward it. Nathan recalled having read somewhere that "the only way out is through," and he was committed to letting the grief have its way with him, no matter what. Sitting on the shore was his communion with the boys and his penance for what he'd done. Perhaps it would eventually become his salvation.

As he sat in silence by the water, Nathan grieved not just for the loss of his sons, but for the damage he'd done to his relationship with Catherine. He wondered what, if anything, the future held for them as a couple. He desperately wanted to be able to fix what had been broken, but his sessions with

Robert were helping him realize that he was powerless to do so. It was against his nature to accept that idea, to truly internalize it. He was a problem solver, a change agent, an innovator. He had never encountered a situation that he couldn't resolve by applying some combination of intelligence and determination. But slowly, week by week, Robert was helping him see that he wasn't going to be able to, in Nathan's words, "figure this out." No mix of grand gestures, strategic planning, and sheer willpower were going to get Catherine to open up to him again. He felt a kind of desperation when he faced this reality, a sensation that was alien to someone who had always succeeded. With growing awareness of his impotence, he began to experience a sense of loss that compounded and complicated the pain of losing Jacob and Joe.

*

Nathan noticed spring coming on fast. There were new birdsongs in the woods on the walk to and from the lake. Ducks and loons returned, gliding across the water's mirrored early-morning surface. As he sat on the shore, he could see the rings from rising fish as they chased emerging nymphs to the surface, the ripples spreading out in concentric circles that slowly, but assuredly, made their way to where he sat. Nathan felt intimately connected not just to this place, but to the change of seasons and to nature itself. He found himself inextricably bound to the world in a way he had never been before. Tragically, yes. But also in a way that made him feel that his life – and those of his sons – were all part of something larger than this pond, or that moment at which it swallowed up his children. Experiencing the change of seasons this way, Nathan gained a vague sensation that his season of grief would someday, somehow come to an end, that a new season of his life would begin somewhere in the future. He tried to hold onto this as a simple act of faith that could sustain him when he woke up in the middle of the night, drenched in a cold sweat from his recurring nightmare.

After weeks of sitting around Jim's house, with only walks to the pond and visits with Robert to distract him, Nathan decided to try establishing something of a routine with his life, an attempt to regain a sense of normalcy despite the maelstrom of his grieving and his estrangement from Catherine. He returned to his office in Portland and began to pick up the pieces of his financial advising practice. Each call he made to a client picked at the tender scab that covered the wounds of that afternoon in March, as he endured expressions of condolence, some more heartfelt than others. He could only handle a few of those calls each day, but he also found that immersing himself in stock reports and running forecasts – the familiar, non-judgmental arena of numbers and spreadsheets – enabled him to escape the loop of regret and recrimination that played endlessly in his head. And it reminded him that there were people counting on him for their future security. It restored to him a measure of the self-confidence that had, too, been a victim of the accident.

*

Nathan sat down to dinner with Jim. The two of them had eaten the evening meal together for more than two months, except when Jim's daughter from his failed marriage stayed with him. Nathan spent those nights at his parents' house.

"I know it's been an imposition, Jim. I can't tell you how much it's meant for me to be here all this time."

"It's no problem, man. I told you that from the start."

"I just don't know how much longer it's going to be. I mean, I really want to move back home, but that's not up to me."

"Yeah, it sucks that Catherine's holding all the cards. And I don't mean that in a bad way. You know I love her, Nate. But I wish there was something you could do, you know?"

"Me too. But like my therapist keeps telling me, all I can do is work on myself. Then we'll see what happens."

"That's a tough pill to swallow, I'm sure." Jim took a bite of his meal. "If it was me, I'd be outside every night under her window holding a boom box like Lloyd Dobler."

Nathan winced a little at Jim's remark. He knew it was meant to be humorous, but his friend's words struck a nerve. *Say Anything* was one of Catherine's favorite movies and, truth be told, he'd always identified with the John Cusack character.

"If I thought it would work, you know I'd be doing it," he said as he cleared the dishes. Changing the subject, Nathan called out over his shoulder from the kitchen sink. "It's Celtics-Lakers tonight, right?"

*

Nathan and Catherine might have missed each other forever, circling in never-intersecting orbits around the small town of Newfield that they both called home. But because Newfield has only one supermarket, the encounter was bound to happen sooner or later. It was late in the afternoon on a day in mid-May when their carts met awkwardly near the check-out line, their first interaction since the funeral of their children.

150

"Hey," was all Nathan could manage, and Catherine reciprocated. They both simultaneously glanced down into each other's carts and then shifted their gazes to their own, realizing that looking at what each other was buying was somehow too much intimacy too soon.

"So, did the wood hold out through the rest of the winter?" Nathan had no idea why he'd asked this, of all things.

"Oh. Yeah." Catherine nodded. "It was fine. Are you and Jim getting along all right?"

"Yeah, yeah. But I'm worried he's starting to get sick of me. I might start to look for an apartment soon."

"Mmmm." Nathan couldn't read the look on his wife's face.

"How're you doing, Cat? I've tried calling you."

"I know. I'm sorry. I just haven't been ready. I'm working on it, though. Okay?"

"I guess it has to be. My therapist is trying to help me let go of the things I can't control, so I'm trying not to push."

"I'm glad you're seeing someone, Nate."

"Me too. How about you? Do you have someone other than Heather and your sister helping you out?"

"Oh, yeah. I thought you knew. The pastor at the church. The one who did the funeral? She's been really great."

Nathan shifted from one foot to the other as he decided how far to take the conversation. "I don't suppose we could sit down and really talk sometime, could we?"

"Maybe, Nate. Just not yet. But maybe soon." Catherine looked down at the contents of her cart. "I have good days and bad days."

"Yeah. Me too. Seeing you makes this a good day, at least for me, Cat."

"Thanks. That's nice to hear. I'll think about getting

together, okay? But don't sit by the phone. If I think that's what you're doing, it's just going to put pressure on me that I don't want or need. I hope you understand."

"Of course"—Nathan drew a cross on his chest— "swear to God. Besides, I've got to focus on getting the office back up to speed. But it's great to see you."

Nathan mustered all his willpower and broke off the encounter, tactfully steering his shopping cart away from the checkout, pretending that he'd forgotten something in the cereal aisle. He looked back over his shoulder before rounding the corner. Catherine was transferring groceries from her cart to the check-out conveyor. Although he longed for it, and he even mentally willed her to do so, she didn't look up from the task.

*

Nathan hung onto Catherine's "maybe soon" as if it were a lifeline trailing a boat in a storm-tossed sea. A window had been opened, if only a crack, to let in a fresh breeze of possibility. He replayed the encounter in the supermarket over and over in his mind. Those two words buoyed his spirits in a way nothing since the accident had. "Maybe" seemed exponentially more hopeful than the terse "No" he had received from her after the funeral. Nathan told Jim of the encounter as he unpacked his groceries.

"I'm glad you can see some light at the end of the tunnel, Nate." Jim reached down and put the dish detergent under the sink. "And I don't want to burst your balloon. But I gotta tell you that I'm worried that you're placing a lot of stock in a pretty vague statement." This brought Nathan up short.

"What do you mean?"

"Look, Nate. You've been telling me that your shrink wants you to find a way to stand on your own two feet, regardless of whether Catherine takes you back."

"Right. And to let go of the things I can't control."

"So, it seems to me that just by running into her, you've fallen right back down the rabbit hole. You're focused on what she's going to do or not going to do. She's the one calling the shots on your emotions. Is that what you want?"

Nathan stopped mid-stride between the grocery bags and the refrigerator, holding a carton of eggs. He cocked his head like a spaniel waiting for a command from its owner, thinking about what his friend had just said. It didn't take long for him to realize the truth in it. "You know, you're right. Wow. That hadn't even occurred to me, Jim."

"Maybe I need to get a fancy office in one of those old Victorians downtown." His friend attempted to lighten the mood after such a serious exchange. "Then I could charge a hundred fifty bucks an hour to listen to other peoples' problems, instead of thirty-five an hour for fixing their transmissions." The two friends got a good laugh at that. Jim went out the front door and down to the garage, leaving Nathan deep in thought.

CHAPTER FOURTEEN
CATHERINE

Catherine loaded the bags into the back of her car. There weren't many, she thought. Not like there had been when she'd been shopping for a family of four. Climbing into the driver's seat, she started the vehicle and immediately called Heather.

"Well, you'll never guess who I ran into at the supermarket."

"No! How do you feel? How did it go? What did you say?"

Catherine considered her friend's questions, especially the first one. As she pulled out of the parking lot and onto the main road, she realized that her answer was "Just fine."

"It's weird, Heather. I've stressed about just this kind of thing happening. I mean, it was bound to, right?"

"Of course. You always run into the people you don't want to see in this town."

"I don't know if I'm just in shock, but I feel really calm. It's not that I don't feel anything." Catherine talked as she made her way up Route 109 toward home. "It's not like I'm dead inside when I think of him. And I won't lie and tell you my heart didn't flutter some when I saw him. But I just feel calm. Like a mountain or something. I don't know how else to explain it."

"Well, that sure beats totally frazzled, or like you want to kill him, I guess."

"Yeah. I don't feel like I need to go home and cry myself to sleep or drink a couple glasses of wine like I thought I would when this happened. He asked if we could get together."

"What did you say?"

"I told him it was still too early, but maybe soon."

"Wow. That's something then."

"He said he was thinking about getting an apartment and moving out of Jim's."

"If I know you, your first instinct was to want to take him in and take care of him."

"That's the thing, Heather. That *wasn't* my reaction. I just kind of received it as information and didn't really have any reaction at all. He told me, and I was, like, 'Oh.'"

"That sounds like a pretty healthy response, Babe. Like you've got some emotional distance and some independence. I think it's a good thing."

"Maybe. I guess. I don't know. I can feel myself wishing that it had been more emotional for me, too. But I can't make that up or force myself to feel something I didn't. It's like I want things to be the way they were, but I also want them to be different."

"Wow, girlfriend. I'm really proud of you."

"Something's definitely shifted. I don't remember ever feeling like a mountain before."

"Catherine, you're one of the strongest, steadiest people I've ever met. Maybe you just never thought of yourself that way."

"Thanks. I appreciate that. And thanks for listening. I'm sitting in my driveway and the ice cream is melting. I'll see you soon."

"For sure." Heather clicked off the call.

*

As a child, Catherine had spent hours glued to her mother's hip in the kitchen. Her mom, who had had a home wedding cake business, had taught her younger daughter all the ins and outs of baking. As a result, Catherine had always found solace baking pies, cookies, and cakes. After she had children of her own, she passed on the family tradition. Jacob and Joe took turns serving as her assistant at the baking island in their large kitchen. They delighted in measuring out the ingredients and sneaking pinches of cookie dough from the bowl. It wasn't unusual to find one or the other of the boys standing on a chair beside their mother, wrapped in an apron and surrounded by a cloud of flour or powdered sugar. Although Catherine could mix and bake a batch of cookies in half the time by herself, she reveled in sharing the knowledge and enthusiasm she'd learned from her own mother. She had just begun to allow Jacob, with some supervision, to use the stove to make scrambled eggs on his own shortly before he died. Catherine remembered the pride he'd shown that first time that he carefully scraped the slightly burned eggs from the pan onto a plate and walked them out to his father waiting in the dining room. Baking with the boys, passing on a piece of her mother that way, was one of Catherine's greatest pleasures as a parent, and she felt the pain of loss acutely whenever she stood alone in the kitchen.

And yet, inexplicably, this morning, Catherine found herself standing at the baking island with all the makings for chocolate-macadamia nut cookies – Nathan's favorite – laid out on the counter. With little demonstrable pleasure and perhaps even less thought, she tossed the ingredients into the mixer, pulled the baking trays out of the cabinet, and scooped out the dough. After putting the cookie sheets in the oven and setting the timer, she grabbed her mug of coffee and sat down in the living room as the house filled with the familiar, sweet aroma that was a near-constant companion in her life "before," as she'd begun to think of it.

Catherine reflected on the urge that had led her into the kitchen this morning. Running into Nathan at the grocery store had shaken her up, for sure. She'd been unable to sleep most of that night. And it had definitely sparked something in her. Was it love? Desire? A longing not to be alone? Or maybe it was simply the pull of muscle memory, like taking those first few turns of the winter after three seasons away from the ski slopes. You don't really think about it, but your body, conditioned from years of practice, knows what it wants and what it needs to do, how to absorb the bumps, how to carve a smooth arc.

Catherine was still miles away from any notion of inviting Nathan back into their home. But seeing him, alone with his sad shopping cart full of peanut butter, frozen pizza, and Cheerios, had cracked the shell she'd so carefully built around her heart. On the one hand, she wanted to see him suffer for what he'd done. He'd robbed her of so much. Her entire life, really. But somewhere inside, if she allowed herself to admit it, there was a spark of sympathy, too. She realized that she wasn't the only one suffering, and she knew that she had the power to alleviate some of his by simply consenting to see him.

Catherine pulled the cookies from the oven and arrayed them on the cooling racks as she tried to parse through her conflicting emotions. She knew she felt bad for him. In some ways, it felt the same as when she looked at a dog in a cage at the SPCA. Little more than pity. But there was something else moving in her, too. An impulse to take care of Nathan and to try to shelter him from harm. Was she simply transferring her maternal feelings to him since she no longer had children toward which to direct them? Or was there, for the first time since the accident, a stirring of compassion in her heart for her husband? An inkling that the devastation she felt was something they actually shared? Could that patch of scorched earth be the common ground they might stand on together?

After they cooled, Catherine neatly stacked the cookies on a paper plate and covered them with plastic wrap. She left them sitting on the end of the counter while she showered, dressed, and considered whether she would actually drive over to Jim's house and drop them off for Nathan.

*

All weekend, the plate of cookies sat on the end of the kitchen island, taunting Catherine. At least a dozen times over the course of two days, she had decided, alternatively, to deliver them to Nathan and to toss them in the trash. She knew better than to consult her sister about her quandary. While Carey was her confidante in all things, the subject of Nathan had been taboo between them since long before the accident. The conflict dated all the way back to the months following their wedding. It was more than sibling rivalry, jealousy, or fear that Nathan would replace Carey as the primary relationship in Catherine's life. Carey accepted that

158

Catherine had chosen Nathan as a life partner. She even wrote a touching Maid of Honor speech for their wedding, in which she invoked the memory of their parents' marriage, drawing parallels between that and the relationship of the newlyweds. The source of the divide lay in Catherine's abandonment of her career as a rising star in one of Boston's biggest law firms. Carey had let her know in no uncertain terms that she felt like Nathan had dragged Catherine, virtually caveman-style, to a remote farmhouse in the Maine countryside where she would forever be barefoot and pregnant, with nothing more challenging to do than make sure there was a hot meal on the table when he got home from work. The fact that Catherine had chosen her lifestyle willingly held little sway with Carey. She blamed Nathan.

Catherine was aware that, as the older sister, Carey felt responsible for Catherine's wellbeing, particularly after their parents' death. It was Carey who had made sure that Catherine stayed and finished college and eventually applied to law school. Carey had helped her arrange the student loans and scholarships that ensured Catherine would get the best legal education possible. She listened sympathetically when Catherine called feeling overwhelmed by her role as an editor of the law review. Catherine could count on her sister to heap mountains of both compassion and confidence on her. Catherine consulted with Carey about internships and, later, job offers, and Carey clearly took pride in her sister's accomplishments every step of the way. She was, to say the least, heavily invested in the arc of Catherine's career.

Then Nathan happened. Carey had watched as Catherine fell hard for him. She listened patiently as Catherine spent hours singing Nathan's praises. Carey even encouraged Catherine to risk her heart, a heart that was still tender and healing from the loss of their parents. And when it became apparent that Nathan was "the one," Carey was careful not to put Catherine in the position of having to choose between them. At the same time, Carey lobbied hard for Catherine to keep working. She encouraged her to persuade Nathan to move from Portland to Boston so that she could continue to pursue partnership in the firm, with its promise of status and financial security.

Catherine pushed back, knowing that, to a degree, Carey was projecting her own stuff onto her. Carey's career trajectory had been a steady ascent since graduating from Wharton with her MBA and going to work for Morgan Stanley, then a boutique private equity firm specializing in tech acquisitions. Carey thrived on the energy and excitement of international investment banking and enjoyed its material rewards. Catherine knew that Carey couldn't conceive of living anywhere other than Manhattan or doing anything that would derail her from her seven- (and sometimes eight-) figure annual income. While she'd had serious relationships over the years, Carey was always clear that her work would always come first.

But Catherine had given herself over to Nathan entirely, had walked away from her career for him, leaving Carey blaming and bitter toward her brother-in-law. Catherine watched as Carey tried her best not to let her resentment show when the three of them got together, but she inevitably came across as cold and aloof toward Nathan. Catherine's decision marred the relationship the sisters shared, too, but only temporarily. The rift between them was healed with the arrival of Catherine's first child and Carey's ready transformation into a fawning and generous auntie. And yet, Catherine had learned from the start that Carey's bias against

Nathan made her an unreliable counselor when it came to matters involving her relationship with her husband. She was sure that Nathan's role in the death of the boys had forever sealed his fate where Carey was concerned.

By Sunday, Catherine was exhausted from the emotional rollercoaster. Earlier in the day she had even gotten as far as putting on her jacket and grabbing the cookies and her car keys. But she couldn't bring herself to step across the threshold from the mudroom into the garage. Instead, she sat down heavily on the bench by the door, the plate in her lap, and sobbed through a maelstrom of emotions. Somewhere deep inside she was desperate to forgive her husband for what he'd done. She wanted him back. Back in her life. Back in her home. Maybe even back in her bed. But wasn't this just wishing for things to return to the way they were before? Back to the happy family life she had led up until the accident? That, she knew, was impossible because she could never have Jacob and Joe back. And when she faced that reality, her yearning dissolved into anguish for all that she'd lost, and then rage for how Nathan had taken it from her. Catherine spent the weekend in an endless emotional loop that took her from pity to compassion to sadness to rage to exhaustion and all the way back again. On Sunday night, she tossed the plate into the trash and went to bed.

*

Catherine had not been so angry in a long time. She had received a call from Nathan's mother. Under the pretense of calling to "check in" on Catherine, she had spent the bulk of the call probing her daughter-in-law about why she and Nathan hadn't yet reconciled or at least resumed living under the same roof. Catherine had reacted vehemently to the interference.

"The mother in me gets where she's coming from." Catherine was pacing around Rev. Susan's office. "I guess the 'Mama-bear' feeling toward your kids never goes away." Catherine paused, realizing that her statement applied, even when your children have died. "But I have a right to make my own decisions without her pressuring me."

"Of course, you do. And, I'll point out, that's exactly what you did. For me, the question is why does she get to you this way? You're telling me that she really pushes your buttons. What buttons are those, and why do you let her near them?"

"She's never treated me like an adult." Catherine plopped down in the chair by the window. "It's like I'm just a kid who needs taking care of. There's no mutuality there. It's the same way she treats Nathan, too, and I can't stand to be in the same room when I see it happening."

"So, this is about protecting Nathan?"

"No. Not at all. There's something about how she makes me feel so small. Like I'm a child. I'm sick of people taking care of me. Like I need protecting or something."

"'People?'"

"Nathan does it too. He's always been the big, strong provider while I've played the obedient housewife. It's like he doesn't see me as a grown woman or an independent person. He buys me nice things like I'm a little kid who needs new toys as a reward for being good." The words tumbled from Catherine's mouth, and the realization shocked her.

"And now, in the worst circumstance of your life, you've decided to stand on your own two feet."

"Yeah. I guess I have, haven't I?"

"You have. And it's bound to feel threatening to the people

who see their job as to take care of you, right? It's upsetting the natural order of things. If they can't be in their caretaker role with you, what role can they play? So, they try to put the genie back in the bottle. They want to keep you in the box you've been in. It's worked for them this long, and they have no idea what to do with this new person who doesn't seem to need them for comfort or validation or security."

"Whew!" Catherine sat back and massaged her neck to relieve the knot she felt there. "Who knew? That's a lot to think about, Susan."

"It's why we're here, Catherine. Sure, we're working through your grief from Jacob and Joe's death. But we're also finding out who Catherine is. And who she's going to be. I think this is why you haven't taken Nathan back into your home yet."

"What do you mean?"

"I don't think what you're doing is trying to figure out if you can forgive Nathan for what he did. I mean, that's part of it, for sure. But I see this time as gestational for you. You're in formation. The house on Mountain Road is a cocoon, or, better yet, a womb, for the woman that's going to be birthed from this horrible incident. I'm betting she won't be the same person who existed before it happened. And, until that new you is born, you won't know how – or if - Nathan, or his mother, or anyone else fits into the picture."

"I like that imagery of the womb." Catherine gazed out the window at the empty courtyard, the glacier from the previous winter long-since melted, as she reflected on the pastor's words. "I think I can work with it. And now that you've said it, the idea of something new growing out of the old really feels right to me. I hadn't thought about it that way before. What I hear you saying is that it's possible that I'm going to come out of this in a way that's more than just a deeply damaged version of what I was before. That actually gives me an inkling of hope for the first time since the accident."

Rev. Susan winked at Catherine and smiled. "That's why I get paid the big bucks."

*

Catherine sat on the deck sipping a glass of wine and watching the sun sink beyond the mountains to the west. Wispy clouds daubed the sky as if placed there by an artist's casual brushstrokes, morphing from white to peach to deep pinks and oranges as the sun disappeared. The air was filled with the music of summer as wrens, martins, jays, and flycatchers made their way back to their perches in anticipation of nightfall. Brown bats that had bided the daytime in hollowed-out trees and under barn eaves swooped and swirled overhead, feasting on the gnats and mosquitos that emerged with the dusk. It was an idyllic time of day, when the earth itself seemed to exhale a contented sigh over all it had accomplished in the preceding hours, as well as over all that remained undone, releasing any lingering tension from its shoulders in preparation for its well-deserved rest.

It was exactly the kind of moment Catherine and Nathan had dreamed about together so many years earlier – a lifetime ago – when they'd selected this site for their future home. They'd spent many such evenings together, sitting beside each other and sharing their own sighs of contentment as they recounted the days' events. These were the moments of intimacy that Catherine treasured with her husband. These were the moments that she feared were now lost to her forever. As she sipped her wine, she thought about her most recent conversation with Rev. Susan. There was something in that talk that she had been turning over and over in her mind, kneading it and working it, letting it rest and rise, like dough that you're coaxing to become bread. It was the convergence of old and new that caught and held her attention, the notion of recapturing something lost to her.

At the same time, Catherine considered what unknown possibilities might emerge. The imagery of the cocoon or chrysalis almost captured it, but not quite. Because, in a true metamorphosis, what preceded ceased to exist. It was lost forever, sacrificed for the sake of what would become. And while Catherine had come to accept that Jacob and Joe were gone, that that part of her life was over, she couldn't fathom letting go of everything that had come before. And then there was the "what was to come," which was still a door that was closed and locked, as dark and inaccessible as the burial chamber of an Egyptian pyramid.

CHAPTER FIFTEEN
NATHAN

Nathan had forgotten the effect that clear mountain air had on him. It had been years – before he'd even met Catherine – since he'd hiked in the White Mountains of northern New Hampshire. His first exposure to these peaks had come as a boy when he attended a summer camp on Squam Lake. He had signed up for an overnight hike up to the Lake of the Clouds Hut, an iconic shelter perched on the broad shoulder of Mt. Washington. For a twelve-year-old boy, the hike up the Ammonoosuc Ravine Trail had been strenuous, but he'd had youth on his side, and the counselors had let them stop and cool off in the pools below the many waterfalls that cascaded off the side of the mountain. To this day Nathan still recalled the moment they'd broken out above treeline, when he had gazed down on the valley floor spread out below and up at the vast sky spread out above. He had spotted a hawk making long, slow circles just about at eye level and felt the pull of the air. It was as though he'd found a kindred spirit, that in a past life he had himself been a bird of prey, an animal capable of soaring for hours on invisible currents of air. It was the first inkling he'd ever had that there might be something bigger than his own small and comfortable world, some greater stream of time that he was a part of, that flowed long before he'd been born and would keep flowing long after he was gone.

Now, more than two decades later, Nathan was scaling the steep and treacherous Lion Head Trail up the spine of Mt. Washington out of Pinkham Notch. His pack, with three days' worth of gear, felt light on his back and the summer day was hot but not stifling. This was his favorite trail to the top of New England's tallest peak because it gained altitude quickly and was the shortest route to get above tree line. Huntington Ravine fell away to his right and, to his left, the famed Tuckerman Ravine with its headwall that tested the mettle of the world's best skiers every spring. He noticed that there was still snow down in Tuckerman's, and he felt a pang of regret that he'd never taken on the headwall when his legs were younger and stronger than they were now, when he spent so much of his time sitting at a desk. That lost opportunity glanced off him like a flat stone skimming across a still pond; Nathan acknowledged it and let it go.

Robert had been working with Nathan on the topic of regret, and the vice-like grip it had on him since the accident.

"How can I not regret my decision to take the shortcut across the ice?" Nathan and his therapist had shifted the locale of the therapy session to the wrap-around porch of the Victorian that housed Robert's office. They sat facing the river as the late afternoon sun dappled the water. "It was the worst decision of my life."

"I'm not saying that you can let go of regret entirely, Nathan. What I'd like to do is see if we can help regret let go of you." Nathan turned and gave Robert a look that conveyed his skepticism. "What I mean is, we all have regrets. We mourn missed opportunities, things we did or didn't do. The question is how much, or to what extent, we let them control our lives. Some people are so controlled by regret that they're unable to make decisions, for fear they'll be wrong, that they'll make more mistakes. They're paralyzed by their regrets and the possibility of piling on more."

"I'm not sure how that's playing out for me."

"Well, let's see...What have you done lately that feels a little risky? Where have you stretched yourself? When have you taken a chance since the accident?"

Nathan reflected on Robert's question as he listened to the river tumble over the dam that lay just upstream from where they sat. Robins hopped around the yard, cocking their heads to listen for worms wriggling below the surface. As he considered his answer, Nathan came up empty-handed. He realized that he'd done nothing since the accident that would fall into the category of "risky" behavior. And not just with taking physical risks, like going rock climbing. Nathan saw that in his work he had become risk-averse in his financial advising, steering clients toward stable and conservative investments, even when some clients had expressed a willingness to roll the dice a bit.

"I've been playing it really safe, ever since the accident, haven't I, Doc?"

"You tell me, Nathan."

"I mean, it makes sense, right? The last time I took a chance, look what happened. Even though I did everything I could to keep things safe, it all blew up in my face. I wish I'd never done it and I'll regret my decision until my dying day. Can you blame me for not wanting to do it again?"

"Of course I don't blame you, Nathan. I don't blame you for anything. See, a healthy sense of regret helps us to grow. It's how we learn from our mistakes. But I think it's important to see how and where regret might be adversely affecting you. Maybe even holding you back."

Nathan contemplated that conversation as he continued his ascent toward the summit.

*

Nathan returned from his 3-day traverse of the Presidential Range feeling renewed and refreshed. With the exception of one windy, foggy morning as he'd made his way along the ridge between Washington and Madison, the weather had been spectacular, and he'd enjoyed his interactions with several thru-hikers along the Appalachian Trail, which extended from Maine to Georgia.

"It was awesome." Nathan unloaded gear from his truck as Jim enjoyed a beer on his porch. He held a bottle out to his friend, who shook his head. "Thanks, Jim, but I'm still on a natural high from my trip."

"Did some soul-searching up there, did ya?"

"Mostly I just enjoyed the scenery and the workout, but yeah, I guess I did."

"Any grand revelations you'd care to share with me?"

"You'll be the first to know. But right now, I need a shower and a shave."

"I'll say you do." Jim joked with his friend, holding his nose and waving him into the house.

*

"I've been mulling over this whole idea about regret."

Nathan sat across from his therapist in the office as a summer downpour soaked the yard outside, the occasional clap of thunder rattling the windows.

"Any conclusions?" Robert asked.

"I think I'm done playing it safe. I mean, I'm not going to go base jumping or anything. But I need to get back in the game."

"What does that look like to you?"

"I think I've waited long enough for Catherine to make the first move. I know that I'm likely to get shot down, but I think I need to at least let her know that I'm ready to sit down and talk with her, and how important it is to me."

"That's a delicate conversation, to say the least, Nathan."

"Oh, I know, Doc. It feels like stepping out into the void. Like a tight-rope walk. But I've been patient. I've been doing the work. And I'm ready to take the chance to push her a little, to see if we can make some forward progress."

"If it would be helpful, we can do a little role-playing to see how that conversation might go." Nathan and his therapist spent the rest of the hour refining his intended approach.

*

The nightmares were getting fewer and farther between, but they hadn't disappeared altogether. There were still nights when Nathan thrashed around in bed as his mind replayed his desperate attempts to free the boys from their harnesses. He would wake up gasping for air, as if he really had been diving down into the murky water as Joe and Jacob sank out of reach, as drenched from the sweat of his terror as he had been when he pulled himself out onto the ice. On these nights, he would lay in bed, panting and shaking, until the sense-memory of the event subsided. And in the wake of each incident, he was reminded that he'd never be able to count on sleep as a refuge from his guilt and his pain.

"Another rough night?" Jim handed his friend a cup of coffee as Nathan emerged, bleary-eyed, from a sleepless night.

"I'm sorry, Jim. I keep waking you up."

"I'll admit that it makes me jump when I hear you howling in the middle of the night, but I get it, Nate. I just feel awful for what you're going through."

"It's my punishment, I guess. What do the Catholics call it? Penance for the sin I've committed? Seems like I'm doomed to relive the worst moment of my life forever."

The two men sat and silently sipped their coffee.

"You know, I could use some help overhauling that V-8 today." Jim nodded toward the garage attached to the house that was his shop.

"I'm all thumbs when it comes to that kind of stuff."

"Might do you some good to get your hands a little greasy. Take your mind off of stuff, maybe even learn a thing or two." Jim winked at Nathan.

"If you don't mind working around a klutz, I guess I'm willing to try." Nathan looked across the table at the man who had taken him in, and he was filled with a deep sense of gratitude. "You know, Jim, I couldn't have gotten through any of this without you. I don't know how I'll ever begin to repay you."

"You can start by shutting your yap." Jim grinned at Nathan. "Your first lesson is that grease monkeys don't get all mushy and sentimental with each other."

Although he was clumsy with the tools, Nathan felt the therapeutic power of immersing himself in tasks that were new to him, that required him to focus his full attention on what was right in front of him. Spending the day this way was a blessed respite from his mind's constant churning about both the past and what his future might hold. The offer of the work's distraction gave him yet another reason to be grateful for his friend's care and attention.

*

"What do you think Catherine's up to?" The question hovered above the meatloaf, mashed potatoes, and gravy that Nathan's mother had set out on the dining room table. Jean gave Frank a remonstrative look at his tactless question. Nathan's fork was suspended halfway between his plate and his mouth.

"It's okay, Mom. We can talk about it if you want."

"Only if it's helpful to you, dear." Jean fretted with her napkin, unfolding and refolding it nervously. "We don't want to pry."

"It's fine." Nathan turned toward his father. "To answer your question, Dad, I don't really know. I told you how we ran into each other in the grocery store a while ago. She asked me to keep my distance, so that's what I've been doing. I want to respect her wishes."

"But what about your own wishes?" Frank pressed his son.

"Frank!" Jean again reprimanded her husband.

"Mom, it's okay. I can handle it." Nathan placed a reassuring hand over his mother's and again turned to answer his father. "I'm getting better every day. It feels like I'm coming back from a long trip. I'm learning what's the same as when I left and what's changed. I'm starting to learn my way around again."

"That sounds like progress, son."

"I think it is. Don't get me wrong, I wish like anything that things could go back to the way they were. But it doesn't help to stay stuck in that fantasy. I've got to accept that we're in a new reality, and I've got to find my new normal."

"But what about Catherine?" Nathan's father returned to the question of his daughter-in-law's position.

"I have no idea, Dad. She's dealing with her own stuff in her own way. I know she's got Carey and Heather and that pastor at the church to help her through. It's not like she's just sitting around the house on some kind of extended vacation." Nathan could feel himself starting to feel defensive on behalf of his wife, an emotion that he'd not experienced any time in the recent past, and he wasn't sure whether or not he liked it.

"But it seems like she's got the upper hand here, Nathan. I mean, it's your house, too."

Nathan could feel his face flushing as his anger – and his voice – rose. "Dad, I'm doing the best I can! I can't make her take me back. I can't make her do anything. There's no switch I can flip to make her see things differently. She's got to come to her own conclusions. And I've got to trust her."

Nathan pushed his chair back, stood up, and threw his napkin on the table. "This is all about trust. Don't you see that? I'm working real hard to trust that Catherine's doing the work she needs. I'm trusting that my therapist is helping me do my work. I'm trying to trust that somehow this is all going to work out in the end. And it doesn't help anything or anyone for you to tell me that you don't trust either one of us." He stormed out of the dining room and out to his car, where he sat in the driver's seat, his hands on the wheel, shaking. After a few deep breaths, Nathan turned the key in the ignition and sped away.

CHAPTER SIXTEEN
CATHERINE

"You got a what?" Heather leaped to her feet and hugged her friend in response to Catherine's announcement. The two women were lounging on the deck at Catherine's house in the long, lingering twilight of a summer evening. The last remnants of the setting sun were bouncing off the base of a few fair-weather clouds, tinting them in soft pinks and purples.

"You heard me. I got a job."

"That's great!" Heather raised her wine glass to toast her friend's news. "I think that's absolutely awesome. What is it? Where is it?"

"It's not a big deal, really. You know that coffee shop on Main Street down in Sanford?"

"The Daily Grind?"

"Yup. It's just a part-time thing, but it gives me something to do and somewhere to go a few mornings a week. I can't just sit around the house the rest of my life."

"Sweetie, I'm so glad to hear you say that! I was wondering

when you were going to bust out of this Fortress of Solitude you've built around yourself. I mean, not that I was watching the calendar or anything. I know you needed time to recover."

"Don't kid yourself. I'm far from recovered." Catherine turned her attention to the darkening sky, searching for the first star of the evening. When she saw it, she made a wish, the same wish she'd been making for the past several months: that she would wake up from this nightmare, climb out of bed, walk down the hall, and find Joe and Jacob safely tucked into their beds. She knew it would be her wish until her dying breath.

"No, no. That's not what I meant. It's just that it's a great first step. I'm so happy for you."

Both women took sips of their wine and sat silently looking out over the trees in the valley below, whose profiles were fading into the encroaching darkness. As they sat, Catherine's thoughts turned to Nathan. She wondered whether the two of them would ever again spend a quiet evening on this deck together, watching the sunset across the valley. She'd found herself thinking about him frequently in the past few weeks. She appreciated that he was honoring her need to call the shots about getting together after their awkward meeting in the supermarket. He hadn't called or texted once to try and force the issue. She knew how hard it must be for him to allow her to be in control of the situation and whether, how, and when it progressed.

*

Catherine was tired of feeling like a victim, like a deer that had been side-swiped by a passing automobile, injured and fragile. While she appreciated all the attention she'd received from Heather, from Carey, from her few other friends in town, she was sick of being coddled and cared for. Of being treated like a delicate porcelain doll that could fall to pieces at any moment. In her conversations with Rev. Susan, she had come to realize that she'd let people do this all her life, not just since the accident. Her parents, before they died. Carey, afterward. Her friends in college and law school. And Nathan. Especially Nathan. Yes, it had been her choice to stop working to raise the kids, but ever since their first date, it seemed, she had handed over the reins of her life to her husband. She didn't resent him for it, exactly. He'd provided her with everything she could possibly want for more than a decade. It was more that she resented herself for letting him lead her down the path with little or no resistance. She allowed him and others to treat her like a child in need of guidance and support instead of an equal partner in an adult relationship. Now that she was stripped of her role as a mother – the only role in which she had real authority over others – she realized just how dependent she'd become on those around her. Even her best friend.

Catherine turned away from the sunset to face her friend. "Can I ask you a favor?" She realized after the words had left her mouth that even how she framed that request was subservient. She tried again. "No, let me rephrase that: Heather, I need you to do something for me."

Heather heard the serious tone in her friend's voice and sat up straighter in her chair. "Sure, sweetie."

"That's it, right there, Heather. I need you to stop calling me 'sweetie.' It may sound like a little thing, and I know it's a term of endearment. But every time you call me that, it makes me feel small and fragile. Like I'm a little kid or something."

"Umm. Okay."

Catherine realized that the woman sitting beside her, who had been beside her every step of the way, hadn't been on board the train of thought that had passed through her mind for the past few minutes, so she explained it. About not wanting to be handled with kid gloves anymore. About wanting to be seen as an adult, an equal in all her relationships. When she was done, Catherine could sense that her best friend in the world was right there with her.

"Wow. You aren't a butterfly coming out of your cocoon. You're a tiger busting out of its cage. I love the fierceness I hear in your voice. Watch out, world!"

Watch out, Nathan, Catherine thought. She wondered whether he'd be able to cope with her newly emerging sense of power and independence, or whether he'd even want to.

*

Catherine was surprised to find that she looked forward to her shifts at The Grind. While she was nearly twice the age of most of the other baristas, she enjoyed hearing about the drama of their young adult lives. Some of them – particularly a couple of women who attended the local community college – latched onto her and actively sought her out for advice. More than the relationships she was making with her co-workers, Catherine found herself enjoying the interactions she had with the customers. With the exception of an occasional mom from either Joe or Jacob's school, Catherine was anonymous to anyone who walked in the door. She wasn't labeled and pre-judged as "the mom who lost her children in a tragic accident." She didn't have to endure the long faces of friends, the well-meaning but earnestly-offered "So, how are you doing?" questions from the women she knew from school or her kickboxing class at the Y. Serving lattes and cappuccinos to customers who knew nothing of her back-story brought blessed relief to Catherine's life. The Daily Grind became the opposite of what its name implied. It was a sanctuary, a place where Catherine could breathe. Where she could be herself without others knowing the baggage she was carrying. Where she could begin to find herself again.

Jeff, the owner of the shop, knew everything Catherine had gone through. But he had the sensitivity not to treat Catherine as fragile. Other than a brief mention of the accident during the job interview, in which he offered his genuine sympathies, Jeff never brought it up. Nor did he walk on eggshells around Catherine the way many of her friends did. He was grateful to have Catherine on board, especially once he saw how punctual and organized she was. He quickly came to rely on her to help him oversee whatever crew was working her shift.

"Catherine, we're roasting that Kenyan blend we got in the other day." Jeff was standing by the large cast-iron roasting machine that stood against the back wall, the aroma filling the shop with a distinctive burnt smell. "Any chance you could stay late to help bag it?"

"Sure, Jeff!" She enjoyed packing the warm beans into their foil bags, sticking the labels on them, and stacking them on the shelves. It was menial work, but it provided her with a sense of control and orderliness she was lacking in the rest of her life.

*

With the early sunrises and nearly endless twilights of Maine in mid-summer, Catherine felt drawn to the outdoors. She began to spend more time in the yard, making lazy circuits around the house. In that grace-filled hour before sunrise, when the earth still held the nighttime's coolness, she would even explore the path that led into the forest, listening to the world awaken. But she never ventured far from the edge of the yard, always keeping her escape route clear. The deeper parts of the forest still felt threatening to her. These trees, after all, had consumed her children. But her trips to the edge of her comfort zone had their own rewards. They reminded her of her childhood when she and Carey would walk out the back door of their home and into the woods for all sorts of adventures. They also reminded Catherine of how much she had enjoyed riding Annie along the trails and streams of her childhood. The muscles in her body held the memory of sitting astride her beloved horse, the pressure of her thighs against the saddle, urging the animal forward, the wind in her face, the freedom of gliding through the trees. Maybe, she thought during one of her walks, this is a part of my past that I can resurrect and reclaim. A quick search of the web revealed a barn that boarded horses in Limerick, just a few miles north of Newfield. As she pulled off the road and onto the long driveway that led up to Sunnybrooke Farm, seeing horses grazing in the fields on either side, Catherine felt the inexorable pull of the place and the longing to love one of these beautiful beasts, as she had Annie.

*

Catherine and Penny, a copper-colored 8-year-old mare, hit it off immediately. Penny nuzzled Catherine playfully whenever she showed up at the stable, and Catherine could lose herself gazing into Penny's chocolate-colored eyes. She loved everything about riding. She loved the physicality of it, the way horse and rider communicated through their muscles, without a word spoken. There was a primal relationship that Catherine experienced whenever she was astride the horse. Not just between a human and a beast of burden, but between two living, breathing animals of different species, working together as one, bringing satisfaction to both. Penny needed to be ridden just as much as Catherine needed to ride. After her first time on Penny, when she found that they were a good match, Catherine signed up to ride her twice a week.

It was a Tuesday afternoon, a day like so many others, when Catherine found herself standing in front of Penny's stall. "Hey there, girl. Wanna get out on the trail today?" She grabbed the halter and gently placed the bit in Penny's mouth, Penny accepting it willingly. Rubbing the horse's silky flanks as she walked around her, Catherine took the saddle blanket and saddle off the rack and hefted them onto Penny's back. She noticed that the horse was standing with one of her rear hooves on tiptoe, a sign of ease and contentment that Catherine translated as trust.

"You're such a sweet girl." She cinched the girth tight around Penny's belly and led her out of the stall and into the late summer sunlight. The mare tossed her head twice as if inviting Catherine to mount her so that they could get going. The rider obliged, and soon they were out beyond the paddock and into the vast fields that made up Sunnybrooke Farm.

Catherine kept Penny at a walk at first, the two of them getting reacquainted. Catherine could sense when the horse wanted to stretch her legs, so with a squeeze of her thighs and a slight lean forward in the saddle, she gave Penny the signal to move first into a trot, and then a canter. When they reached the edge of the field, Penny led them onto a trail between the trees that took them into the adjacent forest. Catherine trusted the horse and gave her free rein to go where she wished. The trees were sparse here, and Catherine found the woods to be inviting rather than threatening. They were filled with sunshine streaming down between branches, and the light had an almost magical quality to it.

Sensing her rider's ease, Penny picked up her gait, and soon the two of them, working as one, were flying along the trail. Pure joy coursed through Catherine's veins, and a wide smile broke out on her face, stretching muscles that had been dormant for months. She realized that she hadn't smiled since the accident. Penny was in full gallop now, yet her stride was effortless. Horse and rider were weightless, sliding between trees that passed by in a blur. They were one organism, breathing together, their hearts beating in sync with each other. They were like two streams that merged into a powerful river, flowing as one through the forest. Astride Penny, Catherine felt free for the first time since. Since when? she wondered. Certainly, since the accident. But maybe since before she'd become a mother. Since before she'd become a wife. Since even before she'd met Nathan for the first time. As she urged Penny onward – they were racing now – it was as if a spell she'd been under for years was breaking beneath her, falling away, being left behind her like a boat's wake that is kicked up, then settles and dissolves with both time and distance.

*

With school back in full swing for the fall, the church courtyard was littered with under-sized bicycles belonging to the children from the preschool program. Eyeing the bikes, Catherine sighed. She thought about how Jacob had been just about ready to give up his training wheels a year ago, and how she had been looking forward to that moment when he put it all together and balanced on two wheels for the first time. Another instance of childhood triumph that was never to be. Catherine let the sadness flow over and through her, and she turned away from the window.

"So, you think you're ready?" Catherine had been telling Rev. Susan that she felt it was time to sit down with Nathan and figure out their next steps, together or apart.

"As ready as I'm going to be. I'm scared, but it feels like it's time."

Catherine was starting to feel the pressure. Not from Nathan, but from some internal clock that she felt ticking away. With her new job at the coffee shop, she felt herself moving again. She wasn't sure whether it was forward or not. But, like a sailboat whose line is untied from a dock, she was starting to drift away. Away from her old life. Away from what she and Nathan had built together. Away from the future she had envisioned for herself for so long. There was freedom in the drifting, for sure. But the further she got from the dock, the harder it would be to get back. If getting back was what she wanted to do. And she was starting to feel that she wouldn't know that, wouldn't be able to hoist her sail and point her bow on an intentional course until she decided how Nathan fit into the equation.

"If you'd like, I could have a conversation with Nathan's therapist to see how he's doing and whether he thinks it's a good idea."

"I don't think that's necessary. I know that he's been waiting for my call."

"Catherine, I've watched you over the past six months, and I've got to tell you that you've been doing some amazing work.

I agree with you that it's time. And I want to warn you that this is going to be hard. Do you have any idea what you're going to say? Where you want this to go?"

"That's the big question, isn't it?" Catherine gazed out the window again and wondered to herself what it was that she really wanted.

*

She wasn't sure if it was coincidence or kismet when, just a few days later, her phone rang, and she saw that it was Nathan trying to reach her. She froze at the sight of his name on her screen, unsure whether she really was ready. At the last moment, before the call went to voicemail, she grabbed the phone off the kitchen counter and answered it.

"Nathan." She tried to sound neutral, though her hands were shaking.

"Hey Cat."

"How're you doing?"

"Oh, well, you know. Um, I just got back from a hike up in the White Mountains. It was spectacular. You could see Boston from the top of Mt Washington."

"Sounds great. I know you love that hike." Catherine fidgeted with a wooden spoon that sat on the counter. "I've gotten back to riding a little. It's fun." She couldn't believe how awkward she felt speaking to the man she'd been married to for a decade.

"Hey, listen, Cat. I've been thinking that maybe we could get together. Talk a little bit. I don't want to pressure you or anything, but maybe we could just open up the lines of communication. What do you think?"

"You know, Nate, I was just thinking the same thing the

other day. I mean, as long as you understand I'm not making any promises or anything."

"No. No. I get it, Cat. Just a conversation. That's all I'm looking for."

They agreed to get together for coffee the following Friday.

CHAPTER SEVENTEEN
NATHAN

Nathan was nervous on the morning he was to sit down and talk with Catherine. Except for the brief supermarket encounter, it would be the first time they'd met since she'd thrown him out of the house. His hands shook as he shaved, and he cut himself on the neck. A small blot of blood stained the collar of his white Oxford shirt as he got dressed. He planned to get to the coffee shop early, to scout out just the right table. But when he walked through the door, he saw that Catherine was already seated at a spot in a small alcove off the main room. Just private enough for an intimate conversation, he thought, but public enough to offer cover and protection. He sat down awkwardly across from his wife, not knowing if he should try to give her a peck on the cheek. He decided against it and instead gave her hand a quick squeeze. It was, he realized, the first physical contact they'd had in more than half a year. He was encouraged that she didn't recoil from his touch, but kept her hand resting on the table. He felt, or maybe he imagined, that she even returned the squeeze with a slight one of her own.

Nathan tried to sound casual as he took a seat opposite his wife, but his heart was nearly pounding out of his chest. "Hey, Cat."

"Hi, Nate. Did you order some coffee?"

"I will. I don't need any right now. I think caffeine would put me over the top."

"Yeah, I'm nervous, too. It feels so awkward."

"At least we're on the same page there."

"How're things at work?" Catherine wanted to start off with a safe subject.

"Well, I could lie and tell you everything's fine. But the truth is that we're just barely holding it together. I mean, I don't want you to worry about it or anything, but we've lost a couple of big accounts, and I'm busting my butt to keep the rest. I think clients are worried that I'm not paying attention."

"I'm sorry." Catherine knew how seriously her husband took his work, and how eager he was to serve his clients well.

Nathan was encouraged by Catherine's concern. He realized in that moment just how much he needed her by his side. An awkward silence fell between them, and they both stared down at the table, fidgeting with their napkins.

Catherine sighed and looked around the coffee shop at the surroundings that were so familiar to her. "You know, I work here now."

"What? Really? Since when?" Catherine couldn't read the tone of Nathan's questions, whether he was expressing amusement, incredulity, or judgment.

"I needed to do something. I couldn't just knock around in that empty house for the rest of my life. Too many ghosts."

"No. I get it. I'm glad you're doing it."

"What's funny is that I really enjoy it. I get to do simple

stuff like stock the shelves and grind the beans. It helps me to be busy and to bring some order to things. Like, at least I can control how the bags are stacked or whatever."

"That's great, Cat. Really."

"I've also gotten back into riding. I've got a favorite horse at a farm up in Limerick. She gets me. It's like we're a team. I'd forgotten how much I like being with horses."

"I'm happy for you." Nathan couldn't think of anything else to say.

"How about you? I mean, besides work. How're you doing?"

Nathan took a deep breath and let it out slowly, trying to decide how he wanted to answer the question. "I dunno, Cat." He looked around the coffee shop as if he were seeing it for the first time as he struggled to find the words to describe how he was feeling. Could he be honest with her? Should he be? For all the hours he'd spent longing to be sitting across from his wife like this, he realized that he hadn't given a thought to what he would actually say to her. For someone who prided himself on always being in control, he was totally unprepared for this moment.

"It's hard." He realized how lame that sounded the moment it came out of his mouth. "I mean, I know I don't have to tell you..." He let his words hang in the air between them. Catherine stared down at the table as he struggled.

Nathan could feel himself unraveling, but he couldn't stop himself. "Cat, I've missed you so much, you don't know. It's like, I lost the boys, which is bad enough, and the baby. But then I lost you." Tears welled up in Nathan's eyes. He had promised himself that he wasn't going to do this.

Catherine squirmed in her seat with increasing discomfort. She caught Jeff's eye, and he approached their table.

"Can I get you two anything?" Nathan used the interruption to sit back in his chair, take a deep breath, and regroup.

"Maybe a couple glasses of water, Jeff," Catherine said. The two sat silently as they waited for the manager's return. After he'd set down a glass in front of each of them, Nathan was able to continue more calmly and deliberately.

"Let me try that again, Cat, okay? Thank you for asking how I'm doing. I'm working hard at trying to grow from what happened. To take responsibility for it, which is totally mine, and to come to terms with the finality of it."

Catherine took a sip of her water and leaned in as Nathan continued.

"Robert – that's my therapist – has been helping me a lot. He's helped me to realize that this experience has changed me and that it's changed you, too. We can't go back to being the way we were. I know that. And I also know that I'd like to try and figure out how we might find a new way to be together. I'm not saying that to push you or anything. I just need you to know that I want to try if you're willing to."

Catherine sat quietly staring down into her glass while Nathan summoned all his strength to sit as patiently as possible. After what felt to him like an interminable silence, she finally spoke.

"Nate, I'm really glad to hear all that. Truly, I am. And I'll be really honest with you and say that I don't know what to do with it. I guess talking today is a start, but I don't know where to go from here."

"I know. We're in uncharted territory." Nathan leaned in. "No one has a map for this. But remember that Tomie dePaola book we used to read to the kids? The one where the grandpa teaches the child to walk, then when the grandfather has a stroke, the tables are turned, and the kid teaches him just the same way?"

Catherine remembered the touching story. *"Now One Foot, Now the Other."*

"I think that's our answer, Cat. The only way to do this is one step at a time, one foot in front of the other. Today's a step. I'm not sure what the next one is, either, but we can figure that out."

This seemed to land well for Catherine. Nathan was sure he saw her nod, ever so slightly, in agreement. He felt that progress had been made, and he didn't want to push his luck. As much as he would have loved to sit and sip coffee all morning with his wife, to walk along the sidewalks of Sanford holding hands, to drive back to their home on Mountain Road and make love, he glanced at his watch as if he had somewhere he needed to be.

"I've got to get into the office. Can we agree to try and keep the lines of communication open?"

"I can do that."

"Thanks, Cat. That's all I ask."

Nathan pushed his chair back and slid into his leather jacket. He kissed Catherine on the top of her head and walked out the door, cradling an ember of hope as if it were a precious jewel.

*

Nathan had nowhere to be, and it was a beautiful early fall day, with a crispness to the air that hinted at the impending change of seasons. He decided to take a walk by the Mousam River, following the footpath through the park and upstream to the dam. He passed by the building that housed Robert's office and he wondered what tragedy had befallen the client Robert was currently meeting. Were they the sole caregiver for a parent with dementia? A young widow, suffering the sudden loss of a husband in a car accident? A middle-aged man, suicidal at the loss of a job? The world, Nathan realized, is full of pain. His, and his role in causing it, was acute. But he wasn't alone. Somewhere long ago he'd heard someone say, "Be kind, for everyone is fighting a great battle." He knew the truth of that statement now. He could feel it in his bones. And how small acts of kindness, of tenderness, of compassion and empathy could go such a long way.

Nathan sat on a bench by the river, watching it flow, feeling relieved that Catherine had accepted his invitation to meet and to start talking again. He felt his lungs fill as he breathed in the clear air. Fill perhaps for the first time since the accident.

"Mr. Osgood?" Nathan hadn't heard the uniformed man approach, his footsteps drowned out by the sound of the water rushing over the dam.

"Yes?"

"Mr. Nathan Osgood?"

"Yes, that's me."

"Please come with me sir. You're under arrest."

Nathan was taken aback. "There must be some mistake. What's going on?"

"We have a warrant for your arrest, sir." The Sheriff took a pair of handcuffs from his utility belt. "Please put your hands behind your back."

"What have I done? What's going on? There must be some mistake."

The Sheriff read Nathan his Miranda rights. "Do you

understand these rights that I've told you?"

"Yes. Yes. Of course." Nathan looked around frantically, but the park was empty. "Tell me what you're arresting me for."

"Two counts of manslaughter, sir. Let's go." The Sheriff led Nathan toward his waiting cruiser, its blue lights flashing.

*

"Can you tell me what this is about?" Nathan asked through the grate that separated him from the Sheriff in the driver's seat of the cruiser.

"I only know what's on the warrant, Mr. Osgood. Two counts of manslaughter. The District Attorney wants to prosecute you for the death of your boys, and a grand jury agreed to indict. I really can't say more."

"How can they do that? I lost my boys. Isn't that enough punishment?"

Nathan watched out the window of the cruiser as the courthouse appeared. He felt the contrast between the beauty of the scene and what he was experiencing. The trees with tinges of their fall colors, and puffy fair-weather clouds dotting the sky as if they'd been put there by a child gluing cotton balls to construction paper for a school project.

The cruiser turned into the courthouse driveway and slid into a parking space at the rear of the building. The Sheriff opened the back door of the car, helped Nathan step out into the parking lot and led him through a door. A deputy stood behind a desk in the basement room, and he efficiently finger-printed Nathan and took his picture for the mug shots. Then he walked Nathan behind the counter, through a door, and down a short hallway where Nathan could see the bars of a jail cell. At the door to the cell, the deputy turned Nathan around and unlocked the handcuffs. Nathan entered the cell without prompting, rubbing his wrists where the cuffs had dug into them. The cell door shut with a loud metallic sound and Nathan was left alone with his thoughts.

*

"You mean I have to spend the weekend in here?" Nathan was agitated and incredulous. He sat at a metal table in a small, nondescript room near his cell. On the other side of the table sat his father and Carter Pierce, the lawyer Frank had contacted when Nathan called him from jail. "This is a nightmare," he sat back in his chair defeated.

Nathan had known the attorney his entire life. Pierce had been his father's corporate lawyer for decades. Notwithstanding the lawyer's familiarity and corporate experience, Nathan worried he might be in over his head. Although a trusted family advisor, Nathan wondered whether Pierce had any experience in criminal law.

"The judge is gone for the weekend. We can't get a preliminary hearing until Monday. I'm afraid you're stuck here until then." Carter Pierce shook his head solemnly.

"I can't believe this is happening," Nathan said, his elbows propped on the table and his head in his hands.

Frank and the attorney rose to leave, and Nathan's father gave his shoulder a squeeze. "Hang in there, son."

Nathan was led back to his cell, where reality set in: he would have nearly seventy-two hours to be alone, without distractions, with only his thoughts for company. At first, he felt like a caged animal. He anxiously paced the perimeter of the small cell, his heart beating as if his rib cage were its own cell, his heart, too, trapped. Without a watch or a window, it was impossible to tell what time it was, and the guard at the desk acted as if he had strict instructions not to engage with the prisoner.

At the very moment he felt like he would jump out of his skin or hurl himself bodily against the cold, steel bars, a memory came to Nathan, clear as day. He and Catherine were newly-married and living in their first apartment in Portland. He had just received word from his accountant that a "tax irregularity" had been found in the prior year's filings. Nathan was in a panic that the possible fines and penalties would bankrupt him, and that the error would permanently ruin his reputation and destroy his fledgling business. He had paced around the apartment then just as he was pacing around his cell now. Like now, he wanted to be anywhere other than where he was. Back then, Catherine had grabbed him by the arms and sat him down next to her on the edge of their double bed.

"Nate." She looked him straight in the eye. "I've been where you are right now. I've had panic attacks almost my whole life. Fortunately, Carey showed me how to get through them." Catherine had proceeded to lead Nathan through the breathing exercises that her sister had taught her, the techniques that had gotten Catherine through so many anxious times in the past.

Nathan forced himself to sit down on the edge of the metal-framed bed and take a deep breath. He let it out slowly. Then he repeated the process. He fixed his gaze at a spot on the floor, just outside the bars, and he breathed in again, this time through his nose. He tried to focus only on his breath. Breath after breath. He cleared his mind of everything else. Slowly, he felt the roaring in his ears subside and his heartbeat began to slow. He stuck with it until his breath returned to some semblance of normalcy, where he could think like a human being instead of reacting like a trapped beast. He finally laid back on the cot and closed his eyes.

Images of Joe and Jacob floated behind his eyelids. Not the images he'd been seeing ever since they'd fallen through the ice. Those images were a constant threat to his sanity, sleeping or waking. This time, instead, he saw the boys happy. Laughing. The four of them were at the dinner table, and it was taco night. Jacob was smiling his crooked smile, having lost a front tooth just the day before. Joe was running around the dining room table wearing nothing but a Superman cape, shouting "I'm Supertaco-man! I'm Supertaco-man!" In that moment, Nathan remembered, he had looked down to the far end of the table at his wife, the mother of his children. Catherine looked bushed, bleary-eyed, and beautiful. Their eyes met, and without saying a word he knew what she was thinking, because it was what he was thinking, too: This is it. This is what we dreamed about and planned for and hoped for. It's loud and it's messy and it's exhausting. And it's just what we wanted. It was this image, this thought, this memory that accompanied Nathan as he drifted off to sleep.

*

On Saturday morning Nathan once again sat across the metal table from his father. He was sleep-deprived and feeling desperate. It had been less than 24 hours since his arrest, and the prospect of spending two more nights behind bars, much less the years a conviction could bring, had him panicked again.

"Nate, I know this is tough, but there's nothing we can do

right now," Frank tried to reassure his son. "I'm sure as soon as the judge comes in on Monday morning you'll be arraigned and can get out of here."

"I know. I know. But Dad, what if I'm convicted and have to do real time? What then?"

"We'll cross that bridge if we ever get there, which I hope we won't. Right now, you've just got to keep it together. Your mother sends her love. There's not much we can do, but I'll stop by again tonight before dinner. Keep hanging in there."

"Like I have a choice."

Nathan returned to his cell, lay down on the metal cot, closed his eyes, and considered his prospects. From where he sat, the future could not have looked bleaker. First, there was the immediate concern about his criminal indictment and the potential for conviction and prison time. Then there was the very real possibility of financial ruin resulting from exorbitant legal fees and an exodus of clients from his firm. Personal and business bankruptcy were very real dangers. And then there was the uncertainty around his marriage and the very real likelihood that he and Catherine would split up permanently. It was a tragedy trifecta. And all because he made a decision – a decision that, in his mind, was both well-reasoned and well-informed – to take a shortcut toward home.

*

"So, here's the deal, Nathan," his lawyer, along with his father, sat across from Nathan at the all-too-familiar metal table on Monday morning. "Judge Perkins has scheduled your arraignment for 10 this morning. We'll enter a plea of 'Not Guilty' and then we'll have a discussion about bail."

"What happens then?"

"We'll agree on a bail amount. It'll take a couple hours to get the bail posted, but then you'll be released."

"I've already got the bank lined up to provide the bond," Frank answered Nathan's question before he had time to ask it.

"The prosecutor will probably make a show of it and ask for some exorbitant amount." Pierce made a note on a yellow legal pad. "But we'll counter with all the ties you have to the community, how you grew up here, etc., etc. and hopefully the judge will be reasonable."

"Whatever it is, I'll cover it," Frank offered, not revealing to Nathan that he had arranged for a loan secured by the family business.

"Thanks, Dad. And thanks for bringing in the fresh clothes. I don't want to look like a homeless man when I appear in front of the judge."

Nathan's father grasped his son's forearm and looked him in the eye. "We'll get through this together, as a family, Nate."

*

"All rise!" the bailiff declared as a be-robed man of about sixty entered the courtroom. "Superior Court of York County is now in session," he announced ceremoniously. "Judge Kenneth Perkins presiding." The space resembled dozens of other courtrooms that Nathan had seen on countless episodes of "Law and Order." He and his lawyer were seated at a long conference table to the judge's right, and the District Attorney sat at a corresponding table to the judge's left. A railing extended the entire width of the courtroom, separating them from the gallery. Frank and Jean were seated in the front row, directly behind their son. There was a smattering of onlookers and about half a dozen people whom Nathan assumed were journalists of some variety. Catherine, he noted, was nowhere to be seen although his father had told him over the weekend that she knew what was going on.

"Counselor," the judge nodded to the District Attorney, "are you prepared to proceed?"

"Yes, Your Honor," District Attorney Tom Shepard rose to make his presentation of the indictment. "This is a pretty clear case of manslaughter, two counts, per the Maine Criminal Code." He handed a sheaf of papers to the bailiff, who turned them over to the judge. "You'll see that a grand jury has indicted the Defendant pursuant to process."

The judge peered down at the paperwork through a pair of black reading glasses.

"Everything looks to be in order here. Would the Defendant please rise?" he said, turning to Nathan. Nathan and his lawyer stood. "How do you plead, Mr. Osgood?"

Pierce looked at Nathan and gave him a small nod, indicating that it was his turn to speak. "Not guilty, Your Honor," Nathan tried to sound strong, definitive, hoping the journalists would translate that into a "confident" statement when they reported it.

"Thank you. You may be seated," the judge instructed, making a notation on the paperwork and handing it to the court stenographer. "And bail, Mr. Shepard?"

"The State requests," the prosecutor stated as he stood up to respond to the judge, "that bail be set at Two Million Dollars."

Carter Pierce jumped to his feet. "Two Million Dollars! That's absurd, Your Honor. My client isn't a flight risk. Absolutely none whatsoever. He grew up in this town. His parents still live here. He owns a business in Portland. He has a home and a wife here."

"Your Honor," Shepard stood calmly and erectly beside his table. "This crime involves the deaths of two young boys. The Defendant faces serious charges. He has already tried to commit suicide..."

Pierce cut him off: "Your Honor, the mental state of the Defendant is irrelevant to this proceeding. Besides, my client was wracked by grief after the accident. He's no risk to himself or to others at this point."

"Your Honor," Shepard proceeded, "the State feels that it's being generous in not asking for the Defendant to be bound over. Two million isn't unreasonable under the circumstances."

"Your Honor, the Defendant is prepared to post One Million Dollars bail, ten percent cash bond. There is absolutely zero risk he won't appear for trial."

The judge looked down from the bench at the two lawyers. Then he turned to Nathan and slowly looked him up and down.

"Bail is set at One Million Dollars. Are we done here, gentlemen?" The judge banged his gavel, rose from his bench, and the court was in recess.

Pierce turned to his client. "I think that went well."

"Really? One Million Dollars is a good result? I can't believe it's that high."

"I didn't want to scare you, but I really was prepared for Shepard to ask the judge to keep you locked up until the trial. He must have decided that that was a bridge too far and that it would make him look bad. He's already walking a tightrope by prosecuting you. Lots of people love an underdog, and they hate to see someone getting kicked while he's down."

"I feel so lucky," Nathan said, with obvious sarcasm.

"No worries, Nate. Your Dad's already on the phone with the bank. He'll have your bail posted in less than an hour. You should be home in time for lunch."

CHAPTER EIGHTEEN
CATHERINE

"What do you mean he was arrested?"

"They're prosecuting Nathan for killing Jacob and Joe." Catherine had thought the big news she'd be telling Rev. Susan was going to be about her recent coffee with her husband. But this took precedence.

"That just seems cruel." The church pastor shook her head.

"Nate's father said that the local prosecutor has his eye on a job in the statehouse, and he's trying to make a name for himself."

"I'm no politician, but it sounds like a risky move to me. I mean, public sympathy for a poor grieving father could backfire in his face."

"Well, I guess he decided it was worth the risk. In any event, Nathan's out on bail now, and it looks like the trial won't be until sometime in the spring."

Rev. Susan shifted her tone as she shifted the conversation. "So, how are you doing with all this?"

Catherine hesitated, took a deep breath, and let it out with an audible sigh. "That's a good question." She looked up at the ceiling, then down at the floor before continuing. "I can't imagine what Nathan is going through. As you said, it feels cruel to put him through this." Catherine paused before she continued. "And I thought I was beyond the 'revenge' stage. You know, really making progress toward moving on. But can I be completely honest with you?"

"I hope by now you know that you can."

"This is hard to admit, but my first reaction when Frank called me was 'Good. He deserves it.' Let's just say that I'm not very proud of that."

"Your reaction is your reaction, Catherine."

"Yeah, yeah. I know. But I always see myself as the one taking the high road. This was not the high road."

"So, that was your initial, visceral reaction. I'm sorry to tell you this, but I'd say that it just means that you're human. How're you feeling now?"

"Sad, I guess. Just plain sad." Tears welled up in Catherine's eyes and Susan passed her a box of tissues. "There's just been too much damn loss. And if Nathan actually goes to jail for this? It's just loss piling on loss."

Susan paused before asking her next question, letting Catherine sit with her emotions. "Is there a loss you're afraid of, that you're not telling me about?"

Catherine gazed out on the courtyard and wiped her nose and eyes. She took a breath and gathered herself, nodding in reply. "If he goes to jail, I can pretty much kiss goodbye any hope of us getting back together."

Rev. Susan knew that it was too soon to ask Catherine to unpack that statement. She sensed that it was too raw, so she let it hang in the air.

*

Catherine left the pastor's office feeling wrung out, like a used dishrag. It had been months since she'd felt this way after a therapy session. Could it be that her heart was breaking over the prospect of not getting back together with Nathan? She hadn't even considered the possibility before his arrest. But if she allowed herself to admit it, Catherine had felt something shift in her as she listened to Nathan talk during their meeting at the Daily Grind. What Nathan had said about doing his own work and not pressuring her was exactly the kind of thing she'd hoped he would say. It was as if one of the tumblers in the lock that she'd secured around her heart had fallen into place. There were a lot more that had to align before the lock was opened, but maybe it was a start. *Was it possible for two damaged souls to find comfort in each other? Was reconciliation possible? If so, what would that look like? Where would they begin? How do you start over when you're both so burdened by so much baggage?*

Although the fall air had taken on a bitter chill, a harbinger of the biting winds of winter, Catherine did what she'd been doing recently when the world was feeling like it was too much to bear, or she just needed an escape from all the thoughts swirling in her head: she went to the barn.

*

Catherine fell into a routine working shifts at the Grind, riding Penny, and sitting ensconced in her easy chair in the living room, sipping wine and trying to keep her grief at bay. Her equilibrium, however, was shaken by the approach of

Christmas. She felt herself sliding back into the black hole of grief as the holiday neared.

"Catherine, it's natural that a holiday, and especially Christmas, would pull you back under. Behind all the commercialism, this holiday celebrates the birth of a child. It's supposed to be a magical time for children, and for parents, too. Of course you'd feel empty-handed." Catherine hadn't taken off her winter parka when she'd sat down in her usual chair, and she tried to burrow down into the coat, shielding herself from the reality she knew she had to face.

"This grieving shit sucks." Catherine's voice emerged from inside her hood. "Just when you think you're doing better, another wave comes rolling in to knock you down."

"That's exactly right. And it's going to be that way for the rest of your life. And not just at holidays."

"Your bedside manner is impeccable. So comforting." Catherine's sarcasm hid a deeper truth: she was deeply grateful for this relationship, which had become something more like sisterhood than therapy over the months since the accident.

"Let me finish, though." Susan leaned in toward Catherine and gently placed a hand on her knee. "What I was going to say was that, over time, both the height of the waves and their frequency diminish, and while they may occasionally knock you down, you don't necessarily fall as far."

"Mmmm." Catherine nodded and turned to stare out into the courtyard whose every detail had become so familiar. An early snow had been shoveled into the corner, the start of the annual glacier.

"What else is going on? You seem preoccupied."

"Nathan wants to meet again."

"How do you feel about that?"

"I know we need to. It's been a while–since the day of his arrest. I know that we can't just keep avoiding each other. Or, I guess to be more accurate, I can't keep avoiding him. He told me that he needs to move out of Jim's place, which I take to mean he wants to talk about moving back into the house. Which means he sees us getting back together and everything getting back to normal."

The pastor reached out and again patted Catherine gently on the knee. "You know, you might just be making a few assumptions there, Cat. You might be right, but all he asked was to talk, right?"

"True, but you don't know him like I do."

"How well does he know you?" Susan probed. "The 'you' that's emerged since the accident."

"Not at all," Catherine knew where this was leading.

"And maybe *you* don't know *him* that well anymore, either. He just wants to talk."

"Mmm-hmm," Catherine said, returning her gaze to the courtyard.

"I could come with you," Susan offered, "and Nathan could bring Robert if he wants."

"No, I don't think so. That feels too much like sitting down with divorce lawyers. I think I can do this on my own."

"I know you can. You're a strong, resilient woman."

"I knew there was a reason I liked you," Catherine said standing up and heading toward the door. "I don't know how you do it, but you challenge me and make me feel like I'm up for the challenge, all at the same time."

"That's why," Susan began, and Catherine took the cue to join her in finishing the now-familiar sentence, "you pay me the big bucks."

The two laughed and hugged before Catherine headed out

the door.

*

Catherine pulled into the Starbucks parking lot, noticed that Nathan's pickup was already there, and eased her Subaru into the free space beside it. She took a deep breath before releasing her grip on the steering wheel and heading for the front door. Nathan was seated at one of the small tables near the fireplace. He rose when Catherine approached and helped her off with her jacket. Two coffee cups were sitting on the table.

"I got you your pumpkin spiced latte." They took seats on opposite sides of the table.

"Thanks, Nate," It took every fiber of her being to hide her nervousness. As they sipped their drinks, they made small talk but then fell into an uneasy silence. Catherine noticed the groovy, coffee house jazz Christmas tunes wafting through the room and could feel herself sinking into a depression, like quicksand threatening to pull her under.

"Fa-la -fucking-la," Nathan muttered, as much to himself as to Catherine.

"Tell me about it," Catherine said, not daring to make eye contact for fear of opening up the floodgates that were barely holding back the tears. She had almost canceled their meeting, it being so close to the holiday. Christmas had always been Catherine's thing, even before she and Nathan had had children. Nathan used to have to beg her not to begin playing Christmas music before Thanksgiving, and Catherine complied with his wishes, at least while he was around. Every year, Catherine would decorate their house in a Colonial Williamsburg style with lots of greens and candles. Early on,

Nathan had come to rely on his wife to "make Christmas" for the both of them and then, later, for the boys as well. Once the kids came along, she had always insisted on making Santa footprints outlined with confectioner's sugar around the tree after they'd gone to bed on Christmas Eve. Just two days earlier, Catherine had flown into a private rage when she'd looked around the house and noticed that there wasn't a single sign of Christmas to be seen anywhere, realizing that, in addition to all the other damage he had done, Nathan had stolen Christmas from her, too.

"This was a bad idea," she said vaguely to Nathan, beginning to rise from her seat.

"Hang on, Cat," Nathan blurted out, reaching into the pocket of his parka hanging on the back of his chair. He pulled out a small, gift-wrapped box and placed it on the table. "I got you something."

"You got me something?" Catherine was incredulous. "You got me something!" Her voice was rising now, and other customers turned to see what the disruption was about.

"Calm down, Cat. It's just a gesture. I know how hard this Christmas is. It is for me, too. I didn't want to let it pass without at least doing something."

"You know how hard this Christmas is?" Catherine was shouting now. "You have no fucking idea how hard it is, so don't even try to pretend," she added. "And you think buying me some trinket or something is going to make me feel better?" She was on a tear now. "What, you want me to wear this around so that it reminds me of the first Christmas after you killed my kids?" Catherine swept the box off the table with a wave of her arm, sending it across the room where it bounced off the stonework around the gas fireplace. Without another word, she threw her coat over her shoulders and stormed out of the coffee shop, leaving Nathan stunned and the other customers staring.

Catherine was so enraged that she dared not try to drive, so she sat in the cold car panting and crying. She banged her hands on the steering wheel and let out a scream like she hadn't allowed herself to do since shortly after the boys' death. She didn't notice Nathan approaching her car and jumped when he unlatched the passenger-side door and climbed into the seat beside her.

"Get the fuck out of my car!" she shouted at him, but he didn't move. She started to shove and hit him, trying to push him out the door. He raised his arms to fend off her feeble attack, and suddenly she felt an overwhelming fatigue wash over her. Nathan opened his arms to her and she fell into them awkwardly across the space dividing the two seats. He held her gently as she sobbed into the fabric of his parka

As her sobs subsided, Catherine sat up in her seat and took some deep breaths. She noticed that all the windows in the car were completely fogged up.

"It looks like someone's gotten all hot and heavy in here," she remarked, trying to break the tension.

"We never were much for 'parking,' were we."

Catherine wiped her eyes with a used paper napkin she'd found in the console.

"Cat, I know this isn't the time or the place, but at some point, we've got to talk about us. It feels like we're just circling each other, working hard to keep things superficial. I've got a ton going on inside me even without the trial, and, if that reaction back there is any indication, so do you. I don't want to have that conversation in a Starbucks parking lot, but can we at least agree that we're going to have it? Maybe after the first of the year?"

Catherine nodded. She was grateful that Nathan both had broached the subject and had had the good sense not to try to push her in the moment.

"I'm sorry about the present," Nathan told her. "It was a stupid idea. I should have known better."

"I over-reacted, and I'm sorry for that, Nate," Catherine said, looking him in the eye. It was like she was seeing him for the first time in a long time, and she realized that there was not just a shared pain between them, but a shared history, too. He was hurting, and lonely, and maybe even a little desperate, just as she was. Her heart broke open to that and she could feel the tension in her body releasing. She suddenly felt softer than she had in nearly a year. Although she knew their shared grief and loss was not the foundation for a healthy relationship, she suddenly and unexpectedly opened herself up to the prospect of a future together.

"Thanks for your courage in opening that door," Catherine said.

"I'm glad you didn't have a gun," Nathan joked. "And I knew I could handle your lame punches. I'm going to go now. But I want you to know that you are on my mind every minute of every day. And I'm going to call you on Christmas morning and on New Year's Eve, even if I can't be with you. You don't have to answer the phone, but I need you to know that my love for you hasn't wavered one little bit through all this."

Catherine nodded and wiped her eyes again. "Thanks, Nate. That means a lot. I love you, too. But I just don't know what that means anymore. Okay?"

If the words stung Nathan, he didn't let it show. He simply nodded, too, leaned across the console and gave Catherine a kiss on the cheek. And with that he was gone.

*

"I won't take no for an answer," Catherine's sister was adamant on the other end of the line. "I'm not letting you spend Christmas and New Year's alone."

"Believe me, Carey. You don't want to be around me right now."

"I've already bought the tickets, Cat. We're flying out of Logan on the 24th and we won't be back until January 2nd. We don't even have to celebrate either holiday. It'll just be a girls' ski trip. It'll do you good to get out of Maine and out onto the slopes."

"Carey..."

"No excuses. I won't hear it. My treat. I'll even supply the wine."

Catherine had no excuse not to join Carey, so in the end she took her up on her offer. The two sisters drank, skied, and slept their way through the holidays. Catherine returned to Maine exhausted and depressed, but she'd survived her first Christmas without Jacob and Joe.

CHAPTER NINETEEN
NATHAN

Nathan tried to put his pre-holiday meeting with Catherine – and how badly he'd messed up – behind him by throwing himself into preparations for the trial. As the relentless grey days of January in Maine bore down on him, he spent countless hours in his lawyer's office discussing strategy and getting updates on the various experts they'd hired to offer testimony.

"It's all about convincing the jury that you weren't negligent in taking the ATV out on the ice," Carter Pierce told Nathan and his father. "We need to show that you exercised reasonable care, and that you couldn't have foreseen the consequences."

"Doesn't the outcome speak for itself, Mr. Pierce?" Nathan could not bring himself to address the attorney, who had represented his father in all his business matters since Nathan was a child, less formally. "I mean, when you see what happened it's pretty hard to say I acted reasonably."

"It's a fine legal point, Nathan. One that I'm going to have to convince the jury to understand. The outcome – the result of your decision – shouldn't matter at all, legally speaking. We just need to show them that a reasonably prudent person in your same situation could have made the same decision. That it was reasonable to think the ice would hold."

Nathan couldn't believe that he was being forced, on a daily basis, to revisit the decision that had ended his young sons' lives. His nightmares, which had finally subsided, returned with a vengeance and sleep became elusive. As the heart of the winter seized southern Maine by the throat, Nathan decided to increase the frequency of his visits with his therapist, which before Christmas had tapered to once a month.

"This just sucks." Nathan saw that the oak tree outside Robert's window was bare of leaves, while a drift of snow climbed partway up the northern side of the trunk. "I thought I was doing better. But all this talk of average ice thickness and tire pressure and visibility just throws everything back in my face."

"It sounds like the nightmares don't come only when you sleep." Robert sat back in his chair and twirled a pen absently with his fingers.

"My lawyer says it's not about what I decided to do." Nathan's gaze was fixed out the window.

"What do you mean?"

"If I understand it, and I'm not quite sure I do, I don't need to prove that I didn't do anything wrong, or even that my own actions were reasonable. He said it's all about an 'objective man' standard. The question is, 'Would it have been reasonable for some hypothetical objective person to do what I did under the circumstances?'"

"It makes it sound so impersonal."

"I guess that's what we need to do. Make it impersonal, so the jury doesn't look at me and ask whether what I did was right. Because, of course, it wasn't. I mean, we know that because Joe and Jacob are dead. If they went by what I did, they'd lock me up and throw away the key."

"But of course, for you, this is all so highly personal." Nathan turned to face him before he responded.

"What good does it do me? It might keep me out of jail, but I'm left without my kids, and my marriage is still in shambles."

"Can I run a thought by you, Nate?" The therapist leaned in and didn't wait for an answer. "What if this is more than just an exercise? What if it's more than simply a trial tactic to keep a jury from convicting you?"

"What do you mean?" Nathan wasn't sure where Robert was going with his line of questioning.

"Is it possible, Nate, that you actually *did* act reasonably under the circumstances? That by any standard – including this 'objective man' standard – you didn't do anything wrong?"

Nathan sat back in his chair and knew that his skepticism was showing clearly on his face.

"Maybe it's not so far-fetched, Nathan. I'm just asking you to try this on for size. I don't expect you to swallow it whole, sitting there. I wonder whether there's a possibility that, while you're working so hard to convince the jury, there might just be room to convince yourself."

Leaving the therapist's office, Nathan chewed on Robert's words. He rolled them around in his mouth like one of the hard caramel candies his grandmother kept in a crystal jar on the coffee table when he was young.

*

The hours Nathan wasn't spending with his lawyer were eaten up by the demands of his financial planning clients. The wholesale exodus of clients he'd feared following his arrest never materialized, and the time between New Year's Day and April 15 was always consumed by the intricacies of tax planning. Between his heavy workload, the trial preparations and his spotty sleep pattern, Nathan returned to Jim's house every night bleary-eyed and exhausted.

"I know I sound like a broken record, Jim." The two men were nursing beers and watching a Bruins hockey game as a fire roared in the woodstove. "But this place has been a refuge for me. I don't know how I could be getting through this without being here."

The large man waved a grease-stained hand at Nathan, dismissing his comment. "Nate, I know you're grateful. You really don't need to keep saying it."

"But I do, Jim. And I know you'd never admit it, but I feel like this has gone on way longer than you ever thought it would, back when you first took me in."

Jim watched the game intently, refusing to acknowledge Nathan's statement.

"I think I should start looking around for a place of my own."

Jim glanced up from the television and looked Nathan in the eye. "Listen, bud. You do what you gotta do. But there's no pressure from me. None. Zip. Nada. I enjoy having company, especially in the dead of winter. I mean, I could do without the screaming and the night terrors, but overall having you around is a plus as far as I'm concerned. And I'll just say one thing. Not to jinx your trial or anything, but are you sure the timing's right? You gonna sign a lease before you know what's gonna happen?"

Nathan slumped back into the sofa and took a long draw on his beer. "Thanks for the vote of confidence, Jim."

"Hey, I'm just being realistic."

"No, no. You're absolutely right. I didn't think about that. I might be moving out soon, whether I like it or not." Nathan hated the thought but appreciated his friend's honesty and willingness to confront reality, even if he himself wasn't prepared to.

*

"The trial starts in three weeks." Carter Pierce, Nathan, and his father were huddled around the conference room table in Pierce's Portland law office. "There are a few things we need to get straight."

Nathan and Frank nodded in unison and waited for the lawyer to continue.

"There are some logistical things that we need to be realistic about. Like, Nathan, have you made arrangements to keep your business afloat during the trial, and potentially after?"

Nathan swallowed hard at the "and after" of his attorney's question. "My clients are aware of the situation. I've got a colleague lined up to serve them in a worst-case scenario."

"That's good. Hopefully, it won't be necessary. But the trial itself could last a couple of weeks and I'll need your complete attention. Now, I know this might be a touchy subject, but what about Catherine?"

Nathan gave Pierce a quizzical look and the lawyer continued.

"Now, we know that she can't be compelled to testify against you. Even though you're separated, she's still your wife." Nathan winced at the statement and Pierce quickly apologized. "I'm sorry. That came across as tactless. But here's my question, Nathan: Is Catherine going to attend the trial? The optics are going to be 1,000 percent better if she's sitting behind you in the gallery."

The question hadn't occurred to Nathan. "I have no idea. I haven't talked to her since before Christmas. And, to be honest, that didn't go so well."

"Well, you'd better talk to her, and see if you can convince her to be there. We need to make you as sympathetic a figure as we can."

"But I thought you said the jury is supposed to use an 'objective man' standard, and not look at me specifically."

"That's the legal argument, Nathan. But when the jury looks over at the defense table, I want them to see a bereft and grieving father who is backed up and supported by his bereft and grieving wife. We want them to do the right thing legally, and I'm fully prepared to pull at their heartstrings to drag them over to our side."

"Do you think you can ask Catherine to come?" Frank placed his hand on his son's arm as he posed the question.

"All I can do is ask. I can't force her to show up." Nathan shifted his glance between his father and his lawyer.

"Well, do what you can to convince her." Pierce shuffled through the pages on his yellow legal pad. "Okay. Here's the last thing: Let's talk about putting you on the stand, Nathan."

Nathan went pale at the mention of this possibility. It was the first time his lawyer had broached the subject.

"Of course, they can't compel you to testify. The Fifth Amendment and all that. But we need to decide whether it's in your best interest."

Nathan looked to his father for guidance. The older Osgood turned to Carter Pierce. "I think the value of Nathan testifying is obvious." He patted his son on the back as he spoke. "He's a sympathetic defendant."

"There's no doubt about that." Pierce nodded in agreement. "What I'm worried about is how this prosecutor is going to treat you if we hand you over to him. He's a bulldog, and he could get you really twisted up, Nate."

"Say more, Mr. Pierce." Nathan sat silently as the two older men exchanged thoughts.

"Look, he's got a fine line to walk. On the one hand, he could do a lot to make Nathan look really bad. Like a neglectful father who casually took a chance and killed his kids. There's a legal theory called 'res ipsa loquitor.' That's Latin for 'the thing speaks for itself.' He could argue that, because Nathan's kids never came home that night, by definition Nathan was negligent. And getting you on the stand," the lawyer shifted his focus to Nathan, "would give him a chance to challenge directly your decision to cross the ice."

"What's on the other side of the fine line?" Frank Osgood probed the lawyer's thinking.

"He can't be too aggressive with Nathan, or it might backfire on him with the jury. Remember, we're starting off with sympathy on our side. He'd have to navigate a minefield to make you look like the bad guy while not turning the jury against him."

The three men sat in silence, considering their options. Nathan spoke into the silence.

"Do we need to decide this now? Can't we just see how things are going with their case and with our defense?"

"Sounds like a plan, Nate." The lawyer tucked his legal pad

into the accordion file folder that held all his trial notes. "But we need to prep you, just in case. I'll line that up with one of my associates so that we're ready to go if need be. And hopefully we won't." Pierce rose from his seat indicating that their meeting was over.

*

Nathan was anxious as he waited for Catherine. He was seated at a booth away from the crowded tables at the front of the pizza parlor. He'd been vague on the phone about his purpose for getting together. He watched the door and stood up to wave to Catherine as she entered the restaurant.

"Here, let me help you," Nathan reached to help Catherine off with her bulky winter parka.

"Can you believe this cold snap?" Catherine's cheeks were rosy from the cold as she took her seat across from Nathan.

"It's bad even for Maine." Nathan nodded in agreement. "I remember a winter like this when I was a kid. My mom's car wouldn't start for a week and there was a morning when I was waiting for the bus that my eyelashes froze together."

Catherine perused the menu in front of her. "I wonder if the meatball sandwich is still good?"

"I haven't been here in a while, so it's anybody's guess."

A server took their order and brought their drinks. "How've you been, Cat?"

Catherine let a long sigh escape her lips. "Christmas was hard." She twirled her straw in her soda. "Carey dragged me out west to ski with her. I guess it was a good distraction. But now we're facing the anniversary."

Nathan was unable to make eye contact. "Yeah, I know. And to make matters worse my trial's about to start."

Catherine sat immobile, impossible for Nathan to read. They sat in their usual awkward silence as he let his words hang between them. The discomfort was broken by the arrival of their food.

"Cat, I don't know how to ask this, exactly, so I'm just going to put it out there. My lawyer has told me that it would really help my cause if you were at the trial. I mean, I would really like it if you were there too, but just strictly as a tactic, he said it would be good."

Catherine put down her meatball sub and chewed slowly. Nathan hoped she was simply considering her answer, and he tried to sit patiently waiting for her reply. She swallowed and took a sip of her soda.

"Let me get this straight, Nathan. You want to use me as a prop?"

"No. No. That's not what I meant. My lawyer hopes that our family can present a unified front for the judge and the jury. You, me, my mom and dad."

"So, I'm just supposed to sit there like the dutiful, sympathetic wife?"

"Cat, I'm not asking you to do anything that you're not comfortable with. Really."

"Did you even think this through before asking me?" Catherine's voice was becoming louder, more strident. "Did you think about how it might make me feel, to have to sit through your trial? To hear in all the excruciating detail about how you drowned our kids? And, what? Am I supposed to sit there behind you, smiling the whole time I'm reliving the worst night of my life?"

"Cat. Wait. I'm sorry." Nathan pleaded as his wife stood suddenly and threw her napkin on the table in front of them. She spoke to him through gritted teeth, barely controlling her rage.

"You know, Nathan. Since Christmas, I've been thinking a lot about what it might be like to start working on getting back together. But this? I can't believe how cruel and selfish it is. It's all about you, isn't it? Well, here's your answer Nathan. And you can give it to your lawyer, too." With that, she raised both hands in front of Nathan's face, the middle fingers pointing skyward. "Fuck you."

Catherine stormed out of the restaurant leaving Nathan stunned and despondent in her wake.

CHAPTER TWENTY
CATHERINE

"Anniversaries are complex beasts." Catherine stared out the office window as Rev. Susan spoke, noticing that the glacier was now fully formed in the courtyard on this late February afternoon. In just a few weeks, it would be a year since the accident.

"I thought Thanksgiving, Christmas, and New Year's were bad, but I don't know if I can make it through this." Catherine's eyes were red-rimmed from crying.

Heather had tried to help her through her first Thanksgiving without the boys by inviting Catherine to share in her family's feast, but before the bird had come out of the oven, she had bolted from the Rockwellian scene. She adored Heather and her kids, but to sit and see how easy and, just, *normal* their lives were caught Catherine by the throat and threatened to suffocate her. Heather claimed afterward that she understood completely, but Catherine could tell that her feelings were hurt, and the guilt over that compounded her grief. Carey whisking her away over Christmas and New

Year's allowed her a brief escape. The diversion helped, but only in the way that a cough drop helps a strep throat. Temporarily. Superficially. Masking a symptom, but not approaching the source of the pain. Despite the distraction, Catherine returned home from the trip depressed at the prospect of another year of emptiness unfolding before her.

Catherine told Susan about her latest conversation with Nathan, where he asked her to show up at his trial.

"I can't believe he would ask that of me. Especially with the anniversary so close."

Susan sat quietly, knowing there was more to come. Catherine dabbed her eyes.

"His self-absorption is monumental. I thought maybe we were getting together to talk about how we might want to mark the anniversary. Like go to the cemetery together or something. But no. All he was focused on was what he needed from me, to save his own skin."

"So, you were blind-sided."

"I guess I thought he'd be in the same head-space I'm in. I guess that's just too much to ask. It feels like we're just spinning our wheels and not getting anywhere. I mean, it's been a year, Sue. What's been the point?"

Susan ignored the question. "If you took off all the filters with Nathan, if you could summon him to *your* meeting with *your* agenda, what would you really say to him?"

"Whew. That's a scary thought."

"I know. But he's not here, and I won't tell him what you might say. So, pretend I'm Nathan and you're going to tell me how you really feel." Susan edged her chair closer to Catherine's as if they were sitting across a table from each other.

"Catherine, tell me how you're really feeling." The pastor

221

role-played Nathan's part. "I really want to know."

Catherine squirmed uncomfortably in her seat. She took a deep breath and let it out slowly, trying to relax the tension in her shoulders.

"Nathan, I really don't know if I can keep doing this."

"Doing what?"

"This dance we're doing. Being stuck in this place. Pretending. Being afraid."

"Afraid of what?"

"Afraid to make a move. Afraid to make a decision. Afraid that we're gonna make a fucked-up situation even worse."

"Worse than what? Being alone and lonely?"

"Yes! I've gotten used to living by myself. I don't like it, but I know it. Right now, I have the space and the freedom to feel how I want to feel, to be how I want to be. If I wake up in the morning and want to cry for an hour, I can do that. If I need to sit and do nothing all day except stare out the window, there's no one around to tell me I can't or I shouldn't."

"And with me there, you can't be yourself?"

"Of course not. Because even if you don't say anything, I know what you're thinking. I can't be around your constant hoping."

"You make hope sound like a bad thing."

"It is when you feel hopeless."

The pastor paused for a beat before continuing. "What else aren't you telling me?"

"I hate you for what you did." The words began to tumble from Catherine's mouth in a torrent, a mountain lake whose dam has just been breached. "And I know that's not fair and that it's not really your fault and it was an awful, horrible mistake that you wish you could take back. But none of that matters to me. You gave me this amazing world, this amazing family, and then you ripped it all away from me. I don't know how to stop hating you, and I don't know if I ever will. And if I can't stop hating you, how could I ever even think of being with you or dream of loving you again."

Rev. Susan sat back in her chair, indicating to Catherine that their role-playing was over. Catherine sat back, too, tears streaming down her cheeks. Susan gave her a chance to regroup and then asked Catherine what she'd learned.

"I'm not ready." Catherine surprised herself with the sudden realization. "Even after nearly a whole year, I'm just not ready to begin to think about any kind of reconciliation with Nathan."

"I think I agree. What would it take for you to tell him that?"

"Clarity definitely helps. It's crystal-clear to me now that I've been trying to accommodate Nathan's timetable. And I'm also clear that we're out of sync as far as that's concerned. I mean, I feel selfish for sitting in that big house by myself, keeping him from coming home while he's paying all the bills. It makes me feel guilty, so I was trying to see if I could work toward giving him what he wants, which is to move back home. But I'm not even close to that decision yet."

"Do you think you could tell him that?"

Catherine nodded as she dabbed the tears from her cheeks and blew her nose into a tissue. "Sitting here right now, I'd say yes. But to actually say those words out loud, I'm afraid I'd probably throw up."

"Catherine, your body, your psyche, your spirit – all of you – has to heal on its own timetable. No one else can dictate that for you. Because if they do, it's a false recovery. And that would just lead to more problems down the road. You said it yourself, in no uncertain terms: you're not ready. While it might be hard to say, no one can fault you for it. It hasn't even been a year. And in that time, you've come farther than a lot of people could. This isn't a race to some imaginary finish line. No one is timing you. And, if they are, they don't have your best interest at heart."

Catherine dialed Nate's number as she left the pastor's office, before her resolve to have an honest conversation with her husband melted like the late-winter snow that lined the sidewalk.

*

Nathan unexpectedly jumped into the conversation after they sat down. "Listen, Cat, there's something I want to say to you." Catherine's heart leaped up into her throat. "It's been nearly a year." Catherine could hear the blood pounding in her ears as he spoke and she started to scope out an escape route, just in case. She had no idea where this was going. "First, I want to apologize for our last conversation. It was really shitty of me to ask you to show up to the trial, and I see that now and I'm really sorry. I'm working really hard not to pressure you about anything, and I backslid. I know I'm not perfect – far from it. But you've got to know that I'm trying to give you space."

Nathan paused to let his apology sink in. The tunnel vision that Catherine experienced from the stress began to subside, and she looked across the table at Nathan. She wasn't sure she could believe him. But she also knew the pressure he was under, between the upcoming anniversary and the trial, so she decided to give him the benefit of the doubt.

"Thanks." She gave a slight nod of her head to acknowledge what he'd said. Nathan had thrown her off her game by setting the tone for the conversation, and she tried to recover by recalling the role-play she'd done with Rev. Susan a few days earlier. But Nathan chose to fill the silence.

"I can't believe it's been a year."

"Don't." Catherine slammed the door shut on the topic of the anniversary. "I can't talk about that, Nathan. When I even think about it, it feels like yesterday."

"Sorry. I get it," Nathan took a sip of his coffee as his wife spoke.

"And I know that we agreed to keep communications going, but it's really not helping me, Nate. I know you want to get back together. Believe me, I know that. But conversations like these, and the last one we had about the trial – all the back and forth and the dance we do, trying to keep our interactions safe, the way your hope hovers over everything – none of this is helping me heal. I know at Christmas I told you I'd keep the lines of communication open, but that's not working for me. Plus, you've got the trial to think about. So, let's just stop talking for a while. I hope you understand." Catherine added the "and I don't care if you don't" silently to herself.

Nathan sat quietly and stirred the foamy milk, tracing the outline of the leaf that the barista had put there. He looked up at her with sad eyes. "Sure, Cat. Whatever you need." With that, he pushed his chair back and walked out the door, skipping the awkward kiss on the top of Catherine's head that had become his parting ritual.

*

Catherine called her sister that evening as she sat in front of the fireplace of the house on Mountain Road. "I feel like I kicked a puppy."

"You did what was best for you. That's all you can do."

"I still feel like shit. I mean, here he makes this whole speech about how sorry he is for the way he acted and I just grind him under my heel."

"You gave him the gift of being honest with him. He shouldn't ask for more than that." Carey knew better than to be critical of Nathan in conversations like these. She decided to change the subject. "Hey, I was thinking we could meet in Boston next weekend. Maybe take in a show or something."

Catherine knew exactly what Carey was trying to do. The anniversary of the accident was fast approaching, and Carey wanted to get her out of town, just as she had over Christmas.

"For a wily wheeler-dealer, you're pretty transparent."

"That bad, huh?"

"I appreciate the offer, Sis. But I think I've got to ride this one out here and not run away from it."

"Want me to come up? I really don't want you to be alone."

"I know. But I think I need to do this myself. If you or anyone else is around, it's just gonna make it worse. I promise to call you if I feel the need. I hope you understand."

"Of course, Cat. I'm always only a phone call away."

"Unless you're in Timbuktu or something."

"True, but I have no travel plans for the next 10 days. Keep it in mind."

"Thanks, Carey. You've been a rock through all this. I don't think I could have survived without you."

"That's what I'm here for, Little Sister." Carey clicked off the call.

*

Catherine had thought about how she was going to spend

the day on the first anniversary of the accident. She had seriously considered staying in bed, hiding under the covers. Now that the day was here, she thought it might be the only way to get through it. Unlike a year ago, it was still bitterly cold, the harsh Maine winter holding on as tenaciously as a dog with a meaty bone. She received a text from Heather early, as they'd agreed a week earlier, that said simply "Thinking of you." Heather had been reluctant to let her friend face the day alone either, but Catherine had insisted, conceding that her best friend could text her as she had, once, and not expect any reply.

Catherine lay in bed and remembered. At first, she remembered the day itself. How it started off like any other Saturday. She remembered in the most minute detail as if she were watching a documentary unfolding. How the boys had been sitting at the table in the breakfast nook as she'd made pancakes. They were still wearing their pajamas, and their hair was tousled from a good night's sleep. How Nathan had walked into the kitchen and poured himself a cup of coffee, sat down with the boys, and talked about their plans for the day. A trip to Home Depot in Sanford for some cabinet hardware. The afternoon unscripted at that point. All three of her boys devouring the pancakes, smothered in syrup and blueberries, with Catherine wondering how soon it would be before the boys were eating them out of house and home.

She remembered how, after they'd left for the store together, she'd stepped outside the slider and onto the part of the deck that faced south. She was surprised at how warm it was. She stepped back inside and grabbed a chair and her coffee and sat soaking up the rays. The sun was gaining strength. In fact, if she weren't careful with her fair skin, she'd get a good burn. But for now, she closed her eyes and tilted her head skyward, listening to the birds, thinking about how happy she was. She hadn't expected this life, really. The one Nathan had provided to her. She had been on the partner track at one of Boston's leading law firms, focused like a laser beam on her career path. And yet, here she was, happy to make breakfast, do the dishes, and relax on the deck of a house in the Maine woods. Catherine felt a deep sense of contentment and peace. And with the sun high in the sky, she could feel her whole life unfolding before her like the leaves on the trees that were soon to bud and blossom. And she remembered the feeling of new life growing inside her and her excitement over the plan to tell Nathan she was pregnant later that night.

Catherine remembered, too, that the boys had eaten some leftover pizza for lunch and that the four of them had played about a dozen hands of Uno afterward. It was such a gorgeous day; Catherine had encouraged the boys to get outside and play in the mud and melting snow. Nathan had thought of taking an early-spring ATV ride, and Catherine had supported the idea. It meant some more quiet time for her, and maybe a nap, so why not? She sent them off in their snowsuits and their helmets all smiles and squirmy excitement. Catherine had spent the afternoon doing some reading, and lots of laundry, and as dinner time approached, she began to prepare the nachos.

And she remembered waiting, and waiting, and waiting. Wondering why Nathan and the boys hadn't returned by the time the sun had set. She recalled how her anxiety had grown into fear, as her mind began to spin out-of-control catastrophic scenarios, and she remembered working hard to quell those feelings. And then the sheriff's cruiser had pulled into the driveway and her whole world imploded.

How could such a perfect day end in such tragedy? How

was the universe so structured that it could, within a matter of hours, take her from the peak of contentment to the pit of utter devastation? If there was a God, why would he do that? But ultimately, it didn't matter. Figuring out the "why" wasn't going to change the "what" of the accident. Even if there was some cosmic reason for it, a reason far beyond her fathoming, her arms were still empty, her heart in shattered pieces on the floor. Catherine lay in her bed as tears streamed down her face and into her ears. If nothing else, it felt good to let go and cry through her pain.

CHAPTER TWENTY-ONE
NATHAN

"Ladies and gentlemen of the jury, this is a very simple case." District Attorney Tom Shepard was standing in front of the jury box, speaking amiably. He made sure to make eye contact with each of the four men and seven women as he proceeded with his opening statement.

"This is a case about a tragedy that befell a family. It tugs at our heartstrings because it involves the death of two young children. Because we are all human, our hearts go out to the defendant. He lost his two little boys. But I say this case is simple because the truth, as the State will show, is that those two little boys would be out enjoying this beautiful spring day had their father done what every father, every parent should do: protect his children from harm."

The prosecutor paused here, and let that sink in. He turned, somewhat dramatically, and pointed toward Nathan, seated beside his attorney at the defense table.

"The State will prove, beyond a reasonable doubt, that the defendant failed in his duty to protect his children. It will prove, beyond a reasonable doubt, that through his own negligence, his failure to act reasonably under the circumstances, the defendant caused the death of those children."

Shepard turned back toward the jury and leaned in, placing his outstretched hands on the railing of the jury box, and continued.

"It may strike you as unfair to hit a man when he's down, to add insult to this most grievous injury that this family has experienced. But we're here today because the law of this State says that if someone negligently causes the death of another, they're guilty of a crime. While the defense will try to characterize what happened on the evening of March 22nd as a tragic accident, it was not. In an accident, we have no agency. No power. Something happens to us that we have no control over."

Another pause.

"But in this case, the defendant was in complete control of what happened. His negligent decisions led directly to the events that unfolded and resulted in two little boys drowning beneath the thin and treacherous ice of Franklin Pond. Over the course of the next few days, I ask you to put aside your emotional reaction to what happened, your pity or compassion for the defendant. It is your duty to listen to the evidence and to see that, beyond a reasonable doubt, he is guilty of causing the death of two innocent victims. Thank you for your service in the cause of justice."

The prosecutor took his seat as the judge thanked him for his statement and turned his attention to the defense table.

"Counselor?" He invited Carter Pierce to proceed with his opener. Pierce stood, buttoning the jacket of his grey pinstripe suit as he approached the jury box.

"Good morning, ladies and gentlemen. I, too, thank you for your service. I'm sure you'd much rather be doing just about anything else than sitting here today. I know I would. The prosecutor has properly laid out the law for you. He's absolutely right that the law says that if someone negligently causes the death of another, they're guilty of manslaughter. We can't and won't argue about that. But he's wrong about the facts of this case, and he's wrong when he says that my client, Nathan Osgood, acted unreasonably on the day that his children died. In fact, we'll prove to you that Nathan's actions were eminently reasonable under the circumstances. We'll show you that his decisions were sound, that he took not just reasonable care but every precaution to protect little Joe and Jacob from harm." Pierce was deliberate in using the names of both his client and the children, as he would be for the entire trial. He had told Nathan that he would, at every turn, attempt to forge a personal bond between the jury and his client.

"Nathan didn't act recklessly that afternoon. He didn't wantonly disregard the safety of his children. We will show, through the course of this trial, that Nathan was doing what any good father would do under the circumstances. We will show that he acted reasonably each step of the way. And we will show that there is no way that Nathan could ever have foreseen the tragedy that would befall him and his family that afternoon."

Pierce was bringing his statement to its conclusion.

"Nathan is not a criminal. He did not act with criminal intent." Then, with as much sadness in his voice as he could muster, the lawyer leaned in toward the jury. "Ladies and gentlemen. We shouldn't be here. None of us. The prosecutor," Pierce waved vaguely toward the district attorney, "wants you to believe that Nathan deserves to be locked up. But the truth of the matter is that little Jacob and Joe, Nathan, his wife, Catherine, and the rest of this family were and are the victims of an accident, pure and simple. About as heartbreaking an accident as any we can possibly imagine. Again, thank you for your time."

With that, the defense counsel returned to his seat. As he did so, he gripped Nathan's shoulder in a gesture of compassion and solidarity, making sure to hold the pose just long enough to let it sink in with the jury.

*

Each morning as they gathered for the trial, Nathan scanned the courtroom to see if Catherine would appear and each morning, he was disappointed. It didn't help that his lawyer had, on the night before opening arguments, reiterated to him the importance of optics, and the significance of his wife's presence to the jury. But there was simply no way Nathan was going to try and twist Catherine's arm. Not after her reaction when he'd last brought it up, and definitely not so close on the heels of the anniversary of the accident.

Nathan had spent that bitterly cold day on the shore of Franklin Pond. He sat on the familiar boulder by the edge of the ice and allowed the cold to settle into his bones. He gazed out on the white, even expanse of the snow-covered lake and was struck by the irony: had the weather a year earlier been anything like this, the ice would have held and his family would still be intact. When the cold became too much to bear, Nathan rose from his perch and began to walk the trail that traced the perimeter of the pond. It was slow going. In places the snow drifted and piled up to his knees, and at others, where animals had packed it, it was slick and icy. This was the trail he hadn't traveled with the RZR, and the words of one of Nathan's favorite poems, really one of the only poems he knew and liked – Robert Frost's "The Road Not Taken" – flashed through his head. The concluding line echoed in his brain: "and that has made all the difference."

By the time Nathan reached the far side of the pond and the place where, a year earlier, he had decided to steer the ATV out onto the ice, he was sweating heavily from the exertion of the hike. As it was a year ago, the sun hung low in the southwestern sky and trees were casting shadows along the shore. Nathan peered down the path that led around the rest of the pond and decided instead that he would do what he'd done on that fateful day. Rather than taking the path through the woods, he would cut across the lake. He was certain that, this year, the ice would hold and he could cross safely as he stepped out onto the snow-covered surface. In places he was trudging through snow and in others the wind had swept the ice clean, and his feet slipped and slid beneath him.

As he approached the halfway point to the far shore, close, he was sure, to the spot where the ATV had broken through the ice, Nathan sank to his knees. The pain of the memory was excruciating, worse than he'd felt since the day it had happened. Tears streamed down his cheeks and froze there in the bitter wind. Nathan found himself hoping and praying that, right then and there, the ice would crack and cleave. That it would open like the mouth of the monster it was and swallow him whole, just as it had his sons. He pounded the ice with both fists, daring it to do so, a roar of despair escaping his lips and echoing across the frozen expanse. But the ice failed to heed Nathan's desperate plea and it held fast in silence, a solid wall between him and his boys' icy grave. Nathan rose, exhausted and spent, and trudged the remaining distance to the shore and back to the refuge of the chair beside the glowing woodstove of his friend's home.

*

The first few days of the trial passed by in a blur for Nathan as the District Attorney presented the case against him. The prosecutor recreated the accident in vivid, painstaking detail for the jury, using aerial photographs of Franklin Pond and the surrounding area, testimony from the sheriff's deputy who had responded to the emergency call, the State game warden who had led the recovery team. He brought in a meteorologist to testify to the weather conditions on the day of the accident and those leading up to it, showing that southern Maine had experienced an early spring that should have alerted the young father to the unsafe conditions of the ice. Through it all Nathan maintained a grim expression, trying to convey to the members of the jury both the pain of having to relive the experience and some kind of confidence that he'd done nothing wrong. Carter Pierce voiced objection after objection, jumping up from his chair each time, if for no other reason than to try and derail the prosecutor's relentless attack against Nathan's judgment and reason. Over Pierce's vehement objections, District Attorney Shepard even led the York County Medical Examiner through testimony describing Nathan's suicide attempt in the morgue on the night of the accident. After three full days of excruciating testimony, the prosecution rested its case.

*

Nathan and his father met with Pierce in a conference

room at his law office, just a few blocks from the courthouse. They wanted to pin down their defensive strategy before morning. The big question still remained: Would Nathan take the stand?

"I really don't think you need to." The lawyer was pacing around the room. This had been his position all along, but now it was bolstered by the weakness of the case the State had presented. "I think we're most of the way home already. We've just got to emphasize to the jury that reasonable people can't tell whether ice is safe or not. And we've got an expert to do that."

Frank and Nathan looked at each other. Frank responded first. "Carter, are you sure it wouldn't be better to let Nathan testify? I mean, he's a sympathetic witness. He's likable. And he's wounded. Won't that play to their emotions?"

"Emotions are unpredictable. I don't want to unexpectedly hand Shepard a gift on a silver platter." The lawyer looked at Nathan. "Putting you on the stand could be just what he wants and needs to save his case."

"Look, Mr. Pierce, I think I handled the mock cross-examination pretty well. Your associate even said so. I've watched this prosecutor in action, and I think I can handle whatever he throws at me."

"It's always a gamble." The lawyer sat down in the chair across from Nathan and held his gaze. "But ultimately it's your call. If you take the stand, at least the jury won't have to speculate about what you might be hiding. Still, I don't think it's necessary."

Nathan looked over at his father, who gave him a slight nod. "If it's my call, I say we do it."

"So be it." The defense lawyer slapped his hands down on the table to punctuate the decision. "Let's go through your testimony one more time." Pierce opened the door to the conference room. He leaned out into the hallway and asked his secretary to order them in some dinner. It would be a long night.

*

As a matter of course, Carter Pierce opened the morning's session with a motion to dismiss the case.

"The prosecution has failed, *prima facie*, to provide sufficient evidence to support a finding of manslaughter." The defense attorney approached the judge, the jury having been excused from the room.

"I object, Your Honor." The prosecutor trailed Pierce to the bench. "All of the elements of this crime have been established. It's time for the defense to do what it can, in front of the jury, to rebut them."

"Counselor." The judge looked down from his lofty perch at Pierce. "You know that the State has a pretty low burden of proof under this statute. He doesn't need to prove criminal intent, and he doesn't have to show any kind of motive. Just negligence, beyond a reasonable doubt. I think we need to let the jury make this decision after hearing your side of the story. Your motion is denied. Let's get the jury back in here and have you call your first witness."

The judge banged his gavel to punctuate his ruling and the lawyers took their places behind their tables across from each other. Pierce hadn't expected the judge to actually dismiss the case. He'd made the motion to let the prosecutor know that he was going to pull out all the stops for his client.

Pierce called his first witness to the stand once the members of the jury had resumed their seats. Carl Scovil was in his mid-seventies and dressed in chinos and a plaid shirt. He looked straight out of the central casting department for a movie that called for a "typical Mainer." He was someone the members of the jury could relate to, not some nerdy scientist talking about climate change. After being sworn in and stating his name for the record, defense counsel began to question him in a friendly manner.

"Mr. Scovil, do you own an ATV?"

"I do."

"And do you ride it in the winter?"

"Sure. All year 'round."

"Do you ever take it across bodies of water in the winter?"

"Of course. I love to ice fish. I'm out on the ice all the time."

"Can you tell us where you were and what you were doing on March 22 of last year?"

"I was ice fishing in Newfield."

"You were out on the ice on March 22?"

"That's right."

"And did you drive your ATV out on the ice that day?"

"Sure. I had to drag my sled with all my sets. I usually drill at least a dozen holes when I fish, so I've got lots of gear."

"So, you drove your ATV out onto the ice last March 22, dragging a sled full of gear, AND you drilled a dozen or so holes in the ice that day?"

"That's right. Caught me some nice perch, too." This drew a chuckle from some members of the jury.

"So, you did all this on March 22nd of last year, and you didn't have any problems out there on the ice?"

"Nope. Just a nice day of fishing."

"And, by all accounts, the ice was perfectly safe?"

Scovil gazed at Pierce, then he shifted in his seat to face the jury. "Look, I've been ice fishing for going on 60 years. I know better than to go out on thin ice. I wouldn't still be around if I didn't."

"Thank you, Mr. Scovil," Pierce said to the witness. "I have no further questions, Your Honor."

"Mr. Shepard?" The judge indicated it was the prosecutor's turn to examine the witness. Shepard rose to approach him, and he asked his questions gently and with deference to the older man.

"Mr. Scovil, you said you were fishing last March 22 in Newfield. Was that on Franklin Pond?"

"Umm, no. I was on Parker Pond."

"So, you don't know what the ice was like on Franklin Pond that day?"

"Well, it's pretty much all the same..."

The prosecutor interrupted him. "But you don't know for a fact what the ice was like that day on Franklin Pond. Whether it was safe. You don't have any first-hand knowledge of that. Is that right?"

"No, I guess I don't."

"Thank you, Mr. Scovil." Shepard returned to his seat and indicated that he was done with the witness.

"Just one other question, Mr. Scovil." Defense counsel rose and approached the witness. "About how many winters out of those 60 or so that you've been ice fishing have you gone out onto the ice in the late part of March, or even to the end of March?"

"I'd say about three-quarters of 'em, roughly."

"And you've never had any problem with the ice?"

"Nope. Sometimes the fish ain't bitin', but that's the only problem I've had."

"Thank you, Mr. Scovil." Pierce sat down, and the judge dismissed the witness.

The rest of the day proceeded in similar fashion. Carter Pierce called a cast of local characters to the stand, all of whom had been out on the ice on the day of the accident. He was trying to show, through sheer volume, that it wasn't at all unreasonable for Nathan to have made the decision to cross the ice that day. Each time, the prosecutor offered the same cross-examination, highlighting that the witness hadn't been on the same stretch of ice as Nathan, and that none of the witnesses could actually know what conditions were like on Franklin Pond.

By mid-afternoon, the defense prepared to shift tactics. Pierce called his own experts – climatologists, naturalists, woodsmen – to reinforce that, under any circumstance, it was reasonable for Nathan to believe that it was safe to cross Franklin Pond on that late winter day. They presented enough evidence to nearly convince even Nathan.

After the last of the defense scientists were finished, the judge consulted his watch and looked into the faces of the jurors. He decided to excuse them for the day, which suited Carter Pierce. Nathan was his next witness, and he preferred to put him in front of a fresh jury and not to have his testimony interrupted. Nathan, his father, and the lawyer all repaired to the lawyer's office to debrief the day's events and perform some final preparations for Nathan's testimony. Pierce kept the session brief in hopes of keeping Nathan's stress to a manageable level.

"Go home and get some sleep, Nathan. Tomorrow's a big day." The lawyer stood up from the conference table and motioned toward the door.

"Fat chance." Nathan shook his head as he and his father stood and walked out the door.

CHAPTER TWENTY-TWO
CATHERINE

Catherine spent a restless night, tossing and turning. At 3 a.m. she abandoned hope of getting any sleep and wandered down the hall to Joe's room. The soft light of a full moon illuminated the space, the branches of a nearby tree casting shadows on the wall. Catherine took Joe's blanket off the end of the bed where she'd placed it so carefully just days after the accident and wrapped it around her shoulders. She eased herself down into the glider that sat by the window, the same chair in which she'd nursed both her boys when they were infants. She stared out the window and rocked herself back and forth, her mind wandering back to happier times. The stone of loss sat heavily in her stomach. It was a tumor that grew and shrank, it seemed, at will.

Heather had been attending the trial and she'd let Catherine know that it seemed to be close to concluding. Catherine was certain that Nathan would take the stand in his own defense. There had never been any doubt in her mind. She knew him too well to believe that he'd ever let his lawyer convince him not to. Nathan, the supremely confident. Nathan, the man-in-charge. Nathan, the master of his domain. Catherine realized that she had, over the years, succumbed to the attraction of his brash assuredness. In doing so, she had relinquished control over her own life because he was so ready to take the reins himself. Catherine thought about the fact that, whenever they drove anywhere, Nathan always automatically got behind the wheel. There was never any discussion about it, and it didn't even occur to either of them to question who would drive. It was a little thing, but the image of Nathan in the driver's seat was so symbolic of their relationship.

All her life she'd been taken care of. First, by her parents. Then, after their death, by Carey. And then, by Nathan. What would it be like to be on her own? The past year was not really a taste of that, given all she was going through. She tried to imagine what her life would be without Nathan. Not just if he was convicted and sent to prison. But if she, through her own act of will, decided that she didn't want to stay in the marriage. Could she actually do that? She feared what it would do to Nathan, and the specter of guilt felt overwhelming. Besides, she wasn't a risk-taker. And walking away from their marriage was about the riskiest thing she could think of. Even imagining it tightened the knot in her stomach and made her pulse race. And yet, she wasn't the person she was before she'd lost her children. Ironically, their death seemed to have awakened her to the possibilities of her own life.

As she rocked slowly in the moonlight, breathing in the lingering scent of her youngest son as it still clung to his blanket, Catherine watched images of her emerging independence unfold before her. Packing up her possessions and driving away from the house forever. Finding a small apartment in an old Victorian on the East End in Portland and filling it with hanging plants. Walking to work at a coffee shop like The Grind, spending her days greeting customers and bagging beans. Nights sipping from a cup of tea with a cat in her lap, reading and knitting. Or maybe she was thinking too small. Maybe she'd get in the car with a few boxes and a suitcase of clothes and head west. She'd never seen most of the country beyond the Mississippi, and she had friends from college dotting the states between Maine and California. Maybe she'd just take some time to see where the winds blew her, landing here and there for a while, then moving on. Maybe she'd find a ranch in Wyoming that needed someone good with horses. As the moon slid toward the hills, images of an open road and driving toward the setting sun filled Catherine's imagination until she finally drifted off to sleep.

*

Catherine sat in her car in the courthouse parking lot, nervously playing with her hair. It had taken all her willpower that morning to get that far, and she already felt emotionally drained and physically exhausted. She sat staring out the windshield at nothing in particular, trying to summon the strength to get out of the car and walk the fifty yards into the courthouse. It seemed like a journey of a thousand miles.

Catherine was startled by a knock on the passenger side window and Heather's face appearing there. Heather opened the door and climbed in next to her friend.

"You're here." Heather angled herself in the seat toward Catherine.

"Well, physically, at least. I think I'm having an out-of-body experience, though."

"Cat, you can do this. I know you can. Maybe it'd help if you thought about the fact that you're not doing this for Nathan. You're doing it for yourself." Catherine gave Heather a skeptical look, so she continued. "I mean, yes, it might possibly help Nathan. But your being here is showing yourself that you're strong. That no matter how you've had the stuffing knocked out of you, you're still standing. To me, it's a huge step forward."

"But forward toward what, Heather? That's what I just don't have a clue about."

"That'll sort itself out." Heather gave Catherine's arm a squeeze. "C'mon. I'll be with you every step of the way." Heather reached for the handle of the door and Catherine mirrored her movements until both of them were out of the car and headed toward the courtroom.

Catherine was surprised at how crowded the room was. Then she realized that this trial, and Nathan's testimony in particular, was big news for this small county in southern Maine, especially because Nathan was a member of a prominent family that had settled there more than two hundred years earlier. Heather urged Catherine forward toward the bar that separated the gallery from the litigants, and Catherine saw Frank and Jean Osgood seated in the front row, right behind a table where Nathan was conferring with his lawyer. Heather eased Catherine into a chair beside her father-in-law, who offered Catherine a wan smile and a nod. Nathan looked up, saw his wife, and nearly jumped the two steps from the table to the bar.

"Cat, you're here."

"Hey, Nate. Yeah. I'm sorry it hasn't been until now."

"But you're here now, and that's all that matters to me."

"Good luck today." Catherine couldn't think of anything

else to say. Her stomach was twisted in knots; she hadn't felt this nauseous since she was pregnant with Joe. She leaned over and whispered to Heather. "I think I'm going to throw up."

"Take a couple deep breaths, Cat. C'mon, breathe with me."

Catherine did as she was told and the nausea subsided slightly, to the point where she didn't feel like she had to bolt from the courtroom.

"All rise," came the command from the bailiff as the judge entered the room.

"Please be seated," the judge ordered. Then, looking at Carter Pierce, said, "Counselor, the floor is yours."

"Thank you, Your Honor. I call to the stand Mr. Nathan Osgood." There were audible murmurs from the gallery. The judge admonished the crowd.

"Folks, this is not a circus, nor is it a ball game. I am telling you now that I will have zero tolerance for any outbursts. If I need to clear the courtroom so that the jury can consider the defendant's testimony with all the gravity it demands, I won't hesitate to do so."

Nathan waited until the judge concluded his speech to walk to the witness box. After he was sworn in, he took his seat and stated his name for the record.

Carter Pierce first led Nathan through a thorough review of his personal history. The fact that he was a Maine native and had grown up in Newfield. His attendance at local schools. The jobs he'd held through high school in Sanford and Saco. His college and graduate degrees, his time on Wall Street, and his return to Maine to start a business of his own. Pierce wanted to humanize Nathan as much as possible. To help the jury see him as one of their own. To gain their personal sympathies so that, when Nathan related the events of that day in March, they would already know and, hopefully, trust him.

Pierce asked questions that invited Nathan to talk about his boyhood and how he'd spent long hours playing outdoors, even in winter. How he and his friends had fished, skated, and otherwise recreated on and around the icy ponds of southwestern Maine for as long as he could remember. He made sure that Nathan included his family history, going back several generations, in the towns in and around Newfield, and noted all the contributions they'd made as citizens and employers. Nathan related one particular tale about how his great-grandfather had kept the family factory going through the depression, taking money out of his own pocket to pay his workers when the orders dried up.

After establishing Nathan's bona fides as a local boy who had followed in his family's footsteps and started a business of his own, Pierce began a line of questioning about Nathan and Catherine's family life. Nathan told the story of their meeting and courtship. He talked about building their dream house on Mountain Road, of the births of the two boys. Nathan talked about working to instill in his children a love of nature, and how he would take them for frequent hikes in the woods around their home.

The questions and answers flowed past Catherine like logs on a river. After the first few, she scarcely noticed them as they washed downstream. She resisted the urge to look around the high-ceilinged room with its white-washed trim and dark wood paneling. She kept her gaze forward, doing her best to appear calm and confident. Occasionally she would glance at the jurors, but their faces gave no hint to what they were thinking. As Nathan and his lawyer tossed questions and answers back and forth between them, Catherine began to speculate about the lives of the men and women who held the fate of her husband in their hands. Did they have children at home? Had they ever experienced tragedy on the scale of what they were hearing about? What did they do for a living? Were their families intact, or had they been through divorce or even death? Did they notice her sitting here? Did it really matter? Catherine was called back to attention by Carter Pierce's next line of questioning.

"Nathan, I want to shift our focus now," Pierce leaned against the witness box. "I want you to walk us through what happened on March 22nd of last year."

Catherine knew this was coming. Why else would Nathan be testifying? But her body went rigid with the question anyway. Heather placed a reassuring hand on Catherine's forearm, leaned over and whispered to her. "Breathe. Just keep breathing." Catherine did her best, but her throat felt tight, like there was a noose around it. Her breath came in sips and gulps until Heather leaned her entire body against hers, and she began to time her breathing with Heather's own deep inhalations. The rushing sound in her ears began to subside as the defense lawyer continued to question Nathan.

"Nathan, please tell us how you came to be lost in the woods that day."

"It was the time of day. With the change of seasons, the sun was higher in the sky than I'd thought it would be. I must have just taken a wrong turn, and we got off the trail."

"But you found your bearings?"

"Of course. I know those woods really well, although it's trickier navigating them in an ATV than on foot. But I got us back on track and was headed home in no time."

"So you knew you were going north, toward Franklin

Pond?"

"Yes. I decided that, since it was getting late, rather than going back the way we came, I'd take a more direct route."

"So, you came to the shore of Franklin Pond. What did you do then?"

Although he tried not to, Nathan couldn't resist quickly glancing at Catherine. He saw the anguish on her face and hesitated. The entire courtroom anxiously awaited Nathan's response. Nathan took another deep breath. Then he let it out slowly and turned his attention away from his wife, looking his lawyer directly in the eye.

"Nathan?" Pierce encouraged him to answer.

"I stopped on the shore. We sat, idling in the ATV as I thought about what to do next. I looked at the time on my phone, and at the sun setting in the west. I knew the trail around the pond, and I knew it was heavily wooded and overgrown, so it would take forever to pick our way along it in the RZR. The kids were complaining about being cold and hungry and they wondered why we were just sitting there."

"And why were you just sitting there, Nathan?"

"Because I wanted to be sure."

"Sure of what?"

"Sure that we could get across the ice."

"So, what did you do?"

"I took a good, long look at the pond. I saw that, in some places, there was snow, in others bare ice."

"What else did you notice?"

"It all looked pretty even. Not like there was any thin ice, and there certainly wasn't any open water."

"So, what did you do next?" Catherine held her breath as she heard the details of what had happened for the first time. It seemed as if the entire courtroom was doing the same, hanging on Nathan's every word.

"I decided to give the ice a test."

"You tested the ice?"

"Yes."

"How did you do that?"

"Well, I know from experience that the thinnest ice is usually around the edges of the pond," Nathan was emphasizing both his experience and his knowledge. "So, I eased the RZR out onto the ice from the shore, with the wheels just barely on. And then I stopped and waited."

"Waited for what?"

"Waited to see if we'd break through. I even turned off the ATV's engine to listen, to try and hear if the ice was cracking or shifting underneath us."

"And what happened next?"

"Nothing. There wasn't any sign that the ice couldn't hold us. It felt solid. So, I started the RZR back up and headed out across the pond."

"Nathan, I know this is difficult, but can you tell us what happened as you made your way across the ice?"

Catherine stared across the distance at her husband. She could see the distress written on his face. She knew that he didn't want to tell this part of the story, not with her sitting there. She had the urge to dash from the courtroom, not just to preserve her own sanity but for his sake as well. Every cell in her body told her to run. But where could she run to? She knew she could never escape the reality of what had happened next. And some part of her, somewhere deep inside, knew that she needed to hear it, in all its excruciating detail, out of Nathan's mouth. She set her teeth, took a deep breath, and broke eye contact with Nathan so that he didn't have to, so that he could tell her how her children had died.

"Everything was going fine. We were making good time. I wasn't speeding or anything. Probably going about five or ten miles an hour. The ice was solid underneath us, and the boys had quieted down."

"Then what happened?"

"We were approaching the far shore and I had sped up a little, going maybe ten to fifteen miles an hour. Then, we hit a bump. It felt like the left front tire hit a large rock, but I didn't see any rocks. Maybe in the low light I didn't see an ice dam or a buckle or something. But whatever it was, it threw the front tire up in the air and it came down hard. Then the left rear tire did the same thing. But when that tire hit, it broke through the ice."

Nathan had begun to take in great gulps of air himself. He searched for Catherine's face, but it was buried in her hands, downcast in grief. Pierce tried to help Nathan tell the story in digestible pieces by offering him small prompts.

"The rear tire of the ATV broke through the ice?"

"Yes. The back end started to sink, faster than you can imagine."

"What did you do?"

"I unbuckled from my harness as fast as I could. Before I could even turn around, the rear of the machine was half-submerged, and the ice all around it was breaking up. I grabbed for the boys as it sank. I went for Joe first, since he's the smallest. I grabbed the buckle of his harness, but it stuck. I couldn't get it released."

Catherine's eyes filled with tears at the image her husband's words were painting. She knew in that moment her decision to come to the courthouse was a huge mistake, and she felt like a trapped animal, unable to escape the ordeal. Catherine couldn't flee and Nathan was forced to continue assaulting his wife with his testimony.

"Joe's harness was jammed somehow, and the RZR was sinking fast. I couldn't breathe, so I broke for the surface."

"I know this is painful, Nathan. But please go on."

"I took a deep breath and tried to dive back down to the boys. I don't know if it was my clothes, or the cold, or what, but every time I tried to get back to them, I couldn't."

Tears streamed down Nathan's face. He was trying to control his emotions, but the pain was overwhelming. "I just couldn't get to them---"

"What did you do?"

"I felt myself going under. I couldn't feel my hands or my feet and knew I was freezing. I knew I needed to get out of the water to go and get help. I managed to climb back up onto the ice and run to my friend's house."

"Your friend, Jim Richardson?"

"Yes, I knew his house was less than a mile up the trail from the pond. I got there, and we called the police. Then we tried to rescue the boys ourselves." Nathan's voice trailed off, as he recalled the unsuccessful rescue attempt.

"Nathan, I need to ask you one last question, okay?" his lawyer prompted him to re-focus on his testimony. "Before the ATV broke through the ice, did you have any indication, were there any signs, that the ice was going to break, that it couldn't support the ATV?"

"No," Nathan said before the prosecutor had a chance to voice his objection to how defense counsel was leading his own witness.

"I have no further questions, Your Honor."

The judge took a deep breath himself. He eyed the jury, many of whom were teary-eyed, and said, "I think this is a good time for a break. Let's resume after lunch. See you all at one o'clock." He banged his gavel and court was in recess.

Nathan stepped down from the witness stand, and his lawyer placed a reassuring hand on his shoulder as he passed. But Nathan didn't stop to debrief his testimony. Instead, he made his way through the gate in the railing and over to where Catherine was seated, doubled over, her face buried in her hands. Heather and his parents were standing in a semi-circle around them as Nathan knelt down in front of his wife. Sensing her husband crouching in front of her, Catherine threw her arms around him and held on for dear life. There, in the gallery of the courtroom, before a coterie of witnesses, they cried together. For the first time, they grieved together the death of their sons and the unborn child they had lost.

CHAPTER TWENTY-THREE
NATHAN

"Mr. Osgood," the prosecutor addressed Nathan once court had come back to order. "I am truly sorry for your loss. It must be an unbearable burden."

"Thank you," Nathan said. Just as his lawyer had suspected, the District Attorney was going to start out with the "good cop" routine. He would address the bereft father with apparent sympathy, appearing to the jury to be a reluctant pawn in the prosecution of this case.

"I'm sorry that you've had to relive this trauma in front of this court, but the law requires me to bring this matter here."

"Your Honor," Carter Pierce stood up, "would the prosecutor please stop making speeches and get on with his cross-examination of the witness?"

Pierce had warned Nathan that he was going to do whatever he could to disrupt Shepard's approach, and he was starting early. The prosecutor shot Pierce a look of disdain but continued.

"Mr. Osgood, you told the jury this morning that you own

a business, is that right?"

"Yes."

"What kind of business is it?"

"It's a financial planning firm."

"So, professionally, you're a businessman?"

"Yes."

"So, you're not a climatologist, or a geologist, or a meteorologist."

"No."

"You're not a glaciologist, either. Is that right?"

"That's right."

"You have no professional training or background in weather or climate, snow or ice?"

"No."

"You're like the rest of us here. Not an expert when it comes to weather or the winter or ice on lakes, correct?"

Defense counsel rose to his feet, feigning fatigue. "Your Honor, I object. My client has answered the question. No need to keep harping on this." The judge sustained the objection, but Shepard continued unperturbed.

"Do you consider yourself an outdoorsman, Mr. Osgood?"

"I like the outdoors," Nathan said.

"Yes, I'd say we all do here in this fair state. It's kind of a prerequisite for living here, especially to make it through the long, cold winters. Let me ask my question another way: In a typical month, how many hours would you say you spend out of doors? And I don't count walking from your car to your office or doing yard work."

"In a month?" Nathan replied. "Probably five to ten. My sons used to love exploring in the woods."

"So, roughly one day a month."

"Umm, I guess."

"Safe to say, less in winter?"

"I guess so."

"You guess so?"

"I spend less time outdoors in the winter than in the warmer months, just like the rest of us."

"Thank you for clarifying that, Mr. Osgood. So, you probably spend less than one full day a month outdoors in the winter months. So, you're not a big hiker or camper."

Pierce again jumped to his feet to object, and the judge sustained the objection.

"My point, Mr. Osgood, is that all-told you spend, maybe, about seven or eight days a year in the outdoors, in terms of total time, right?"

"It's hard to put a number on it."

"But you're certainly not like a park ranger or a game warden, who basically lives outdoors."

"No."

"You would say that your own 'natural environment' is indoors, either at home or in an office."

"Yes."

"And if you were looking for some expertise on an issue or question related to the outdoors, would you consider yourself an expert?"

"I've done my fair share of camping and hiking," Nathan said, tiring of this line of questioning.

"But do you consider yourself an expert the way, perhaps, you consider yourself an expert in stocks and bonds, or running a business?"

"No, not to that same degree."

"If, for example, you wanted to know whether the ice on Franklin Pond was thick enough to cross, then you would need to consult someone, is that right?"

"Umm. I guess so."

The prosecutor turned to the judge and asked, "Your Honor, would you please instruct the witness to answer the question?"

The judge turned to Nathan. "Mr. Osgood, 'I guess so' is not responsive to the question. Please answer the prosecutor's questions either affirmatively or in the negative."

"I'm sorry, Your Honor," Nathan said. "I'm doing the best I can."

"I'm sure you are, Mr. Osgood. Please continue Mr. Shepard."

"So, I was asking you, Mr. Osgood, whether you have the necessary expertise to determine whether crossing the ice on a pond is safe."

"I'm not an expert in that field, if that's what you mean."

Shepard looked at Nathan with exasperation and turned again to the bench.

"Your Honor---"

"Mr. Osgood, please answer the question directly," the judge scolded Nathan.

"No, I do not have expertise in that area."

"So, when you were sitting on the bank of Franklin Pond in your ATV last March, and you were thinking about whether to try and cross the ice, you had no way of knowing whether the ice would support you and your vehicle, isn't that right?"

"I don't think anyone could be 100% certain."

"Your Honor, the witness continues to be evasive," the prosecutor approached the judge. "Would you please instruct him to answer my questions and refrain from editorializing?"

The judge reprimanded Nathan, it seemed, half-heartedly.

"So, Mr. Osgood," Shepard returned to his line of questioning, "Were you one hundred percent certain that the ice would support you and your ATV before you went out onto it that day?"

"No."

"In fact, you were really unsure, weren't you? I mean, you said earlier that you sat and thought about it. Then you tested the ice near the edge, isn't that right?"

"Yes."

"So, you must have had some doubts." The prosecutor was getting warmed up now, and the jury was paying close attention.

"I was being cautious. I wanted to be careful, to make sure it was safe."

"But the safest thing to do would have been to stay off the ice, isn't that right, Mr. Osgood?"

"Of course."

"And yet, without any professional knowledge or background, without consulting someone like a game warden, as a complete amateur and with no information and no experience, you decided to cross the ice instead---"

Carter Pierce jumped to his feet, interrupting the prosecutor. "Your Honor, the State is testifying here. He can save this for his closing argument, but right now he's supposed to be cross-examining my client."

The judge looked over the top of his glasses at Shepard, who held up his hands in mock apology.

"I'm sorry, Your Honor," he said, knowing full-well that he had made his point with the jury.

"Mr. Osgood, can you tell us again what you were thinking as you sat on the shore of Franklin Pond on the afternoon of March 22?"

"I was thinking that I needed to get my boys home. I was thinking that my wife would be worried about where we were.

I was thinking that it was safe to cross the ice."

"So, with the setting sun, you were feeling pressed for time?"

"Yes."

"But your ATV had headlights, didn't it?"

"Yes."

"So, you could have navigated the woods after dark."

"Yes, but---"

"But you were concerned for your kids and for your wife."

"Yes."

"And crossing the ice was a short-cut."

"Going around the pond would have taken a whole lot longer."

"Which is the definition of a short-cut."

"I guess so."

"So, you decided to take a short-cut that put the lives of your children at risk, even though you could have taken a safer route."

"Objection!" Carter Pierce again leaped to his feet.

"Sustained," the judge replied, looking down at the prosecutor sternly. Shepard, his point having been made, decided to shift tactics.

"Mr. Osgood, before March 22 of this year, had you ever driven an ATV across lake ice?"

"No."

"Did you know how much your ATV weighed as you sat on the shore of Franklin Pond that afternoon?"

"I knew it was about 1,000 pounds."

"Actually, as testimony has shown, it was closer to 1,500 pounds, fully loaded as it was. That's about 50% more than you thought."

"If you say so," Nathan said. The prosecutor was beginning

to get to him. He tried hard to refocus and calm himself down.

"Can you tell us, Mr. Osgood, how thick a sheet of ice needs to be to support a 1,500- pound vehicle driving across it?"

"I don't know."

"Is it two inches or ten?"

"I don't know."

"Or is it twenty? Does the ice need to be three feet thick to be safe?"

"I said, I don't' know." Nathan said through gritted teeth.

"So, if you didn't know how much your ATV weighed, and you didn't know how thick the ice needed to be, how could you even assess whether it was safe to cross that day? If you didn't know those basic facts, even if you had drilled a hole and determined how thick the ice was, you still wouldn't have known if you could safely drive across it in your ATV, isn't that right?"

Nathan sat glaring silently at the prosecutor. After he failed to offer any response or explanation, the prosecutor asked the judge to instruct Nathan to answer the question.

Nathan replied with a barely audible "No."

"In light of all these circumstances, Mr. Osgood," Shepard zeroed in for the kill, "wouldn't the reasonable thing to have done, the *safe* thing to have done, have been to take the trail *around* Franklin Pond, instead of trying to cross it when you had no idea whether it was safe?"

"I did what I could to determine it was safe," Nathan said. "Do I regret my decision? Of course, I do. And I will until my last breath. I made a mistake, pure and simple. And I would give anything to take it back."

"So, Mr. Osgood, you admit that you made the wrong decision."

"Of course. Hindsight is 20/20."

"And that decision was, on its face, unreasonable."

"Objection!" Pierce shouted from the table. "Calls for a legal conclusion."

"Sustained," the judge replied.

The prosecutor walked back to his table and turned toward the judge. "I have no further questions."

Nathan dared not look up as he stepped out of the witness box. He was fuming mad at the District Attorney and he was wrung out from having to publicly relive the accident. He didn't want the jury to see that he was a beaten man. But more than that, he wanted to be sure that he didn't make eye contact with Catherine, who had sat rigidly in the gallery through the whole thing. He knew that if their eyes met, he'd again dissolve into a puddle on the courtroom floor.

The wound from causing his children's death was as fresh in that moment as it had been in the first days following the accident. Nathan fell heavily into the chair beside his attorney, who was informing the court that his defense had concluded. The judge adjourned the court, calling for closing arguments the following morning. Nathan stood with his lawyer as the judge exited the courtroom, his palms flat on the table and his head hanging below his shoulders.

CHAPTER TWENTY-FOUR
CATHERINE

As the rest of the courtroom cleared, Catherine remained in her seat in the gallery. Heather gave a look to Nathan's parents indicating that they should go on without them. They gathered up their despondent son and left. Catherine stared straight ahead, her body rigid. Her unblinking eyes were fixed on a point on the far wall of the courtroom, and her breath was shallow but steady. Heather sat patiently beside her, her own breath coming to match that of her friend. The mid-afternoon sun slanted in through the tall, west-facing windows, illuminating dust motes that danced, unnoticed, around them.

Suddenly, as if waking from a spell, Catherine took in a deep breath of air, and slowly let it out. She turned to her friend.

"Let's go."

The two women rose from their seats and made their way to the parking lot, where theirs were the only cars left.

"I'll follow you home," Heather held her friend in a long

embrace.

"Actually, Heather, I'm going to head over to the barn and take Penny out for a ride. I think it'll do me good." Catherine could see the concern written all over her friend's face.

"I'll be all right. Really, I will." She took Heather's hand in hers and gave it a squeeze

"Will you promise to call me tonight? If you don't, I'll be forced to come over and check on you."

"Sure, Heather. No problem. I'll give you a buzz when I get home."

Heather reluctantly parted company with her friend. Catherine pulled out of the parking lot and pointed her car in the direction of Sunnybrooke Farm. Over the past few months, it had become her refuge and her home away from home.

*

Catherine was grateful that Penny was available to ride that afternoon. She changed into her jeans in the bathroom of the farmhouse, grabbed some tack, and headed to the mare's stall. There, she found Penny standing patiently, as if she'd been expecting Catherine all along. Catherine immediately sensed the horse's gentle presence, a feeling that brought her a deep and immediate sense of peace. Staring into Penny's large brown eyes, Catherine felt the tension of the day begin to melt. Instead of placing the bit in Penny's mouth, Catherine dropped the bridle to the floor and flung her arms around the horse's warm neck. She buried her face in the coarse coat, inhaling its familiar equine aroma. She could feel the horse's heartbeat through her own cheek. Penny stood patiently, accepting the odd gesture, glad to be providing whatever it was that her human companion was receiving from her in that moment.

The two stayed like that until Penny finally shuddered her flanks and broke the spell. Catherine took a step back and wiped her damp eyes with the back of her hand. She reached down to pick up the bridle, saddled up the mare, and led her out of the barn. Catherine mounted Penny and turned her toward the field that led to the vast network of trails that lay beyond the edge of the woods. The bitter cold of the weeks before had shifted into the warmth of an early spring day. The maples and birch trees were showing the soft light green of early buds, and puffy clouds floated on the horizon. Penny knew exactly where it was that Catherine wanted to go, and soon horse and rider were cantering into the woods. The two worked as one, each responding to the feedback of the other in a silent dance between seasoned partners. The steady rhythm of the horse beneath her and Penny's even breath allowed Catherine to leave the trauma of the day's events behind her, at least for a time.

*

Catherine made the obligatory call to her friend as she poured herself a glass of wine. She assured Heather that Penny had worked her magic and that she was okay. As she hung up the phone, she asked herself if it was true. Was she okay? She grabbed her wine and walked from the kitchen to the living room where she sat down in her favorite chair. *Am I okay? What does 'okay' even mean?* She sipped her wine and recalled a recent conversation with Rev. Sue about grief and recovery.

"It feels like people think that, now that it's been a year since the accident, I should be all better." Catherine noticed that the glacier had begun to melt. Rivulets of melting snow and ice stained the sidewalk of the church's courtyard.

"I'm not surprised." The pastor took a sip of tea from the stoneware mug that was her constant companion.

"Someone even asked me the other day if things were 'getting back to normal.' Like I had the flu or something, and that I'm over it."

"People who haven't been through something like you have don't know what to say, because they just don't get it. Grief isn't like a cold that you have for a while, and then it just goes away and you pick up where you left off. Grief is more like an amputation. It's like losing a limb. You're never going to be the same again. You never get 'back to normal.' The pain of the loss is always there, and you've got to learn to live with it, to accommodate and work around the part of you that's gone and will never come back. A football star who loses a leg in a war is going to find a way to adapt, but he's never going to play football again."

As she sipped her wine and considered Rev. Susan's words, Catherine thought about what that might mean for her relationship with Nathan. Was he part of the limb that she'd lost, or was he a part of the body that survived?

*

In the weeks leading up to the anniversary of the accident, Catherine had begun to dream again. She'd always been a dreamer, literally. She was someone who had elaborate and sometimes wild dreams while she slept, and she remembered them vividly when she woke up. As a little girl, she would tell her dreams to her father every morning as they sat together, having breakfast. She didn't have brief flashes, short glimpses of dreams. Hers were full-blown tales that frequently included encounters with dinosaurs, dragons, and other mythical creatures. She dreamt so vividly and so often, and she remembered her dreams so well, that as she got older, she read voraciously about how to interpret them. Over the years, she filled volumes of dream journals that she kept on her nightstand. As a mother, her dreams had shifted and often included her children in some future state of development. Joe as an inventor, making some great discovery. Jacob bringing home his fiancée to meet the family. But when the accident happened, Catherine had stopped dreaming. She didn't even realize it until her dreamlife suddenly resumed and took root.

"I had the most amazing dream last night." Catherine and Rev. Susan were standing in the large church kitchen, waiting for their tea water to boil. Catherine had elected not to return to the trial, knowing that all that was left were the lawyers' closing arguments. "I wasn't in Maine anymore. I was standing on a dock on the shore of Jenny Lake in Wyoming."

"That's pretty specific."

"Yeah, well, I've been there before, when I was a kid, and my parents took us on a summer road trip to visit the National Parks." The pastor poured the water for both their tea and the women walked the short hallway to her office. Catherine sat down, blew on her tea, took a sip, and forged ahead. "In the dream, I was standing there looking at the Tetons soaring above the lake. The lake was so still that I could see the perfect reflection of the mountains in it. It was like the sky and the water shared the same deep blue. The reflection was so perfect it was disorienting. I couldn't really tell which way was up."

Another sip of tea. "What I remember most from the dream is how I felt. It was like I was whole. Like, somehow, I'd put the pieces of my life back together and I could breathe again. It's hard to put into words, but I felt light.

Unencumbered. Free. It was like the memories of the boys occupied a small space in the back of my mind, but they didn't dominate me. It was as if my brain was this really big house that included a small room set aside just for Jacob, Joe and the baby, where I could visit them without feeling destroyed."

Catherine paused to catch her breath.

"That's quite a dream."

"And there's more. As I was standing there by the water, I felt someone walking up behind me. The dock was shaking a little with each approaching step. Then I felt an arm reach around me and offer me a steaming cup of coffee prepared with just the right amount of cream, exactly as I like it. Then another arm wound around my waist and, whoever this was, leaned their chin on my shoulder. We just stood there like that for a while, kind of breathing together. And I felt this deep, deep sense of peace. In my dream, I took a sip of the coffee and turned around, away from the mountains and toward the person who was holding me. I looked up into their face, but it was backlit from the sun rising behind them, so I couldn't tell who this person was."

Catherine sat back in her chair, letting Susan know that she was done with the telling. Susan held the silence and waited for Catherine to offer up her interpretation of the dream.

"That feeling of contentment, that peace, has really stuck with me. That's the biggest takeaway, I guess. The fact that the boys' absence wasn't a searing, open wound anymore. It gives me hope that someday that might actually be the case. I can't imagine it now, but I guess there's something inside me that thinks it could happen."

"I'd say that's pretty significant. What else?"

"Well, when I think about the open expanse of the lake and

its reflection of the sky, it feels like those things could represent the possibilities for the future. The Tetons themselves, being such imposing mountains, might represent obstacles that I need to overcome. They're big, and they're daunting, but they're also not insurmountable."

"And what about the 'mystery man?'"

"I'm frustrated not to have been able to see his face. In fact, I'm not sure it was a man or a woman. It could have been Nathan – he knows how I like my coffee. But it could have been someone else. Anybody, really."

"Maybe not knowing who that was tells you something about where you are right now, with all the uncertainties about reconciling with him."

"I guess. But maybe the bigger idea is that, at some point in the future, there'll actually be someone who makes me feel safe."

"And happy, it sounds like."

"Happiness. Now there's a concept."

*

"Nothing yet?" Catherine had called Nathan to see whether the jury had returned a verdict. It had been three days since the trial concluded and the panel had begun its deliberations.

"Nope. Nothing. My lawyer thinks that, the longer it goes, the better my chances are. It must be that there are some hold-outs who aren't ready to find me guilty."

"I hope so, for your sake, Nathan." Catherine truly wished for Nathan's acquittal, her initial impulse for revenge now tempered by empathy and compassion.

"The waiting is killing me, though. Every time my phone

vibrates, I jump out of my skin."

"I'm sure. Would you rather me not call?"

"Oh, no. That's not what I meant. I'm really glad to hear from you."

Catherine thought it might help her husband if she changed the subject. "Remember those bulbs I planted with the boys? The daffodils are just starting to bloom and the tulips are about halfway up."

"Oh, that's great, Cat. Maybe I could stop by and see them?

Catherine kicked herself for the opening she'd offered Nathan and wondered, in that moment, whether her subconscious was working ahead of her rational brain. "Um, sure. We can work something out."

"I think I'm driving Jim crazy. I mean, he's been great having me here, but especially waiting for the jury I feel like a caged animal. And he's stuck in that cage with me. If this thing goes my way, I'm gonna have to find another place to live."

Catherine felt a surge of adrenalin at Nathan's statement. Was he asking to move back into the Mountain Road house? She took a breath before responding.

"One step at a time, Nate. One step at a time." It was the best she could do under the circumstances.

"Yeah, you're probably right. Have you been riding much, now that the weather's getting warmer?"

Catherine was relieved that her husband had moved the conversation to safer ground. She told him all about Penny and her long rides in the woods, about how good they made her feel, both physically and mentally. The estranged couple exchanged a few more pleasantries before Catherine wished Nathan well.

"I'll keep my fingers crossed, Nathan. Let me know as soon as you hear."

"I will if I can. I'm glad you care, Cat.

"Of course I care, Nathan. You're still my husband."

"Thanks. That means a lot."

After she hung up the phone, Catherine thought about their awkward ending to the call. Did she even know what it meant to say that Nathan was still her husband? Was it merely a statement of their legal status, or something more? And why had she told Nathan about the flowers coming up in the beds around the house? Maybe it was as simple as the fact that she'd spent the day mulching the beds, so they were on her mind, but maybe it, too, was something more.

Catherine had spent that afternoon gardening, digging her hands in the dirt, feeling the grit under her fingernails, getting back to the earth, back to some sense of feeling grounded. She needed to be here, too, to remember a glorious autumn morning she had spent with the boys, more than eighteen months earlier, planting the bulbs that were now bringing color to her world. Jacob was serious and determined in the task. He wanted to be sure that the holes he dug were precisely six inches deep, in a perfect grid, and that the bulbs he planted went in with their roots pointed down. Joe, true to form, was haphazard in his approach. He'd excavate one hole like he was digging to China and the next would be little more than a divot. He'd grab a bulb and toss it in, not caring if it was right-side-up, upside-down, or sideways.

Catherine had smiled at Joe's willy-nilly approach, thinking ahead to a spring with bulbs sprouting every which way or not at all. And once again, she marveled at the contrast between her two boys. They'd come out of the womb two entirely different kids, and this was just one of many ways it showed up in their lives. It certainly had made motherhood interesting and challenging, to say the least. Each of her children demanded a different skillset from her, and they never failed to keep her guessing.

The memory had rocked Catherine back on her heels. She wiped her brow with the back of a muddy hand, leaving a streak across her face. She let the sadness wash over her, not fighting it. She allowed herself to feel the pain as it burrowed deeper and deeper into her belly and spread out through her body. The tears came again, and, leaning forward to spread more mulch, she let them water the garden she'd planted with her boys when they all had had their whole lives ahead of them. And there, on her knees in the garden, surrounded by the flowers her boys had planted, she offered up a silent prayer of gratitude for the beauty that they had left behind.

CHAPTER TWENTY-FIVE
NATHAN

"Ladies and gentlemen of the jury, have you reached a verdict?" The judge wore a weighty expression as the foreman handed a slip of paper to the bailiff. Nathan had met Carter Pierce and his parents in the courthouse parking lot a few minutes earlier and the lawyer had explained what to expect.

"Okay, Nate," Pierce and Nathan walked into the courthouse side by side, Frank and Jean trailing close behind. "Here's what will happen. If the verdict's 'Not Guilty,' then we hightail it out and go celebrate. If it's 'Guilty,' the bailiff will escort you to the cell you were in after you were arrested. I'll make a motion for your release pending sentencing, and the judge should hear it immediately. With luck, you'll be released before dinner time. Got all that?"

Nathan nodded. "Let's hope we're having a celebration lunch and not a last supper." His gallows humor didn't raise anyone's spirits. They turned as a group and climbed the stairs to the courtroom.

The process was just as Nathan's lawyer had described it.

What he'd failed to mention was the knot in Nathan's stomach that formed the moment the foreman handed the bailiff the slip of paper that would determine his fate, and the way his legs felt like jelly when the judge asked him to stand for the reading of the verdict. It took all his effort to get to his feet and stay upright.

"Mr. Foreman, what is your verdict?"

"We find the Defendant guilty on two counts of manslaughter." Out of the corner of his eye, Nathan saw the prosecutor give a quick pump of his arm, like he'd just completed a game-winning pass. Then Nathan's knees started to give out, and he felt his attorney grab his elbow to steady him.

*

The two weeks between Nathan's conviction and his sentencing passed quickly. As the hearing date approached, Nathan received a call from Catherine. Nathan was glad that she'd reached out and offered words of encouragement, but the call had been awkward, leaving him feeling unsatisfied and estranged. He had decided not even to ask whether she would attend the hearing. He feared that she would receive any request as an expression of need or, worse yet, an attempt to exert control over her. He was relieved when she closed the conversation with the words, "See you at the hearing."

The buzz of the courtroom was abruptly suspended when the judge entered and took his place on the bench. The District Attorney was looking relaxed at the prosecution table. He had gained his conviction and it was now in the judge's hands to mete out an appropriate punishment. There was virtually nothing the prosecutor could do to influence his decision.

Across the aisle, things were different. Nathan appeared haggard, as if he hadn't slept at all in the time since he'd last been in court. Carter Pierce was all business, ready to lead a parade of character witnesses through their paces in an attempt to sway the judge toward leniency. Notwithstanding his determination to paint his client in the best possible light, the lawyer's pessimism peeked through.

"We'll do what we can, Nathan," Pierce told his client before they'd sat down beside each other. "But the truth is, we're at the mercy of the court here, and there's no telling what the judge will do."

The judge seated himself and the rest of the courtroom followed, while Pierce remained standing, prepared to call his first witness.

"Please be seated, counselor." The judge surprised Pierce, who instantly obeyed. "I want to keep this hearing as short as possible."

"Your honor," Pierce rose again from his chair. "I assure you we have just a handful of witnesses, and we'll be as brief as we can be."

"I asked you to be seated, Mr. Pierce." The lawyer obeyed and glanced over at Nathan with a shrug of his shoulders. He was as perplexed as his client.

The judge peered over the top of his glasses down at the courtroom. "I have followed this trial with the greatest of interest, and I believe the jury reached a verdict that was warranted by the evidence. Mr. Osgood." The judge looked straight at Nathan. "You showed extremely poor judgment that day in the woods, and with obviously tragic consequences." Nathan nodded slightly at the judge's words but stayed silent.

"And so, you stand convicted by your actions in accordance

with the laws of this State." The judge continued to direct his remarks at Nathan.

"As a jurist, I am committed to principles of justice and fairness. Over the years I've seen people from all walks of life sitting in that chair you're sitting in today. Some very bad people, to be sure. People from whom I need to protect the public, people who need to be protected from themselves, people who, frankly, make me question my faith in humanity." The judge paused to take a breath.

"You, sir, are not one of those people. On the contrary, you are, in my opinion, one of the good ones. A good one who made a bad choice, to be certain, but someone who is trying to do something with his life, to become someone who adds value to our community." Nathan, while still tense, could feel his shoulders relax just a little at these words.

"I have thought long and hard about what an appropriate sentence is in this case. There are basically three reasons for incarcerating a person. First, to keep the public safe from harm. Second, to punish an individual for their actions. And third, to attempt to rehabilitate someone so that they can become a productive citizen. You, Mr. Osgood, are a threat to no one. Rehabilitation seems meaningless in this case, since I doubt you'll ever be in a position similar to the one you were in last March. Besides, I'm sure you've learned that lesson. That leaves us with punishment. And I dare say that waking up every day, knowing that your actions resulted in the death of your children, is punishment far beyond any that I can mete out."

"Would the Defendant please rise," the judge ordered. Nathan and his lawyer obeyed. Nathan's hands were shaking, and he tried to conceal his anxiety by leaning them against the defense table.

"Mr. Osgood, removing you from the community that you're a part of seems, to me, counterproductive and excessive. I therefore sentence you to five years' probation and three thousand hours of community service, of a form and nature to be approved by this court."

The courtroom, populated largely by supporters of Nathan and his family, erupted at the news. They were quickly brought back to order by the banging of the judge's gavel. The prosecutor had jumped to his feet at the announcement and was attempting to get the judge's attention.

"Your Honor!" he shouted over the din. "Your Honor! This is a travesty! The Defendant killed two innocent children. A complete miscarriage of justice!"

"Mr. Shepard, I'd watch your step." The judge was clearly irritated by the prosecutor's outburst.

The District Attorney walked back his remarks. "Your Honor," he continued in a more measured tone, "the jury convicted the Defendant of manslaughter. You can't just turn him loose. What kind of signal does that send to the community?"

"It sends a signal that justice has been, can, and will be done. Your objection is duly noted." The judge returned his attention to Nathan. "Mr. Osgood, you are to report to your probation officer within 30 days. You are free to go." With that, the judge banged his gavel one last time and left the courtroom.

Nathan turned toward the gallery and his eyes met Catherine's. She reached out across the bar separating them and he walked into her embrace. His parents joined them in a group hug, while Carter Pierce looked on, a broad grin spread across his face. Amidst the celebration, Nathan realized just how good it felt. Not to be free, but to be in his wife's arms. He let himself melt into her.

Expecting to see Nathan carted off to jail, no one had planned a celebration. The phalanx of loved ones, business associates, and childhood friends whom Carter Pierce had called to testify milled about in the courthouse parking lot until Nathan called out that he would treat them all to a celebratory lunch at Tito's. The crowd broke for their cars and drove the short distance to the restaurant. It wasn't until the large party was seated around several tables pulled together for the celebration that Nathan noticed that Catherine was not among the celebrants.

*

"I'd like to propose a toast," Nathan's father said after everyone had ordered lunch and drinks had been served. "First, to Carter Pierce," he said, looking down the long table at the lawyer who had seen his family through good times and bad over the years. "Carter, it was touch and go for a while there. You had us concerned. Although this may go down in your books as a loss, we all take it as a win. You are our Perry Mason. Here's to you." Frank raised his glass and, along with everyone else, took a sip. Then he turned toward the end of the table.

"Nathan," he said, momentarily choking up. "Nathan, I'm glad the judge saw in you what all of us know, and what all of us were prepared to testify to: You are a fine man, a good friend, a man of integrity and honor. I am proud that you're my son, and I am glad that you are free. Here's to Nathan. Here's to freedom." Everyone raised their glasses in Nathan's direction, then took another drink. As his father took his seat, Nathan eased his chair back from the table and stood.

"To say that the past several weeks, the past several months, hell, the past year, have been challenging would be an understatement. I want to say first, thank you to the best lawyer in all of New England." Nathan tipped his glass toward Pierce. "I also want to offer a special thank you to my good friend, Jim Richardson." Jim was seated halfway down the table, opposite from Frank and Jean. "Jim, you took me in when I had no place to go, you've been here for me, every step of the way. I don't know how I would have survived all of this without you." Everyone around the table gave Jim a round of applause.

When it had subsided, Jim interrupted Nathan's toast by saying, with good-natured gruffness. "Yeah, but pretty soon I'm gonna start charging you rent."

"Here's to my mom and dad, whose love and support I can always count on," Nathan continued, "and here's to all of you, who have showed up every time I've asked. As they say at the end of *It's a Wonderful Life*, 'No man is a failure who has friends.' I will always remember what you've done for me, and what you've been willing to do." Nathan raised his glass. "Here's to all of you." He put the glass to his lips, and drained it, as the others around the table did the same. "Now, let's eat!"

Nathan took his seat as the servers brought out piles of steaming tortillas and sizzling fajitas. Nathan spent the next hour enjoying his freedom and a good meal with family and friends. For the first time in more than a year he was able to live in, and enjoy, the moment, notwithstanding the absence of Catherine, and of Jacob and Joe.

*

Nathan and Jim sat on the porch of Jim's house watching

the sunset. The air had turned unseasonably warm, to the point where a few mosquitos buzzed around the men's ears. Nathan was feeling content, the pressure of the trial and possible prison time lifted from his shoulders.

"I meant what I said back at the restaurant today, Jim."

"Yeah. Yeah. I know."

"Really, you saved my life."

"C'mon, Nate. You know I don't go in for all that Dr. Phil/Oprah stuff."

The two men sat in silence as the sounds of the forest dissipated with the setting sun.

"I guess I'm gonna have to figure out what's next." Nathan dug in the cooler for another couple of beers, twisted the caps off and handed one to Jim. "I'll start by looking for an apartment."

"Nate, I told you. You don't need to do that. You're not that big a pain to have around."

"No, Jim. I've got to do it for myself. It's part of moving forward, getting on with my life. I can't sit around here waiting and hoping for Catherine to make a move. I need to start mapping out my own future."

"Sounds like a plan. But there's no rush, far as I'm concerned."

*

"Thanks for getting together with me, Cat." Nathan stood as Catherine entered The Daily Grind and gave Jeff, the manager, a wave.

"How've you been doing since the trial?" Catherine was genuinely interested to hear. They hadn't spoken in nearly a month, since the sentencing hearing.

"I guess you could say I'm kind of adjusting. I don't like the phrase, but I'm trying to figure out what a 'new normal' looks like. That's why I wanted to get together." Nathan took a sip of his iced coffee. "I've been camped out at Jim's house all this time, and Jim's been great about it. But it's like an escape from reality if you come right down to it. It's part of the holding pattern that I've been in since..." He let his voice trail off and noticed Catherine shift in her seat uncomfortably.

"No. No, Cat. This isn't about me wanting to move back to Mountain Road." Nathan saw her relax at the statement. "I just wanted to tell you that I've found an apartment. It's up in Saco, so it's closer to work for me. And it's away from Newfield and all the ghosts."

"Ghosts can travel," Catherine spoke the words into her latte.

"I know. I know. But you know what I mean. I've been walking down to Franklin Pond every morning for more than a year. And it's been good for me. But that lake is like a magnet, the hold it has on me. It keeps pulling me back. I think getting some physical distance from it will help me move forward."

"I get it, Nate. Just don't expect a new place to work some kind of magic."

Nathan was frustrated with the turn the conversation was taking. He'd only wanted to let Catherine know about his plans. He tried to get things back on track.

"Anyway, I was thinking that there was some stuff at the house that I could use. The lease starts June first and I was hoping I could come by at the end of the month and pick up some furniture and dishes."

"Of course. Just give me a call when you want to do that."

"Thanks, Cat. I'll let you know." Nathan looked around the

coffee shop. "Something's different in here."

"Oh, yeah. About two weeks ago we did a complete reset of all the shelving and displays." Catherine told Nathan about organizing the shop by continent, region, and country. Nathan saw how her eyes lit up as she spoke, a light he hadn't seen in her in a long, long time.

"I know it's silly to get excited about displaying coffee beans on a couple of shelves, but you know how I've always loved organizing things."

"I do, Cat. Believe me, I get it. I'm pretty happy – maybe 'relieved' is a better word – when I have just a run-of-the-mill, ordinary day at the office. Speaking of which, I've got to get going. Thanks for getting together. I'll let you know when I want to swing by and pick up the stuff."

Nathan rose from his seat, grabbed his iced coffee, and stepped out into the sunny spring day.

*

"Mr. Osgood?" A heavy-set man who looked to be in his mid-50's stood over Nathan with his right hand extended. "I'm George Marshall, your probation officer." Nathan was surprised to see Marshall wearing jeans and a polo shirt. He'd expected a law enforcement officer in uniform. "Why don't you come back to my desk." The man guided Nathan past several government-issued desks occupied by men and women either on the telephone or punching at their computer keyboards.

"Here, have a seat." Marshall gestured to a chair beside a desk like all the others in the room. The probation officer opened a file folder and reviewed its contents briefly. "So, three thousand hours of community service. That's no small commitment."

"It beats the alternative." Nathan was nervous about the process. He didn't like it when he wasn't in control and didn't know what to expect.

"So, let me first say that I'm sorry about what happened and about your boys."

Nathan was thrown off balance by the man's apparent empathy. "Uh. Thanks."

"Mr. Osgood –"

"Please, call me Nathan."

"Okay, Nathan. I want to make one thing clear right up front. I'm here to help you and support you. While you're technically accountable to me, and I have the power to pull your probation if you step out of line, ultimately your success is my success. So, I want you to succeed."

Nathan was again taken aback. He didn't expect to have an ally in this process. He let his probation officer continue.

"So, you don't strike me as a "pick up the trash by the side of the road" kind of person, and three thousand hours would be a lot of trash. Let's talk about how you might serve your sentence that could benefit folks and possibly even be a little rewarding to you."

Nathan and George Marshall brainstormed ideas for nearly an hour before the officer's next appointment showed up.

CHAPTER TWENTY-SIX
CATHERINE

On a Wedensday in late May, Catherine's phone vibrated with a text from Nathan.

Moving Saturday. OK to come by around 8 to pick up some stuff?

Catherine texted back: **Sure. Morning is better. Riding in pm**

In the weeks since their last meeting, when Nathan had told her about getting the apartment, Catherine had spent time collecting items that she thought Nathan might need: Bookcases, lamps, a set of silverware, some of his favorite CD's and DVD's, and a pile of clothes that she'd pulled out of his side of their closet. In one of the boxes, she included several framed photographs of the boys, of the two of them as a couple, and one of the four of them as a family. She didn't do this to be cruel, but to be sure that her and their presence was tangible for Nathan in his new setting. If she were being completely honest with herself, she would have admitted that she wanted to make sure he didn't just "move on" in a new place with a new life without her. She wanted him to be reminded on a daily basis of what he'd lost, just as she was when she walked by the boys' rooms morning, noon, and night.

*

Catherine was cleaning up the few breakfast dishes when she heard a vehicle coming up Mountain Road. She wiped her hands on a towel and went out to the garage to meet Nathan. He got out of his truck and approached her. She allowed him to give her a hug and a friendly peck on the cheek, but she didn't reciprocate.

"Moving day, huh?"

"Yeah. I got a bed and a couch from my folks, so I just need a few things from here."

"Before you start loading up, do you want some coffee? We just got a great new Guatemalan at The Grind."

"You know me; I never turn down coffee." The two of them walked in through the garage and made their way toward the kitchen. Catherine realized that this was the first time her husband had been back in the place since he'd come to see her after his release from the hospital. Their last encounter had been anything but pleasant, and Catherine noticed how different she felt this time. She speculated that Nathan might be sensing the change as well. She pointed out the pile of household goods in the corner of the mudroom.

"I pulled together some stuff I thought you'd want for the new place."

"You didn't have to do that, Cat." He walked into the kitchen and took a seat at the bar just like it was any other Saturday morning. Catherine pulled a small bag out of the pantry and scooped the aromatic beans into the grinder.

"I know." As the coffee brewed, the two looked around awkwardly. Catherine moved to the sink and busied herself there, keeping her back to Nathan as he took in the scene. She wondered what he was thinking. Was he trying simultaneously both to remember and to forget as she often found herself doing? Nathan noticed the sheet of poster board sitting on the table in the breakfast nook and walked over for a closer look.

"I put that together on the anniversary." Nathan held up the collage that must have had a hundred pictures glued to it.

"It's beautiful." The words caught in his throat. He returned the colorful assemblage of memories to the table and sat down again at the bar and they fell into another one of their uncomfortable silences as the coffee brewed.

"Well, this is awkward." Catherine thought that naming it might break the tension.

"Sure is. Where is that big, old elephant? I know he's right here in the room, but I can't spot him."

"Yeah, he's here all right." Catherine poured them each a mug, adding milk to hers and handing Nathan his black, the way he liked it.

Nathan blew across the top of his mug and looked at his wife. "Is it hard? Living here, surrounded by all this stuff? The stuff from our old life?"

Catherine hadn't anticipated having a heartfelt conversation with Nathan this morning. She had planned to help him load up his truck and send him on his way. But she's the one who had invited him in for coffee, so she had set herself up for this.

"It's gotten easier. And in some ways, I'm glad I'm here. It keeps me close to the boys. Or, I should say, it keeps them close to me. For a long time, I couldn't walk by their rooms or look at a picture without turning into a puddle – and I still do sometimes. But now, for the most part, I take comfort in being around their stuff." They sat in silence then, staring into their coffee cups.

Nathan tried to stifle them, but as he sat there in his old home, drinking coffee from his favorite mug, sitting close to his wife, tears welled up in his eyes. When he tried to sniffle them back, Catherine looked up at him, and her heart broke. She could see the depth of his pain. She could see how the weight of his guilt was pressing down on him. As their eyes met, both of them broke down.

"I'm sorry, Cat. I'm so, so sorry."

Catherine set down her mug and went to him, taking him in her arms and holding his head against her chest.

"I know you are, Nate. I know you are." She stroked his head as if he were one of her sons who had come home from school having been bullied, offering as much comfort as she could. Nathan curled his arms around her waist and held on for dear life. Catherine let him cry it out, her own tears dripping onto the front of her blouse and mingling with his.

Catherine made a decision. It might be one she later regretted, but it was her conscious choice, and in that moment, it felt good. She separated herself slightly from Nathan's grasp and took his hand. Without a word, she led him out of the kitchen and into the front hallway. As she gently tugged his hand – he didn't resist in the least – she led him up the stairs and through the door of the master bedroom. Still in silence, as he stood in the middle of the room, Catherine slowly and deliberately undressed in front of him until she was wearing only her panties. Then, with the same deliberation, she slowly undressed him. Once Nathan was naked before her, she again took his hand and led him to the bed, where she gently laid him down. Still, without a word between them, with equal measures of pathos and passion, she climbed on top of him and made love to him.

*

"You did what?" Heather could not believe her ears when Catherine called that evening and told her what had happened.

"Shhh. Keep your voice down. I don't want you to wake your kids!"

"You drop that bombshell, and you expect me to keep quiet?"

"I know. I know."

"So, how was it? And how do you feel now?"

"It felt good, Heather. I mean, we fit so well together. We always have. So physically, it felt really good. But this time it was different, too. I was the one calling the shots. I was the one in control. And that felt *really* good."

Heather couldn't resist the temptation to prod her friend good-naturedly. "Watch out. Catherine, the Dominatrix is on the loose!" She quickly turned serious again. "So, what's next?"

"I have no idea. And I told Nathan that. When he left, I told him not to read anything into what happened and certainly not to think that things are magically all okay between us. I've probably given him more hope than he had when he pulled in the driveway, but I went out of my way to try and manage his expectations. He's still moving into the place in Saco, and we didn't make any firm plans to see each other again. So, who knows? I've got time and space to sort it out."

"The plot thickens..." Catherine could almost feel her

friend's smile over the phone as she spoke.

"We shall see." Catherine hung up and went to the doors leading out to the deck. As she looked out over the valley, she could feel the seeds of doubt about what she'd done taking root.

*

Catherine spent the next several weeks replaying in her head what had happened, trying to figure out her motivation and how she felt about it. Eventually, she settled on the simplest explanation: two people with a shared pain had sought comfort in each other's company. But what really stuck with her about it was that she felt like she was in charge of her actions. *She* had made the decision to take Nathan in her arms. *She* was the one who led him upstairs. *She* had exercised the power to decide how far to take it, and she took it as far as she wanted. It wasn't lost on her that Nathan had acquiesced each step of the way, but that was insignificant compared to how she had claimed her own agency. And how empowered she felt by it. It was almost like a drug. She wanted to feel that way again and again.

*

As spring gave way to summer, Catherine's life took on a rhythm of its own. She worked at The Daily Grind four days a week, and she went out to Sunnybrooke Farm to ride Penny as often as she could. She and Penny had become fast friends, and riding, too, helped her claim her own power. Horse and rider were partners, yes. But when she was atop Penny, Catherine was in control. She decided where they would go, and how far and how fast. Through the most subtle pressure in her thighs and her heels, she directed the 1,000-pound beast. She was like the conductor of an orchestra, and Penny the first violin. Yes, Penny could do everything she did without her, but it was Catherine who controlled the pace and direction.

By the Fourth of July, a relentless, muggy haze had set in, enveloping all of New England in an oppressive torpor. This happened every summer in Maine – a blast of tropical weather that lasted a couple of weeks – but this year it arrived earlier than usual. Catherine found it impossible to sleep. She got out of bed and padded down to the kitchen and made herself a cup of herbal tea. Even though it was the dead of night, it was warm enough to curl up on one of the deck chairs and to gaze up at the sky. It was a moonless night and due to the humidity, the stars were hazy dots, each one adorned by a halo. In the distance she heard the familiar call and response of a pair of great horned owls.

As she sat, Catherine's thoughts turned to Nathan. They'd seen each other twice since he'd moved into his apartment. Both meetings had felt less awkward than when they'd gotten together earlier in the spring. He seemed to be finding his footing, from what she could tell. He'd told her how things at the office had stabilized and even turned around, and how he was thinking about volunteering for the local rescue squad. She saw in him glimmers of the old Nathan. The one that had drawn her in a decade ago. She felt pangs of jealousy that his recovery seemed to be moving forward while she languished in her grief. Then she remembered something Rev. Susan had told her:

"There is no such thing as the 'Grief Olympics.' Recovery is not a competition."

It was times like these that Catherine felt like she'd never be healed. She drained the last of the tea from her cup, called out to the owls with a "who-whooo" of her own, and went back to bed.

It was mid-morning before Catherine rallied. Although the oppressive heat was still bearing down on the region, there was a hint of a breeze that signaled a change to more seasonable weather. She called Heather and invited her over that evening to watch the sunset. "I'm going to head up to the stable this afternoon and take Penny out for a ride." Catherine balanced the phone between her ear and her shoulder as she pulled on her riding jeans. "But I should be home by six or so." It had been several weeks since she and Heather had gotten together, and Catherine was anxious to share with her best friend some of her recent thinking about her future.

Catherine had the sense that Penny was waiting for her when she walked into the stall. The horse nuzzled into her shoulder as Catherine patted her on her neck. As she offered Penny the bit, Catherine stroked the rubbery muzzle of the animal, its whiskers prickling the palm of her hand. Everything about Penny felt familiar to Catherine. Her ruddy aroma. The coarse hair of her mane. The swishing sound her tail made to chase away the barn flies. Catherine felt as much at home here as any animal did, from the barn cats to the horses themselves. She saddled Penny up and led her out of the barn into the steamy summer sunlight. Catherine mounted her and guided her at a walk past the riding rings and toward the trails that wound their way through the woods.

*

Horse and rider were both breathing heavily, Penny flying along at a full gallop. Sweat glistened on the mare's flanks and Catherine's shirt was soaked with her own perspiration. She was bent low over the horse's neck as they threaded their way through the trees. Dappled sunlight filtered through the pine boughs, creating pools of light and shadow that lit the pair like a strobe. They both knew this trail well, having traveled it often over the past few months. Catherine trusted Penny and surrendered the reins willingly. She squeezed the horse's flanks with her thighs, crouching above the saddle as it rocked beneath her in a steady rhythm. Astride Penny, Catherine's mind was emptied. Emptied of the grief of losing her children. Emptied of agonizing over her future. *This is what freedom feels like.*

Catherine sensed the horse's panic just a split-second after Penny herself reacted, but that instant made all the difference. The horse unexpectedly broke its gait and veered sharply off the trail to avoid some unseen hazard. Catherine, unable to react in time, suddenly found herself hurtling through the air. At first, the sensation of flying was enjoyable, even serene, just an extension of her movement through space atop the horse. But her flight came to a bone-crushing end against a large outcropping of granite that knocked the wind out of her and cracked several ribs. Catherine's head glanced off the rock, and she saw stars. As her body landed at the foot of the boulder, everything went dark as suddenly as if someone had flipped a switch.

*

Catherine lay on her side with her back against the large rock that had broken her fall, her aching head cradled in her arms. She had no sense of how much time had passed since she'd been thrown from the horse. She inhaled in shallow sips, trying to minimize the searing pain of her broken ribs. Her head pounded, and she knew from her blood-stained blouse that she must have cut open her scalp when she hit the unforgiving granite. She had trouble focusing her eyes.

Concussion. Call for help. She patted the pockets of her jeans, then remembered that she'd left her phone in her car.

Catherine tried to stand up, but even the slightest movement sent lightning bolts of pain through her body and set her head spinning. Her thoughts, like her breathing, came in short bursts.

Not. Going. Anywhere.

Thirsty.

Penny. Help. She clucked her tongue, hoping the horse was nearby.

No answer.

Gonna be sick. Catherine vomited onto the ground beneath her.

That's not good. Should have worn a helmet.

So sleepy.

Catherine closed her eyes and again slipped into unconsciousness.

CHAPTER TWENTY-SEVEN
NATHAN

"Nate, I'm worried that Catherine might be in trouble." Nathan had picked up the call from Heather as he sat reading a prospectus in his apartment. It was a hot summer night, and he was grateful for the air conditioning in the renovated mill building. The fact that Heather was calling him had given him cause for concern before he'd even heard the strain in her voice.

"What kind of trouble?" Nathan was on high alert.

Heather told him about the plans she'd made with Catherine to meet for a drink and how Catherine was nowhere to be seen. Then she told him how she'd driven to Sunnybrooke Farm and found Catherine's car in the parking lot with a riderless horse standing beside it.

"I called 911 and a sheriff's deputy came right out to the farm. She alerted some rescue folks and I think they're assembling a search party out there. But she told me that they're not going to start to look for her until daylight."

"Well, I'm not waiting for the sun." Nathan was feeling his

own surge of adrenalin, and his voice took on a "take-charge" tone that was familiar to her. "Thanks for calling, Heather." He didn't wait for his wife's friend to say goodbye before clicking off the line and immediately calling Jim.

"Catherine's in trouble. Can you load your four-wheelers and meet me at Sunnybrooke Farm, up in Limerick?"

"See you there in twenty."

Nathan clicked off the call, grabbed his truck keys and a jacket and headed out the door.

*

Jim and Nathan arrived at the farm nearly simultaneously, and they were bathed in the pulsing blue lights of the sheriff's cruiser as they strode toward the farmhouse. Nathan was relieved to know that emergency personnel were already there. The men walked into the farmhouse. Nathan immediately recognized the sheriff's deputy who had shown up at Jim's house more than a year earlier, and he saw a flash of recognition pass her face.

"What's the latest?" Nathan approached the deputy, who was seated at the dining room table along with two other uniformed men and a man in jeans, none of whom he recognized. They were all gazing at a large map spread out on the table. The intricate network of trails reminded him of an anatomy book he'd once seen illustrating the human circulatory system.

"Mr. Osgood, we're just going over the trail map with Lee, here." She nodded toward the one civilian at the table. The man extended his hand to Nathan. "Lee Gordon."

The deputy pulled Nathan aside. "Lee owns the farm and much of the woods behind it."

"But there's no sign of Catherine?"

"All we've got to go on is the fact that the horse she usually rides showed up at the barn without her, and her car is parked in the driveway." The deputy pointed out the window. "It's a safe bet she was thrown and is out there somewhere."

Nathan turned his attention to the map on the table. "There's got to be fifty miles of trails."

"More like 150." Lee shook his head slightly.

Nathan ran his hands through his hair in frustration. "So, where do we start?"

Everyone around the table looked to the sheriff's deputy. "That's what we were just talking about."

Lee pointed to several areas on the map. "The good news is that we can eliminate a lot of these trails. Some are too steep and rocky. Others are old and overgrown."

"We should probably prioritize the most heavily-used trails, don't you think?" The deputy looked around for agreement. "Can you highlight those for us, Lee?" She handed him a marker, and Lee leaned over the map, pausing to think it over. Then he began to run the highlighter along a matrix of trails.

"There are a few main intersections where we won't know which way she went."

Nathan leaned over the map, and an idea occurred to him. "This might sound stupid, but could the horse tell us?"

"That's not out of the question. Penny's got a good head, and she and Catherine are a good team. We could certainly take her out on the search."

Nathan turned and directed a question to the deputy. "What about a chopper?"

"I've asked the Staties for one of theirs, but it won't be airborne until first light."

Nathan began to pace around the small dining room. "We need more manpower."

"Mr. Osgood, we can't responsibly start the search until morning. If you want to round up some folks to help, be my guest. But we're not sending people out into those woods until sunrise. Got that?"

Nathan stood toe to toe with the deputy. He was a full six inches taller. "What do you mean? Catherine might be injured. She might be in shock. We can't wait another eight hours to start the search."

"That's our policy."

"Screw your policy!" Nathan was shouting now, his face a deep crimson. "Jim and I have ATVs right outside, and we're not gonna sit around twiddling our thumbs waiting for daylight."

The deputy was unfazed by his aggression but took a conciliatory step back. "The best thing you can do to help your wife would be to round up everyone you can for the morning so that we can set up an organized search party. Please, Mr. Osgood, don't complicate this for everyone."

Nathan was having none of it. He stormed out of the farmhouse, Jim trailing behind him. Nathan strode toward the ATVs on Jim's trailer.

"Nate, there's a reason they have these policies in place."

"I don't give a flying fuck about their policies." Nathan wheeled around on his friend. "If you're not going to help me look for Catherine, why don't you just go back inside and sit around sipping coffee like the rest of them."

"Look, Nate, I'm on your side, okay? Here's what I think we should do. Most of this is Lee's land, right?"

"Right."

"So, if it's private property and the property owner gives

us permission to take a ride around, no one can stop us, can they?"

"I see where you're going with this."

"Right. Let me go inside and see if I can get a private word with Lee. I'm sure he'll agree to let us go. You start untying the rigs from the trailer, so we're ready to take off."

Ten minutes later, Nathan and Jim were riding across the open fields of Sunnybrooke Farm, headed toward the woods on the far side. Jim was right. Although she strenuously objected, there was nothing the sheriff's deputy or anyone else could do to stop them.

*

Nathan and Jim were armed with a copy of the trail map that Lee had handed them in the driveway. The farm's owner had marked a handful of trails on this version, indicating the ones that he guessed were among the most likely Catherine had taken earlier in the day. As the two men left the open field behind them and entered the woods, they pulled up, side-by-side, dismounted their machines, and consulted the map by the light of their headlights. The trail diverged just after it entered the forest and they needed to make their first and most critical decision: whether to turn right or left.

"Looks like there are more good trails down this way," Jim indicated toward the left on the map. Although a few trails to the right were highlighted, there were more in the other direction.

"Makes sense." The two men climbed back aboard their ATVs and took the trail to the left. They rode slowly, scanning the sides of the trail for any sign of Catherine. Because the machines were noisy, every few hundred yards they shut them down, took off their helmets, and shouted her name. They only heard their echoes in response.

It was slow going. After an hour, they'd only gone about a mile and a half from where they had entered the woods. Within that distance, they'd had to make three different decisions where the trail had forked, and each time it was basically a coin toss. Nathan began to feel the futility of their little sortie. He realized that they were just taking a shot in the dark and that it would take massive amounts of manpower to cover all the possible routes that Catherine might have taken. As they sat astride their machines during one stop, calling Catherine's name out into the void, Nathan acknowledged as much to his friend.

"This is starting to feel hopeless."

"Yeah, but we're here, and we're trying. It beats sitting around staring at each other back at the farmhouse."

Nathan nodded, donned his helmet, and started up his four-wheeler. The men continued to pick their way along the trail that wound endlessly through the woods.

*

The two men switched off their machines. They were perched at the top of a hill, with views in every direction. This was the western end of the network of trails they had painstakingly followed for the past several hours. Nathan took off his helmet and turned toward the east, where the sky was turning from black to a dull grey. The sun would be up in another hour or so. Both men were wrung out from the search. Having reached the end of the trail, they felt the full impact of its futility.

"We knew we were looking for a needle in a haystack,

Nate." Jim clapped his friend on the shoulder. "We gave it our best shot."

Nathan gazed off into the distance and nodded. His body was here, but his mind was elsewhere. Through the fear of what might have happened to Catherine, he was thinking that the night's excursion was a metaphor for his attempt to reconcile their relationship and save their marriage. Catherine was somewhere out there, and Nathan was desperately seeking to reunite with her. He was doing what he could but wasn't sure Catherine was reciprocating. He was riding around in the dark, turning this way and that, hoping by some miracle to find her. He wanted desperately to show her how much he still loved her, but he couldn't get to her. It was almost like she didn't want to be found, that a reunion wasn't what she was looking for.

Jim broke into his friend's reflection. "I guess we'd better start making our way back. They'll be gearing up for the official search, and we'll want to be in on that."

Without saying a word, Nathan strapped on his helmet, started his ATV, and wheeled it back in the direction from which they'd come. Just as it's always quicker to follow a maze from the center to the start, the ride back to the stable took only a fraction of the time that it had taken them to get to the hilltop. They stopped several times along the way to shout Catherine's name and to listen for a response, but at this point, Nathan was prepared to hand over the search to the experts.

*

Nathan and Jim went back to Jim's place to crash for a couple of hours, but Nathan was too anxious to sleep. He slipped out the front door, down the porch steps, and made his way down the familiar trail to the shore of Franklin Pond. Nathan sat down on the boulder that had sat there for millennia, a silent sentinel on the shore, and watched as a loon with a lone chick paddled across the serene surface as the sun peeked over the horizon in the east.

This is where it all started. It looks so calm, so peaceful. How could it be the site of such devastation? What has my life become? What will it become if Catherine is seriously injured, or worse? Is life just a random series of events? The luck of the draw? If I had steered the RZR just a few feet either way, I'd have missed whatever it was that I hit, and none of this would have happened. Is that it? Do we hang onto life just by a matter of a few inches, within the slimmest margin of safety?

In that moment, for the first time since he'd lost Jacob and Joe to the icy depths of the lake, Nathan realized – really felt down in his bones – that what's done can never be undone or even fully atoned for, no matter how hard he tried. With this revelation, he experienced a kind of release from his guilt and his constant self-flagellation. Not that he absolved himself of responsibility for what had happened. But the yoke of remorse and regret that had for so long weighed him down felt lifted from his shoulders. His future, which had looked only grey and dismal, held for the first time the possibility for sunshine.

Nathan's phone vibrated in his pocket, and he answered Jim's call.

"Lee just called. The chopper's on its way and the search parties are ready to fan out. Let's get back to Sunnybrooke and see what we can do to help."

*

The farm was a beehive of activity. Emergency vehicles

from around the county and the state were scattered along the driveway, and a large crowd was huddled in the parking area. Their heads turned as one to the throbbing sound of a helicopter approaching from the north.

The sheriff's deputy looked at her watch. "Right on time." The State Trooper helicopter settled into the paddock, and the aerial search team disembarked.

The searchers, about thirty in all, gathered in a circle around a state game warden, who was obviously the officer in charge.

"We've got a lot of ground to cover. We're lucky that a lot of daylight and good weather are on our side. Lee Gordon here, the owner of the farm, is going to get a head start leading the horse that Mrs. Osgood was riding yesterday. We're hoping she'll lead us to the right spot, or at least help us to narrow the search parameters."

Lee had already mounted his horse and was holding Penny's lead in his hand. He turned them toward the field that led to the trails. The warden continued: "When we get to the edge of the woods, we'll fan out along the trails according to the plan we discussed earlier."

The blades of the helicopter began to turn slowly as the engine whined to life. The phalanx of state and local authorities shouldered their backpacks and began hiking toward the forest. Nathan and Jim approached the warden.

"I'm Nathan Osgood, Catherine's husband. We rode the full length of this trail overnight." Nathan traced their route out on the map. "Out and back. We didn't see any sign of her there. Where would you like us today?"

"Thanks, Mr. Osgood. I know you're concerned about your wife, but we've got this covered. The best thing you can do is sit tight and wait. With this many people looking, and with the chopper, I'm sure we'll find her pretty quickly."

Nathan looked at the warden blankly, not knowing how to respond. He wanted to share in his confidence, but he was tired, frustrated, and worried. "But we can just gas up our machines and head back out."

"Truly, sir, we've got this. To be honest, you'd probably kinda complicate things if you went back out. Then I'd need to worry about you in addition to your wife. Please, go home. Take a shower and get some sleep. I'm sure we'll find her within a few hours."

Jim tugged at his friend's elbow. "Nate, I think we need to listen to the pros here. Let's load up our machines and head back to my place." Before walking away, Nathan gave his cell number to the warden.

"We'll be sure to call the moment we find her." Jim and Nathan turned back to their ATVs and began loading them onto Jim's trailer.

CHAPTER TWENTY-EIGHT
CATHERINE

Catherine had no idea what time it was. The woods were quiet, which meant that it was late, past the time when the insects were most active. She was thankful for the absence of mosquitos. She wondered whether anyone had noticed her absence and realized that Heather was the only one who knew where she'd gone that afternoon. She prayed that her friend figured things out. She'd never let her down, and Catherine rested in the assurance that today wouldn't be a first.

She lifted her head slightly and noticed that the nausea-inducing dizziness had subsided. The pain in her ribs was still sharp, but she managed to struggle to a sitting position with her back against the rock. She was dying to suck in a deep breath of the night air, but she resisted the urge. The shallow breathing had dehydrated her, and she began to feel desperate for water. Fear crept up from the pit of her stomach and into her throat. How long will it take for someone to find me? *Don't panic. It won't do you any good to panic.* With her cracked ribs, she couldn't use the deep breathing techniques Carey had taught her long ago as a way to calm herself. She was on the edge of losing it.

Catherine tried to estimate how far she and Penny had ridden from the trailhead. *Two miles? Maybe three?* Not an insurmountable distance under normal circumstances. She also tried to assess her options but found it challenging to put together a string of coherent thoughts. *Sit tight. Walk back. Which way is 'back?' Where's the trail? Can I follow it? I can't breathe. How can I walk if I don't know the way?* Catherine could feel the cold hand of despair gripping her shoulder, holding her down.

*

Catherine's need for water became intense and all-consuming. The pain from her ribs radiated throughout her body, and her arms and legs felt heavy. All she wanted to do was go back to sleep. Instinct told her that this was a bad idea, so she fought off the fatigue and tried to formulate some kind of a plan.

She deduced that, since her back was against the rock that she'd hit when Penny threw her, the trail back toward the barn should be right in front of her. She was facing the way toward water, toward home, toward the warmth of her own bed, where she could sleep for weeks to her heart's content. She pressed her hands against the rock and slowly levered her legs under her until she was in a standing position. Her body swayed like a palm tree in a hurricane. She held a hand against the rock for balance and tried to peer down the dark trail. When she felt steady enough, she took a few tentative steps.

*

Without a flashlight on a moonless night, it was impossible for Catherine to know whether or not she was keeping to the trail that would lead her back to the barn. She had to stop every few steps and lean against a tree or a rock to regain her strength and balance. Each time she paused, fatigue threatened to drag her under. It was as if the earth itself was pulling her down, calling to her to rest in the soft bed of pine needles and succumb to sleep. Her throat was parched, and the few times she shouted for help, her voice was reedy and weak. Her head was pounding now, and she feared she might be doing damage to her already-injured brain by stumbling along the trail as she was. Every breath drew a stabbing pain as her lungs pressed against her shattered ribcage. She held one arm wrapped tightly across her chest in a vain attempt to hold things in place. She stretched her other arm out in front of her to ward off unseen, low-hanging branches and to find purchase on a rock or tree when she needed to take a break.

Because her vision was impaired by the impenetrable darkness, Catherine had no idea that she had veered far off the trail that might have led her to safety. All she knew was that, with every step, her determination waned and her fatigue grew in inverse proportion. Just as she was giving serious thought to sitting down and resting, her foot caught on a protruding root, and she tumbled toward the earth. She saw stars as her body bounced and slid down a tree-lined slope and came to rest at the bottom. She could hardly breathe for the pain she was in, and tears leaked from her eyes. She didn't have the strength to pick herself up, and she allowed herself to be swallowed up by the ground beneath her, which held her close as she quickly lost consciousness.

*

Through closed eyelids, Catherine could tell that the sun had risen. She'd made it through the night. Her head was pounding, but she also felt like there was something else throbbing outside of her body, somewhere above her. She couldn't even lift her head for the pain, and her breathing was erratic. *Am I hallucinating? Are those voices?* She tried to raise her own, but she only emitted a weak squawk through her dry, cracked lips. She tried to raise an arm to wave, but even that effort exhausted her. Then she felt hands on her, gently pressing on her neck, her wrist. Was she dreaming this, or had she been found? A voice, disembodied and distant: "We've got you, ma'am. Stay with me." And then, as if someone had drawn a curtain across her eyes, everything went black.

*

Catherine loved it when she had dreams that she could fly. She hadn't had one in a while, but she always awoke from them feeling light and breezy, as if she were a feather dancing on air. They usually followed the same pattern: She was spending an ordinary day, doing ordinary things like running errands or chasing the kids around the yard. At some point in the dream and for some unexplained reason, it would occur to her that instead of walking, she could simply lift off from the ground. Her flying was like a magic trick; by a simple act of will, she would levitate from wherever she was standing, and soon she'd find herself soaring high above the treetops. She didn't fly like a plane or a bird. She floated, more like she was in a hot-air balloon, with the world passing serenely beneath her. It was a peaceful experience that she would wake up from refreshed, delighted, and a little bit disappointed when she realized that she was actually an earth-bound creature.

This dream was different. She was flying, yes, but the air was turbulent. Instead of floating and feeling free, she was being buffeted about, and she felt hemmed in. Like she was tied down. She had no control over where she was going. Instead, she was a puppet being held up by strings in the hands of an unruly child. And unlike her usual dream, where it was always quiet, this one was noisy. The din was deafening. She longed to escape this dream but couldn't. She didn't know how. She felt a gentle but firm hand on her shoulder, startling her.

"Just try to be calm, ma'am." *Why is a man shouting in my ear? And why is it so loud?* "We're almost there."

What kind of dream is this? Her head, neck, and arms were strapped down tight. She felt trapped, which added to her rising anxiety. When she tried to move, she felt a sharp, stabbing pain in her chest. She realized that struggling was futile, and she quickly gave up. As she relaxed, she drifted down into a deeper level of sleep, and soon the bad dream dissolved beyond the edges of consciousness.

*

A team of emergency medical professionals dashed to the helicopter the moment it touched down in the hospital parking lot. They loaded Catherine onto a gurney and rushed her to the emergency room, where the doctors and nurses went to work hooking her up to IVs, oxygen, and multiple monitors, trying to stabilize her vital signs. After taking a series of x-rays, they bound up her broken ribs. Their primary concern was her head injury. The x-rays revealed a skull fracture. With her vitals stabilized, the doctors hurried Catherine off for a CT scan, which showed a significant swelling of her brain. The team administered drugs that they hoped would reduce the inflammation, which was pushing against her skull. Stabilized, but still unconscious, she was transferred to the ICU. All they could do now was watch and wait.

*

Catherine lay out on a blanket on the desert floor. The vast expanse of the Universe spread out beyond her field of vision in every direction. The Milky Way extended from horizon to horizon like a garden path splashed across the sky. Catherine breathed in the dry desert air and released it slowly, lowering her gaze. She noted the dark silhouettes of the rock formations of Joshua Tree National Park that surrounded her. She couldn't remember the last time she'd felt this relaxed. Gazing up into the heavens, it felt like her body was rising up and becoming one with the stars. She reached out to take the hand of the person lying next to her. The simple touch grounded her, reassuring her that the laws of gravity were still in effect, still holding her fast to the earth.

"There's a Native American legend that says that every one of those stars is the spirit of someone who came before us."

The voice was soft and comforting, but Catherine felt herself tense up at the thought, remembering her two boys. She took a breath and felt the tension dissolve as quickly as it had arrived. She couldn't pinpoint when it had happened. But now she could bring to mind memories of Jacob and Joe, hold them tenderly, and then release them without falling into the gaping abyss of grief. She realized that she had survived the loss that had threatened to drag her under forever. That she had visited

Hell itself and returned. Not unscathed, but alive. She knew she wasn't the person she once was. The fabric of her life had been irreparably rent and, although it was expertly patched, the tear would always be there, like a scar. But now, from this vantage point where distance and time stretched to infinity, she saw that the cloth was far larger than she could ever have imagined. And she knew that it continued to be woven on the loom of her own life and of the larger Life of which she, and they, were but a small part.

Taking in another breath, Catherine scanned the heavens to see if she could pick out the two stars that she could call her own. A sense of deep contentment overtook her when she realized that those two stars – any two stars – were cast up in the firmament not as single points of light, but as part of vast constellations that would be whirling through the Universe forever. Each star, she thought, is a single entity unto itself, but it's not alone. Every star draws planets and comets into its gravitational field. Each one radiates life-giving light and heat across unimaginable distances. They are related to everything and everyone who has ever been and will ever be, including me. There is nothing that can separate us. Even death. In that moment, Catherine felt closer to her two boys than she had at any time since she'd lost them, maybe even since the times when each of them was barely a seed growing deep inside her womb.

*

Nathan was dozing in the chair beside the bed when Catherine's eyes fluttered open.

"Nate, can you turn the lights off?" She recognized her husband by scent before sight. "They're giving me a headache."

"Hey, there." Nathan reached for the switch on the wall of the hospital room. "You gave us all quite a scare." He gripped Catherine's hand.

"I'm so tired."

"You took quite a beating." He stroked the back of his wife's hand. "The best thing you can do is rest. I'm just glad to have you back." Nathan bent down and kissed her on the forehead, just below the bandages that wrapped her fractured skull. "Carey is on her way up from New York. She should be here tonight."

"I don't even remember what happened." Catherine's voice was a feathery whisper, all she could manage. "But I had an amazing dream. Remind me to tell you about it."

"It'll all come back to you. The doctors said it would just take some time."

Catherine tried to gain her bearings. She could tell she was in a hospital bed. She had a splitting headache and sharp pains every time she took a breath. She had a vague memory of a noisy, bumpy helicopter ride. But beyond that, her memory ended abruptly.

"Nate, what happened to me?"

"You don't remember?"

"Right now, I couldn't tell you if I fell out of an airplane or wrecked the car. Are the boys okay?"

Nathan squirmed in his seat and avoided answering his wife's question.

"The most important thing is you're all right. Why don't you close your eyes and get some rest?"

Catherine didn't need to be coaxed. She released her tentative hold on consciousness willingly, as easily as dropping a stone in a lake.

*

Catherine found herself in the familiar surroundings of Rev. Susan's church office. She was sitting in her usual seat, facing the window that looked out over the courtyard, and sunlight was streaming in, warming her face. Outside, the trees were in their soft-greening stage, that time in spring when empty branches are just about to burst forth into full leaf. As she watched the children of the church school file into the muddy courtyard, she noticed that the glacier that formed in its shadowy corner was dingy and half-melted. She conversed with her confidante.

"It really feels like I've turned a corner. Something has shifted inside me, and I can't really describe it. It's like I'm more future-focused now. Not dwelling on the past as much. I spend a lot less time thinking about what might have been. More of my energy is pointed toward what could be."

Catherine turned away from the window to look her pastor in the eye and gauge her reaction, but Rev. Sue wasn't sitting there. Instead, it was Penny who sat patiently, listening attentively to Catherine's revelations. Rather than being taken aback by the sight of a horse sitting in the minister's office, it seemed to Catherine the most natural thing in the world. Penny didn't respond to Catherine's disclosure but gazed at her with her large, compassionate eyes.

When their session concluded, Catherine excused herself. As she walked through the anteroom to the study and down the hall, she saw a long line of people. They were all, Catherine sensed, in one stage of grief or another. Some sat hugging themselves, their eyes red from crying. Others were stone-faced, dazed and disoriented as if they were collateral damage from a drone strike. As she walked past, she noticed that each person was clutching a photograph and that the image in every picture was of a young child. Catherine realized that all of them were grieving parents just as she was. And they were all there to be healed by Penny.

*

Catherine felt lighter after meeting with Rev. Susan just days after her release from the hospital. In all, she'd been a patient for more than a week. Susan had laughed out loud when Catherine told her about her dream of Penny playing pastor, but as their mutual amusement subsided, she invited Catherine into a serious conversation about its deeper meaning.

"I've known for a long time that being around horses was therapeutic for me."

The minister nodded her agreement. "And the dream seems to say that you're not alone in that. I think this dream, and the one about your night in the desert are important, Catherine. It would be good to pay attention to them."

Catherine mulled this over as she drove home from the church. Their conversation had kindled a spark in Catherine that she hadn't felt for some time, one that had been there long before she'd lost Jacob and Joe, long before she'd become a mother, even before she'd married Nathan.

Without conscious thought, Catherine found herself at Sunnybrooke Farm. She made her way up the lane and, out of habit, parked her car in the same spot where she'd left it the day of her fateful ride. She walked into the barn, drawn to it by a force she neither fully understood nor tried to resist. Because her fractures hadn't fully healed, she wasn't able to ride. But she felt the need to simply be in Penny's company.

"Hey, girl." Catherine approached the stall, and the horse's ears perked up at the sound of her voice. She stroked her equine friend's rubbery, whiskered muzzle and felt the warm breath of her easy exhalations. Catherine inhaled the familiar, welcoming scent of the barn in breaths as deep as her ribs would allow and felt herself relaxing. She grabbed a curry comb, let herself into the stall and began to groom the horse in long, rhythmic strokes. It was a meditative experience for both of them. Catherine took pleasure in her companion's uncomplicated presence. Susan was right: horses are good therapists. With each gentle stroke of the brush, Catherine could feel her broken life being stitched back together. When she was done, Catherine pressed her cheek against Penny's silky, muscular neck. Tears came to her eyes. This time, they weren't tears of grief. They weren't tears of anger. And they weren't tears of regret. They were tears of relief. Tears of gratitude. Catherine realized that her life was opening up to the future, a future that held good things, that had potential and even, just maybe, the possibility of happiness.

*

As the first bracing winds of autumn wove through the rolling hills of southern Maine, Catherine could nearly feel her ribs healing, her strength returning. On one particularly crisp morning, when a heavy frost glimmered on the lawn around her home, Catherine realized she could finally breathe easier. She took in a deep lungful of air without pain or constriction and knew that her body had healed itself. At the same time, she knew her heart was healing, too. She couldn't describe how or why it was happening. There were no discernible milestones in her recovery, no particular moments of restorative revelation. There was simply a subtle mending, a weaving together. She felt like a jigsaw puzzle that sat on a table in the den, visited and worked on sometimes intently for hours and other times casually in passing, that was being pieced together by some unseen hand. And like a puzzle, each piece added clarity to the picture that had theretofore remained mysterious and concealed.

Against all of this healing, all this recovery, one question always hung in the background: *What about Nathan?* But truth be told, Catherine spent much more time reflecting on the two dreams that she'd had following her accident. The first dream, of her time in the desert gazing up into the night sky, had become a source of enduring comfort. She had come to embrace the image of her boys as stars in the sky, and there were many nights in which she found herself wandering out onto the deck to look up. While she didn't have the expansive desert view she'd seen in her dream, Catherine could still see part of the Milky Way from where she stood. She would let her imagination transport her into the heavens, to walk along its path in the company of her star-children. At one point, she had downloaded an app for her phone to learn the names and compositions of the various constellations, but she found that she had little interest in the science of the night sky. She preferred to scan from horizon to horizon, picking out two particular stars that caught her attention along the way. Looking up into space this way, she felt connected to Jacob and Joe in a way she didn't when she visited their graves (which she'd mostly stopped doing months before her riding accident). Their spirits weren't buried underground. They were soaring through the heavens, part of the infinite celestial dance.

While that dream was ethereal, the other had much more down-to-earth implications. As Susan had pointed out, the healing power of horses was not an experience unique to Catherine. The dreamed-of image of the "horse as therapist" led Catherine to explore the possibility of establishing her own therapeutic riding center. She spent hours scouring the web to find and learn about existing facilities, which were dotted around the country. The places she found were all aimed at children or adults with some kind of disability. None specialized in treating adults who had suffered the trauma of loss. The meaning of her dream was clear and specific: therapeutic horseback riding for parents who had lost a child or children. From what she could find, such a place didn't exist anywhere. Catherine was energized by the prospect of starting something new, and her interest began to border on obsession. Whenever she was with Susan or Heather, she would go on endlessly about her vision.

"Think about it. A farm that caters to bereaved parents." She paced around Susan's office, unable to contain her excitement. "Someplace that might even help surviving siblings. Maybe it could be a place that parents could come and stay for a week or two to immerse themselves in the healing energy of the horses."

Her concept unfolded as she thought about it. Late one night she called Carey, with whom she'd shared her dreams from her hospital bed months earlier. "It could be a destination resort. Kind of like a dude ranch, but with purpose. We could do more than horse therapy, too. The place could have massage therapists, Reiki practitioners, herbalists."

"It sounds very cool, Cat. How can I help?"

"Right now, I'm just starting to map out what this might look like, so stay tuned."

"It's really good to hear you sounding so positive, Sis. This is progress."

"It sure feels that way. I'll keep you posted."

Catherine clicked off the call and realized that she was feeling a subtle but pronounced shift inside herself as her dream took on the characteristics of a mission. Or, to use Rev. Sue's language, "a calling."

*

Catherine found herself spending all her free time scouring the internet both for existing facilities and for farms or ranches that were for sale that might be suitable for the operation she had in mind. As she searched, she felt some of her lawyerly skills reignited. As a bankruptcy attorney, she had worked with countless clients to restructure their companies. She knew what a business plan looked like and she had an instinct for what a sustainable project required. It felt good to revive a long-dormant part of herself. It felt like she was on familiar, solid ground.

Catherine knew the importance of due diligence, of fact-gathering. As part of hers, she sat down with Lee Gordon, the owner of Sunnybrooke Farm, to learn about some of the economics of running a horse farm. She realized that, for all her love of horses, and her involvement with them over a lifetime, she'd never been financially responsible for their care and feeding. When she explained her concept to Lee, he expressed a thinly veiled skepticism.

"It's a tough business, Mrs. Osgood. Even if you don't own the horses yourself, and you get some income from boarding, you're always teetering on the edge of ruin. And I own this parcel free and clear. If you have to take out a mortgage to buy a farm, well, let's just say that I wouldn't advise it."

Gordon noted the look of discouragement on Catherine's face and tried to lighten the mood. "There's a running joke in the horse community that goes like this: 'How do you make a small fortune in horse farming? Start with a large one.'"

There had been a time when Catherine would have let this kind of roadblock derail and defeat her. But no more. Catherine accepted the information as just that: useful data. She would not be denied.

CHAPTER TWENTY-NINE
NATHAN

Catherine's accident spooked Nathan.

"Robert, I don't know what I would have done had I lost her, too." Therapist and patient were in their usual spots in the office. It had been more than two months since Nathan's last session. "Seeing her lying there in the hospital bed, her head all bandaged. It was like my worst nightmare."

"Mmm. I can imagine. And I'd also like to remind you that your worst nightmare has already come true."

"Yeah. I guess you're right. But you know what I mean."

"I do, Nathan. And I think it's important for you to appreciate that your worst nightmare happened and that you survived it. That's no small task."

Nathan sat quietly, chewing on his therapist's words.

"I guess what I'm saying is that it reminded me of how important Catherine is to me. And how much I still want and need her in my life."

"That's an interesting phrase, Nate: 'want and need her in my life.' Tell me about it. Are 'want' and 'need' the same thing?"

Robert waited patiently as his client considered the question.

"No, of course they're not. To 'need' something means that it's essential. That you can't live without it. To 'want' something is an expression of desire. It's more like a wish, I guess."

"So, how do you feel about Catherine?"

"Well, I've learned to live without her these past 18 months. Not that I like it, of course.

*

Nathan worked hard not to let Catherine's actions dictate his emotions, but each text, each call from her kindled a spark of hope. When she called him a month after the accident asking that they get together, he couldn't help but cross his fingers and pray that she would be offering him something he could hang onto. His pulse quickened just to see her car in the Starbucks parking lot.

They exchanged pleasantries and small talk sitting at a wrought iron table on the sidewalk until Nathan couldn't stand it any longer.

"So, how are you doing, Cat? Really." He waited patiently while Catherine formulated her answer.

"There's so much that's happened, Nate. Since then. To me."

"And I want to hear all about it. It feels like we've been on these separate paths all this time. I have no idea where you are now, and there's no way you can know where I am, because we haven't talked or tried to figure it out."

"I know. But I needed the space. I'm grateful you gave it to me."

"I'm glad we're talking now. It feels...I don't know, natural."

"I agree." Catherine paused and took a sip from her latte. "But, Nate, we can't just fall into old patterns, old habits. In one way, it would be easy. But things aren't like they used to be. I'm not like I used to be, and I'm glad for that."

"I know, I know."

"It's like this latte. You ordered it for me like you always have, and I'm drinking it like I always do. We know each other so well, and things just come automatically. We don't have to think or talk. It would be easy to fall back into our old life without thinking. But I don't want to do that. Do you?"

Nathan sat with the question. "To be totally honest with you, there's a big part of me that does. I just want to pretend these last 18 months never happened and go back to being the way we were." Nathan took a sip of his coffee, and Catherine waited, hoping for more. "But that's not what I expect, Cat. That's a fantasy. Fantasies are fun to hold onto, but they're not real. That life, our old life, doesn't exist anymore."

Nathan felt good that he was being as honest as he was with Catherine. He wasn't holding back, but he wasn't begging and pleading with her the way he would have been a year earlier. He felt the shift inside himself and hoped that his wife would, too. The silence that followed wasn't as uncomfortable as the many awkward moments they'd sat together since the accident, either.

"Nate, I really appreciate how honest you're being with me, so I want to be honest with you, too. I'm not ready to have you move back in yet."

"And I'm not asking. The place in Saco works right now."

Catherine nodded, looking down into her latte.

"Do you think, though, that we can talk 'big picture,' here, Cat?"

"What do you mean?"

"I mean, like, what's your sense of our overall trajectory? Where do you see yourself headed? And where do I fit in?"

Catherine's face flushed at Nathan's question. "Nate, I wanted to see you today because I really feel like I'm getting better. Like I'm actually recovering from what happened. And I wanted to let you know that. But to be perfectly honest, and I know it's not what you want to hear, I have no idea what that means for us."

Nathan allowed a flash of disappointment to show itself, but he quickly regained his composure. "I'm happy to hear about the first part, Cat. And I can't lie. I was hoping there might be progress on the other. I'm not telling you this to put any pressure on you or anything, but when you were out there in the woods, and I thought that I maybe had lost you for good, that you might have died, well, I thought it would end me."

"Oh, Nathan." Catherine reached across the table and placed her hand on top of his.

"I want us to be together, Cat." Nathan put his free hand on top of Catherine's. "Somehow, whatever that looks like. I know you know that that's what I want, but I haven't said it out loud in a long time. I want there to be an 'us.'"

Catherine slid her hand out from between Nathan's. "Nate, if I could see a way through to that, I'd be the first one to make that happen. But right now, even with all the other things opening up in my life, I still haven't found the key to unlock that door."

Nathan leaned back in his chair, let out a sigh, and nodded.

"I'm sorry. I wish it were easier." Catherine looked into his eyes, and Nathan felt that she meant it.

"You and me both." Nathan was unable to hold her gaze for fear she'd read the depth of the disappointment on his face.

*

At his second meeting with his probation officer, Nathan spent the bulk of the time relating the events surrounding Catherine's accident, rescue, and recovery. The officer listened intently, and when Nathan was done telling the story he sat back in his chair.

"You've sure had your fill of drama, Nathan. I'm glad your wife is going to be all right."

"Thanks, Mr. Marshall."

"And I appreciate that you've been prompt in showing up for our meetings so far."

"I hear a 'but' coming."

"You're right about that. The 'but' is: But you've got to get going on your community service. I know the judge didn't specify when you had to start, only how long, but in our last meeting I thought we had some pretty good ideas."

Nathan looked down at his hands. "I know. I know. But, to tell you the truth, none of those really grabbed me."

Officer Marshall chuckled, mostly to himself, then turned suddenly serious and leaned in toward Nathan. "You know how that sounds, don't you Nathan? Like you're a rich sumbitch who gets to call the shots. Like you're entitled or something. Let's remember who's who around here."

Nathan quickly realized that he'd overstepped, and quickly apologized. "George. Officer Marshall. That's not what I meant. I'm fully prepared to do my service. I'm just saying that I think I can do more for the community than help clean out the dog kennels at the animal shelter."

"While you're thinking about it, I'd suggest you get started." Officer Marshall slid a piece of paper across his desk toward Nathan, who saw that it had the name and address of a food bank in nearby Springvale. "They're there two days a week. I talked to the Director today and she's expecting you on Thursday."

Nathan folded the paper and tucked it into his jacket pocket.

"I'm not saying you'll do all three thousand hours there." The probation officer was shuffling through a pile of other papers on his desk as he dismissed Nathan. "But it's a good place to start."

*

Nathan arrived a few minutes early at the church that housed the food bank. Springvale was one of the thousands of small towns on life support that dotted the New England landscape. Its heyday, when factories producing shoes and mills churning out miles of woolen fabric, had long-since passed. Unemployment typically ran at near double the national average and the opioid epidemic had hit hard there. When Nathan was a teenager, Springvale had the reputation as a miniature "sin city," its main street lined with bars and strip clubs where they were loose about checking IDs. But now, even those were mostly boarded up.

Nathan approached the basement door which was marked by a hand-lettered sign that read, "Springvale Food Bank" and the hours they were open. He passed by small clutches of men and women, some bouncing infants on their hips, who were waiting in a haphazard line. None made eye contact with him and Nathan could almost feel the desperation dripping off of them. The door was unlocked and he entered into a brightly lit room that appeared to take up most of the basement. Folding tables were lined up across the width of the room, separating it from a large kitchen. Nathan noticed that half a dozen volunteers were already at work, organizing food donations on the tables.

He approached the nearest volunteer. "I'm looking for Claire Macomber."

"She's the one in the denim work shirt." The woman nodded toward the kitchen.

"Thanks." Nathan saw the Director of the food bank on the far side of the kitchen, up to her elbows in an industrial-sized chest freezer, handing out bags of frozen vegetables to another volunteer.

"Hi. I'm Nathan Osgood." The Director looked up from her work but didn't stop what she was doing.

"Nathan. Good to meet you. Here, would you please put these out on that table over there?" She nodded toward a table that held other frozen foods. "I'll be with you in a minute."

Nathan did as he was instructed and returned to the kitchen, where the Director was removing the insulated gloves that had protected her hands while she worked in the freezer. She extended her right hand to Nathan, who shook it. "Glad to meet you. Let's go in here." She motioned Nathan toward an office that looked like it had been a broom closet in a former life. "Have a seat."

Nathan sat in the folding metal chair beside a card table piled with paperwork as the Director slid into a matching chair on the far side. "I'm glad you're here. We can use all the help we can get." Claire Macomber appeared to be in her mid-50's, her hands red and raw despite the gloves. Her long, greying hair was swept up in a loose bun at the back of her neck, with a pencil sticking out of it. Her glasses, which hung on her chest by a beaded necklace that looked like it was assembled by a four-year-old, were fogged from the temperature change between the freezer and the office. She grabbed them with one hand and waved them absently-mindedly in front of her as she searched the table for something.

"I'm happy to do what's needed."

"First things first." Claire put the glasses on and found what she was looking for. She handed Nathan a small packet of papers. "I'll need you to read and sign these. Standard liability waivers and confidentiality agreement. We take the privacy of our guests very seriously."

"Guests?"

"You were probably expecting 'customers' or 'clients,' maybe. No, we refer to those we serve as our guests. And anyone who works here is a 'host.' Those other terms are dehumanizing, and the last thing anyone needs who shows up here is to feel further dehumanized." The Director peered at Nathan over the top of her glasses as she spoke.

"Okay. That makes sense."

Claire spent the next ten minutes giving Nathan a quick rundown of the operation. To say it was running on a shoestring was an understatement. The church offered up the basement space for free, but every other aspect of the organization, including its leadership and coordination by the Director, was entirely dependent on volunteer donations and good will. Each week they distributed nearly everything they had received through the kindness and generosity of residents in the community, except for a small emergency stash they maintained for the family who occasionally showed up *in extremis* outside normal hours.

"That's all the time I can spare this morning, Nathan.

Nothing too complicated here. We take the food that's donated and store it on the shelves or in the fridge. We take it out and put it on the tables on Mondays and Thursdays for our guests. You'll need to check in with me every day you're here, both when you arrive and when you leave, so that I can report your hours to your P.O. But as far as I'm concerned, you're just another volunteer doing good work to support those in need. Let's get to it."

The work was as simple as Claire Macomber had described. For the next three hours Nathan moved boxes, cans, and the sparse stash of fresh produce from the kitchen to the tables, and he helped the "guests" load food into their shopping bags. At noon, the door was closed and the small amount of food remaining on the tables was returned to storage. Nathan helped to wipe down the long folding tables and put them away in a closet. He checked in with the Director.

"How was your first day?"

"Eye-opening. I can't believe how many people showed up."

"And today was fairly light. Wait until you see it around the holidays. Fortunately, donations usually pop then, so we can help more people out. But come January it can get pretty bleak around here."

"I can imagine." Nathan shook his head. Until today he had no idea there was so much need in this small town, and it made him wonder how, growing up just a few miles away, he could have been so clueless.

"I'll see you Monday. Thanks for what you do here. I'm glad I can help."

Nathan tried to process all that he'd experienced in the preceding three hours as he drove to his office in Portland. He felt guilty that he'd dismissed working at the food bank as a form of community service that he was willing to undertake when his probation officer had suggested it. And it dawned on Nathan that, for the past three hours, and for the first time in more than eighteen months, he'd not once thought about Catherine, or the accident, or even Joe and Jacob.

CHAPTER THIRTY
CATHERINE

It was probably one of the last warm days before the long, cold winter set in, so Catherine and Susan decided to take a walk around the neighborhood near the church as they talked. The pastor sensed that Catherine had something serious on her mind and she waited patiently for her to open up.

Catherine looked down at her feet as she shuffled through the fallen leaves.

"Susan, what does forgiveness look like?"

"Whew, that's a huge question, Catherine. In true Unitarian Universalist fashion, I can tell you what it isn't." Susan smiled at her client as they walked. "It's not giving permission or saying that what someone did was okay. It's not letting them off the hook for their own responsibility for what happened."

"But it's got to be more than that, right? I mean, what does it look like? What does it feel like?"

"One of my favorite sayings about forgiveness comes from Anne Lamott. She says, 'Forgiveness means that it's finally unimportant that you hit back.'"

"I haven't wanted to hit Nathan in a long time." Catherine paused on the sidewalk and turned to the minister with a smirk. "It's been at least a few days."

For once it was Catherine's turn to wait patiently for Susan to find her voice.

"I think of forgiveness as more of a process than an outcome." Rev. Sue looked out at the passersby enjoying the day. "It's not a 'one and done' kind of thing. It's more like a snake shedding its skin. At one point, the snake was comfortable in that skin. It fit, and it served a useful purpose. But eventually, it starts to feel constricting, and at some point, if it's going to keep on living, keep on growing, the snake's got to leave that old skin behind. Holding and letting go of a grudge, or resentment, or anger is like that. Getting to forgiveness means getting comfortable in your own skin, shedding all that other stuff. Does that make any sense?"

Catherine considered the metaphor and nodded. "It does. I know I've done a whole lot of growing over this past year and a half. And holding onto the blaming and the hatred felt good for a while. It *was* really useful, I think, as a defense mechanism if nothing else. But it feels like I'm done with it now, or at least I want to be. I don't think I can ever completely let Nathan off the hook for what he did, but I don't want to let those feelings hold me back, either. I've got to be able to set them aside or leave them behind somehow. I don't like snakes, but that image of shedding my skin is a good one."

"I'm glad it works for you."

"It's the 'how' of it that's got me stuck, though."

"How to forgive? How to shed that skin?"

"Right. I mean, I can't just wake up one morning and decide, can I? It can't be as easy as that." The two women drifted to a nearby park bench and sat down.

"But that might be where it starts." Rev. Sue angled to face Catherine. "If you're telling me that you've outgrown the skin, that it's not serving a useful purpose to blame or to hate Nathan anymore, then that's the first step. You recognize the need. Maybe the next step is to make the choice to forgive. I know it's mixing my metaphors, but maybe at first, it's like trying on a new dress or pair of jeans. You can decide to wear them for a while, see how they fit, see how they feel. It doesn't mean you get rid of everything else in your wardrobe, or that you're even going to find that they're comfortable at first. If they're not, you can hang them back up and try again later. But maybe they'll actually feel like they fit. Maybe you'll like the way they make you feel. If you do, well, then you can go from there."

"First I shed my skin, then I try on new clothes. Got it."

"Don't forget that, in between, you make the choice to try it out." Susan rose from the bench, and Catherine followed her lead. The two walked on until Catherine broke the silence once more.

"Nathan is looking for some answers from me. He wants us back together, to start over, or to start something new. But to tell you the truth, Susan, I feel like I've shed my skin and emerged a totally different person than I was before. I feel like I want to move forward into something really new. And I don't think it includes him."

*

Catherine was vexed by the problem of financing the purchase of a farm and the discouraging information that Lee had shared with her. Although she had experience as a bankruptcy lawyer, she didn't have any experience actually starting and running a business. Practically her whole adult life, she'd had Nathan around to take care of their finances, but she couldn't talk to him about this. In fact, he was the last person she wanted to approach. One chilly November evening, as she curled up in her favorite chair by the roaring fire, Catherine placed a call to her sister.

"How are things in the tundra?" Catherine knew that her sister was thrilled to escape the "dreadful winters" (as Carey called them) when she was old enough to move out of their house in upstate New York.

"I hear the Big Apple isn't much better." Catherine was defensive of her beloved New England winters.

"Yes, but at least we have the theatah, dahling." Carey had perfected the fake high-brow accent after her first few trips to London. "What's up, Sis?"

"Have you got time to talk about something serious?"

"Sure."

"You remember the dreams I had after my accident, right?"

"Of course. The desert and the stars. Your therapist being a horse."

"Right. Well, that second one has really taken hold." Catherine proceeded to tell Carey about the investigations she'd been making about therapeutic horse programs. She concluded by relating her conversation with Lee about the costs of running a farm.

"Wow, Cat. It sounds like you're really serious about this project."

"You have no idea. I really feel like it's what I'm meant to do. Something good's got to come out of this whole thing. And I think it could really help people."

"You've been doing some great due diligence."

"Thanks, but I'm kinda stuck. I mean, I've got this great idea, but I have no way to make it happen. I've even put together a basic business plan, but when I include the cost of financing the purchase of a ranch and the stock, it just doesn't work."

"What does Nathan have to say about it?" There was a telling silence on the other end of the line. After waiting for a response, Carey realized none would be forthcoming, and she understood why. "Oh. Got it. Okay. So, you're looking to me for some business expertise."

"Exactly."

"Well, I think the answer is obvious."

"I'm listening."

"We need to form a foundation. You'll be the executive director. It'll be a non-profit that people can make donations to. You've got a compelling story to tell, even if it might strike people as a little flaky that it came to you in a dream."

"Carey, that sounds awesome!" Catherine's mood improved immensely at the glimmer of hope her sister was offering. "I would never have thought of that."

"I've got a friend here in the city who would just love to host a fundraiser for this kind of thing. She knows a lot of big-wig donor types, and they're always looking to throw their money at a good cause. This is like the summer camp that Paul Newman started. The 'Hole-in-the-Wall?' Obviously, you don't have the celebrity draw for it, but it's the same sort of venture. People love investing in feel-good projects like this. Especially if their contributions are tax-deductible."

"But do you think we could raise enough? I mean, buying a place, stocking it with horses, hiring people, running the place as a resort. It could cost millions."

"You leave the money to me, Sis. The streets here are paved with gold, and I'll get you more than you need. Go find a farm that works for you and let me know how much it'll cost. And I'll tell you right now; I'll donate the first half-million to get you started."

"Oh my God, Carey!" She had no idea her sister had that kind of money. "You'd do that?"

"To help make my little sister's dream come true? You bet I would!"

Catherine was so excited when she hung up the phone there was no way she was going to sleep. She spent the rest of the night combing the internet for horse farms for sale.

*

In the weeks that followed, Catherine threw herself into the project with missionary zeal, to the point where she hardly noticed Thanksgiving had passed, and another Christmas was approaching. She called a former associate at her old law firm in Boston to help her process the paperwork needed to set up the non-profit foundation and she searched the internet relentlessly for the perfect site. This felt like more than just busywork that kept her mind off the upcoming holiday. It was forward movement that felt positive and productive. She checked in regularly with her sister to let her know what she'd done and to brainstorm her next steps. When Carey offered a repeat trip to Park City for Christmas, Catherine declined and offered instead to host her sister in Maine for the holiday.

*

Catherine made the trek down to Logan Airport to pick

Carey up after her long flight from Hong Kong. She had a special present for her sister and hoped she could keep the surprise until Christmas morning, two days away. She was also glad to have her sister there for moral support. While Catherine didn't feel the same devastating emptiness she had for her first Christmas without the boys, she could tell that she would by no means simply skate through this one.

Catherine waved to Carey as the older sister emerged from the customs checkpoint. Carey ran into her arms, and they shared a long hug.

"That flight was a bitch." Carey let her younger sister lead her toward baggage claim. "I don't even know what day it is."

"Two days before Christmas. I can't tell you the mixed emotions I've got."

"I'll bet. What do you hear from Nathan?"

"He's checked in with me a couple times the past week." Catherine recognized Carey's beaten-up suitcase and retrieved it from the carousel. The women headed to the parking lot and Catherine's waiting Subaru. "He knows how much I used to love Christmas with the boys. He was glad to hear that you were going to be here, and I wasn't going to be flying solo, like I did over Thanksgiving."

"We'll get through this one together, Sis. I assume you're well stocked with wine?"

"I'm hurt that you even felt the need to ask." It was good to have Carey in the seat next to her as they drove north up 95 toward the Maine border. They easily fell into habits of speech and mannerisms that they'd established all the way back when, as little girls, they'd shared a bedroom together in Saratoga Springs.

*

The two sisters made a deal that Carey wouldn't bother Catherine on Christmas morning while she stayed in her bedroom, and she could stay as long as she wanted. Catherine knew she would need some time to mourn privately on the biggest family holiday of the year. And grieve, she did. As on the anniversary of their deaths, Catherine lay in bed and let the memories wash over her. Of Joe pretending to swim across the living room floor, through the sea of wrapping paper after all the gifts were opened. Of Jacob's excitement over receiving the train set that had been his father's as a boy. Of family photo sessions in front of the tree. All the ordinary moments that, when taken together, make up the history, the texture, the shade, and shape of a family. Catherine opened her heart up to the loss, and her tear ducts followed. As her crying subsided, she heard Carey padding around the kitchen and soon the familiar and comforting aroma of freshly brewed coffee wafted up to the bedroom. Catherine said a silent prayer, a prayer of thanksgiving for all the joy her children had given her, and a prayer for their souls, wherever they were, and climbed out of bed. After splashing her face with some water, she pulled a neatly wrapped box from her nightstand and headed downstairs.

"Merry Christmas," Carey said, handing Catherine a large mug of coffee, with just the right amount of milk, as she entered the kitchen. "What have you got there?"

Catherine could tell that Carey was working hard to keep things upbeat for her benefit. "Give me a minute. I need at least one cup of coffee before we can do this." She sat down at the table in the breakfast nook, which supported a ceramic Christmas tree with translucent colored lights. It was a relic from their home in New York, something that their grandmother had given the family when both girls were little. It was rather hideous, but every year their parents would cart it out before Nana arrived. Catherine had chosen to hold onto it when they'd cleaned out the family home after their parents had died. As ugly as it was, she couldn't bear to think of it broken to bits in some landfill somewhere. Now, it held a place of honor, the only Christmas decoration Catherine had the heart to put up for the holiday.

"I can't believe you kept this monstrosity." Carey nodded toward the tree as she sat down across the table.

"Oh, come on, it's not that bad."

"Neither is dengue fever." The two sipped their coffees as a bitter wind blew outside, sending steel-colored clouds scudding across the sky. It looked like it might start to snow at any minute.

"I honestly don't know why you'd ever choose to live here."

"It's home."

"I didn't mean it like that, Cat. I'm sorry how that sounded. You know me: I just don't like the country. Especially when it's cold and bleak like this."

"It's okay, Sis. I understand. I'm not a fragile teacup, ready to shatter at a moment's notice anymore. Don't worry about it. But if you don't like the country and you don't like the cold, you're probably going to hate your Christmas present." Catherine slid the box across the table. Her sister grabbed it and greedily tore at the wrapping paper. Inside the box was a thick manila envelope which Carey tore open, pulling out the papers inside.

"Ennis, Montana? Where the hell is Ennis?"

"It's in Montana." Catherine knew that Carey's entire life revolved around her office in Manhattan, her home in the trendy Park Slope neighborhood of Brooklyn, and all the glamorous financial capitals of the world. As far back as high school, Carey had set her sights on getting out of Saratoga Springs and seeking her fortune on Wall Street. Catherine remembered that her sister had had a single poster on her bedroom wall in high school. It was "A New Yorker's View of the World," which showed America west of the Hudson River as nothing but a vast wasteland until you reached Los Angeles. Catherine took a breath to begin to try and sell her on this spot smack in the middle of nowhere.

"It's about 50 miles southwest of Bozeman."

"Oh, that helps."

"No, look." Catherine grabbed the papers and sorted through the printout of the online real estate listing. She passed them across to Carey one by one. They showed a 300-acre dude ranch for sale, with frontage on the Madison River. The ranch had a main house with a large commercial kitchen, several small cabins, paddocks, and a barn that could board 15 horses. The listing showed sweeping views of the property as it rolled down to the Madison, a premier fly-fishing river. Carey zeroed in on the price-tag: a cool $7.5 million for the turnkey operation.

"See?" Catherine pointed to a site map. "There's plenty of room for additional outbuildings for a spa and other healing spaces."

To her sister's annoyance, Carey turned her attention away from the sales flyer and fiddled with her phone.

"What are you doing?"

"Booking us flights to Bozeman. We've got to go check this place out and get it locked down if it looks right."

Catherine jumped up and screamed with excitement. This wasn't an emotion she'd planned to experience on this particular day. "You're going to fly to Bozeman, Montana in the dead of winter with me?" She couldn't believe this was happening.

"Ennis, dear. Not Bozeman. Ennis."

The two sisters watched the online sales video for the ranch several times, with its aerial views of the rolling ranch land that swept down to the river. Catherine could tell Carey was as taken with the place as she was. After they'd refilled their coffees, with their reservations made to fly to Boseman, they sat together on the couch.

"So, Montana. That's a bold move."

"I've looked all over the country. There's nothing available east of the Mississippi. I tried. Really, I did."

"So..."

Catherine knew exactly where Carey was going without asking it, so she decided to bite the bullet and just say it out loud: "And, yes. This means I'm leaving Nathan."

She was surprised by how harsh and cold the words sounded coming out of her mouth, especially on this day. It was only the third time she'd said them out loud. First to Susan, then, a few days later, she'd confessed it to Heather. She hadn't yet broken the news to her husband, a task that she was understandably dreading.

"And no, he doesn't know it yet."

Carey stayed quiet giving her sister space to say what she wanted to say.

"I know it's a big deal. Really, I do. And I'm not taking any of this lightly. But if there's one thing that I'm sure of, it's that I'm not the person I was two years ago. And I don't need Nathan or anyone else coddling me while I sit around here drowning in sorrow. It finally feels like my life has meaning and purpose and direction. And that direction is West, apparently."

Carey leaned over and gave her little sister an affirming hug, then she got up from the couch and went out to the kitchen, returning with a present of her own. Catherine had always been one of those people who unwrapped gifts as if preserving the paper was as important as the gift itself, and her deliberate motions drove Carey crazy as she waited for her sister to see what was inside. Catherine opened the box and pulled out a manila envelope identical to the one she'd given her sister. When she gingerly opened the envelope and looked at the lone sheet of paper inside, Catherine burst into tears.

"You told me you'd come up with the name when you formed the non-profit." Carey took the paper from her sister's hand to keep it from getting soaked with tears. "So, I went to a graphic artist I know in Brooklyn, and he came up with this logo. I really like it. Do you like it, Catherine? I mean, it's just an idea, and if you don't, we can do something else ---"

"Shut up, Carey." She grabbed the paper back and gazed at it. "I absolutely love it!" Catherine tried to focus through her tears on the printed image: Two stars linked together, each with a capital "J" in it. Below that, the profile of a horse sticking its head out of a stall, and beneath that, the name of the Foundation: "J-Star Ranch for Healing and Hope." Catherine clutched the paper to her chest, grabbed her sister's hand, and shed more tears of joy.

CHAPTER THIRTY-ONE
NATHAN

Nathan was shocked by both the volume of donations and the magnitude of need that surged at the food bank over the holidays. The deluge of contributions threatened to overwhelm the small cadre of volunteers, who diligently stuffed the storage shelves to overflowing. Borrowed refrigerators and freezers bulged beyond capacity. Then, within the space of a few hours three times a week (the organization added an extra day this time of year), with the line of guests snaking through the church parking lot and spilling out onto the adjoining sidewalk, the larder was nearly completely wiped out. The term "feast or famine" took on new meaning for Nathan, as the cycle repeated itself from the second week of November and into the Christmas season. Nathan devoted as much time as he could to the effort, despite the demands of his own business which always saw a spike in activity at year-end. Between his work at the food bank and his paying job, Nathan hardly had time to miss Catherine and the boys over the holidays. He texted Catherine on both

PETER FRIEDRICHS

Thanksgiving and Christmas, and was glad to receive a response, but didn't find himself longing for more.

"I had no idea hunger was such an issue, right here in our own backyard." The irony didn't escape Nathan's notice as he piled his plate with turkey, stuffing, and mashed potatoes, sitting at his parents' dining room table on Christmas Day. Frank and Jean exchanged bemused glances.

"I know. I know." Nathan put the serving spoon down and leaned back from the table. "But, you know, you guys always gave me everything I wanted, and I've always just taken it for granted. You don't know what privilege is until you hand over a can of beans to someone who might not have anything else on their kitchen shelf. If they have a kitchen at all."

*

Nathan was equally shocked by the precipitous decline in donations the food bank experienced after the New Year. While demand tapered a bit, supply fell off a cliff. Claire and the other volunteers did their best to mete out the meager supplies equitably among those who showed up.

"We need to prioritize families with children." The Director spoke with Nathan after the doors were closed and tables stored one Monday in January. "But everyone has needs. About the only good thing that happens this time of year is that some of our seasonal and itinerant workers head south to find work."

"And it's like this every year?" Nathan was having a hard time adjusting to the reality of food insecurity in his hometown.

"I've been doing this for twelve years now, and it's been just like this every time."

The memory of parsing out the meager allotment of food to so many families in need haunted Nathan. He wished he could figure out a better way.

*

"You're a smart guy," Jim had his head buried in the engine of a Ford Escape in his garage as Nathan handed him tools one Saturday afternoon in late January. "Didn't they teach you anything at those fancy schools?"

"I've been wracking my brain, Jim. It's like an Economics 101 problem. Demand outstrips supply, which creates a shortage. There are only two ways to fix it. Increase output or decrease the need."

"Maybe you're looking at it with a microscope. You're too close to it. Maybe it's not just about a food bank in Springvale. Hand me that spark plug wrench, would ya?"

Nathan handed his friend the socket wrench. "Oh, so I'm supposed to go out and fix the problem of world hunger?"

"Maybe not the whole world. But maybe a little bigger piece than what you're looking at."

The conversation prompted Nathan to get to work cataloging all the food banks in York County, and he was amazed to find that there were more than two dozen. As he dug into the problem, he found that virtually every one of them operated on the same model and virtually every one of them struggled with the same problems.

*

"What do you think recovery looks like?" Nathan was back in his therapist's office as a dusting of snow swirled around the grassy expanse that led out to the river, which Nathan noticed was partially iced over. He knew that, in a matter of just over a month, he'd be facing the second anniversary of the accident and he wanted to be prepared.

"I know you hate it when I do this, but what do *you* think recovery looks like?" Robert sat back in his chair and waited.

"You're right. I do. I don't know. It feels like a mellowing, I guess. The ups and downs are moderating. They're not as frequent or as intense. It's less of a roller coaster and more like flying in a plane, where most of the time it's pretty smooth, but every once in a while you hit some unexpected turbulence."

"That sounds like a pretty good metaphor, Nathan. From what I've observed, you're not as anxious a flyer as you were in the past either. For long parts of the flight, you seem better able to relax. To let your guard down."

"To beat this metaphor to death, I'd say that I still keep my seatbelt buckled in case of turbulence, but overall I think you're right." Nathan proceeded to tell his therapist about his work at the food bank and how it had helped him cope with the holidays.

"It sounds like this 'community service' is serving more than just the community, Nathan."

"It feels really good to be helping out. But on another level, it's so damn frustrating. There are definitely bigger problems that need to be fixed."

"Well, maybe you're just the guy to fix them."

Nathan felt better leaving Robert's office than he could ever remember. And he realized that Catherine's name hadn't come up even once.

*

Nathan threw himself into the inefficiencies of food bank operations in York County as if it were a business school problem. He brought to bear all the skills he'd learned during his MBA program at Babson and the knowledge he'd gained since earning his degree. He interviewed food bank directors all over the county, obtained data about populations they served, and crunched numbers until he was bleary-eyed.

"There's got to be a better way." Nathan was telling George Marshall, his probation officer, about all the work he was doing in addition to the few hours he put in at the Springvale food bank each week.

"You know, Nathan, if you were able to really get a handle on this, and figure out that 'better way,' we might be able to persuade the judge to reduce your sentence."

"That would be great, George. And I've been keeping track of the hours I'm spending on the project." Nathan handed a spreadsheet across the desk. "If I could get credit for those hours, that would help, too. But to be truthful, all that feels secondary right now. It's like someone's handed me a puzzle and challenged me to solve it. I'm not sure I've even got all the pieces in my hands yet, but I'm starting to see the picture coming together."

"Keep tracking these hours, Nathan. I think we can get them to count." Officer Marshall had never seen anyone immerse himself so enthusiastically in his community service.

*

Nathan was driving back to Saco from his Portland office when he got the urge to reach out to Catherine. He wanted to tell her about how the business was doing, but more than that he wanted to share with her everything he was doing with the food bank project. It felt to him like such a positive move forward, and he hoped she'd appreciate that. Plus, he wanted to share his excitement over the progress he was making with the person he still considered his partner and helpmate. He spoke a voice-command into the car's system to call Catherine and was disappointed when the call went to voicemail.

"Cat, it's Nate. I just wanted to say 'hi' and see how you're doing. It's been a while and I wanted to tell you about a new project I'm working on. Give me a call when you have a chance."

Nathan hated putting himself in the position of waiting to hear back from his wife. The powerlessness of hoping to receive a return call made him anxious and it sucked him back into a funk like the ones he experienced almost daily a year earlier. When he got home, he poured himself a large glass of bourbon and found a Bruins game on television. The food bank project went untouched that night.

Nathan hauled himself out of bed the following morning nursing a slight hangover, with a dull throbbing at the base of his skull. He took three aspirin and was making a pot of coffee when his phone buzzed to notify him of an incoming text. He read the message from Catherine:

Sorry I missed your call. Glad to hear you've got a project. So do I. Talk when I get back.

Nathan was glad to hear back from his wife, but the news that she was working on something of her own made him anxious. He wondered what it was and where it had taken her. And where it might take her in the future. He wondered, too, whether she had experienced a similar reaction to his voicemail from the previous night. Would she be happy at the thought of him moving forward separately from her, or would it disturb her? He tried not to let Catherine's cryptic message tie him up in knots, but he still felt like he'd launched himself into a bumpy part of the flight that he now had no power to escape from. He took a long, hot shower, allowing both the pulsating water and the aspirin to work their magic on his headache.

*

Working at home one evening several days later, with spreadsheets and charts strewn across the dining room table that doubled as his workspace, Nathan had a revelation about "The Food Bank Problem," as he now thought of it. It was all about the decentralization of the current system and the way every little operation was acting independently from all the others. While the people each food bank served by necessity came from within just a few miles of each distribution center, each food bank was scrapping and scraping for donations from their hyper-local populations. *Did the fact that the guests of each food bank had to be physically close to the source dictate that the donations needed to be? What if there were one central depository for donations that then distributed them to each food bank, making those distributions in response to the varying needs of each food bank's guests?* The prospect excited Nathan and he began to crunch numbers again to see whether a centralized collection and distribution point could add efficiencies that would lead to fewer shortages and fuller bellies.

*

Nathan made a pilgrimage to Franklin Pond on the second

anniversary of the accident that was much like the one he'd made to mark the first. Winter had released its icy grip on southern Maine ahead of schedule, and when he'd gotten to the familiar boulder by the shore, he could see open water in the middle of the lake.

If only things had been that clear two years ago.

Nathan felt a tightening in his chest as he remembered the worst day any parent could possibly have in their life. The tears flowed easily, but they were not the gut-wracking sobs of the past. The grief he felt was real and deep, but not debilitating. Gone was the crippling sense of guilt that for so long had been his constant companion and, with it, the urge to walk out into the middle of the pond and submerge himself in its icy depths. With a deep breath, he hauled himself up off the rock and began his annual trek around the pond. This time he didn't pause at the point on the far shore where he'd made his decision – the decision that had changed everything. He just kept walking the perimeter path until he was back where he began.

CHAPTER THIRTY-TWO
CATHERINE

Catherine could hardly contain her excitement as she and Carey drove out of Bozeman in the rented Jeep Cherokee. The small city quickly gave way to snow-covered grassland sparsely dotted with houses. After a two-hour drive, they rounded the curve on Route 287 to begin the descent into the Madison River Valley, with the frozen expanse of Ennis Lake below. The small town itself was nestled in the distance, smoke from dozens of chimneys curling into the endless Montana sky.

Catherine's dream was coming true. She could feel it. Big Sky country, even in the dead of winter, spoke to her soul. The scale of the mountains, the absence of trees, and the vast, expansive views were already a balm to her broken heart. She remembered her dream of standing at the foot of the Tetons and felt the same sense of contentment wash over her.

"Carey, it feels like I can breathe for the first time since the accident." They descended the hill and entered the town, where they found the real estate broker's office without need of the GPS. Its sign hung prominently along the one main street.

"Now, remember: When it comes to the financial stuff, I'll do all the talking." Carey was in "business mode," and her younger sister was glad to have her play the role of the big-city financier. "And try not to seem too eager when we get to the ranch. I want to cut the best deal we can with this guy."

The broker and the two women exchanged pleasantries in the office, and the sisters endured a brief sales pitch. The broker then led them out to his truck, and they climbed in. Carey rode shotgun, and it occurred to Catherine that, in this part of the world, the term had a more literal meaning than it did back East. From her perch in the back seat, Catherine gazed out a side window as they drove out of town, making the twelve-mile trek south to the ranch. They passed the local airport, and the broker told them about plans to expand the lone terminal and to increase flights in and out. Carey took this information with a grain of salt, assuming it was part of the sales job.

Catherine was hardly listening. She was staring out at the mountains soaring above the river valley. The broker informed them that they were looking at the backside of Big Sky Resort, the largest ski area in the state. "Of course, you can't get they-uh from he-yuh." It was a horrible impression of a Downeast Maine accent. "You'd have to drive most of the way back to Bozeman to get to the east side of the range." The broker turned right off the road onto a lane that had been freshly cleared of snow.

"You've got about a two-mile access road off the highway. Lots of privacy, for sure." They passed through a gate with a sign hung above it that read "Madison-South Ranch." The broker explained that the spread had been in the same family for four generations, but that the current owner had moved on after college to business on the West Coast. "He works for Google or one of those companies. Tech is his thing, not horses. That's why he's selling."

As they made their way up a small rise toward the west, the ranch came into view. It was just as the brochure had depicted it. Dusted with a fresh blanket of snow, it gleamed in the crisp, midwinter sunshine. Catherine was instantly enchanted, and she gave her sister's shoulder a squeeze from the back seat. Carey tried to pretend it hadn't happened, although she was sure that the broker had noticed. She had told the broker over the phone that they were scouting out a location for a new non-profit. She hadn't shared her own family's very personal connection to the group's mission.

"A couple is living here over the winter, taking care of the property and the stock. They've got eight horses right now, I believe." Catherine was anxious to poke around in the barn and see what condition the animals were in. She would be able to tell how well the overall ranch was maintained from how the horses were treated. The broker pulled up in front of the main house, and a couple that looked to be close to Catherine's age stepped out the front door to greet them. After a cursory tour of the house, Catherine asked to see the barn.

The warm, moist breath of the animals steamed the air around the stalls, and Catherine immediately felt at ease around the familiar smell of horse, hay, and manure. The woman in the couple led Catherine down the row of stalls, introducing her to each horse in turn. Catherine felt an instant kinship with her and described to her the intended use of the ranch going forward.

"Would you two consider staying on beyond the winter if it worked out?"

The woman nodded enthusiastically. "We were hoping you'd ask. We love this place, and I love these horses." She gave Catherine a little background on each horse: how long they'd been at the ranch, how old they were, their current medical condition. Carey and the broker stood uncomfortably in the cold as the horsewomen chatted, oblivious to the chill of the barn. Finally, the two women rejoined them, and they all returned to the main house, where the male caretaker gave them a rundown on the condition of the outbuildings.

"The place needs a few repairs. The equipment shed needs a new roof, for example. But the basic structures and systems are sound."

After an hour poking around the property, they retraced their drive down the lane toward the highway. The broker turned to Carey as he stopped at the end of the lane, where it met the highway back to town. "I told you it was a clean operation."

"It certainly looks that way."

Catherine leaned forward between the two front seats. "And I can tell the horses are well-loved."

"So, let's head back to my office and talk turkey."

*

Catherine felt like things were happening at hyper-speed. She'd sat in awe as she watched her sister negotiate a six-month option to buy the ranch, and her jaw dropped when Carey wrote out a personal check for $100,000 to bind the deal. They'd flown back from Bozeman feeling giddy, their mood intensified by the champagne they'd split in their first-class seats. Carey spared no expense when it came to travel and creature comforts. With a location secured, the sisters turned their attention to planning the fundraiser in earnest. Carey enlisted the help of a friend to assemble a professional-looking slide show with photographs they'd taken during their visit to the ranch and others that the caretakers had provided of the place in full bloom in spring. Catherine worked hard on her speech for the event, receiving generous coaching from her sister.

"You can't be shy with this group. You've got to state your case and make a clear ask for their financial support. It's a language they all understand. We don't just want to pull on their heartstrings. We want to pull on their purse-strings, too."

Catherine felt overwhelmed by the idea of speaking in front of a few hundred wealthy socialites, especially about something so personal. She thought about how she had flushed crimson and lost her train of thought the one time she spoke up at a local PTA meeting. Then her sister pointed out how many motions Catherine had argued in front of a bankruptcy court judge, with millions of dollars on the line. That memory gave her a much-needed shot of confidence.

What wasn't getting done was having "The Talk" with Nathan. He had tried to contact Catherine several times since the holidays. She knew that it was unfair to keep putting him off, especially since all the plans for the ranch were coming together so quickly. It felt like she was doing it all behind his back, and that made her feel terribly guilty. She shared her concern with Rev. Susan.

"If it makes it easier, Robert and I can be there when you tell him."

"I appreciate that, Susan. But this is something I've got to do on my own." The thought of actually telling him, though, made Catherine's stomach turn.

"I know you can do it, Catherine. But I'll back you up if you need help."

"I can't tell you what it's meant to me to have you supporting me through all this. I couldn't have made it through without you."

"That's nice of you to say, Catherine. But there's been a strong woman lurking inside you all along, waiting to break out. I'm just sorry it took something as awful as the accident to uncover it."

"Yeah, well, there's that, isn't there? You know, amidst all the excitement of getting ready for the fundraiser and buying the ranch, there have actually been a few moments that I haven't thought about the boys. When I realize it, I'm shocked, and it makes me feel guilty. Especially with the anniversary coming up."

"That's all part of the healing process."

"It feels like they're starting to fade away." Catherine's eyes welled up for the first time in weeks. "I don't want to lose them. What happens when I move to Montana, for God's sake?" It was like her resolve was melting away.

"Catherine, stop right there. You're never, ever going to lose Jacob and Joe." Rev. Susan spoke in a stern tone Catherine hadn't heard before. "Remember that dream you had, about being under the night sky in the desert? The boys are stars, always watching over you. They're a part of you, no matter where you're living. But that's what you've got to do: live. Live your life. You're moving forward into your future. It's not your choice that they're not here to share that future with you. But you can't put everything on hold forever."

"I know, I know." Catherine nodded, sniffling back the tears. "I've just got to get this over with, with Nathan. It's going to hurt him so much. "

The pastor placed a reassuring hand on Catherine's knee. "It's going to be hard, and it's going to hurt. No doubt about it. But don't forget he's been in limbo for a long time himself. Maybe this will give him permission to start moving forward with his own life, too."

Catherine knew that Susan was doing her best to comfort and support her, but she also knew that, when she finally delivered it, the news would cut Nathan to the core. She decided to defer the conversation for one more week, until after the fundraiser for the foundation.

*

"I don't know if I can do this." The two sisters were standing in the doorway of the hotel ballroom. Carey had reserved a room that would comfortably fit 250 people, and through her vast networks, she'd filled it to capacity. Catherine noticed that most of those in attendance were women, which gave her some comfort. But she also knew that these women, draped in thousand-dollar dresses and dripping with jewelry, were not her people. Catherine was comfortable with the folks who wore flannel and jeans and hung out in barns. And, to make matters worse, she knew it was these people who held her future in the palms of their hands.

"You've got this, Cat. I'll be glued to your hip all night."

Together, they mingled with the guests, as servers offered drinks and elegant finger foods. A quartet played soft jazz to accompany the cocktail chatter. Catherine noticed right away that the wait-staff's white jackets were embroidered with the foundation's logo. Carey had spared no expense. The two sisters floated from one clutch of impeccably coifed women to another, Carey introducing her sister and smiling broadly. As nervous as Catherine was, Carey was clearly in her element, among her people, and this put Catherine more at ease. They slowly made their way to the front of the room, where a raised platform and a microphone awaited. A large flat-screen television was mounted on the wall behind it, cycling through pictures of the ranch.

"There's an art to this." Carey leaned in to be heard above the din. "We want them to drink enough to loosen their wallets, but not so much that they forget why they're here. Timing is everything." She let the band finish the song it was playing and nodded to the guitar player to let him know she was ready to speak. The two women stepped onto the platform, and Carey moved to the microphone.

"Good evening, everyone. Thank you for accepting our invitation to be here on this beautiful evening. It's great to see so many familiar faces, and I look forward to meeting those of you I don't know. My name is Carey Sims, and I am proud to be speaking to you tonight. Proud not just because we're here to support a wonderful cause." Carey gestured toward the screen, which now displayed the foundation's logo. Then she nodded in Catherine's direction. "I'm proud because I am here with my sister. My little sister, who means more to me than anything or anyone in the whole world. I am proud to be able to support her in the tremendously important work that she's doing. And when you hear her story, I know you'll want to support her, too. Everyone, please meet my amazing sister, Catherine Osgood."

Catherine stepped forward, and Carey gave her a quick hug. She was greeted by polite applause and hundreds of expectant faces. She looked out at the crowd and took a deep breath, trying to settle her nerves. "Thank you, everyone, for coming out tonight. If you'll indulge me, I want to tell you a story." Another deep breath. A glance over at Carey. A wink of reassurance.

"Two and a half years ago, I was working in the garden with my sons, Jacob and Joe. We were planting bulbs – daffodils and tulips. It was a spectacular fall day in Maine, the trees in full color, the sky dotted with puffy clouds. It was the kind of day you see on calendars and screensavers, and you wonder whether a place can actually be that beautiful." Catherine's eyes drifted upward with the memory. The audience followed her gaze as the screen behind Catherine shifted. A picture of Jacob and Joe, wide grins spanning their faces. Jacob missing one of his front teeth.

"Jacob, my older boy, was six at the time. He was my future engineer. Everything needed to be precise with him, whether it was the amount of milk on his breakfast cereal or needing to follow his exact bedtime routine every night. So, Jacob being Jacob, worried about how each bulb was planted. He had to make sure the holes were evenly spaced and that every one of them was exactly six inches deep. He made sure that each bulb was nestled into the soil just right, with the roots pointed down. Joe, who was my wild child and every bit the troublemaker, was four. True to form, he was digging holes where and how he wanted. Some were halfway to the center of the earth, and others no more than a shallow divot. And he would just toss bulbs in, every which way. Then, when he covered them up, he'd stomp on the ground to make sure they didn't go anywhere."

A slight chuckle from knowing parents rippled from the crowd.

"All I could think about was how beautiful those flowers were going to look in the spring. Given their ages, the boys had no idea what the fruits of their labor, six months later, would be. But as their mother, I was excited to teach them about the change of seasons and about how sometimes hard work doesn't have a payoff right away; that good things are worth waiting for. I've also always loved the first shock of color that daffodils and tulips offer in the springtime, so I was looking forward to the joy they'd bring after a long Maine winter, and how we'd all bask in that beauty together as a family."

Catherine choked on her next words. She paused to take another breath and regain her composure.

"That wasn't to be."

She let the words hang in the air as the screen showed a field of tulips in full bloom.

"The flowers bloomed, all right. But no one was there to enjoy them. By spring, Jacob and Joe were gone, and I was too blind with grief to notice them."

Catherine heard a few sniffles from women in the audience.

"My boys were the victims of a terrible accident. A parent's worst nightmare. I died the day they died. What happened to them happened to me, and I never thought I would find a way back. I admit, there were times I really didn't want to."

Another deep breath.

"But life has a way of persisting. Of pressing on. Spring follows winter, and the snow melts and the flowers bloom. A few weeks ago, it was the second anniversary of the day I lost them, and miraculously, I'm still here. And instead of wanting to mow down those flowers before they bloomed, like I did last spring, I'm actually looking forward to their blossoming. While it's still bittersweet, the memory of that fall day in the garden has become a joyful one. I can't wait to see the orderly rows of Jacob's flowers and the random ones from Joe. It's like they left a piece of themselves in the soil for me to enjoy."

Catherine shifted her focus and her tone.

"I have returned from the brink of death – theirs and mine. And it may sound strange, but my life was saved by a horse."

Penny's image flashed up on the screen.

"As city-dwellers, you may not understand that statement, so let me try and unpack it. After the accident, I spent hours with this big, beautiful girl." She pointed up at the screen, a smile now radiating joy to her audience. "Her name is Penny. She was every bit the healer that my therapist was. Just spending time with Penny saved me. Looking into her big, brown, understanding eyes, I could tell she knew me better than I knew myself. Horses have this gentle, persistent presence. That's why they're used as therapy animals for kids with autism and other disabilities. People who've suffered traumatic brain injuries. Scientists have proven their healing power, although they can't explain it."

Catherine could feel herself gaining confidence now.

"I don't know why no one has thought of it before, but horses can help to mend broken hearts, too. Broken hearts like mine. The broken hearts of parents who have lost their children. Every year in this country, we lose nearly fifty thousand children between infancy and age eighteen, from accident and illness. That's one hundred thousand parents whose lives are shattered. One hundred thousand people who desperately need help, like I did, putting the pieces back together."

Photos of the ranch in Ennis scrolled by as Catherine continued.

"The J-Star Ranch will be the only place of its kind in the country, maybe even the world. As the logo says, it's a place of healing. And it's a place of hope. A place where horses and humans can help parents find a way back. A way out of the deepest darkness of their lives. Out of a nightmare that they might otherwise never escape."

Catherine gazed out over the crowd and took one last deep breath as the screen cycled back to the slide of the foundation's logo.

"You have the power to make all this a reality. With your generous financial support, we'll be ready to begin operations at the ranch in just a few months. We have a staff in place, and the horses are there. They're ready and waiting to offer their healing powers to parents desperately in need. All we need is you. Thank you for listening to my story and thank you for your support."

*

The fundraiser was a success beyond even Carey's wildest dreams. Catherine's speech had captivated the well-heeled audience, and they couldn't line up fast enough to write their checks. Although the inspection of the ranch and its facilities revealed the need for more serious repairs than they had anticipated, the foundation took in more than enough to cover them and the purchase price. Two months after the fundraiser Catherine and her foundation became the proud owners of the newly named J-Star Ranch.

CHAPTER THIRTY-THREE
NATHAN

"Thank you for coming today." Nathan greeted the heads of more than twenty local food banks whom he had invited to the Comfort Suites in Sanford. He'd offered them a modest buffet lunch, both to entice attendance and to express his gratitude for their service to the community. "I think this is the first time we've had so many people dedicated to eliminating food insecurity in one room at the same time."

Nathan was up-front about how he'd gotten involved in the issue. "I'm afraid to admit that hunger wasn't even on my radar. My family has always been comfortable. I've been blessed with the privilege of never having to worry about where my next meal would come from." He went on to briefly summarize the tragedy and the trial that had brought him to become aware. "I didn't exactly walk into the Springvale food bank of my own volition. As many of you know, I was prosecuted and convicted of manslaughter in the death of my children." Nathan paused to take a breath, both for those hearing this news for the first time and for himself. "The judge, in his infinite and compassionate wisdom, sentenced me to three thousand hours of community service, and it was my probation officer, George Marshall," Nathan gestured to a man seated in the corner of the room. Officer Marshall offered a little wave, "who gave me the assignment. What I saw was both heartening and heartbreaking."

Nathan described his experience at the food bank. "But I'm not telling you anything you don't already know. You've been doing this far longer than I have. So, I've called you here to this 'summit' today to see what we might be able to do collaboratively to support each other in the work that we're all committed to." Nathan turned and pointed his remote at the small projector, which sprang to life at his direction. "I have some ideas I'd like to share with you." After Nathan had completed his presentation, he facilitated a discussion that lasted for more than two hours and, to a person, everyone stayed until the end. When the meeting concluded Nathan stood by the door and shook hands with each of the participants, offering them his most sincere thanks. Claire Macomber was the last to leave.

"Nathan, I don't consider myself a religious person, even if the food bank is housed in the basement of a church. But I need to say that you are a gift from God. Tragedy may have sent you to us, but this project has 'triumph' written all over it." She leaned in and gave Nathan a hug. "See you Monday, as usual!"

The meeting gave Nathan all the confirmation he needed to take the project to the next stage.

*

"Jim, you're a great friend."

"Oh, geez, Nate. Don't start that again." The two men were sitting on Jim's front porch on an unseasonably warm April afternoon.

"Let me finish, would ya? What I was going to say is that you're a great friend, and I'm really glad you're willing to listen to me go on and on about the food bank stuff. But I really miss sharing this kind of stuff with Catherine."

"Yeah, I get that Nate. I mean, my wife and I haven't been together for eight years, and we still share the important stuff."

"I feel like I'm living in this vacuum or something. I have no idea what's going on with her. It's a void. Like I'm floating in outer space."

"But at least you're not still just sitting around doing nothing but waiting for her to call."

"No, I know. I guess that's 'progress.'" Nathan used air quotes as he spoke the word. "But are we just gonna circle around in different orbits for the rest of our lives? Maybe hoping they cross every once in a while? I've left her probably 3 or 4 messages in the past month and all I get back is silence. It sucks."

"Do you want me to talk to her? I mean, I don't relish the thought of being a go-between. But before the accident, we were all pretty close."

"I appreciate the offer, but I don't think that's gonna work. It's bound to backfire. She knows how close we've become, and she'd probably see it for the end-around that it is."

"Have you talked to your shrink about this?"

"Nah. I know what he would say. 'Be patient, Nate. You can't force her hand.'"

"Couldn't hurt to ask."

"Mmm. Maybe not." Nathan sipped his beer and thought about it.

*

"What do you think I should do, Robert?" Nathan had related his frustration to his therapist in a mini-rant as he paced around the office. "And please don't tell me to be patient. I feel like I've been patient long enough."

"You know, Nathan, I'm hearing something different from you today. It's not about recovering what you had with Catherine or going back to a past that you can never have again. I think what you said is that you're anxious to share something that's important to you now. Something current. Something that's pulling you forward. That's a very different message than I've heard for the past two years."

Nathan hadn't thought about it that way. Robert was right. His impulse to be with Catherine and to share what he was working on was coming from a vastly different place. *Maybe this is what was meant by recovery.*

"Here's what I'd like to propose." Robert leaned in and touched Nathan on the knee. "Why don't I get in touch with Catherine's therapist and see if she can meet with me. With your permission, I can let her know how you're feeling. Maybe I can prime the pump a bit, so that Catherine gets a sense of where you are these days. Maybe that'll bring her to the table. Knowing it's not about reliving or regaining the past but exploring the future."

"That sounds good to me, Robert. You can tell her therapist whatever you want about me. If I can't be transparent at this stage, I don't think I could ever be."

Robert agreed to report back to Nathan once he and Catherine's therapist had met.

*

Nathan threw himself into the food bank project while he waited to hear back from Robert. The summit of directors had confirmed both that they were willing to consider a collaborative venture and that his idea of centralizing the collection and distribution of donations made logistical sense. He related all this to his parents one night over dinner.

"I think my next step is to find a location for a warehouse. It's got to have easy access to highways, but needs to be near a population center so that we can promote donations."

Nathan's father looked thoughtful for a moment. "What about that barn up on Shaw's Ridge? You know, the old dairy farm?"

Nathan remembered the location from his childhood when his parents would take him for ice cream and miniature golf. "I thought they tore that down."

"Nope. Old man Shaw left it to his kids, but it's just sitting there now. If it's structurally sound, it's probably in a good location. Everybody in York County knows about Shaw's Ridge from back in its ice cream days. They know how to get there and it's pretty much in the center of the county."

"That's a great idea, Dad. I'll have to go check it out."

Nathan drove the short distance from his apartment in Saco to Shaw's Ridge the next morning, just to scope it out. Sure enough, the barn was still standing. He decided to knock on the door of the farmhouse, on the off chance that someone was home.

"Can I help you?" A woman who appeared to be about

Nathan's age opened the door and spoke to him through the storm door.

"Hi. I've got kind of a crazy question for you. Do you own that barn?" Nathan pointed to the mammoth structure with peeling paint and sagging roof.

"That's not a crazy question. I do. I mean, my husband and I do."

"Oh, great! My name's Nathan Osgood. I live over in Saco, but I was raised in Newfield.

"I'm Jean. Jean Shaw." She pushed open the storm door and held her hand out.

Nathan shook it. "Here's the crazy part. Do you mind if I come in and tell you about an idea I have?"

Because they were in rural Maine and because Nathan had a friendly face, the trusting woman let him in, offered him a cup of coffee and listened closely as he described his vision to her.

"That sounds really interesting. I know we've got some neighbors who visit the food bank in Alfred from time to time. It's a shame so many people have to. I don't think we can let you have it for free but let me talk to my husband and we'll see what we can do."

"Can I take a look inside?"

"Sure." The woman grabbed her coat and a set of keys off a rack on the wall by the door. Nathan followed her out and traipsed the 50 yards or so over to a side door to the barn. The woman fiddled with the keys until she found the one that unlocked the padlock and let them both in.

As Nathan's eyes adjusted to the dim light filtering in through cracks in the walls and ceilings and his nose adjusted to the smell of generations of cow manure ground into the floorboards, he let out a long whistle. "This is more space than we'll ever need. Or I should say, more than I hope we ever need."

"Yeah, she's a big, old eyesore. Used to house more than 100 Holsteins here in its heyday."

Nathan's mind was churning about the possibilities the cavernous space held. *This just might work.* "Thank you, Jean. For your hospitality and for not running me off your farm for a fool." He handed the woman his business card. "Please talk it over with your husband and give me a call. I'm happy to come back out to meet with him, too." This time he extended his hand first. It was nice meeting you." *Yes, this just might work.*

*

Let's get together. Can you do tomorrow at 3? Robert texted Nathan and Nathan confirmed. He was nervous as he drove to his therapist's office, as nervous as he'd been in months. What news, he wondered, would Robert have? Somehow it felt like his fate was hanging in the balance.

"I don't want to keep you in suspense, Nathan. Catherine is willing to meet with you.

Robert filled Nathan in on his conversation with Rev. Susan. "It was very cordial and pleasant, but she was a little guarded. I get that, because she was upfront in telling me that she did not have blanket authority from Catherine to disclose everything, like you gave me."

"It sounds like she's hiding something."

"I wouldn't assume that, Nathan. I think all it means is that Catherine is a bit more guarded than you are. But we already knew that from the fact that she's not returned your calls or texts lately."

"I guess that's right. What else did she say?"

"She did a lot of listening. I tried to communicate where you were, where you are now, how far you've come. I wanted her to understand that you're beyond simply longing to re-establish a relationship that's now in the past. I think she heard me."

"She must have if Catherine has agreed to get together with me."

"Susan wanted me to be clear with you about one thing, Nate. And it's probably why, when she called me yesterday, she told me that Catherine wanted you and me to talk before she'd call you to get together."

"This sounds ominous."

"Again, I don't' think so. But we'll see. What Susan told me is that, when you and Catherine meet, she wants to talk first. She needs your assurance that you're going to listen to what she has to say."

"That sounds okay, I guess. But it also sounds like she has something specific she wants to say, and I gotta tell you, that makes me nervous."

"Look, Nathan, the reality is this: She may want to tell you that she wants a divorce. She may want to tell you that she wants you to move back into the house. Or what she has to say may fall anywhere between those extremes. But you need to be able to assure me, so that I can assure Susan, so she can assure Catherine, that you're going into this meeting in "receiving" mode."

"Okay."

"I think I was able to communicate to Susan, and by extension to Catherine, where you are. I wasn't specific about your food bank project, but they both know now that you've actively reengaged with your life, that you're pursuing new goals, and that you're not just stuck in the same loop you were in for months after the accident. So, there's not a lot you need to tell Catherine at this point. Which means that instead of talking, you need to listen."

Nathan agreed, but thought to himself that it would be easier said than done.

CHAPTER THIRTY-FOUR
CATHERINE

"Nathan's agreed." Rev. Susan was on the phone with Catherine. "Robert has assured me that he understands that you're willing to meet as long as he listens while you talk."

Catherine wasn't sure whether she was relieved at the news or panicked. Was she really able to do this? Could she cut the feet out from under her husband and tell him she was moving to Montana without him? She knew in her head that she was too far down the road to turn back, but now that it was going to happen, it felt like her heart was still harboring doubts.

"I don't know if I can do this to Nathan." Catherine swallowed hard.

"Catherine, you're not 'doing this to him.' You're standing on your own two feet. You're claiming control of your life. You're choosing to pursue your dreams. Every person has a right to do that. If Nathan loves you, he'll see all that. He may not be in a place right now to root you on and celebrate it, but if he truly loves you, he'll see his way clear to easing the path."

"I hope to God you're right, Susan."

*

Catherine picked up her phone, took a deep breath, and pressed the number for Nathan.

"Hello, stranger!" He was trying just a little too hard to sound cheerful. "How've you been?"

Catherine took another deep breath to calm herself. "Hey, Nate. Look, I'm sorry I've been MIA these past months. There's lots of stuff going on. I was wondering if we could get together so that I can tell you about it."

"I appreciate you wanting to get together, Catherine. I'm ready to hear all about it."

"I was thinking Mario's for dinner tomorrow night. Say, 7 o'clock?"

"Sure. I'll be there."

"Okay, see you then." Catherine ended the call. Short and not-so-sweet. She had picked Mario's because she wanted to be sure to have this conversation in a public place, and the restaurant was one they'd eaten at before but never particularly favored. It wasn't packed with memories like Tito's or Romeo's Pizza, places they'd often gone as a family.

Catherine tossed and turned the entire night, anxious about the coming conversation. She rehearsed the scene over and over in her mind. She envisioned scenarios that ranged from Nathan storming out of the restaurant in a rage to her having to leave him sitting at the table, crying like a baby. None of the scenes had a happy ending. By five o'clock the following afternoon, Catherine was a complete wreck. She stood in her closet, paralyzed, trying to pick out an outfit. A familiar voice echoed up the front hallway.

"I'm up here, Heather!" Her best friend always knew just the right moment to show up. Heather walked into the bedroom, carrying two wine glasses and a bottle of Pinot Grigio.

"So, this is it." Heather uncapped the bottle and poured some into a glass. "I thought you might need a little fortification." She waved the glass in front of her friend.

Catherine put up her hand in the universal "Stop" sign. "I sure could use it. But I need my head to be crystal clear tonight."

"I understand." Heather sipped from the glass. "How're you feeling?"

"Like I'm gonna throw up any second now."

"Look at it this way. In a few hours, the band-aid will be ripped off."

"That's what I'm afraid of. That it'll be a bloody mess."

"Bad analogy. Sorry." Heather took another sip of wine and joined her friend in pawing through her wardrobe. In the end, they agreed on a striped, button-down top and a khaki-colored skirt. Neutral as could be. Heather gave Catherine a hug before the two of them climbed into their cars and went their separate ways. Catherine's hands were shaking as she placed them on the steering wheel.

*

As was his habit, a habit that both infuriated Catherine and endeared him to her, Nathan had arrived early. When she entered the restaurant, she noticed that he had secured a table in the corner that offered a modicum of privacy. Clearly, he knew they were there for a serious talk. Nathan rose from his seat as Catherine approached and helped her off with her jacket. He gave her a friendly peck on the cheek, and they sat down.

"It's been a while. I'm sorry about that." Catherine offered her husband an olive branch.

"No worries, Cat. I hope you've been okay. I was worried about you on the anniversary."

"Did you go down to the pond?"

"I did." Nathan chose not to say more about his experience that day.

Silence fell between them and Catherine wondered how many times since the accident they'd endured such awkward moments. They both consulted their menus and took advantage of the break in conversation to place their orders.

"And, Nate, I want to thank you, too, for not pushing at all this whole time. Really. I know it's been hard to be apart all this time, but it's what I needed. And you gave it to me. That means a lot."

Nathan had a hard time looking Catherine in the eye. "Cat, you know I'd do anything for you. And I don't just mean that out of guilt for what happened. Since the day I met you, I knew that I'd jump off a cliff if you asked me to."

"Nate, we agreed that I'd talk and you'd listen." Catherine was irritated that he had already breached their understanding. But that irritation gave her the impetus to plunge ahead.

"It means the world to me that you feel that way. You've been so good to me for so many years. We built a nice life together. We had it all, didn't we?" This was not going according to the script that Catherine had rehearsed in her head. But at least they seemed to be speaking from their hearts.

"It doesn't have to be over."

"I know it doesn't for you." She took a deep breath. "But it does for me."

There it was: the simple, gut-wrenching truth, out on the table before them, as real as the water glasses and the silverware.

Catherine saw Nathan tearing up. He leaned across the table and whispered urgently. "Cat. Don't do this. We can work this out."

Catherine didn't want to give him room to start begging, so she cut him off. "Nate, you need to let me tell you how I'm feeling. I'm sorry if it hurts you." It would be so easy, she thought, to just melt into his arms and make him happy. She fought back the urge and continued.

"This isn't about the accident. Not really. I want you to hear this very clearly, okay? While that may have set the wheels in motion, I think those wheels needed to start turning at some point. What I'm telling you is that being alone the past two years has changed me. I know you want me back, but you hardly know the 'me' that I am now. I'm not the person I was when we lost the kids. I'm not even the Catherine I was when we met."

"That's fine. I want to know the new you."

"Please don't interrupt me, Nate," Catherine spoke through gritted teeth. She could feel herself settling into the power of her hard-won truth, the truth that she wouldn't deny herself. "I need to get this all out, and if you love me, you'll listen and let me finish."

Nathan fiddled with the paper from his straw and remained silent.

"Nate, I loved being your wife, and I loved being Jacob and Joe's mother." Catherine realized that this was the first time either of them had said their children's names out loud between them since the day they'd died.

"You need to know that, okay? Nothing I'm about to say changes that. We had a wonderful life together. A life anyone would envy. I was happy. Truly, I was. You made me happy. I don't want you ever to doubt that."

Nathan nodded slightly but kept his mouth shut as Catherine continued.

"But in the process of becoming your wife, and then the boys' mother, I lost myself. Or to be more accurate, I never found myself in the first place. We were just kids when we met, and you swept me off my feet, and you had our lives all planned out. And I went along because the plan was so perfect. Your plan became *our* plan, and we were happy. I know I was happy, and I think you were, too."

"Of course, I was."

"But here's the thing: through all that, I never had time to figure out who *I* was or what it was that *I* wanted. At first, I was too young to realize it, and then I was so caught up in living our life together that I really didn't even notice that anything was missing. Until it all came crashing down."

Nathan couldn't help himself. "Cat, I would do anything to take back that day. That moment when I decided to cross the ice. There's nothing I can do, nothing I can say to change it. I know that. I know I can't make it up to you, ever, in a thousand lifetimes. But I'd trade my life for theirs if I could."

Catherine reached out and gently placed a hand on Nathan's. "I know that, Nate. I know that the accident is never going to leave you, and that's a terrible burden to bear."

"But I'm moving forward, too. I'm discovering new opportunities, new passions to pursue. I'm not just looking to go back."

Catherine pulled back and looked him in the eyes. "I'm

glad to hear that, Nathan. So maybe you'll understand that that's exactly what I'm doing, too. What you have done since the accident is given me a great gift. By giving me space and time to heal, and to deal with the grief and the pain, you've helped me to find *me*. And I know that's not what you want, but I hope, if you love me, that it's something."

Nathan continued to stare down at the table, but he didn't interrupt Catherine as she continued.

"Remember the dreams I said I had after my riding accident?" When Nathan nodded, Catherine told him how she had been working to find a farm where she could open up a therapeutic riding program for grieving parents. She told him about Carey's help in setting up a foundation and about the fundraiser. Then she told him about the ranch outside Ennis.

"Montana! You're moving to Montana? Cat, your home is here. *Our* home is here. You don't know anyone in Montana, not even close. And what do you know about running a ranch, much less a foundation? Why not just build a barn and put some horses on some land here in Maine? I could buy the land. We could build on it. Sell the house if we want. Do this therapeutic riding thing together. As a team. We'd have income from my business to keep us going until we saw that the farm was financially viable, and then when it is, we could sell that and expand. Or maybe then move somewhere bigger, together. Montana. Wyoming. Anywhere."

"I know that all makes logical sense, Nate. But you're missing the point. This is something I need to do for myself. It's like something is pulling me towards it. Rev. Susan says it's a calling. Whatever it is, I need this to be *mine* and not *ours*. I don't want or need you to figure it all out for me."

"Montana?"

"Nate, this is happening. It's real. I've incorporated the

foundation. We've raised the cash and I've got a Board of Directors. We just closed escrow on a ranch outside of Ennis. I'm getting ready to move."

Catherine could see the look of incredulity etched on Nathan's face. "I need you to see that it feels really good just to have gotten this far on my own. It's something I need to do. And whether it succeeds or it falls flat on its face, it will be *my* success or failure. It's the only way I know to take my pain and channel it into something positive. It's healing for me. It's a way to honor the kids, too. To keep their memory alive and with me."

Catherine pulled a sheet of paper out of her purse and slid it across the table. Nathan picked it up and looked at the foundation's logo, the linked stars with the letter "J" in each.

"This is beautiful, Cat." Nathan let out a long sigh as he sat back in the booth. "I don't know what else to say." She could read the defeat that was written on his face.

"I know it's too much to ask you to be happy for me, Nate. But can you at least tell me that maybe someday you will be? Maybe you'll see your way to understanding why I need to do this?"

"I'll work on that, Cat, if you tell me that someday you'll forgive me for what I did."

"Oh, Nathan." Catherine reached out and took his hand. "Don't you see? I *do* forgive you. It doesn't mean that I'm not wracked by grief and even rage over what happened. My heart will always be broken by it. I don't know exactly what forgiveness feels like, but I think it has something to do with moving on. Not in a mean or vindictive way, but in a way that releases both of us from these prison cells we've been living in. So that we can go on with our lives. It might mean life together or lives apart, but either way, it's about getting un-stuck."

Catherine held Nathan's gaze and continued.

"Nathan, I'm un-stuck now. I feel like, somehow, out of this awful thing, my life's purpose has been revealed to me. Susan calls it 'grace,' but whatever it is, I've found it. Or it's found me. And the only way I can respond to it is to forgive what's been done and what's happened and the part you played in it. Nathan, you have my forgiveness. I just hope that someday you can learn to forgive yourself."

"So, this is it? Will I see you again?"

"We'll always keep in touch, Nate. I still love you. Maybe someday you can come out and see the operation. But for now, yeah. This is it."

"I want only the best for you, Cat. I hope you know that." Nathan slid out of the booth, kissed Catherine on the top of the head, and walked out the door.

*

The house was a jumble of boxes. Catherine was leaving for Montana in just a few days. Kurt and Isabel, the caretakers who were now her employees, were supervising the repairs and awaiting her arrival. Catherine wasn't taking much with her, mostly just clothes and photo albums. The house in Ennis was fully furnished, and she didn't want to be weighed down with a lot of extraneous stuff. *I've got plenty of baggage I'll be taking anyway.* She undressed and climbed into bed for her last night in the house on Mountain Road.

Catherine and Nathan had gotten together twice since their conversation at Mario's. She was grateful that Nathan hadn't tried to dissuade her from her plan. She even detected a new energy in him, and a light in his eyes that she'd not seen since the accident as he told her his plans about setting up a central donation and distribution center for area food banks. They talked about the mundane details of their separation and divorce. Catherine neither wanted nor needed anything from Nathan, but he insisted on providing her with a small stipend.

Nathan had told her that he planned to move back into the house after she left. He said he was thinking about putting it on the market in the fall, which made her sad. Nathan asked her about some of the business aspects of the ranch, and Catherine was proud that she was able to address nearly all of his concerns. She had launched the new website and was scheduled to attend a national conference of family counselors and therapists to talk up the ranch in hopes of finding referral sources for their first clients.

Catherine's farewell meeting with Rev. Susan was a tearful one. Sitting in her familiar position in the pastor's office—the glacier gone for another year—she tried to express the depth of her gratitude for all that Susan had done for her.

"You've seen me at my worst."

"And I can't wait to see you at your best, Catherine. Two years ago, who would have thought that this is where you'd be? You're going to do great things."

"Small things with great love. That's what you taught me, right? We don't do great things, just small things with great love."

"The student has become the master. My work here is done." The two of them laughed as they hugged through their tears one last time.

*

Heather was there, of course, to help Catherine pack up

her car and to say goodbye. The two friends were teary-eyed as they held a hug that would have to last them a long time. Heather assured her best friend that she and her family were going to take a road trip to Montana, and she made Catherine promise to teach her how to ride a horse.

"Heather." Catherine choked on her words.

"Don't say it." She held Catherine's face in her two hands and gazed deeply into her eyes. "I know."

They hugged again, and then Heather shoved her closest friend in the world into the driver's seat of her Subaru. They said, "I love you" to each other simultaneously, and Catherine drove out of the driveway cautiously, trying to see through her tears. She waved to Heather, as her friend stood in the driveway waving back, and turned down the road. She didn't dare look back at the house that had been her home, the center of her entire life, for so many years. She had one more stop to make before heading down the Maine Turnpike.

*

Some would say she was being melodramatic, or at least overly sentimental. Who needs to say goodbye to a horse? I do, Catherine thought. She couldn't leave without feeling Penny's warm, rubbery muzzle in her hand, without gazing into her soft, knowing eyes, without breathing in her deep, earthy scent one last time. Yes, in just a matter of days, she would be living a life surrounded by horses. But Penny was the horse that had set her on this path.

Catherine turned in the long driveway of Sunnybrooke Farm. She was surprised to see a pickup truck hitched to a horse trailer parked by the barn. It was a beefy, silver Ford F-250 crew cab, and it looked brand new. Lee came out of the barn and stood in front of the pickup as Catherine drove up.

"What's with the truck, Lee?"

Lee walked around to the driver's side of the vehicle and pointed to the front door. Catherine gasped when she saw the two linked stars with the letter "J" inside each of them, the picture of the horse and barn below it, and the ranch's name beneath. Without saying a word, Lee pulled open the door of the truck and then walked toward the barn. Catherine saw an envelope sitting on the front seat, next to a set of keys. She opened it and read:

"Dear Catherine,

A real Montana rancher doesn't drive a Subaru. She needs a pickup truck, so I got you this. You always said I was a man of grand gestures, and I hope you'll allow me this last one.

You changed my life forever, for the better, and for that I will always be grateful. I hope you find what you're looking for.

I will love you always,
Nathan"

Catherine leaned back against the side of the truck as tears filled her eyes. But before she could catch her breath, she was distracted by the sound of hoofbeats. She turned toward the barn and saw Lee leading Penny toward the horse trailer.

"He bought her for you, too." Lee wore a conspiratorial grin on his face. Catherine ran to Penny. She laid her face against the silken coat of Penny's cheek and threw her arms around her neck. As always, Penny patiently received Catherine's affection. When Catherine finally released her embrace, Lee loaded Penny into the trailer, then helped Catherine transfer the boxes and clothes from her car into the truck.

Catherine gave Lee a hug, which startled him, and he returned it awkwardly. She climbed into the truck, started it up, and shifted it into Drive. She made her way down the lane, Nathan's note sitting open on the passenger seat beside her. At the end of the driveway, she stopped and tucked it into her shirt pocket, setting it close to her heart. Then she turned onto the main road and drove west toward the new life that awaited her. A life not of her choosing, but one that would be of her own making.

EPILOGUE

Catherine stepped out of the barn into the frigid February night. In her three winters on the ranch, she had come up with only one word to describe what the air was like on nights like this: "Brittle." Like a glass Christmas ornament, pulled from a vat of liquid nitrogen: one false move and it would shatter into a million jagged-edged pieces. Carey had joined Catherine for her first Christmas in Montana – before the worst of the season had seized the Madison River valley by the throat – and vowed never to return between the months of October and April. Even Kurt and Izzie, the J-Star's caretakers, took a few weeks off this time of year to escape to warmer climes.

Catherine had come to embrace the elemental force of the cold. She loved the way her breath caught in her throat when she stepped out into it and the tingly feeling of tiny icicles forming in her nostrils when she inhaled. But what she most adored were the night-time skies. With no humidity in the air, the stars shone with a crispness she'd never seen back in New England. It was as if someone had turned up their brightness on some great cosmic dial. Whenever she looked up on nights like this, she recalled the dream she'd had in what felt like a whole different lifetime. The dream where she had gazed up at the night sky from the desert floor in Joshua Tree National Park, the first time she'd heard the legend that our ancestors are stars gazing down on us. On nights like this those stars, which she knew were light-years away, felt as close as her own beating heart.

As she did every night as a silent, solo ritual after bedding down the horses, Catherine stopped on her walk back to the house and looked up to the heavens. She allowed her gaze to settle on a single pair of stars. It didn't matter which two, as long as they appeared to be close to each other, traversing the firmament together. She allowed her shoulders to relax and a tender, bittersweet smile to crease the corners of her mouth as she remembered Jacob and Joe. The memory of their death still stung. The hole in her heart would never be filled. But the edges of her pain had begun to smooth, like a sharp stone that's worn down over time by rushing water. Now, mostly, when she thought of the boys, she thought of the hours of joy they'd given her. Joe's antics and Jacob's earnestness. She raised the fingers of one hand to her lips, kissed them tenderly, and raised them skyward, sending her love out into the universe.

*

Catherine had decorated the master bedroom of the ranch house in a western pioneer style. Her queen-sized bed had a tall wooden headboard carved with scrolls and vines. A simple oak bureau sat against an opposite wall, with a mirror above it held in a similarly carved frame. A Native American woven rug covered the small expanse of hardwood floor between the two pieces of furniture. In the dead of winter, the room was cold – nearly frosty – as the heating system struggled to offset the effects of the relentless arctic winds that buffeted the ranch. The warmth of the woodstove in the living room didn't reach this far corner of the house.

Catherine loved sleeping in the cold, with three layers of quilts piled on top of her, only her nose exposed to the chill. She didn't waste any time shedding her clothes and climbing into her nighttime ensemble: sweatpants, rag wool socks, and a ratty Mount Holyoke College sweatshirt she'd owned for more than a decade. She stood before the bureau and pulled the elastic from her hair, noticing as it fell that its tawny color had begun to mellow with age. She grabbed her hairbrush from the bureau and began to pull it through the knots accumulated through the day's activities. Looking toward the mirror, her eyes landed on the note wedged between the glass and the frame. She had placed it there more than three years earlier, when she'd first arrived at the ranch and introduced Penny to the resident horses. The note had begun to yellow with age and the effects of the harsh Montana sun that blazed through the bedroom window during the summer months. She rarely even took heed of its existence these days. It was like an old photograph that you pass in the hallway every day without seeing, a fixture that becomes invisible through its familiarity. But for some reason, tonight it held her gaze. The sharp strokes of Nathan's handwriting and the memory of his generous gesture when she'd left him pulled her mind back to the hills of southern Maine.

Catherine thought about the stars in the Montana sky she'd just seen, and about nights sitting on the deck of the house on Mountain Road with her husband, holding hands and spinning out the dreams of the life they'd build together.

She returned the brush to its place on the bureau and walked to the bed. The nightstand beside it held a lamp retrofitted from an old kerosene lantern and a novel about women who had helped settle the high plains of the American West. Catherine climbed under the covers and reached out to turn off the lamp, but instead, her hand-picked up her cell phone. She dialed the number that she still knew by heart, and he picked up on the first ring.

"Cat?" Nathan's voice was groggy, and she remembered that it was two hours later there.

"Nathan," Catherine whispered into the phone, thinking of the stars staring down from the frozen Montana sky. "There's something I need to show you."

ACKNOWLEDGEMENTS

I have run a few half-marathons, and that experience has taught me that to go the distance we need fans and friends both on the sidelines and in the trenches. Throughout the marathon of writing this book I've been blessed to be accompanied by a cadre of dedicated and enthusiastic supporters – a great cloud of witnesses, if you will – without whom I never would have reached the finish line.

First and foremost is my family. My wife Irene has always believed in me far more than I have believed in myself, and from the start of our relationship knew that I had a book in me. My daughters, Rebecca Wallace and Julia Bean, have encouraged me every step of the way and given me beautiful and rambunctious grandchildren with whom to wrestle and play. I thank, too, my parents, Jim and Aline, and my siblings, Nancy, Anne and Jeff, who offered many insights and much encouragement.

My running partners Don Garfinkel and Marylin Huff have put up with countless hours of my angst and uncertainty around this project. Their optimism and good counsel as we've run, jogged, plodded and slogged along the streets and parks of Delaware County have been invaluable.

I want to thank David and Serena Kolb for offering their constant love and friendship. It was at Blue Loon, their camp on the shores of Madagascal Pond in northern Maine, that I penned the first several chapters of what would eventually become this book. The real Robert Heasley, therapist and friend extraordinaire, offered me not just his name but his constant guidance on the therapeutic process, as well as some therapy for me along the way.

There were many early readers of different versions of this work whose input helped give shape and texture to Nathan and Catherine's lives. Among them: Kent Matthies, my brother in ministry and inexplicably devoted fan of the Philadelphia Eagles. Judy Welles, who sadly didn't live to see this book published, and her husband Duane Fickeisen. JP Dunn, whose friendship I have cherished for the past 40 years. Darcy Costello, who wanted Cat and Nate to get back together and who, I hope, finds some consolation in the Epilogue.

I also want to thank the members of my congregation, the Unitarian Universalist Church of Delaware County. The pain, grief, joy and achievements of their lives are reflected in those of the characters in these pages. I thank them for the great gift of allowing me to pastor them through all the challenges and all the celebrations of their lives.

Professionally, I want to thank Nick Courtright, Trista Edwards and all the great folks at Atmosphere Press for recognizing the potential in this work and helping to get it out into the world. My developmental editor, Katie Kennedy, helped wrestle the monstrosity that was the first draft down to something resembling a coherent narrative. And Deborah Hoffman has offered ongoing insight and guidance on the mysterious and often frustrating world of book publishing, as well as enthusiastic encouragement every step of the way.

BOOK DISCUSSION

1. Can Nathan claim to be a victim of the accident? Why or why not? Why might it matter?

2. Who were you rooting for most in the story, Nathan or Catherine? To whom do you more closely relate? Why?

3. How does Nathan's guilt affect his grieving? How does it affect his ability to reconcile with Catherine?

4. Experiencing pangs of compassion for Nathan following the accident, Catherine considers the possibility of reconciliation: "[Was there] an inkling that the devastation Catherine felt was something they actually shared? Could that patch of scorched earth be the common ground they might stand on together?" Can a healthy relationship be built, or rebuilt, upon a shared tragedy? What would it take for a relationship to survive such a devastating event?

5. Dreams play a big role in Catherine's recovery, guiding her toward a new life. What role do dreams play in your life? Do you listen to your dreams? Trust them? Follow them? What's a dream that you've followed, or wish you had?

6. Rev. Susan says "Grief isn't like a cold that you have for a while, and then it just goes away, and you pick up where you left off. Grief is more like an amputation. It's like losing a limb. You're never going to be the same again. You never get 'back to normal.'" Does that ring true to your experience with grief?

7. Rev. Susan tells Catherine that she thinks of forgiveness "as more of a process than an outcome. It's not a 'one and done' kind of thing." Does this resonate with your experience? How do you get to forgiveness? What stands in the way of forgiving?

8. Were you hoping that Nathan and Catherine would reunite and find a way forward together? Discuss your desire for a "happy ending."

9. In the Epilogue, Catherine reaches out to Nathan three years after her departure. "Nathan, there's something I want to show you." What do you hope happens next?

ABOUT ATMOSPHERE PRESS

Atmosphere Press is an independent, full-service publisher for excellent books in all genres and for all audiences. Learn more about what we do at atmospherepress.com.

We encourage you to check out some of Atmosphere's latest releases, which are available at Amazon.com and via order from your local bookstore:

Comfrey, Wyoming: Birds of a Feather, a novel by Daphne Birkmyer
Relatively Painless, short stories by Dylan Brody
Nate's New Age, a novel by Michael Hanson
The Size of the Moon, a novel by E.J. Michaels
The Red Castle, a novel by Noah Verhoeff
American Genes, a novel by Kirby Nielsen
Newer Testaments, a novel by Philip Brunetti
All Things in Time, a novel by Sue Buyer
Hobson's Mischief, a novel by Caitlin Decatur
The Black-Marketer's Daughter, a novel by Suman Mallick
The Farthing Quest, a novel by Casey Bruce
This Side of Babylon, a novel by James Stoia
Within the Gray, a novel by Jenna Ashlyn
Where No Man Pursueth, a novel by Micheal E. Jimerson
Here's Waldo, a novel by Nick Olson
Tales of Little Egypt, a historical novel by James Gilbert
For a Better Life, a novel by Julia Reid Galosy
Big Man Small Europe, poetry by Tristan Niskanen
The Hidden Life, a novel by Robert Castle

ABOUT THE AUTHOR

Through his writing Peter Friedrichs attempts to peek behind the curtain of our collective lives and strives to help us understand more fully what it means to be human. He holds degrees from Amherst College, Georgetown Law, and Andover Newton Theological School and his career path has taken him from practicing law in Portland, Maine to pastoring a Unitarian Universalist congregation in suburban Philadelphia. Peter lives in Swarthmore, Pennsylvania with his wife Irene. This is his first novel.

Website: https://peterfriedrichs.net/
Facebook: @PeterFriedrichsAuthor
Twitter: @PAFriedrichs

CPSIA information can be obtained
at www.ICGtesting.com
Printed in the USA
LVHW031756170521
687666LV00007B/272